MORTAL RITES

COMPANY OF STRANGERS, BOOK 3

MELISSA MCSHANE

To Jay—
I'm sorry the Princess got killed all those times and nearly derailed the campaign.
In my defense, stirges are wicked nasty when they all attack at once.

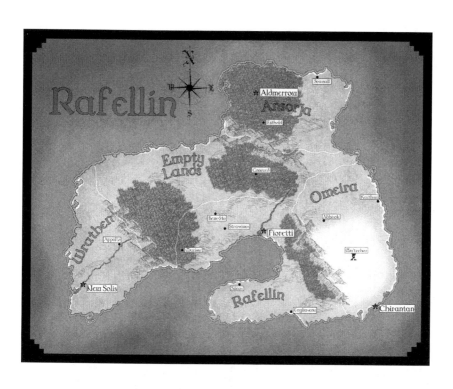

1

Sienne stood at the villa's window and looked out over the Jalenus Sea to where the ocean met the sky, two shades of blue blending into one another. Waves crashed against the rocky cliff, far below, their ebb and flow a soothing rush of noise that harmonized with the higher notes of the constantly blowing wind. One pane of thick, bubbly glass remained in the window; the rest were long gone. The glass transformed the vista into a dreamscape in which bulbous waves humped and bulged their way inland, tinted rosy pink. Sienne preferred the unaltered landscape. It wasn't as pretty, but at least you knew where you were.

She inhaled deeply, closing her eyes to enjoy the scents of sun-warmed air and salt breezes. The air was tinged with the sweet smell of the tiny pink flowers that covered the short stretch of ground from the house to the cliff's edge. They were strongly scented for something so small, and she wished she knew their name. Her father the Duke might know, dedicated gardener that he was in his spare time, but if he were standing beside her, he'd be more interested in criticizing her choices than in delivering a horticulture lecture. She scowled and turned away. And it had been such a pleasant day, too, until her past intruded on it.

"I take it you have had as little luck as I," Perrin said from across the room. The small library had less than a thousand books, but when each had to be examined closely, that was an even more daunting number. Perrin had made three neat stacks of books on the floor beside him and was in the process of beginning a fourth.

"The owner loved plays," Sienne said, returning to the bookcase she'd cleared of most of its books. "They're easy to eliminate, but I admit to becoming bored. I didn't know there were so many ways to retell the story of the Seven Pilgrims."

"I have found histories. Very dull ones." Perrin flipped open another book, skimmed its pages, and set it on the new pile. "But this collection is so disorganized it is impossible to simply ignore a shelf on the basis that one has found five histories there, and therefore the other books must be the same."

Sienne reached the end of the final shelf. The last book was slimmer than the rest, bound in magenta-dyed leather that time and the sea air had worn to pink along the spine. She flipped through the pages. "Poetry," she said. "*Sappy* poetry."

"I take it you are not a lover of verse."

"Not modern verse. I like old long-form epics about the before times." She set the poetry book back and stooped to gather up her piles to restore them to the bookcase. It probably wasn't necessary, since nobody was likely to come along insisting they clean up their mess, but she'd been too well trained at school in the dukedom of Stravanus to be able to leave books on the floor.

She heard footsteps overhead, making the ceiling creak. Alaric, probably, searching the upper floor for more books. The previous owners had let their collection spill over into every room in the house upstairs and down. On the ground floor they'd found, in addition to the actual library, decorative shelves in both formal sitting rooms and a pile of cookbooks in the kitchen, and there were a couple of loose volumes of the epic *What Dreams Remain* in the outhouse. Missing pages from the latter indicated it hadn't been used for reading material, or at least not ultimately so.

Sienne began on the next bookcase. There were eight in total, all of them packed full. Exposure to the damp, salty air had caused most of the books to swell, compacting them further. She wormed her fingertips between the first and second volumes, stretching high to reach the top shelf, and pulled out a book. "*Desert Plants of Omeira.* That bores me just thinking about it. Honestly, I don't know why we're bothering. It's unlikely Penthea Lepporo left any necromantic treatises lying around where anyone might find them."

"How better to hide something dangerous than in plain sight?" Perrin swept his long, dark hair out of his face and began shifting his piles back onto the bookcase. "And the manner in which she left the house suggests she did not have time to hide any books that might draw the attention of the guards."

"I think it's sad that her family never came back after she died. It's not as if she died here, and it's a beautiful house. Or was, thirty years ago." Sienne closed her book with a snap and stared out the other window, the one that overlooked the overgrown patio and concrete urns that once held tiny fruit trees. The trees had all died from neglect, but creeping vines had taken over their corpses, their white star-like flowers giving the dead trees a false impression of life. Since they were at the Lepporo estate looking for evidence of necromancy, it seemed an appropriate image.

Their quest to find a ritual that would free Alaric's people, the shape-changing race called Sassaven, had taken an unexpected turn four weeks earlier. Having acquired two ritual objects, they'd begun searching for the recipe for a potion containing the sedative herb varnwort, in hopes it might lead them to evidence of the ritual itself. Almost immediately, they'd discovered that varnwort was used in many, many rituals. All of them were necromantic.

Sienne had pointed out that so far as anyone knew, the only rituals that had survived from the wars that had all but destroyed civilization four hundred years ago were necromantic, so that was no real surprise, but it had still been disturbing. They were looking for a ritual that would invert the one binding the Sassaven to their evil creator, not one that would raise the dead. But it was their only lead.

So for the past four weeks, they'd turned their search toward finding a necromantic ritual that both used varnwort and had something to do with binding. It was delicate work; studying necromancy wasn't illegal, only the practice of it, but the law didn't always discriminate between the two, and people who studied necromancy didn't advertise the fact.

They'd found Penthea Lepporo's name in the correspondence of a known necromancer who'd died forty years ago, and Alaric had gotten permission from Penthea's son to examine the Lepporo library at the abandoned estate. Which was why Sienne was digging through old, damaged, boring books when she could be back in Fioretti reading something exciting.

She set the book down and reached for the next. It was taller than the others on its shelf and wedged tightly in place. Cursing softly, Sienne stepped back and tried using her small magic called invisible fingers on it, tugging at it without touching it. It stayed stuck as solidly as if the shelf had been built around it.

She cast about the room for a solution. Two armchairs positioned near the window looked as if they'd break if she put even her slight weight on them, but the table between them, low and square, looked hewn from granite rather than built of solid oak. With some effort, she dragged it over to the bookcase and hopped up. This put her at eye level with the shelf and the row of books. Grabbing hold of the offending tome, she wiggled it back and forth, trying to loosen it.

Something snapped, and the book came free so rapidly she nearly lost her balance. "By Averran," Perrin exclaimed, "what did you do?"

"This book was stuck, that's all."

She glanced down at Perrin, who had his hand on a bookcase neither of them had examined yet. "That is not all," he said. He took hold of the bookcase's side and pulled, making it swing gently toward him. A gaping square hole in the base of the wall lay beyond it, dark and smelling of dust.

Sienne and Perrin stared at each other. "This is far more interesting than poetry, epic or not," Perrin said. "Shall we investigate?"

"Are you kidding? It would be the midge hive all over again."

Sienne drew in a breath and shouted, "Alaric! Dianthe! Kalanath! We found something!"

Hurried footsteps sounded on the stairs, and Dianthe appeared in the doorway. "Found—oh, by Kitane's left arm," she said, staring at the hole. "What is it?"

"There was a secret switch Sienne cleverly found," Perrin said.

"Just so you didn't go in there on your own. Remember the midges?"

"Is no one going to let me forget about them?" Sienne demanded.

More footsteps announced Kalanath's arrival, followed immediately by Alaric, who had cobwebs in his short blond hair. "Attic," he said. "But this is far more promising. Sienne, you didn't go down there alone, did you?"

Sienne rolled her eyes. "I *am* teachable, you know. What should we do?"

Dianthe crouched next to the hole. "There's a ladder going down, and it smells like a large room. Sienne, why don't you make some lights, and I'll see what I can see."

Sienne concentrated, and half a dozen white lights the size of small apples popped into existence, floating around her head. She directed them into the hole. Dianthe leaned farther forward. "It's definitely big, and the ceiling is remarkably high. Wait here." She turned and descended the ladder, disappearing out of sight. The others gathered around the hole and peered after her. Sienne couldn't see anything but the ladder and, far below, a black wooden floor that shone in the magic lights as if highly varnished. Dianthe's boots made sharp tapping noises that quickly receded to nothing.

"What do you see?" Alaric called out.

"We have our proof that Penthea Lepporo, or someone who lived in her house, practiced necromancy," Dianthe said. "Come on down. Whoever it was didn't leave any nasty surprises."

"Probably didn't have time," Alaric said, moving back to allow Kalanath access to the ladder. "Penthea's illness came on suddenly, her son said, and they all left for Fioretti with her."

"Yes, and don't you think that's strange?" Sienne said. "That they never came back to retrieve all their things? I realize the Lepporos are wealthy, but even wealthy people aren't generally that wasteful."

Alaric shrugged and offered Sienne a hand. "Their town house is far more opulent than this, remember?"

"I remember." It had been opulent enough to make Sienne uncomfortable, despite her upbringing as a duke's daughter. She'd feared knocking over some priceless vase or smearing mud on an antique rug. "Even so."

"Who knows why the rich and powerful do what they do?" Alaric held her hand a few moments longer than necessary to help her onto the ladder, and she smiled at him and received a smile he reserved only for her. It still made her giddy when he looked at her that way, weeks after they'd acknowledged their mutual attraction. Giddy, and something deeper and warmer she hugged close to her heart. Falling in love with Alaric had been unexpected, and wonderful. But he never gave any indication that he cared more for her than casual affection, and she wished she knew if he was concealing some more profound feeling. She was the last person in the world who'd know love when she saw it. Her ex-lover Rance was proof of that.

She hurried down the ladder into a space several degrees cooler than the house above, which was warmed by the afternoon sun of late first summer. Dianthe was right, the ceiling was surprisingly high, at least ten feet—much higher than Sienne would have expected from a basement. The walls were painted the same black as the floorboards, providing a stark contrast to the white lines of script covering them. A wooden butcher block table stained with dark residue occupied the center of the room. Dianthe stood at the room's far side, next to a couple of flat-topped chests fastened with leather straps. Sienne crossed toward her as she unbuckled the first one and opened the chest.

"Ugh!" Dianthe exclaimed, stepping back and pinching her nose shut. A foul stink like rotten meat wafted to Sienne's nostrils, and she imitated Dianthe's gesture. "That's far too ripe for something that's been locked away for thirty years."

"What is it?" Kalanath asked, prodding the chest with the tip of his steel-shod staff.

Dianthe leaned over, her nose still plugged, and shook her head. "I can't tell. I think it might have been a trap. But it doesn't look like the contents of the trunk are damaged, so I'm not sure what the point was. Take a look. I'll be more careful opening the other one."

Sienne walked over to the wall and examined the lines of script. They'd been painted on rather than written in chalk or ink, and in places the letters were too blurry to make out. Alaric came to stand beside her. "What does it say?" he asked.

"Nothing," Sienne said. "It's gibberish. Maybe it's a code? Or it could be a necromantic ritual, except all the ones I know about use actual Fellic words."

"This appears to be a list," Perrin said. He stood a short distance away, looking at another patch of writing. Sienne and Alaric went to join him. "A list of ingredients. Varnwort is not on it, before you ask."

Alaric let out a sigh. "I didn't expect this to be easy, but I still hoped—"

"Me too," Sienne said.

"Come and look at the books," Kalanath said.

The trunk was, in fact, full of books, jumbled together in no particular order. Kalanath handed them out to the others while Dianthe circled the second trunk, muttering to herself. Alaric whistled. "Necromancy books."

"And a journal," Perrin said, flipping the pages of one of the smaller books. "Whoever it was kept detailed notes."

Sienne shivered. "It's really cold in here. Let's take everything up to the library. There's better light there."

Alaric began stacking books in the crook of his arm. "Dianthe, what's in the other trunk?"

"I don't know. I'm afraid to open it. There's something off about the latch that I think is another trap—a nastier one." She shivered. "Sienne, can you give me a little more light over here?"

Something slammed nearby, making Sienne jump. A patter of

sharp thumps followed. The room grew marginally darker. "What was that?"

Kalanath crossed to the ladder. "The hole is covered. A bookcase fell over it."

Alaric set down his armful of books. "I'll get it open."

The short stack of books shifted, then tumbled over, spilling across the floor. As Alaric crouched to pick them up, they rose into the air, circling him like a pack of wary dogs. "Sienne, stop that!"

"I'm not doing it!" Sienne exclaimed.

One of the books flew at Alaric's face. He batted it away as two more dove in after it. Sienne's armload of books darted away to join their mates, and the air was suddenly full of flying books, wildly careening in all directions. Sienne covered her head with her arms and cried out as a large book cracked her on the back of the skull, making her vision go blurry briefly. She ducked away from another assault and ran for the ladder. As Kalanath had said, a bookcase had fallen diagonally across the hole, blocking it so only slivers of light shone through.

She turned to tell Alaric to get the bookcase out of the way, and froze. Behind Alaric, emerging through the lid of the second trunk, was a wispy, nearly invisible figure of a child about seven years old. It wore an old-fashioned night shirt that floated around it as if blown by an intangible breeze. The contours of its body shimmered, here one moment, gone the next, giving it the appearance of a sketch by an artist who couldn't make up her mind what to draw next. Its small face was drawn up in a silent wail, and its hands scrubbed invisible tears out of its eyes.

"Alaric, look out!" Sienne screamed. Alaric looked up, then turned. The child grasped his shoulders and wailed. This time it was audible. The shriek filled the chamber, sending the flying books to the floor and making Sienne clutch her hands over her ears in a futile attempt to block it out. She could barely hear, over the sound of the wail, the exclamations of her friends. Alaric flailed at the thing, unable to get a grip on it even though it held him solidly in both small hands.

Kalanath stepped forward and swung his staff at the child's body. It passed through, making the form ripple with its motion but otherwise having no effect. At the same time, Dianthe drew her sword and thrust at it, but was forced to pull up sharply when she met no resistance and nearly skewered Alaric. Her eyes watering, Sienne snatched up her spellbook where it hung in its harness at her side and opened it to *force*.

The child wailed again, and Sienne gritted her teeth and wiped tears out of her eyes. Taking two long strides to the side for a clearer shot, she read off the evocation *force*, feeling it burn like acid inside her mouth. As the last syllables left her lips, a bolt of magical energy blasted away from her at the creature. It struck the thing in the side. This time, its wail was one of pain and fury. It released Alaric and flew straight for Sienne.

2

S he gabbled out *force* again, as quickly as she dared without ruining the spell. The magical energy hit the child full in the face. It staggered mid-swoop, but kept coming. Sienne screamed and dropped to the floor. It whooshed past her head, causing her hair to ruffle in the wake of its passing. She rolled and got to her feet. It had turned around and was headed for her again. Sienne spat out the hard-edged syllables of the evocation, but it was too fast, it would hit her before she finished the spell—

A pearly light flared before her eyes, and the child slammed into Perrin's shield and dissolved in a cloud of sparks. Breathing heavily, Sienne lowered her spellbook. "Thank you."

"That was a temporary solution," Perrin said. "A phantasm cannot be stopped so easily." He had his riffle of blessings out, but was scanning the room rather than looking through them.

Sienne raced to Alaric's side. The big man lay on his back, blinking up at the ceiling. "Are you hurt?" she asked, her heart in her throat.

"Can't breathe...easily..." Alaric rolled to his knees and paused there, panting like he'd run ten miles without stopping. "Like it... sucked the air...out of...my lungs."

"It returns!" Kalanath shouted. Sienne's head snapped up. A knot of movement near the ladder slowly resolved into the floating figure of the child. Sienne opened her book and began reading off *force*. She wished she knew if the spell made any difference, or did any damage.

The shield blessing popped like a soap bubble. "How do we kill it, Perrin?" Alaric called out, then coughed, a hacking dry sound that made Sienne's chest ache. A *force* bolt shot away from her and struck the thing, making it scream again in anger.

"We must disrupt its connection to the material world," Perrin shouted over the screaming. "There will be a thing here—an object, or a piece of its body—"

"How about the whole damned thing?" Dianthe cried out. She had the second chest open and was staring into it with a look of horror.

Sienne backed toward her, not taking her eyes off the phantasm. Behind her, she heard the others gathered around the chest exclaiming, then Alaric was at her elbow, saying, "Perrin, shield us!"

Sienne turned and ran for the chest as the phantasm once again exploded against Perrin's new shield. "It is the last shield blessing," Perrin said. Sienne put both hands on the edge of the chest to steady herself and bit back a horrified shriek. Tucked into the chest was the mummified body of a child, its knees drawn up beneath its chin.

"Kitane's eyes, it's in here with us!" Dianthe shouted. Sienne looked up and saw the thing reforming within the shield, not five feet from her.

"You have to burn the body!" Perrin exclaimed. Sienne whipped open her spellbook and gabbled out another evocation, this one *burn*. Her mouth felt raw, her tongue numb, but she managed not to tangle herself on the sharp syllables. A ray of blue fire shot away from her as she finished casting the spell, striking the tiny body and sending blue flames scattering across it.

Something struck her in the back of the head, something cold and sharp-edged like a mouthful of needles. Instantly her throat and lungs were filled with frozen fire, numbing and burning at the same time, and she gasped for air and found nothing. She dropped to her knees so the blue flames were at eye level. *Burn*, she thought at them, willing them to spread, *burn*, and as if they could hear her thoughts, they went wild, consuming the small body until it looked like a funeral pyre.

A wail shook the chamber, pain and anger warring with each other. Air rushed into Sienne's lungs, cool and soothing. She coughed, sucked in air again, and sagged against the chest, heedless of the fire burning inches from her face. Hands dragged her away and helped her to sit upright. "Better?" Alaric said. She nodded. Her tongue felt swollen to three times its normal size, between the acid burn of her evocations and the freezing attack of the phantasm.

She wiped blurry tears out of her eyes and blinked at the chest. "I thought," she wheezed, "there were no such things as ghosts."

"Not as they are portrayed in popular literature, souls who are rejected by God and condemned to wander the earth," Perrin said. "Most ghosts are summoned back from their eternal rest by necromancers wishing to avail themselves of the spirits' knowledge. If a necromancer loses his or her control of the ghost, it becomes trapped in the material world, unable to return to the presence of God and unable to walk the world as it did in life. These are called phantasms."

"I'm starting to understand why the Lepporos never came back," Dianthe said. "And what Penthea Lepporo's mysterious illness actually was. Do you suppose it killed her here?"

"I'm considering paying them a visit," Alaric said darkly. He helped Sienne rise and steadied her when she wobbled. "They must have known what we'd find."

"Surely not," Sienne protested. "What would be the point of sending us off to die? We hardly know them. And it's been thirty years. Penthea's son would have been a child when this happened."

"It nearly killed you, Sienne."

"I don't see any point in looking for vengeance on someone who wasn't at fault. This was entirely Penthea's doing, assuming she was the necromancer." Sienne gave his hand a squeeze and stepped away.

"Let's get these books upstairs and see if any of them have what we need."

Alaric grimaced, but climbed the ladder and shoved the fallen bookcase to one side. Sienne gathered up an armload of books and waited for him to move aside before climbing out one-handed. Her vision swam as she climbed, and her breathing felt labored, as if she had one of those chests strapped to her back. She held tight to each rung and tested her footholds carefully. It wouldn't be much of a fall if she slipped, but that was small comfort.

She clambered out of the hole, took a few steps into the room, and sank into one of the chairs, which groaned alarmingly under her weight. Setting her stack on the floor, she took the topmost book and leafed through it. "Ew. An anatomy book."

"Nothing wrong with that," Dianthe said, dropping her books on the floor next to Sienne's and sitting cross-legged beside her.

"It is if it's a guide to dismembering someone. Oh, how exciting, there's a section on exsanguination. With diagrams." She set the book aside and picked up the next one.

"Look at this one," Dianthe said, handing her a fat tome about twice the size of Sienne's spellbook. "It's in Sorjic."

Sienne flipped through it. "Looks like necromantic theory. I don't see any rituals."

"I've found something," Alaric said. "This contains a number of rituals for raising the dead, all of which include recipes for potions."

"That seems unlikely," Perrin said. "The dead cannot imbibe, so cannot consume potions."

"Ointments, then. It's very clear that they're meant to be included in the rituals. Some of them specify varnwort. We should take a closer look at this later." He tossed it to Sienne, who caught it and put it away in her pack.

"We're not going to tell Stefen Lepporo what we found, are we?" she asked. "And ruin his image of his mother?"

"I do not think it is a good idea," Kalanath said. "But we agreed to make the ruin safe for him to return. What can we say?"

"That we cleared away a nest of wereboars, and it's perfectly safe,"

Alaric said, turning the pages of another book. "We'll put the book-cases back, destroy the opening mechanism, and let Penthea's memory rest. Besides, we don't know it was her. It could have been any number of people."

"Who all had to be complicit in the cover-up," Dianthe said. "I feel sorry for Stefen. He seemed like a nice man. Not like that old manservant whatever-his-name-was. In hindsight, he looked like he might have known the truth. He certainly went out of his way to dissuade Stefen from agreeing to our proposal."

"In which case, he'll have to stay silent, or explain why he knows we're lying," Alaric said. "Perrin, is there any way to verify that there aren't any more ghosts haunting this place?"

"Phantasms, and yes," Perrin said, "provided that Averran is willing to bless this place with his presence. I think I will make that request now. Please excuse me, I should find a central location from which to pray." He handed his stack of books to Kalanath and left the room.

"This one is different," Kalanath said, holding up the top book from Perrin's stack. "It is a diary."

"Perrin said he'd found a journal," Sienne said. "May I see?"

Kalanath handed the book to Sienne. "Well, that confirms it, Penthea was our necromancer," Sienne said. "Her name's inside the front cover, and it starts with a reference to trying a new ritual to summon a ghost. The first entry is dated about thirty-two years ago, and..." She skimmed through the pages. "The last one is three days before the Lepporos left the estate, and four days before Penthea's death. I think we should read this carefully. That necromancer's letters suggested she was researching ancient ritual, and this might be where she kept her notes."

"If we're not going to tell Stefen the truth, what are we supposed to do with all these necromancy books?" Dianthe said.

"Dump them into the basement before we seal it up," Alaric said. "Now, this looks interesting. It's not a real book." He showed them what looked like a large book, its leather binding cracked with age. A ribbon bookmark dangled from between the pages. When Alaric tugged on it, they heard a click, and the cover of the book popped open. Alaric lifted it and revealed the book was actually a box, stuffed full of folded papers. "Looks like letters."

Kalanath took one and unfolded it. "The handwriting is too messy for me to read." He handed it to Dianthe.

"It's from...I can't make out the signature," she said. "Looks like... he's answering some question she has about a binding ritual."

"Binding?" Alaric exclaimed.

"That's all it says."

"This letter isn't in the same handwriting," Sienne said, unfolding another one. "It looks like Penthea shoved all her letters into this box."

"It's getting late, and I want to be back in Fioretti before sunset," Alaric said. "We'll take these with us."

Sienne closed the book-box and put it into her pack with the other book and the journal. "Is that all?"

"Not quite," Dianthe said. "Hurry, though. Denys and I are going dancing tonight."

"I still don't know what you see in him," Alaric grumbled.

"He's handsome and clever," Sienne said.

"He's also a guard lieutenant," Alaric pointed out.

"Nothing wrong with that. And he was just promoted to captain," Dianthe said. She gathered up the books they'd already discarded and tossed them into the hole to land in a series of thumps far below. "It's not like we're not law abiding citizens, just because we're scrappers."

"Your skill set isn't exactly lawful." Alaric handed her a few more books for throwing away.

"I'm no thief. Just because I could be if I wanted doesn't make me a criminal."

"Of course not," Sienne said. "You're the most honest person I know."

Perrin appeared in the doorway. "I am assured there are no more malign influences on this house," he said. "I hesitate to ask, but do we know whose poor body we burned?"

"It might be in the journal." Sienne shuddered. "I'd almost rather not know. Who could do that to a child?"

"Necromancers aren't known for caring about morality," Alaric said. "Or for their compassionate natures. I wouldn't be surprised to learn Penthea had a child who died of a mysterious illness, or an unfortunate fall, when he was seven or eight."

Sienne shuddered again. "Don't let's talk about it, please?" She set down the last book in her stack. "The rest of these are all necromancy theory, ideas about why necromancy works when it's not magic, things like that. Nothing we can use."

Dianthe dumped the final books down the hole. "Let's seal it up and get back to town. This place makes me ill."

Sienne climbed back on the little table and examined the book that had started everything. "There's a hook here this book—it's not a book, it's wood painted to look like a book—connects to. I think, if we snap it off—"

"Let me," Alaric said, reaching past her. With a twist, he broke the mechanism and tossed the bit of metal down the hole. "Are all the incriminating things accounted for? Kalanath, help me move this bookcase."

With the bookcase back in place and the books restored to their shelves, there was no evidence that anything was hidden in the library. Sienne moved the table back to its original position and took one last look out the window. The sun's rays slanted across the ocean, gilding the waves and the whitecaps. "This is a beautiful place," she said, "but I can't help hoping Stefen won't choose to restore it."

"I can't stop seeing that tiny body," Dianthe said.

"We set the child's spirit free," Perrin said. "Try to see that for the blessing it is."

"I can't help feeling God failed that child," Sienne said. "I don't mean to blaspheme, but how can She abandon one of Her creations like that? Leaving it trapped for thirty years and more in that basement?"

"It is why necromancy is so evil," Perrin said, holding open the front door to allow the others to precede him. "Necromancers interfere with the natural progression of life and death. I know little of the details, Averran not being overly concerned with the state of the soul after death, but I am aware that God gathers Her creations to Her bosom when they die, and the spiritual laws that make that possible also allow humans to warp them to their own ends. For God to make necromancy impossible would mean preventing human spirits from reaching their eternal home."

"Well, it seems unfair. But I feel that way about a lot of things."

"You have a highly developed sense of justice, Sienne. That is not bad."

Sienne mounted her horse, Spark, and turned her toward the road leading home. "I guess if everything were truly, perfectly fair, a lot of us would get fates we didn't like. It's not like we're perfect."

"Very sensible," Alaric said, with another one of those private smiles that made Sienne's heart beat faster.

The Lepporo estate was half an hour's ride east of Fioretti, capital of Rafellin, and the sun was in Sienne's eyes all the way back. By the time they reached the eastern gate, she had a headache on top of her growing hunger. She said goodbye to Spark at the stable and trudged after Alaric toward their lodgings at Master Tersus's house. She never minded walking behind him, particularly at this time of day, when the streets were flooded with men and women returning to their homes after the day's labors. Alaric, over six and a half feet tall with broad shoulders and an imposing physique, broke the crowds far more easily than she could have done.

"Are you all right, Sienne?" Dianthe said, glancing back at her.

"Headache. And I'm hungry."

"You're not still suffering from that phantasm's attack, are you?" Alaric asked.

"No. But I'll be ready for an early bedtime."

"That makes sense."

Alaric sounded disappointed. Had he had something else in mind? She already knew he would never go dancing with her—he claimed he looked like a performing bear when he danced—and their relationship was still a secret from everyone but Dianthe.

Sienne wasn't sure how she felt about that. Maybe he wanted to keep their relationship secret because it didn't mean very much to him.

Her initial relaxed attitude toward her attraction to Alaric had faded as her feelings for him had changed. She'd been in love exactly once before, with someone who hadn't loved her in return, and she couldn't tell if Alaric felt for her what she felt for him. She loved being with him, loved talking to him or just sitting quietly hand in hand, and kissing, and he seemed to like that too...but what if all he cared about was the physical intimacy? What if she was just the one who was available?

She felt so stupid. Love was one of those basic things you ought to recognize when you saw it, right? So what was wrong with her?

The back hall of Master Tersus's house smelled deliciously of roast chicken with rosemary, one of Sienne's favorite dishes. Leofus, the cook and general manservant, waved his familiar spoon at them as they entered the kitchen. "Just in time," he said. "Go get cleaned up."

Sienne exchanged looks with Kalanath. Leofus believed scrappers needed to be reminded of the basic etiquette of civilization, or they'd do things like come to the dinner table covered in the grime of whatever expedition they'd been on. Kalanath shrugged and propped his staff against the wall. "It is not as dirty as last time," he murmured.

"I still feel grimy," Sienne replied as they all crowded into the bath house where the sink and pump were. "I don't know how much of it is real dirt."

"Not much," Alaric said, working the pump. "But try convincing Leofus of that."

Sienne splashed water on her face as well as her hands, just in case. Maybe after dinner she could take an actual bath. It might help her lose some of the uncomfortable feeling hanging over her like a shroud.

She stayed quiet during the meal, not feeling much like talking. Nobody seemed to notice, since their meals at Master Tersus's house were excellent and not the kind of thing that encouraged conversation over eating. Dianthe finished first and cleared her plate. "Tell

Denys I'll be right down if he arrives soon," she said, and vanished out the door.

"I know," Sienne said. "You still don't know what she sees in him."

"He's so law-abiding you could use him as a plumb line," Alaric said.

"So is Dianthe. Just because she knows how to pick locks—"

"It's not that. Dianthe is flexible. She obeys laws because they make sense, not because laws are intrinsically worth following. Renaldi never met a law he wouldn't follow, no matter the circumstances." Alaric sighed. "I'm just afraid it will hurt her someday."

A knock sounded at the back door. Sienne swiveled in her seat to watch Leofus leave the kitchen. A few moments later, he returned with Denys Renaldi following him. Tall and dark-haired like a typical Rafellish, Denys had a pleasant smile and hazel eyes that crinkled at the corners. Tonight he wore, not his customary guard lieutenant's uniform, but nice suede trousers and a fine linen shirt under an embroidered vest, more expensive than Sienne would have thought someone on a guardsman's salary could afford. He turned his smile on Sienne and nodded a greeting.

Alaric stood when Denys entered, prompting Sienne to hide her smile behind her hand. If Denys knew Alaric was trying to intimidate him, he showed no sign of it. "Alaric," Denys said politely.

"Renaldi," Alaric said in his deepest voice. "Going dancing?"

"That is the plan, yes." Denys nodded at Perrin and Kalanath, who were still eating. "How are things? Still engaged in finding artifacts for those with too much money and not enough sense?"

"We are. You still busy hunting down petty criminals and treading them underfoot?"

"More or less. You haven't heard the latest scandal?"

Alaric raised his eyebrows. "Apparently not."

"I was sure you'd know about it, scrapper and all that."

"We've been busy."

Silence fell. Alaric studied his nails. Denys clasped his hands behind his back and examined the ceiling. "Oh, for heaven's sake,"

Sienne exclaimed. "*I* don't mind showing my ignorance. What's going on, Denys?"

Denys's lips quirked in a wry smile. "Funny you should ask, Sienne," he said. "There have been ghoul sightings at some of the larger cemeteries, both inside Fioretti and outside the city walls."

"Ghoul?" Kalanath said. "What is a ghoul?"

"Masterless undead," Perrin said. "Corpses raised to unlife by necromancers who then lose control of them. Without a link to their master, they must consume human flesh to avoid a second death. Hence their haunting of graveyards—they prefer to eat corpses—"

Sienne dropped her chicken leg and pushed her plate away.

"My apologies. This is not the conversation for the supper table," Perrin said.

"You're right, though," Denys said. "But ghouls will attack living people if they can't get their, um, preferred food. Sorry, Sienne. At any rate, the guard presence has been increased near the cemeteries, just in case. The ghoul sightings haven't been confirmed, and nobody's been attacked, but after what happened three years ago, the king has ordered us not to take chances."

"What happened three years ago? Or is that another conversation not fit for the dinner table?" Sienne asked.

"Three years ago a coven of necromancers—"

"I believe the collective noun is 'blight'," Perrin said.

"I can't believe you know that," Alaric said.

"I can," Sienne said. "Anyway, there was a blight of necromancers three years ago?"

"They tried to raise an army of undead to destroy the Duchess of Marisse," Denys went on. "The plan, as it came out at their trial, was to take advantage of the many cemeteries here in Fioretti and march the undead across country to Marisse. Stupid, given how far away Marisse is, but nobody said you had to be smart to be a necromancer. They didn't get very far before they started losing control of their creatures. Once that happened, and the ghouls began attacking people here in the city, the guard easily tracked them down and put an end to the plot. But some people were killed, and the king came under attack for not doing enough to prevent it. As if there were more he could have done."

"Like hunting down necromancers more diligently?" Alaric said.

"It's not illegal to study necromancy, just to perform it," Denys said icily. "And even then necromancers are entitled to a fair trial. The king's laws are just without being unfairly punitive."

"He's not my king," Alaric said. "But it doesn't matter. You say you haven't seen any actual ghouls?"

"Not one. But I have a feeling about this. I think it's legitimate."

"What is?" Dianthe said. She took Denys's arm and kissed his cheek. She'd changed into a full-skirted calf-length dress of sapphire blue that would swirl nicely while she danced. Sienne, who didn't like dresses, felt a pang of envy she immediately suppressed. It wasn't as if she was fond of dancing, anyway. Much.

"Rumors of ghoul attacks," Alaric said. "Nothing for us to worry about."

"I should think not," Dianthe said. "And nothing for *you* to worry about either, Denys. For tonight, anyway." She squeezed his arm. "Don't anyone wait up."

3

When Dianthe and a rather starry-eyed Denys were gone, Sienne picked up her plate. She still felt weary, but her mind was alert and sleep was far from it. "I think I'll make a start on that journal before I go to bed."

"And I'll see if I can organize those letters," Alaric said.

"As I can provide no assistance with those tasks, I intend to go for a walk," Perrin said. "Good evening, all."

Sienne cleared her place and retrieved her pack from the corner where she'd left it. "Good night, Perrin."

The back door had barely closed behind Perrin when Kalanath said, "I do not like it."

"Like what?" Alaric scraped the bones off his plate into the scraps bucket.

"He walks frequently in the evenings."

"There's nothing wrong with that."

Kalanath shook his head. "I fear he goes to taverns."

Sienne paused in the kitchen doorway. "No. He wouldn't. Do you have some reason to believe it?"

"No reason. But he returns late and avoids us when he does. I cannot think of some other thing he might do on these long walks."

A shiver of dread ran down Sienne's spine. Perrin's drinking had become such a problem that he'd come under chastisement of his avatar Averran, with the result that he'd sworn to Averran he wouldn't drink at all. As far as Sienne knew, he'd kept that vow, but Kalanath was right; Perrin had gone off by himself frequently these last few weeks. She remembered how he'd looked, those days when Averran refused to speak to him. Falling back into those habits would be devastating not only to him personally, but to all of them. "He doesn't smell of liquor."

"Unless he's avoiding us until the smell wears off." Alaric looked grim.

"No. I don't believe it. Besides, what could we do if it were true?" Sienne shook her head. "And if it *is* true, don't you think Averran would chastise him again? We'd certainly know about that."

"I did not think of this." Kalanath looked more cheerful. "Then it is something else."

"You're right, though. Perrin has been going off on his own a lot lately," Alaric said. "But that's none of our business."

"If there's something bothering him, he'll tell us when he's ready. If he wants to talk about it at all," Sienne said. "Will you join us?"

"My reading in Fellic is slow. I think I will not be much help," Kalanath said. "I will practice and then go to sleep." He retrieved his staff, saluted them with it, and went out the back door.

"I guess it's just us," Sienne said with a smile. The idea made her tiredness and lingering aches fade.

Alaric smiled back. "That's the nicest thing I've heard all day."

They walked down the back hall to a flimsy wooden door that separated the kitchen and bath house from what Sienne thought of as the public areas of Master Tersus's house. Stairs just past the door led up to Master Tersus's bedroom, his private study, and the second bedroom he used as a showcase for part of his art collection. Beyond the stairs on the ground floor were the formal sitting room, the library—devoid of books and full, again, of art—the dining room, and a small room overlooking the side garden that Master Tersus had no use for.

It had a sofa and armchair that didn't match, a short oval table too low for the comfort of anyone sitting in the sofa or armchair, a bookcase of some exotic hardwood that was too big for the room, and a gaudy floral rug woven in blue and pink that remained vibrant and unfaded despite its being about twenty years old. Sienne's theory was that it was so ugly it would never wear out. Sienne and her friends rented the room from Master Tersus along with their own bedrooms and use of the bath house. Since Master Tersus received the benefit of the team's presence as a theft deterrent for free, Sienne thought he was getting a tremendous bargain.

She dropped her pack next to the sofa and squeaked as Alaric put his arms around her and drew her down to sit beside him. "Shouldn't we—" she said.

"It can wait," Alaric said, and kissed her, a long, slow kiss that made the room spin. She put her arms around his neck and returned his kiss. She never felt so safe and happy as when she was in his arms, and not just because he had arms nearly as big around as her waist. It was because he was the man he was, the man she loved, and if he loved her too, everything would be perfect. There had to be some way to figure out how Alaric felt, short of being the first to say those three little words. She hated herself for her cowardice.

"Something wrong?" Alaric murmured, tucking her under one arm in a gesture that never failed to make her feel warm all over.

"Just remembering the ghoul story," she lied. "It's horrible and disgusting. I hate that we have even the most academic connection to necromancy. I know it's foolish, but I can't help feeling...complicit, maybe."

"I understand. The idea that the potion we're looking for might be necromantic worries me. If the ritual we want is tainted, should we really pursue it?"

"But it can't be. Don't you think you would know if the Sassaven ritual, the one the wizard uses to bind your people, was necromantic? Given all the searching you've done? This has to be a coincidence." Sienne sighed. "My hope is that we'll stumble on other rituals hidden among these necromancy books, and one of them will be the one we need."

"I like that hope. I'll borrow it." Alaric kissed her forehead and released her. "Let's see if we can make some progress."

Sienne reached into her pack and brought out the book-box, handing it to Alaric. "I'm going to go through the other book first. The one with the rituals. I can mark the ones that call for varnwort—that shouldn't take long."

Alaric nodded. He popped open the box and stirred through its contents. "I wonder how necromancers ever find other necromancers. They can't possibly advertise their profession to the world."

"I suppose they start by pretending they're only interested in the theory, and dance around the question of practice."

Sienne opened the book of rituals and tore out the last page. Alaric made a startled noise. "It's blank. I need something for marking the pages. The only other paper I have is cut to exactly fit my spellbook, and I'm not sacrificing that."

"You could turn the corners of the pages down."

"Only savages do that." Sienne tore the paper into narrow strips and put them on the cushion next to her.

Alaric unfolded the letters one by one and put them in piles on the table. "So far I see three—no, wait, there's a fourth handwriting—four correspondences. Too bad they're so old. I imagine at least some of the writers are dead by now."

"It's still worth looking into." Sienne turned the pages of the book, scanning the elegant writing. "Have you noticed none of the necromancy books, the practical ones I mean, are printed?"

"That makes sense. I can't imagine a publishing house being willing to print a book on practical necromancy. There's a fifth letter writer." Alaric started a new pile.

"Here's a recipe including varnwort," Sienne said, marking her place. "Do you suppose Dianthe will spend the night with Denys? Why doesn't she ever bring him here?"

"What, and have sex surrounded by her family? Renaldi lives

alone in a very nice house he inherited from his grandmother. Much more congenial."

"That makes sense." She'd thought about sex with Alaric—of course she had—and had come to the conclusion that even if she was ready for sex, which she wasn't sure she was, knowing Dianthe slept next door and had very good hearing had thrown cold water on that nascent plan. "You do like Denys, really, don't you?"

Alaric sighed. "He's not who I'd choose for her, but even if she were really my sister, my opinion wouldn't be any more relevant. And yes, I can admit he's a good man, even if I wish the stick weren't quite so firmly embedded in his ass. He's never held it against Dianthe that she's a scrapper, and I know he knows she has some...extra-legal talents, and that doesn't bother him either."

"I'm glad. I like him. Dianthe is so happy with him." She marked another spot.

They worked in silence for a while, until Sienne reached the end of her book and set it aside. "I found six references to varnwort. I'll examine them more thoroughly tomorrow."

"You're not going to bed already, are you?"

"No. I want to read Penthea's journal. Well, 'want' is the wrong word. I have a feeling it will be disturbing. But I'd like to get it over with."

"Someone else can do it, Sienne."

"There's no reason I can't. 'Disturbing' isn't justification for chickening out."

Alaric chuckled. "I might have guessed you'd say that."

Sienne opened the journal, thought about leaning on Alaric, decided that would impede his work, and started reading. "Do you want to hear any of this?"

"Only if it's relevant. Are there blank pages in that? I want to take notes."

Sienne tore out a few of the pages from the back of the journal. "It's only about two-thirds written in. I should have used these instead of the ritual book's end pages." She rummaged in her pack and pulled out a stick of charcoal, which she offered to him. "Sorry I don't have a pencil."

"That's fine."

They settled into silence. Penthea's handwriting was clear and well-rounded, not what Sienne expected from a necromancer. Though she didn't know why she thought that, since it wasn't like there was some handwriting requirement for becoming a necromancer. It was probably because as a wizard, she was familiar with the four spell languages, whose script reflected the sound of the words: hard and staccato for the curt, short words of a summoning, for example, or flowing gracefulness for the sweet peace of a transform. Necromancy didn't have any such conditions.

7 Vipoletze 384

The star anise is useless. Nevalainin was either lying or deluded. I suspect the former. She never did like to see others succeed. I will have to remember this when I refer to her work again.

9 Vipoletze 384

Acacia, bladderwrack, rose hips + new beer = failure

Acacia, bladderwrack, rose hips + red wine = failure

Acacia, bladderwrack, rose hips + white wine = failure

Acacia, bladderwrack, rose hips + brandy = failure

Acacia, bladderwrack, rose hips + moon spirits = sedative, but not strong enough

Increase proportions of bladderwrack?

10 Vipoletze 384

The latest summoning lasted longer than the one previous by two minutes. Unfortunately, the ghost refused to answer my questions. It pretended no knowledge of the subject, but I know better. Ghosts are privy to secrets beyond what they knew in life, and I will prove it.

"I'm starting to get a feel for the kind of woman Penthea was," Sienne said. "Focused, driven, and impervious to the evidence of her own eyes."

"If she was focused and driven to the extent of finding the ritual we need, then I say good luck to her," Alaric said. He scribbled something on his paper and added, "In the abstract, anyway. As far as performing necromancy goes, I hope she failed."

"She succeeded in summoning ghosts occasionally. But most of her experiments were failures." Sienne turned a few more pages. Seeing Penthea's foul experiments laid out with such precision made her feel dirty. She'd collected body parts, dug up graves in secret—how could she bear to condemn herself in writing like this? Or did she think herself so far above common morality that she didn't care if people knew what she did?

24 Vipoletze 384

The potion works. My trial on Triumph was successful beyond my greatest hopes, though the dog's ghost provided no useful information, naturally. I will proceed with my experiment tonight. Philippus is an ideal candidate, and I do not know why using a child never occurred to anyone. My sons are young enough that any information Philippus provides must necessarily prove my theory, since he lacks the experience that would otherwise justify him knowing those facts. He will feel no pain—Triumph is evidence of that. Just a short sleep, and then a blessed death, and my child will vindicate me. If not, I have Stefen as well.

Sienne sucked in a sharp breath. Blessed death. A child. The lines on the page blurred together, preventing her from reading further.

"Something wrong?" Alaric said. He dropped the letter he held. "You're crying."

"We guessed it," Sienne said, her voice shaking. "The phantasm was her own child—she poisoned him with one of her foul potions, some experiment—Alaric—"

Alaric took the book out of her hands and gathered her into his arms. "We freed the child. He's beyond torment now."

"How could anyone do that to another person, let alone the child she carried inside her body and nursed and raised?"

"I don't know," Alaric murmured into her hair. "I think you need to be done for tonight. You're shaking. It's been a long day, and you're probably still suffering the effects of the phantasm's attack. It could have killed you."

"The phantasm attacked you, too. Don't you feel it?"

"I weigh more than twice what you do, and it wasn't in contact with me for as long. Come with me. I'll draw you a bath, and you can have a nice soak and then go to bed. The journal will be there in the morning."

She leaned into him and sighed with happiness. *Rance would never*, she thought, and the rest of the thought was swallowed up in a blinding revelation. Of course Rance wouldn't have had such care for her needs. He hadn't loved her.

Sienne turned and put her arms around Alaric's neck, drawing him close for a kiss that had her whole heart in it. He cradled her cheek in one large palm, brushing her hairline with his fingertips. "What brought that on?" he said when she released him. "Not that I'm complaining."

"Because of who you are," Sienne said. "And because I love you."

His eyes widened. "Sienne," he said, then kissed her fiercely, his hands settling low on her waist to pull her close. Her arms went around his neck once more, and she kissed him, moving from his lips to his cheek and then to his ear. He buried his face where her neck met her shoulder. "I love you," he murmured. "I've wanted so long to hear you say it."

"You have? You could have said something. I didn't know—I was afraid I was the only one. How long?"

He let out a short laugh and nuzzled her throat. "I've loved you since the night we first kissed. But that ass Rance Lanzano hurt you so badly, I knew you weren't ready to hear any declaration of love from me. So I waited. Not very patiently."

"You were patient. And you told me you loved me, every day, with every kiss and every tenderness. I just didn't realize until right now."

"I'm glad you realized it." Alaric caught her around the waist and lifted her into his lap. "Much better. We fit together so perfectly this way."

"I love it. I love *you*. I can't believe you love me."

"Can't you?" His lips touched hers again in a long, lingering kiss that filled her with an unexpected rush of desire. "Are you so unlovable?"

"I keep thinking how I disliked you, and you hated that I was a wizard—"

"We've come so far from those days. You're right, it's unlikely. And wonderful." Alaric kissed her again, his lips tender on hers, and once more desire filled her, a need to feel his skin against hers. She hesitated, and he drew back. "What's wrong?"

"I want you, but I'm not ready for sex. I hope you don't—that's all right, isn't it?"

His eyes narrowed. "Of course. You didn't feel I would insist on it, did you? Ten minutes ago I didn't know you loved me. Going from that to sex in half an hour is a little much."

Sienne sighed and rested her cheek against his. "I wasn't sure."

"We have all the time in the world. I love you, Sienne, and I only want you to be happy."

"I am. More than I can say."

He took her hand and squeezed it gently. "Then—bath, bed, and in the morning I intend to kiss you where everyone can see, so there's no question of how I feel about you." He laughed. "Though I doubt it will be a surprise to anyone."

"I thought we were being discreet."

"Discreet, yes, but it's hard to conceal affection from people you share such close quarters with. I wager Perrin and Kalanath have been politely pretending not to notice the way I look at you for the last several weeks. Or the way I'm prone to putting myself between you and danger."

"You do that for everyone."

"I do it far more often for you, sweetlove."

The endearment made Sienne tingle all over and briefly reconsider the no sex decision. "You have to be careful or one of these days I'll hit you with a *force* bolt meant for an enemy."

Alaric shrugged. "I try. But it's who I am."

"I know. I love that about you." Sienne stood, retaining her hold of Alaric's hand. "I don't think I'll need that bath to relax. I feel as if I could float away."

"So do I. But I still don't like the tremor in your hand." He took her by the wrist and held her hand up to her face. He was right, it trembled visibly. "I'll draw that bath, and then I'll finish sorting these letters while you soak."

"All right. Did I say I love you? Because I do."

He smiled. "You can never say it enough."

4

Alone in the bath house, half-submerged in hot water, Sienne tried to think of anything but the dead child in the chest. Unfortunately, everything she'd been doing for the last few weeks was related to necromancy, and she couldn't escape those thoughts. She wrapped her arms around her chest and let herself weep for the child. Though he had had his revenge, if he'd killed his murderer. Saved his brother Stefen too, probably, which was a cheering thought.

She heard the back door open and shut. Kalanath, or maybe Perrin. She stood and let the tub drain, then dried herself and put on her nightdress. The hot water had relaxed her enough she thought she might be able to sleep, and time would make memory fuzzy.

When she emerged from the bath house, she heard Dianthe and Alaric talking in low voices in the kitchen. She thought about stopping in to say good night, then decided not to interrupt their conversation. But as she walked past the door on her way to the stairs, she heard Dianthe say clearly, "But I am a murderer, Alaric. It's all true."

Sienne jerked around and took three rapid steps into the kitchen. "*What?*"

Dianthe and Alaric turned at her entrance. A scowl of epic

proportions transformed Alaric's normally pleasant expression into that of a furious force of nature, ready to explode. Dianthe looked as guilty and miserable as Sienne had ever seen her. "Nothing," Alaric said.

"She said—"

"Don't try to protect me, Alaric," Dianthe said, "there's no point in it anymore. She deserves to know the truth."

"What truth?" Kalanath said, entering behind Sienne. He held a small plate strewn with crumbs, the remnants of a bedtime snack.

"Never mind. Go to bed. We can discuss it in the morning," Alaric said. The back door opened and shut again, and Alaric closed his eyes as if praying for divine patience.

Perrin appeared in the doorway. "I hope you are not all waiting up for me." He was steady on his feet and didn't smell of alcohol.

Dianthe shook her head. "Sit down, everyone. Something's happened, and I...might need to leave Fioretti for a while."

"Leave Fioretti?" Sienne took a seat, her eyes still fixed on Dianthe. "But we're still doing research."

"Not you. Just me."

"This sounds dire," Perrin said, sitting next to Sienne. "I hope you will explain. I will otherwise imagine the worst."

"I doubt you can imagine this."

Dianthe waited for the others to take their customary places, then drew out her chair. Instead of sitting, she gripped its back and leaned slightly on it. "I don't talk about my past, and until tonight that was fine, because it didn't matter to any of you. But tonight...things changed." She drew in a deep breath and let it out slowly, her eyes focused on something far from the kitchen.

"I'm from Sileas, born and raised," she said. "When I was seventeen, I worked as a maid in the ducal palace, where my mother was head cook. It was never meant to be permanent, but I didn't know what I wanted to do with my life, so there I was. Light work, nothing too tedious, and I always had plenty of time for fun.

"There was...a man. A noble at court. You can guess where the story goes from there. He wanted me, I said no, he persisted. I learned to avoid him, and I thought I was in control. Until the night he and a friend followed me into town, got me alone and...I've never fought so hard in my life. All I had was a knife, but it turns out that's all you need to kill someone.

"My knife found his heart, he fell, the friend ran one way and I ran the other. I knew the story the friend would spread—that I'd tempted them both and then attacked them."

"But that's ridiculous! Who would believe anything so stupid?" Sienne exclaimed.

"The duke of Sileas isn't as honorable as he should be. Whenever it's a question of a noble's word against anyone else, no matter the evidence, the noble always wins. It wouldn't matter that it was two against one or that all the staff knew how that man had been after me. I killed him, and that made me a murderer. I got out of Sileas as fast as I could, but news of my deed had already spread, and I had to use every trick I knew to escape. Then I went as far north as I could get."

Kalanath stirred. "If you were a servant, how did you know to fight two men and survive? Or to escape the guard?"

Dianthe smiled. "I was only a servant because I didn't want to be a thief. I had a friend, Corbyn—actually, he was one of my mother's friends, and I think he was sweet on her, though he never did anything about it. He used to hang around the kitchens, cadging food and entertaining me. Corbyn played games with me when I was a child, seeking games and puzzle games...I didn't know he was teaching me his skills until the first time he gave me a padlock and showed me how to open it without a key. I think I was fourteen. He showed me how to conceal a knife where even the keenest guard wouldn't spot it, and how to strike with that knife from the shadows. It saved my life, though there were times I almost wished it hadn't."

"Never say that," Perrin said. "Your life is precious. We are all of us grateful you survived."

"At the cost of another's life. And at the cost of my own, if you figure I had to leave my mother, my friends, and everything I knew behind when I fled." Dianthe sighed. "I made my way to Concord, the free city, and then I met Alaric. So it wasn't all bad."

"I had to talk hard to convince her to come south with me," Alaric said. "Fioretti is a big enough city for anyone to lose herself in, and we couldn't make a living hiring out as bodyguards from Concord—too many other people looking for the same work."

"This is what I always feared," Dianthe said. "Being found."

"Did someone identify you?" Perrin asked.

"Wanted posters. Big ones, all over the south side, offering a thousand lari reward for information leading to my capture. Looking for Dianthe Katraki, not Dianthe Espero, granted, and it's not like the drawing looks much like me, but it's just a matter of time before someone puts it together."

"But it's so unfair!" Sienne exclaimed. "Are you saying in Sileas it's illegal for a woman to defend herself? That's not murder!"

"Nobody knows the truth but me and that other man," Dianthe said, "and he wouldn't speak up to defend the low-class bitch who killed his friend. There's nothing I can do but get out of town and wait for this to blow over."

"That's not a solution," Alaric said. "Are you going to keep running every time the search heats up? It's been nine years, Dianthe —why would they come looking for you now?"

"Who knows? Maybe the dead man's family experienced a sudden surge of familial pride and decided it was a matter of honor for them to find me and bring me to justice. It doesn't matter."

"Wait—where's Denys?" Sienne asked. "What happened when he saw the posters?"

"He didn't see them. I steered him out of that area and then faked an illness. I don't think he believed me. He's too smart sometimes. I'm afraid I hurt his feelings, but—" Dianthe buried her face in her hands. "My worst nightmare is him putting me under arrest. I've done everything I can to stay on the right side of the law, because it would kill him if he had to do that."

"He won't," Alaric said. "You said those posters look nothing like you, and he doesn't work that side of town, anyway. Dianthe, you don't have to run."

"Not forever. Just for a few weeks. A month, maybe." She didn't look convinced.

"Then I guess we should pack up," Sienne said. "I'm sure we can find a job that will take us out of the city for a while."

"Sienne, this is my problem. None of you should have to uproot because of me."

"You are one of us," Kalanath said. "If we were in trouble, you would not wait to help. You should not be alone."

"Exactly," Perrin said. "Now, I would suggest we tear down all those posters, but it seems to me that would suggest to someone they are looking in the right place. Sienne is right, packing is the next step."

"We're not going anywhere," Alaric said. "Dianthe, Fioretti is three times the size of Sileas. There's no way anyone will find you here. We'll stay out of the south side and you won't go out alone, just in case. Whoever is funding this search won't be able to keep it up forever; they'll run out of money. We just have to stay out of sight until that happens."

"Oh!" Sienne exclaimed. "I must be more tired than I thought. I can cast *shift* or even *imitate* and you won't look anything like yourself!"

"An excellent idea!" Perrin exclaimed. "Have you never dreamed of being an Omeiran redhead?"

"I don't speak Meiric," Dianthe said, laughing. "But...yes, that would make me feel more comfortable. Even so, you shouldn't—"

"Do not say it is a thing we should not do because it is dangerous," Kalanath said. "It is what we do for each other."

"Then I won't say it," Dianthe said. "Thank you, all of you. The idea of running again...it was so hard, last time, and it's even harder now."

"I suggest we all go to bed," Alaric said. "I've done some reading of those letters, and I have five names I want us to track down in the morning. They were all in correspondence with Penthea Lepporo about practical necromancy, and at least one of them knew something about binding rituals. Probably some of them are dead now, but it's worth pursuing."

Sienne pushed back from the table. "I'll read more of her journal tomorrow. She seems to have wanted the binding ritual to trap a spirit without turning it into a phantasm, and one of her experiments might have succeeded."

"You don't have to be the one to read it," Alaric said.

She smiled. "I don't mind, really. It will be easier in the morning. I feel we're getting closer, don't you?"

"I will be happy when we have the ritual and must no longer study these things," Kalanath said, wrinkling his nose with distaste. "I fear what I will dream tonight."

Sienne watched him covertly. This was not the first time Kalanath had complained of bad dreams, and Sienne suspected him of being superstitious about them. She didn't know if it was an Omeiran thing, or if it was personal, but so long as he never talked about them, she didn't feel comfortable prying.

She followed Dianthe up the stairs, and at the top, she hugged her friend and said, "You wouldn't have just left without saying anything, right?"

Dianthe returned her embrace. "I might have. I'm glad I have all of you to keep me sensible."

"You're usually the sensible one. This makes a nice change." She smiled at Alaric, whose smile in return was warm but absent, as if he were thinking of the next day's plans already.

Safely in bed, she curled on her side and searched for thoughts that weren't a small body wedged into a trunk. Even remembering Alaric's arms around her, the feeling of being loved and cherished, wasn't enough to dispel the images. It took her an hour to fall asleep.

———

THE NEXT DAY DAWNED BLEAK AND CHILLY, WITH RAIN HAVING FALLEN THE previous night and threatening to do so again. Sienne ate her porridge and stared out the window at the side garden where Kalanath was practicing despite the weather. He whirled his staff through a complicated routine of blocks and thrusts that dizzied Sienne. She didn't know enough about fighting to tell if his routine included an invisible partner. Surely he'd trained against real opponents, back in Omeira.

"Good morning," Alaric said, leaning down for a kiss. She returned it, feeling horribly self-conscious and aware that Perrin was seated opposite her even as her heart beat a merry welcome to her love. Perrin eyed them both, but said nothing, instead taking another long drink of hot coffee. Dianthe didn't say anything either. Maybe Alaric was right, and this was something her friends had known all along.

Alaric's plate overflowed with two slabs of ham, a pile of bacon, and three fried eggs. Sienne's stomach revolted at the idea of solid food so early in the morning. She spooned up more comforting porridge and said, "I hope there's something we can do for research that keeps us indoors today. I hate the idea of trudging around Fioretti in the rain."

"Unfortunately, trudging is on the schedule," Alaric said. "Three of the five letter writers live in Fioretti, or did thirty years ago. We're going to visit each of them and see if we can get them to open up about their knowledge of necromancy."

"I fear that will test even my well-known diplomatic skills," Perrin said. "Do we have a specific line of inquiry to pursue?"

"We'll start by mentioning Penthea Lepporo and the correspondence each had with her. If we present ourselves as fellow researchers into necromancy, without hinting that we believe them to be practitioners, we should come across as innocuous enough that they'll open up."

"So what's our interest in Penthea?" Dianthe asked. "They'll want to know why we care about a thirty-year-old correspondence."

"We're scrappers." Alaric took another large mouthful of food. "We're working on behalf of the family to recover Penthea's records, and we hope her old friends might know something about where she stored them."

"Isn't that a little flimsy?" Sienne asked.

"Yes, but that's part of the plan," Alaric said. "If one of them knows more about necromantic practice than he's willing to admit, he'll believe we're hiding a similar interest under our threadbare cover story. It's a signal that we're fellow initiates, or something like that."

"Clever." Sienne scraped the last of her porridge from her bowl and stood to take it to the sink. Kalanath came in, his red hair beaded with rain, and she said, "Is it raining, then?"

"A little," Kalanath said, running his fingers through his hair. "Not enough to be a trouble."

"Then I'm changing my clothes," Sienne said, and hurried upstairs.

When she returned, the table had been cleared of dishes, and five stacks of papers lay atop it. Alaric still sat at the head of the table, but now he had a sheet of paper in front of him. He held a stick of charcoal loosely in his fingers. "Here's the names we know, and their addresses," he said as Sienne came to his side. She read the list over his shoulder:

Drusilla Tallavena, The Havens, Fioretti
Pedreo Giannus, 15 Sunrise Alley, Tagliaveno
Ivar Scholten, 2 West Gardens, Onofreo
Uriane Samretto, Gloriosa, Fioretti
Pauro Murtaviti, 34 Carissima Lane, Fioretti

"We'll look the ones in the city up first," Alaric said. "Onofreo's not far, but there's no sense going out of town, or starting a correspondence, if what we want is one of those three."

"Do we know where they are?" Kalanath said. "What is 'The Havens'?"

"Rich people sometimes name their houses fancy things," Dianthe said. "It's stupid, but it can make them easy to find if you know what neighborhood it's in. Unfortunately it doesn't narrow the neighborhood down like a street address and a number does." She prodded the last name with her finger. "I know roughly where this is."

"And I am familiar with the residence Gloriosa," Perrin said. He didn't look happy about it.

"Is it going to be a problem?" Alaric said.

"Unlikely. I am not personally acquainted with the Samretto family, but the Deluccos do business with them. It is possible Mistress Samretto will not wish to admit me into her home. Or she may welcome me with open arms, if she is at odds with my father. It is impossible to say."

"It's a chance I'm willing to take," Alaric said. He picked up one of the piles and shuffled through it. "Pauro Murtaviti's letters to Penthea focus on necromantic theory. My feeling is that Master Murtaviti is not a practicing necromancer, because there wasn't any discussion of raising spirits in the letters, but he might just have been extremely careful. He mentions binding rituals a few times, again in the context of theory, so it's worth pursuing." He picked up a different pile. "And Uriane Samretto is the one who specifically instructed Penthea in binding rituals. She was definitely a practicing necromancer, and not cautious. Her letters suggest certain books Penthea could use, and it's possible she owns these books. If we could get her to let us look at them, that might be valuable."

"So we should see her first," Kalanath said.

"She does sound like the likeliest prospect," Alaric said. "And I was thinking we could ask Renaldi if he knows The Havens."

Dianthe laughed. "Wait, you're serious? You're considering going to Denys for help?"

"No, I was going to send you. Renaldi goes all over his part of Fioretti and I imagine he knows it well. It would save time if we don't have to go to the records hall and look it up the hard way, or send a letter and risk spooking our target."

"I'll ask him. But I'm telling him it was your idea."

Alaric grimaced. "Fine. Whatever makes you happy. But first, let's tackle Uriane Samretto."

5

The rain fell just heavily enough that Sienne was grateful for her rain cape and her waterproof boots, well-worn from months of travel and very comfortable. For once she walked beside Alaric and marveled at how different the view was when she didn't have him looming before her. People scuttling along the street, hunched into their cloaks or clutching coats over their heads, veered out of his path as if he were a rock they might otherwise dash themselves upon. Alaric strode along without seeming to notice their behavior.

"How does that feel?" she asked.

Alaric looked down at her. "How does what feel?"

"Being the one everyone gets out of the way of."

"Do they?" His eyebrows went up. "I hadn't noticed."

"You are rather like a ship breaking the waves," Perrin, on Alaric's other side, pointed out.

"Really?" Alaric focused on a couple coming toward them, holding hands. The man tugged the woman to one side when they were a few feet in front of Alaric, glancing up at the big man with something like awe in his eyes. Sienne giggled. Alaric reddened. "I don't see what I can do about it," he said.

"I didn't mean to make you self-conscious. I think it's...endearing," Sienne said.

He smiled. "Well, if that's what you think, then I won't let it bother me."

"We are grateful to bask in your reflected impressiveness," Perrin said with a grin.

"You're welcome."

There weren't many pedestrians to step out of Alaric's way, and even fewer horses. A carriage or two passed them, sending up splashes of water that prompted Alaric to trade places with Sienne so she wasn't walking on the street side of the pavement. Even that little, casual gesture made her feel like she was flying. How had she not noticed, all these weeks, that he never stopped looking out for her? And yet he never tried to protect her from herself, or stop her doing things "for her own good." So that was what love looked like. It was better than she'd ever dreamed.

Perrin led them across the Sancorus Bridge, past the palace on its isle in the middle of the Vochus River, and into a gated enclave where private guards examined them closely, but didn't call for them to stop. "Security is rather lax," he murmured, "though as we are the beneficiaries of that laxity, I hesitate to draw attention to it."

"Maybe we don't look disreputable enough," Dianthe said. "Or maybe we look like the hired help, and they have orders not to interfere with the servants. I know I'd be angry if the guards kept stopping and delaying my cleaning people." Her normally dark blonde hair was currently chestnut like Sienne's, her face was plumper, and her eyes were bright blue. Sienne had opted for small *shift* changes rather than the full-body confusion *imitate*, reasoning that anyone looking for the woman on the wanted posters, which she still hadn't seen, would be fooled just as well by the little things, and it took less of her magical resources and lasted longer. Hearing Dianthe's voice coming out of a stranger's face still gave Sienne goose pimples, as if she'd contributed to her friend's disappearance.

The houses within the enclave sprawled rather than rising high the way the houses in Master Tersus's neighborhood did. Stone and glass and wrought iron gave the impression of houses hewn from a mountainside rather than built, their roofs of colored slate tiles the only mark of individuality among them. At the moment, those roofs were dull with rain, but they would be bright and cheerful when true summer came. Gardens surrounded each house, the property lines defined by evergreen hedges that rose no more than four feet high. Despite the gate guards' lack of initiative, the residents clearly counted on them to keep out undesirables.

It took five minutes of walking to reach the Samretto home, during which time Sienne assessed the architectural qualities of each residence they passed. She'd grown up dividing her time between the ducal palace in Beneddo and her parents' estate in the country some ten miles north of the city, both of which were over a hundred years old. New construction like this, the kind that tried to pass itself off as old, didn't impress her, but the gardens were lovely. One of them had an ivy-twined gazebo Sienne almost wished she could sit in, drinking a glass of wine and enjoying the sights and smells of her garden. So long as someone else tended it. She didn't so much have a black thumb as an entire black fist when it came to gardening.

The Samretto home looked just like all the others, though its roof was greenish-gray slate and its garden looked rawer than its neighbors, as if it had been planted more recently. She followed Perrin up the path, careful not to slip on the round stones that were slick with rain, and waited beside Dianthe as he struck the door with the heavy brass knocker. Alaric stood at the back of their little group, next to Kalanath, on the grounds that this was not the kind of conversation where they needed to intimidate someone. Yet.

Presently the door opened, and an elderly woman in a long-skirted black dress peered out. "Yes?"

"Good morning," Perrin said with a bow. "We desire to speak with Mistress Uriane Samretto. Is she in?"

"Mistress Uriane?" The woman sounded surprised. "Mistress Uriane has been dead these five years."

Sienne's heart sank. "I am sorry to hear that," Perrin said, sounding genuinely regretful. "Thank you for your time."

"Would you like to speak to Master Samretto?" The woman held the door open wider. "He does so love visitors."

Perrin didn't hesitate. "That would be most kind, yes." He glanced back and made a "follow me" gesture with his eyebrows, then walked through the door.

Sienne cast a glance at Alaric, whose expression was neutral. What did Perrin think they could achieve in talking to the woman's widower?

She followed Perrin into the small entry and wiped her feet on the mat just inside. Two doors to the left and right were closed, and a hallway led deeper into the house. The room smelled of floor polish and mildew, as if someone had started cleaning at the bottom and hadn't made it as far as the corners of the ceiling. Two flower arrangements in alabaster vases flanked the front door, but they were either long dead or intentionally dried out. Sienne had never seen the point in dried flowers; they lacked scent and color. So much better to use live flowers, or better yet, leave the flowers uncut and appreciate them in their natural habitat.

The old woman gestured to them to wait and disappeared down the hall, moving in the halting way of someone whose joints pained her. Alaric took a few steps after her, then turned on Perrin. "What are we supposed to say to this old man?"

"I had not thought that far, frankly," Perrin said. "It is unlikely Master Samretto can tell us anything of his late wife's necromantic pursuits, even if he was aware of them. But if she had a library, and he has not gotten rid of it, he might permit us to look through it."

"Good point. It's worth asking, anyway."

Alaric stepped back as the old woman made her slow, careful way down the hall toward them. "Master Samretto will be happy to speak with you. If you'll follow me?"

Perrin took the lead, with Sienne close behind him matching the woman's short, limping stride. She hoped she didn't look like she was trying to mock her. But the woman didn't look back. Sienne had plenty of time to observe the paintings on the walls, which were mostly still life oils done by the same hand. The one exception was a landscape done by the artist Penaco Muretti, whose signature and style Sienne recognized. It was of far higher quality than the rest. How had a Muretti ended up in this narrow, dark hall where no one would ever see it? It was a mystery, and one that didn't let her draw any conclusions about the owner.

There were no doors along the hallway, just one at its far end that had no latch and never had done as far as Sienne could tell. The old woman pushed it open, and it swung freely on its hinges. "Master Samretto, your guests," she said.

A wave of heat struck Sienne in the face as she entered, starting her sweating under her arms and beneath her hair. A fire too large for the small fireplace burned hot and bright, and even though Sienne was sure a lot of the heat was sucked up the chimney, there was more than enough left over to turn the room into a furnace. Two windows that might have been opened to give some relief were shuttered tight, with drapes drawn over them so the fire was the only light in the room. A couple of bookcases flanked the fireplace, and a high-backed armchair and footstool were drawn up so near the flames any sitter would have his feet roasted.

In the armchair sat a frail old man, with pale parchment-like skin over thin bones like a starving wisp. His thick white hair seemed too heavy for his head, which nodded on a skinny neck that should not have been able to support it. Smoked glass lenses the size of coffee cups covered his eyes, which were buried in wrinkles. Sienne thought he was asleep until he turned his head and smiled at them, causing a cascade of wrinkles like ripples on the surface of a still lake. "Welcome, welcome," he said, his voice as thin as his bones. "No one's come asking about Uriane for years. Sit, please—there are chairs—"

Sienne looked around. There was another armchair in the corner, placed facing the wall as if it were being punished, and a couple of ladderback chairs more suited to a kitchen than a drawing room. She pulled one of these forward and sat. Perrin took the armchair and turned it around. Dianthe and Kalanath sat on more of the kitchen chairs. Alaric, left without a seat, took up a watchful stance just inside the door.

"There, that's better. My, aren't you big. Ansorjan?" The old man looked Alaric up and down. Alaric nodded once. "They seem to grow them larger every year. And—but where are my manners? I'm Myles Samretto."

"Perrin Delucco," Perrin said, bowing in his seat. "These are my companions Alaric, Dianthe, Sienne, and Kalanath."

Myles Samretto's eyes gleamed beyond the dark glasses, and the wrinkles deepened. Sienne held her breath, certain they were about to be kicked out because of Perrin's surname. But instead, he said, "An Omeiran! *I welcome you to home mine,*" he added in halting Meiric.

"*Thank you,*" Kalanath said in the same language. "*It's an honor to speak with someone so graced with years. The heat's quite comfortable.*"

"Not everyone appreciates it," Samretto said, "but I spent many years in Omeira when I was young and grew to love the desert and its dry heat. But you didn't come to talk about me. This is about Uriane's avocation, isn't it?"

"Her...avocation?" Perrin said.

Samretto nodded at Perrin, but addressed himself to Kalanath. "The necromancy. I never could persuade her to give it up. She never would have hurt anyone, you know, none of this raising the dead business. She simply felt more at home with dead people than with living ones, with the exception of myself, thank Kitane. And she was good at it, too..."

His words trailed off, and his head drooped. Perrin opened his mouth to speak, hesitated, then made a face at Kalanath that said clearly *He likes you, you talk to him.* Kalanath shook his head. Perrin glowered at him, his lips tightening. Kalanath rolled his eyes and said, "You are not afraid to admit it?"

Samretto's head came up with a jerk. "Admit what?"

"That your wife did necromancy."

"Oh, that. Well, she's been dead five years, so who's to be hurt by the admission? And, as I said, she never hurt anyone. Helped people, really. Someone's beloved auntie dies unexpectedly, and grieving relatives want a last word with her—well, how is that anything but a blessing?"

Sienne could see Perrin's face from where she sat, and his expression said clearly that he wouldn't call summoning a ghost from its eternal rest just to chat about old times a blessing. But he kept his peace. Kalanath said, "She was good at it?"

"The best. Ghosts she summoned stayed longer than other necromancers were capable of maintaining."

"How did she do it? With a binding ritual?"

Samretto shrugged. "I never understood the details. I'm sure it was in her books."

"Master Samretto—"

"Please, call me Myles."

"Myles," Kalanath began again, "we wished to speak to Mistress Samretto because she used to write to a woman named Penthea Lepporo. Another necromancer. It is a difficult thing to explain, but it is that we hoped to look at some of Mistress Samretto's books that Penthea Lepporo knew of. Do you have these books?"

"Oh, goodness, no," Samretto said. "I sold off her library so the government wouldn't confiscate it. They don't like private citizens owning necromantic texts, and when Lidia—that was my wife's, well, I suppose you could call her a partner in necromancy—when Lidia and Uriane fought just before Uriane's death, I was sure Lidia would inform on her to the government. They weren't my books, but you know how the law is about conjugal property. I couldn't take the chance that they'd decide I was complicit."

Weren't you? Sienne thought.

"I don't suppose you know who bought the books?" Perrin said.

"They were anonymous purchasers, for the most part. Her friend Annegret Loewen bought a few, for old times' sake, and that nice young man, Pauro something, I sold him a couple when he came looking for books he'd loaned her."

"Not Pauro Murtaviti?" Alaric said.

"Goodness, I forgot you were there. It's rather like having a mountain speak to you, isn't it? It might have been Murtaviti. I've never been good with names." The old man stretched. "Can I offer you something to drink? Coffee, or water? I'm afraid I don't keep spirits readily to hand."

Perrin caught Alaric's eye. "No, thank you. We should be going. We appreciate your help."

"So soon?" Samretto struggled to sit up more fully. "Must you?"

"*I will come another time,*" Kalanath said in Meiric. *"I'd like to have someone I can talk to about my country. If you don't mind.*"

The old man's face creased in a smile. *"That I would like,*" he said. "*If it be not much trouble.*"

"Not at all," Kalanath said, offering Samretto his hand with the palm flat toward him. Samretto, still beaming, raised his own gnarled hand to press his palm against Kalanath's.

Sienne rose when her friends did and followed Alaric down the dark hall to the entry chamber. Once outside, she said, "Were you serious?"

Kalanath shrugged. "He is old and lonely, and I was taught to respect those who have passed through the years. And I do not often speak with people who have been to my country."

"Well, it's nice of you, that's all."

"And we learned some valuable information," Alaric said, "namely that the next name on our list has a connection to Uriane Samretto as well as Penthea Lepporo. I don't believe in coincidence."

"It may mean nothing, even if it is no coincidence," Perrin said. "Necromancers may mostly work in solitude, but if they have a society, it will be of other necromancers. And I cannot believe there are so many of them that they do not know each other."

"Still, I'm eager to meet this Pauro Murtaviti, who we now know was alive at least five years ago." Alaric slowed his steps to allow the others to catch up with him as he reached the end of the street. "Dianthe?"

"South side," Dianthe said. "Are these confusions still active?"

"You've got at least another six hours before they wear off," Sienne said.

"Then let's go."

The rain had diminished to heavy mist while they were in

Samretto's house, and Sienne pushed back the hood of her rain cape and let the mist build on her face and bead along her eyelashes and eyebrows. It was the kind of weather that encouraged you to stay inside with a good book, and part of her resented having to be out in it. But listening to Myles Samretto had piqued her curiosity. She wondered who this Paulo Murtaviti was, and what books had he bought from Uriane Samretto. If he had the answers they needed, he needed to be convinced to share those answers—and that might be difficult.

Fioretti's south side was older than the rest of the city, the original heart of Fioretti before the Fiorus rulers had taken power and moved much of the government's offices nearer the newly constructed palace. Carissima Lane, like many of the streets in the south side, marked an ancient cow path along which houses had grown up. It meandered at random, taking unexpected turns and in one place doubling back on itself. "I would suspect a drunkard of laying out this route, did I not know differently," Perrin said.

"Lovely. There's one," Dianthe said.

"One what?" asked Sienne.

"One of the posters. No, don't look!"

"Why not?" Kalanath said, crossing the street to look at where several handbills and posters had been plastered to the side of a tavern. One of the larger ones had REWARD printed across the top in bold black letters, with 1000 LARI in smaller but more distinctive red lettering just below.

"Oh, you're right," Sienne said. "That picture looks nothing like you."

"It's so embarrassing. Like being caught with your trousers down." Dianthe stood with her back to the poster, denying its existence.

"It's already been partly covered over by this announcement of some performing troupe coming to Fioretti in a week," Alaric said. "Two more weeks, three at the outside, and it will all be forgotten."

"Can we just move on?" Dianthe said, her voice high and plaintive. Alaric put an arm around her shoulders and steered her up the street. Sienne cast one last look over her shoulder at the poster. She knew what it was like to be afraid of your past catching up with you, but she was certain her own troubles paled beside Dianthe's. Wanted for murder. What a nightmare.

Like in many old neighborhoods, house numbering was erratic on Carissima Lane. Number 34 was tucked between numbers 15 and 27. Alaric knocked at the door. "The kind of people who live in these places aren't generally receptive to friendly strangers," he told Perrin. "So we're going to try unfriendly first."

Nobody answered the door. Alaric knocked a second time. Sienne looked up and down the street, which was virtually empty. She caught a flicker of movement out of the corner of her eye, a few houses down, just the flutter of a curtain where someone had twitched it aside to look at them. She resisted the urge to smile and wave.

Alaric let out a deep breath. "We'll have to try again another time," he said, half-turning away.

The door opened. A middle-aged woman wearing a plain dress of maroon cotton and a white wraparound apron stood there, holding a scrub brush like a weapon. Her hair was covered by a scarf, but wisps of black escaped from it, softening the lines of her face. She took in the five people standing on her doorstep with wide eyes. To Sienne's astonishment, tears began flowing down her face.

"Thank Lisiel," she said. "What took you so long?"

6

"Excuse me?" Alaric said.

"I reported Pauro missing five days ago. Does the guard care so little about us ordinary citizens that they just ignore our pleas?" The woman lowered the brush and dashed away tears with her free hand. "Never mind. I'm just glad you've come."

"I'm sorry, mistress, but I think you've mistaken us for someone else," Alaric said. "We're not with the guard."

"Of course not. But—you mean to say the guard didn't send you?" The tears returned. "Then there's no hope for my husband."

"Are you Mistress Murtaviti?"

The woman nodded.

Alaric cleared his throat and shifted his weight. "We came because we wanted to speak with your husband, Pauro. I take it he's missing?"

She nodded again. "It's been five days. I sent word to the guard, asking for help, and I hoped...I'm sorry to disappoint you. I wish I could tell you to return later, but I don't—" Her tears turned into loud, uncomfortable sobs like someone choking.

"Why did you think the guard sent us?" Sienne asked.

The woman shook her head and swallowed another sob. "I asked them to contact a scrapper team who might be willing to go out looking for Pauro. It's just the road between here and Tagliaveno, well-traveled, but there are always bandits."

"Are you sure he didn't take ship? It's faster," Dianthe said.

"Pauro hates ocean travel. It makes him violently ill." She wiped her eyes again. "I don't suppose...you *are* scrappers, yes?"

"We are," Alaric said, "but—"

"I'm so sorry. Please, come in. Let me get you something hot to drink. Why did you want to speak to Pauro?" The woman stepped back and held the door open. Alaric caught Sienne's eye. She shrugged, the barest hint of a gesture. Probably the woman wouldn't be any more helpful than Myles Samretto, but it was worth the time to find out.

The tiny entry chamber was whitewashed and felt colder than it was because of it. No furniture or artwork relieved its starkness, and all six of them crammed into it made Sienne feel unexpectedly claustrophobic. "This way," the woman said, opening a door directly opposite the front door.

The room beyond was much larger and better lit, with plenty of sofas and chairs that said the Murtavitis liked entertaining guests. Sienne admired the framed charcoal drawings covering one wall, all of them portrait studies of people's faces. "These are very good," she said.

"They're my husband's. He's fond of sketching likenesses. Please sit, I'll bring coffee."

"Wait—" Alaric began, but the woman was already gone through a second door. "We don't even know her name," he added.

"She's going to ask us to hunt for her missing husband," Dianthe said. "What should we tell her?"

"Maybe we should find this man," Kalanath said, "if he is the one who knows what we want."

"We'll talk to the woman, and find out what she knows," Alaric said. "Then, if it turns out we need Master Murtaviti's knowledge, we'll agree to find him."

"There are three other names on our list," Sienne said, gazing at the portraits. "Maybe we should focus on finding them before we go haring off into the wilderness after someone who might just have taken the long way home." One picture in particular intrigued her. It was of a man with strong cheekbones and a well-defined jaw. His eyes were deeply set under a heavy brow. The overall impression was of someone who refused to give up even when the whole world was against him.

"Master Murtaviti has a connection to two people we know knew something about a binding ritual," Alaric said. "He may be harder to find than the others, but I have a feeling his knowledge will prove useful. And we'd have to leave the city to talk to two people on our list anyway."

Murtaviti was good; the heavy-browed man's eyes followed Sienne as she walked from one side of the portrait to another. "Good point. Though what do you think the odds are that Mistress Murtaviti knows anything about her husband's avocation?"

The door swung open. "Please, sit," Mistress Murtaviti said. She bore a large silver tray in both hands, laden with a coffee pot, six cups, a small pitcher of cream and a bowl filled with lumps of sugar. "I'm sorry, I didn't introduce myself. I'm Bernea Murtaviti." She set the tray on a low table at the center of a grouping of chairs and began pouring.

"Alaric," Alaric said. "This is Dianthe, Kalanath, Perrin, and Sienne."

"I'll do my best to remember, but I feel so scattered lately, I can barely remember my own name."

Sienne accepted a steaming cup and poured a liberal amount of cream into it. "I'm sure this must be very difficult for you," she said.

"I just don't understand it. This isn't the first time he's made this journey between Fioretti and Tagliaveno." Bernea sat back in her chair with her own cup, but didn't take a drink. "He sent a message when he left so I would know when to expect him, but he didn't return on time, and he didn't send any other messages. He always sends messages when he's on the road. It's an expense, I know, but I hate worrying."

"You said he didn't like ocean travel. Is there some reason he didn't use *ferry* or *transport*?" Alaric asked.

"That really is a terrible expense. And, as I said, this journey is practically routine. I never thought...oh, by Lisiel, if it was bandits..." The tears began flowing again. Dianthe, sitting next to Bernea, put a comforting hand on the woman's hand.

"Was he traveling alone, or in a caravan?" Perrin asked. "Because a caravan might have any number of reasons to be delayed that have nothing to do with bandits."

"He was with a caravan." Bernea wiped her eyes and blinked at Perrin. "You think it might have been that? Animals lamed, or a wagon foundered?"

"It is entirely possible," Perrin said. "And I believe I may be able to help. Averran granted me two scrying blessings this day, and I can attempt to discover Master Murtaviti's location."

Bernea drew in a quick breath. "Would you? I can pay—anything you like—"

"We're interested in information," Alaric said.

"Information? What information?" Bernea sounded more alarmed than Sienne felt the question justified.

"Let us discover Master Murtaviti's location first, and then pose our questions," Perrin said, shooting a warning glance at Alaric. Sienne guessed he was thinking they should put Bernea in their debt before asking uncomfortable questions about whether her husband was a practicing necromancer.

"I will need a map," Perrin said.

"I have a few," Bernea said. "I suppose you want one showing the area between here and Tagliaveno?"

"You have it exactly," Perrin said.

Bernea rose and set her untouched cup on a nearby cabinet. "I'll be right back."

The moment she was gone, Dianthe said, "Should we have pressed her for details first?"

"She will be more receptive if she has some reassurance," Perrin said.

"I think she's more nervous than she should be," Sienne said. "She doesn't like the idea of us asking questions about her husband."

"I noticed that, too," Alaric said. "And did you notice the strange thing about the portraits?"

"That none of them are smiling, and many have their eyes closed?" Kalanath said. "I did not know it was strange, because it is that your customs are different, but in Omeira it would be unnatural. It looks like a wall of the dead."

"They might just show a progression in his ability," Sienne pointed out. "Portraits are hard, my artist sister Phebe says, because people can't hold still like vases and fruit do. He might have started out needing his subjects not to smile, and maybe he wasn't good at eyes at first." But she thought of the heavy-browed man, and her theory felt flat.

"Even so—"

The door opened. "I found two that might work," Bernea said, handing them to Perrin. Dianthe moved the coffee tray, and Perrin unrolled the maps and examined them.

"This one," he said, indicating a map that showed all of Rafellin. "It will not give us an exact location, but it will be sufficient to show us where he went astray."

And prove whether he's still alive, Sienne thought but did not say aloud. Probably Bernea had had the same thought, and Sienne didn't want to upset her.

Perrin used three empty coffee cups and the cream jug to pin down the corners of the map. "Pray, step back, this is delicate work," he said, and everyone took a step back from the table. "Is Pauro Murtaviti his full name?"

"Yes." Bernea gripped the skirt of her dress in both hands.

Perrin reached into his belt pouch and brought out a charcoal pencil with a fine tip, which he set on the map. He removed his riffle of blessings from inside his vest and flipped through it until he found one with a dark blue smudge on the corner. Tearing it off, he took up the pencil and wrote the name PAURO MURTAVITI in neat, clear letters around the complex sigil burned into the rice paper. The pencil went back into the pouch, the blessings were tucked into his vest, and Perrin held the rice paper square in both hands over the map's center.

"O Lord Averran," he muttered, "have patience in your crankiness, and grant me this blessing."

Blue flame consumed the paper, licking across Perrin's fingers without provoking a reaction from him. More fire ignited at the corners of the map, spreading inward until the surface was a sheet of blue fire. Bernea cried out, and Dianthe put a restraining hand on her arm. "Just wait," she murmured.

The fire covering the map flickered and then went out, here and there. It left behind, not charred paper, but an unmarked surface that gleamed newer than it had been when Perrin laid it down. Finally, only one spot on the map still burned. The fire rose and thinned until it looked like a blue, flickering needle. The bottom of the needle touched the map, and Sienne finally smelled burning. Then the fire was gone, and scorched into the map was a bright blue dot.

"Is that...where he is?" Bernea breathed.

"Indeed," Perrin said. The dot lay east and a little south of Fioretti, near the shore of the Jalenus Sea. "There are no landmarks nearby."

"But it's on the highway between here and Tagliaveno," Alaric said. "That suggests that something went wrong with the caravan."

"But he sent no messages. Wouldn't he have sent a message if he knew he'd be delayed?" Bernea's dress was twisted into a mass of wrinkles.

"If no priest traveled with them, he could not have done so," Perrin said. "Truly I think you have nothing to worry about."

"I suppose." Bernea's anxious gaze traveled from one of them to another. "I'd still like to be sure. Would you go? Find Pauro and bring him home? I can pay...it would mean so much to me..."

Alaric alone among them didn't meet her eyes. He was staring at the map. "I don't see what good we could do," he said. "He'll probably return home in a few days, once the delay is over."

"But what if he's ill, and that's why he hasn't returned? No caravan would wait on his illness. If he has to travel alone, Lisiel knows what might happen to him. Please. Find him and bring him home."

Alaric pursed his lips in thought. He tapped the blue spot. "We came to ask your husband some questions. Maybe you know the answers."

"But if you make the journey, you'll be able to ask him yourself!" Bernea sounded pleased at this solution to both their problems.

Alaric looked up and focused his pale blue eyes intently on her. "How long has your husband studied necromancy?"

Bernea sucked in a sharp breath. "What—that's ridiculous! Pauro's no necromancer!"

"I didn't say he was. I said he studied necromancy. That's not illegal. I just want to know how long."

Bernea's eyes darted from Alaric to the portrait wall and back again. "Since before we were married. But it's just theory! He's interested in why necromancy works when it isn't magic or blessings. If you try to claim otherwise, I'll—"

"Calm down, Mistress Murtaviti, we're not interested in getting Pauro in trouble." Alaric stood and wandered through the room, picking up a porcelain figure and setting it down again. "Master Murtaviti was in correspondence with a woman whose necromantic studies went beyond the theoretical. Again, we're not accusing your husband of practicing necromancy, but these letters suggested Master Murtaviti had certain books in his possession that contained information relating to one of our jobs. We just want to look at the books."

Bernea stood. There were two spots of color high on her cheekbones. "Bring him back to me, and you can look at anything you like," she said.

"But surely—" Dianthe began.

"No. I won't let strangers into Pauro's library. Besides, I don't know anything about necromancy. I never paid attention when Pauro talked about it." Bernea was breathing heavily. "He'll be able to answer your questions better than I."

"All right," Alaric said. "We'll bring back your husband. Payment is fifty lari. Up front."

The color vanished, and Bernea's eyes widened. "I don't have that much."

"I'm sorry, that's the standard rate for a journey of that length." Alaric never looked away from her stunned expression. "We'll return tomorrow—that should give you time to get the payment together."

"But—how do I know you won't just take the money and not go?"

Alaric smiled. "You don't know our reputation, or you wouldn't think that. Ask around, if it makes you more comfortable. Talk to Captain Denys Renaldi, he'll vouch for us. But it's fifty lari or we don't make the trip."

Bernea made one last attempt. "You won't get your answers if you don't bring back Pauro."

"You may not get Pauro if we don't go."

Bernea sagged. "All right. Tomorrow morning."

The others rose. "Don't worry, Mistress Murtaviti," Dianthe said. "We'll find him."

"For fifty lari, I hope so," Bernea said, somewhat bitterly.

Bernea escorted them to the door and shut it sharply behind them. "We could have pushed harder," Sienne said.

"She will not tell more," Kalanath said. "It is in her eyes. She is determined."

"That was my impression too," Alaric said.

"So why the fifty lari up front?" Dianthe said. "You know we usually work for half now, half at delivery."

"To see how desperate she really was," Alaric said. "She's not worried about her husband being in trouble. She's afraid he might *be* trouble. She lied when she said Master Murtaviti was only interested in theory, and she lied when she said she didn't know anything about necromancy. Something else is going on here, and I want to know what."

"So we're heading east tomorrow," Sienne said. "On the trail of someone who might be a practicing necromancer, and is almost certainly in trouble or causing it."

"That sums it up nicely," Alaric said.

"I shall petition for several scrying blessings tomorrow," Perrin said. "We will need to keep a careful eye on Master Murtaviti, in case he takes to the road again."

"I'll check the market one last time," Sienne said. "If I can find someone selling *ferry*—"

"You still wouldn't be able to get us there any quicker," Dianthe said. "Don't you have to know the location you're going to?"

"If Perrin can use the scrying blessing to show me the location, I can *jaunt* there and get to know it well enough for *ferry*. It probably won't matter. Nobody's had *ferry* the last two weeks I've been looking."

"Don't worry too much about it," Alaric said. "Let's get packed and warn Master Tersus we'll be gone for a while."

He headed off down the street, and Sienne hurried to take her usual place behind him. Much as she liked her horse, now that she knew *ferry* and its more powerful cousin *transport* were possible, she couldn't help feeling reluctant to take the overland journey. Wouldn't it be wonderful if they could reach their destination in hours rather than days? Less time, fewer supplies needed, and no sleeping on the ground. Of course, that meant no early morning watch, seeing the sun rise, and cooking breakfast for her friends, but those were small sacrifices compared with the comfort of her nice, soft bed. *Maybe someday*, she thought, and trotted along after Alaric.

7

A warm wind blew Sienne's hair around her face, bringing with it the scent of green grass and pine trees. The road unrolled before and behind her and her friends, curving gently to follow the contours of the forest. Sienne guided Spark away from the verge again, sighing inwardly. The horse, normally well-behaved, kept trying to nibble the soft grass that grew by the side of the road. "You're not hungry," she told the animal. "You've eaten a good meal and now you're just being greedy."

Spark tossed her head in a gesture that clearly meant "I am too noble to argue with you." Sienne laughed and stroked her mane.

"That's right, keep up the good spirits," Dianthe said. She squinted at the sun in the clear sky and groaned. "I have not had enough coffee for this."

"You've said that every morning for the last three days," Alaric said. "I don't think there's enough coffee in the world to wake you thoroughly while we're on the road."

"I can quit any time I want."

"Sure you can," the others chorused.

Dianthe scowled. "Well, I can."

"Today is a shorter travel day," Alaric said. "There's an outpost a few miles down the road that we should reach by late afternoon, and we'll stop there for the night."

"And at noon I will perform another scrying," Perrin said. "We draw ever nearer, and yet...I confess something about this disturbs me. I realize these maps are not as accurate as we might like, but our target appears to be moving."

"I thought you said that was an illusion, created by the imprecision of the maps," Sienne said.

"That is what I believed yesterday, yes. But I have looked again at the pattern formed by three scrying attempts, and there is more...'intent', I believe is the correct word. Deliberate movement. I have an idea I intend to attempt when we stop at noon that may confirm my hypothesis."

"And the problem is, if he's moving, he's not moving west?" Alaric asked.

"That is it exactly. Then we must ask ourselves where else he might go."

"Something to worry about when we've confirmed it," Alaric said, "but you're right, it's concerning."

"There are too many possibilities," Dianthe said. "He may have been kidnapped. He may have had to detour when his caravan left the road for some reason. He may have fallen in love with someone and decided to abandon his wife. What are we going to do if we find him and he doesn't want to come home?"

"Return to tell Bernea Murtaviti the truth," Alaric said. "We aren't contracted to haul him bodily back to Fioretti."

"That would be just as sad as if we found him dead," Sienne said. "Maybe more so, depending on how Mistress Murtaviti thinks."

"But how likely is it that he fell in love on the road? You said Mistress Murtaviti fears he is the trouble. What trouble can a necromancer cause?" Kalanath said.

They all fell silent. Sienne couldn't help imagining all the ways a necromancer could cause trouble and guessed her companions were thinking along the same lines. She nudged Spark away from the verge again. "I think we should pick up the pace. Maybe that will stop Spark from snacking, if we're going fast enough."

"And it will get us to our rendezvous sooner," Dianthe said. "I'm trying not to think of hordes of ghouls descending upon us."

"You had to say it, didn't you," Sienne said.

"How is a ghoul killed?" Kalanath said. "Do they look human?"

"I've never seen one," Alaric said.

"I have," Perrin said. "They look much as they did in life, but their skin is pasty and dull and their eyes are white, as if filmed over. They cannot walk a straight line because they have trouble controlling their limbs—they move much like puppets in the hands of an inexpert master. In that they differ from undead still commanded by the necromancer who raised them, who except for their appearance move as easily as any living person."

"That makes me shiver," Sienne said. "Can you really call it killing, if they're already dead?"

"My mentor called it destroying them," Perrin said. "And it is quite difficult. They can continue moving, and attacking, having taken blows that would fell a living man. I was told certain kinds of magic, such as *force*, have little effect because ghouls do not depend on a working nervous system to function—they are fueled by some form of dark energy no one fully understands. There are only two ways to destroy a ghoul. One is to batter it until it stops moving, which, as I said, is difficult. The other is divine intervention. There are blessings that invoke the powers of an avatar to interrupt the flow of dark energy and return the corpse to its inert state. I have seen it done once. It was...remarkable."

Sienne wanted to ask Perrin about his teacher, but Kalanath said, "You do not have such a blessing, do you?"

"Thank Averran, no. I do not think we will encounter ghouls today." Perrin smiled. "Or we will, and Averran believes we can defeat them without his intervention."

"Let's hope not," Alaric said. "I'm not interested in discovering how much damage it takes to drop a ghoul."

————

At noon, they stopped for bread and cheese, and Perrin dismounted and took the map from his pack. "This may work, or it may not," he said, weighting down the corners of the map with stones, "but I think it is worth trying. First, the usual scrying."

Sienne and the others watched as the now-familiar blue flame flickered across the map, ending with a sharp fiery needle that marked a spot near the other blue spots already there. They did seem to be marking a line heading east from the highway, but it was so short a line it might be an illusion. Sienne followed the line's progression, extending it along its logical course. There was a ruined city in that direction, but nothing else for miles until you reached the distant Bramantus Mountains, and beyond that, the desert and Omeira.

Perrin traced the same imaginary line with his finger. "I really do feel our quarry is moving. Slowly, only a few miles a day, but definitely moving."

"Which means we'll have to leave the highway soon," Alaric said. "Damn it."

"We can leave the horses at the outpost," Sienne said, "and we're almost certainly faster on foot than he is."

"Yes, but I was hoping this would be easy." Alaric sighed. "You said you had one more thing you wanted to try?"

"Yes." Perrin rolled up the map and stowed it away, then walked a few paces into the meadow that bounded one side of the road. Pines lined the other side, cool and shady and growing thickly right up to the road, but the meadow was empty of everything but long grasses and wildflowers, fragrant and warm. Perrin trod down a patch of long grasses and sat. "Stay back."

Sienne stroked Spark's shoulder. The horse was nibbling grass from the verge again. Probably it tasted better than hay.

Perrin crossed his legs and removed another scrying blessing from the riffle of papers, scribbling on it and then setting it in his lap. He rested his hands loosely on his knees and closed his eyes. "O good and crotchety Lord," he said in a clear voice, "I wish to express my gratitude for your manifold blessings, and ask your divine favor to extend one of them slightly. I would like to see the face of the man whose name I have inscribed on this blessing. I—"

He stopped, and tilted his head as if listening to something none of them could hear. "Yes, o Lord, he is missing. His wife—" He paused again, longer this time. "Forgive me, o most cantankerous one, but I do not understand. We are not in opposition to him; we seek only to restore him to his wife."

Perrin's eyes flew open and stared, unblinking, at something in the middle distance. His breathing became labored, as if he were running instead of sitting. Sienne held still, afraid of distracting him if she moved. After nearly a minute, Perrin blinked, and relaxed. "That was unexpected," he said.

"Did you not see Master Murtaviti?" Dianthe asked.

"Yes, I saw him. I expected the scrying to be visible to us all, but it seems Averran in his wisdom granted it only to my inner eye. He is a rather ordinary-looking fellow, which is irrelevant. I had hoped to make some determination as to his condition, whether he is under duress of some sort. But he looked perfectly placid. I could see little of his surroundings, but he was definitely surrounded by pine trees."

Alaric looked off to the east, toward the forest. "So he is moving east."

"Presumably."

"Damn it." Alaric let out a deep breath and mounted his horse, the big gelding Paladin. Sienne still thought it was a little strange that Alaric, whose people could transform into horses or unicorns, was comfortable riding a horse. She'd have thought that would feel odd. But it didn't seem to bother him.

"I hope this man has the information we need," Alaric grumbled. "He's certainly putting us to enough trouble."

"It won't take that much longer," Dianthe said. "Another day, maybe two, and we'll catch up to him."

"You're so optimistic it's sickening."

"Cheer up," Sienne said. "At least we get one more night in real beds."

"*Two* optimists. Sisyletus spare me." But Alaric was smiling.

The day wore on toward evening as they headed south and east. It was one of those beautiful first summer days that made Sienne happy to be alive, riding along with friends. All their problems—Pauro Murtaviti's disappearance, Dianthe's wanted posters, the possibility of ghouls—faded into the distance, like nightmares that lose their power in the gleaming light of day.

She watched Alaric's back and felt a silly smile spread across her face. They weren't sleeping together now—the outposts didn't have bedrooms, just men's and women's dormitories, but even if that weren't the case, how awkward to make Dianthe sleep elsewhere, or insist on an extra room for Alaric and Sienne to share. But when they got back to Fioretti...they would need to figure something out. Sienne still didn't like the idea of having sex next door to Dianthe and her keen hearing. But she felt increasingly ready in a way she hadn't four days ago.

She smelled the outpost before she saw it, the delicious scent of roasted meat wafting toward them on stray breezes. She hadn't realized she was hungry, but now she was ravenous. That bread and cheese hadn't gone nearly far enough toward filling her.

She sniffed the air again, and wrinkled her nose. Another odor, this one awful, cut across the delicious scents. "What *is* that?"

Dianthe turned her head like a dog catching a scent. "It smells rotten, but only just. Like meat that's gone off."

"I sincerely hope that is not supper," Perrin said, "or I will be forced to stage a revolt. Outposts may not provide more than one item on their menu, but surely that one thing ought to be edible."

Kalanath reined in his horse, somewhat awkwardly. "Look at that animal. It is not well." He raised his staff and pointed.

Sienne followed his gaze. A creature approached them from the south, moving slowly and in short, jerky steps. Its back was hunched high, and as she watched, it reared up on its hind legs and took a few staggering steps before falling back to all fours. "What is it?" she said.

"A dog?" Dianthe suggested. "Though it would have to be a sodding enormous dog."

"A wounded deer, I think," Perrin said.

"It's no deer," Alaric said grimly. He drew his sword from where it was sheathed on his back and dismounted. "It's a man."

"A man?" Sienne gasped. "But—we should help him!"

"Stay back. I have a bad feeling about this." Alaric moved forward a few cautious steps at a time, holding his sword at the ready. Dianthe and Kalanath slid down and followed him. Frustrated, Sienne pulled out her spellbook and opened it to *force*. Alaric's hunches were usually accurate, and she wasn't going to sit still and watch this strangely-behaving man attack her friends.

The man—now that she knew what to look for, she could see the shape of his head and hands—stood upright again, weaving to keep his balance. He gripped his head with both hands and howled, an eerie, spine-chilling sound that made Sienne grip her spellbook more tightly. Then he rushed the three in the front, the howl growing in intensity until it shattered the stillness of the peaceful afternoon.

Kalanath ran to meet it, bringing up his staff to take the man in the stomach. Sienne had seen this strategy before; Kalanath's attack was less intrinsically lethal than Alaric's or Dianthe's, and when they were facing humans, he would strike first to give the opponent a chance to choose other targets. Usually this blow made the victim double over, knocking the wind out of him.

The man didn't pause in his charge, didn't bend or release his breath in a single loud *pah*. Instead he moaned, "*Death*," the word so garbled it was barely recognizable. He grabbed Kalanath's staff in both hands and jerked it to one side, stepping around it and inside Kalanath's guard.

Kalanath took a step back, but the man raised a hand and swiped at his face, making Kalanath cry out and bring his staff up sharply to drive the man away. Then Alaric and Dianthe were there, threatening the man from both sides. Alaric swung a heavy two-handed blow at the man, who staggered backward to avoid it and ran directly into Dianthe's blade.

The stink of rotting meat grew tenfold. Dianthe stepped back, withdrawing her sword from where it had pierced the man's lower back, and waved her hand in front of her face to dispel the odor. Sienne's stomach revolted, and she had to swallow hard to keep the bread and cheese from coming back up. Then she screamed, "Dianthe! Watch out!"

Dianthe brought her sword up just in time to block the man's next swing at her. Black fluid oozed from the wound in his back, which should have knocked him down. It hadn't even slowed him. He clawed at Dianthe, forcing her back. "*Kill*," he moaned, again almost unintelligibly.

"Dianthe! *Drop!*" Sienne screamed, and read off the evocation *force*. As Dianthe hit the ground, the man flailed and nearly lost his balance, and a bolt of magical energy shot from Sienne to hit him squarely in the chest.

"Not *force!*" Perrin shouted, maneuvering his horse to Sienne's side. "It is undead! You need fire!"

The man was still up, showing no signs that *force* had hurt him at all. Dianthe scrabbled crab-like away from the ghoul as Kalanath battered at him repeatedly with his staff. Sienne whipped the pages open to *burn* and began reading, nudging Spark to where she had a clear shot.

Dianthe rolled out of the way, abandoning her sword. The ghoul followed her, drooling black fluid to match what flowed from the wound in its back. "Back," Alaric shouted, and Kalanath stepped gracefully to one side as Alaric aimed a mighty thrust at the thing's spine. His sword spitted the ghoul neatly, making it spasm and twitch. It flung itself forward, off the sword, fell to its hands and knees, then pushed itself upright again just as Sienne's *burn* took it right between the eyes.

The dark blue flames flowed over its head and down its neck to its back. The stink, now charred as well as rotten, was overpowering, and Sienne gagged and vomited uncontrollably. Shaking, she recovered herself to find the creature was still up and mobile, though not stable. It staggered in a tight circle, its hands outstretched as if it were blind. Dianthe retrieved her sword, and she and Kalanath and Alaric stood in a circle around it, poised to attack.

"I do not know what more to do," Kalanath said. His cheek was bleeding from four parallel scratches, one of which touched the corner of his eye. "It cannot be killed."

"It's slowing down. We're doing *something*," Alaric said.

The ghoul dropped to its knees and clutched its head again. It said something unintelligible and howled again. "Stand back," Alaric said, and raised his greatsword high. The thing lifted its head and seemed to look at him. Alaric swung and took its head off. The head, still burning, bounced away into the fields. "Burn it again, Sienne," Alaric said.

Swallowing the last taste of bitter bile, Sienne read off *burn* once more, this time striking the ghoul's battered body in the stomach. Even without its head, the thing flailed about, looking for a victim. It burned darkly for more than a minute before it collapsed and lay writhing on the ground. After another few minutes, the flames died, and the ghoul gave one last convulsive shudder and was still.

Sienne slid off Spark and had to clutch the saddle to keep from falling over. Her legs trembled from having gripped the horse so hard, her hands shook from the excitement and terror of combat, and her stomach wanted to turn itself inside out again. Perrin came to stand beside her, holding the ghoul's head, now a misshapen, stinking lump of flesh. She shrieked and stumbled away. "What are you *doing*? Don't touch it!"

"It was human, once, and no less deserving of respect than any victim of evil," Perrin said. He walked forward and laid the head next to the collapsed body. "And it was most certainly a victim. It must have been murdered, and horribly so."

Sienne sidled around the corpse to stand next to Alaric, feeling obscurely that his presence would be a shield against her returning nausea. "Maybe so, but it's disgusting. And it stinks."

Alaric put an arm around her and hugged her close. "A ghoul on the highway means nothing good. We should reach the outpost as quickly as possible and make sure everyone there is all right. Then return to deal with the ghoul's corpse."

"This was no ghoul," Perrin said.

"It's a masterless undead, Perrin. You said that was what a ghoul was," Dianthe said.

Perrin shook his head. "Indeed, but ghouls are incapable of speech, whereas this creature uttered more than one word, albeit not very clear ones. I believe this is not a ghoul, but a revenant, and that strikes terror into my heart."

"Then what is a revenant?" Kalanath asked, touching the scratches on his face gingerly.

Perrin noticed the gesture and his lips thinned. "We should care for your injury first, my friend."

"It is just scratches."

"Yes, but the undead can contaminate the living, causing fevers or even diseases. Ghouls in particular carry marrowblight, which can be fatal if infected wounds are left untreated. I cannot imagine what sicknesses might have been transmitted by that revenant." Perrin removed a blessing from his riffle of papers and pressed it to Kalanath's cheek, muttering an invocation. The paper went up in a bright green flame, but Kalanath didn't flinch, merely closed his eyes and sighed as green light filled the scratches and then vanished, leaving smooth, dark skin.

"He wouldn't turn into an undead, would he?" Sienne asked. "Or is that a story, too?"

"Only a dead creature can be raised to unlife," Perrin said, tucking the riffle of papers away. "And that can only happen intentionally. It is not possible for someone killed, for example, by marrowblight to spontaneously arise from the grave. In fact, revenants are the only creatures who return from death without the intervention of a necromancer."

"Mount up. Let's talk on the way. I'm concerned about the outpost," Alaric said.

But no talking occurred, thanks to the rapid pace Alaric set. In just a few minutes, they rounded a curve in the road and saw the outpost, a large log building with a wooden shingled roof and a brick chimney from which issued pale smoke. Bodies lay in the road and on the wide porch circling two sides of the outpost. Alaric cursed and urged Paladin on faster. Sienne followed him, fear knotting her abused stomach further.

8
———

Alaric came to a stop beside the first body, which lay crumpled beside the well-worn path leading from the highway to the outpost's front door. He dismounted and crouched beside the victim, rolling her onto her back. Sienne came to join him. The woman was clearly dead, her throat torn out and her neck and chest bloody. Alaric took her wrist. "Still warm," he said. "This happened recently. It makes sense, given where we encountered the thing. Maybe there's still hope."

"This man is also dead," Perrin said, bending over another body some few yards up the road from where they stood.

"He's alive!" Dianthe cried out. She was crouched beside another man, who judging by the smears of blood had dragged himself from where he was attacked to the outpost's door. "He's fading fast, though."

Perrin ran up the path to the door and dropped to his knees beside the victim. "One moment," he said, removing a blessing and pressing it to the man's abdomen, which was slick with blood and showed signs of intestines bulging out. Sienne covered her mouth in horror. It seemed impossible that the revenant had caused so much damage with just its hands.

Bright green light flared, blinding Sienne briefly. She blinked away tears and focused on the injured man. The green light filled each of the deep wounds, overflowing them like water pouring from an overfull pitcher. As it faded, the wounds sealed over, and Sienne could see unmarked skin beneath the rents in the man's shirt. His breathing, which had been almost imperceptible, became the deep breathing of sleep. Perrin sat back and wiped his forehead, leaving a smear of blood. "That was the most complex healing I have ever taken part in," he said, breathing heavily.

Dianthe knelt on the man's other side and shifted him into a more comfortable position, though it was unlikely he noticed in his unconscious state. "We should get him inside," she said.

Alaric came forward and picked the man up easily. "Someone get the door."

Kalanath put his hand to the latch and rattled it. "It is locked."

"That's impossible. Outposts are never closed," Dianthe said. She knocked hard on the door.

Kalanath tried the latch again. "It feels like something is blocking it." He put his shoulder to it and shoved. The door moved half an inch before stopping.

Dianthe pounded on the door. "Hey! We've got a wounded man out here! Open up!"

Shuffling, and the sound of something heavy sliding across a wooden floor, came from inside the outpost. Then someone said, "Prove you're not undead!" The voice was high and querulous, and it annoyed Sienne instantly.

"Undead don't speak," Alaric said. "Now let us in before we break the door down."

There was silence. Then the querulous voice said, "Is it gone?"

"We have killed it," Kalanath said. "It is gone."

More shuffling. The door swung open. Several people crowded around it. "Thank Kitane," an elderly man said. He looked at the unconscious man in Alaric's arms and his eyes widened. "Don't you dare bring that into this house! He'll turn undead and kill us all!"

"That is impossible, I assure you," Perrin said, stepping past

Alaric and taking the elderly man by the arm to steer him away. "He has been healed of his injuries and needs a place to rest. You *do* provide such lodgings, do you not? Or am I wrong, and you turn away those who do not fit your idea of a worthy guest?"

"Of course not!" The elderly man craned his head to look over his shoulder at Alaric. "Take him to the men's dormitory. There's only a few occupied beds today. Pick whichever you like."

"Our thanks," Alaric said.

The outpost door opened on the large room filled with tables where visitors ate and conversed, and a hall extended in both directions from it. Alaric took the left-hand hall without needing to be told where to go; all outposts were built along the same lines. Perrin followed Alaric. The other three hesitated just inside the doorway. Sienne didn't think they were needed to put the revenant's victim to bed, but sitting and asking for food seemed callous.

The crowd surrounding the door all spoke at once, their words tangled together into unintelligibility. "Stop, stop!" Dianthe exclaimed. "What happened here?"

"Didn't you see the thing on the road?" The old man was shaking hard enough that Kalanath had to close the door for him. "It tore through those three like they were nothing. We had to lock the doors for our own safety, don't you see?"

"How did they get trapped outside?" Dianthe asked.

This prompted silence in a way her demand had not. Suddenly no one wanted to meet their eyes. "Orlan went toward it when it came near, thinking he could help," a woman said. "It tore him apart in seconds. The rest of us ran, except for those other two. They tried to fight it."

"We tried to make them come inside, but they were sure they could kill it," a man said. He had black hair that stood up on his head like a brush and a bony face. "It wasn't our fault."

"Of course not," Dianthe said. "It took four of us to destroy it."

A few mutters went up. Sienne caught the looks they were giving each other and concluded they were thinking about how a little cooperation might have saved at least two of those victims. "It doesn't matter now," she said. "But maybe some of you could bury the dead?"

The muttering grew louder. A couple of men and one woman left the outpost and shut the door behind them. Others stepped aside to allow Perrin and Alaric back through the crowd. "Someone should retrieve the revenant's body and bury it as well," Perrin said.

"Revenant?" the old man said. "I thought it was a ghoul."

"How were you able to kill it?" the first woman said. "It shrugged off every attack those others threw at it."

"Teamwork," Alaric said shortly. "We'd rather not discuss it, if you don't mind." He pushed through the crowd and made straight for a corner table. The others followed him, with Sienne coming last. She didn't like the way the crowd looked at them, as if they'd done something impossible. It wasn't impossible, just difficult. But having seen the bodies of the revenant's victims, she couldn't help wondering if they were right to be awed.

She sat next to Alaric, who unstrapped his sword and propped it against the table. "So what's different about a revenant that worries you?" he asked Perrin.

"When someone is murdered horribly, on rare occasions his spirit is not content with God's justice in the afterlife. Someone who feels he has been wronged beyond God's capacity to punish can under extraordinary circumstances re-inhabit his body and pursue his murderer. That is a revenant."

"But...isn't God's justice perfect?" Dianthe said.

Perrin shrugged. "It only matters that the spirit believes he has not received justice. Such spirits are so driven by anger they are rarely rational."

"That's so sad," Sienne said. "If it hadn't killed those people, I'd feel sorry for it."

"We have released the spirit to its eternal rest, and destroyed its body past its ability to return to it." Perrin pushed his long hair back from his face and let out a deep breath. "I find it disturbing, though, that we are pursuing a necromancer and have happened upon a revenant."

"The two don't have to be related," Alaric said. "The necromancer doesn't have to be the murderer the revenant was pursuing."

"But if Master Murtaviti is a practicing necromancer, which I find increasingly probable, he will almost certainly have taken lives in the pursuit of his avocation," Perrin said. "He is the only murderer we are certain has passed near this vicinity in the last week."

Alaric opened his mouth to say something, then closed it, his brow furrowing in thought. Dianthe said, "We can't be sure Master Murtaviti is anything more than a scholar with an unpleasant field of study."

"But we can be sure Mistress Murtaviti lied to us about how seriously her husband took his hobby," Sienne said. "And he was in communication with two necromancers who *were* practicing necromancers. Doesn't that make it more likely that he was, too?"

"What's certain is Pauro Murtaviti's disappearance just got a whole lot more sinister," Alaric said. "If he is a true necromancer, then it's possible his raising the dead has gotten out of control, and he could be in danger. That's assuming he *is* out of control, because it's also possible he's doing something evil intentionally. Something that might prompt a vengeful spirit to return from its eternal rest to seek him out."

"This is all a lot of supposition, though," Dianthe said. "We need more facts."

"If we seek Master Murtaviti in the forest, as the map says, we will do better to know if we seek an innocent or a villain," Kalanath said.

"I don't see how we can figure that out, though," Sienne said.

"I do," said Perrin. "And I am extremely reluctant to do so."

"Why is that?" Alaric's eyes were narrowed.

"Because speaking with the dead is frowned upon by all six avatars, when it is not done within a court of justice," Perrin said. "And although I am prepared to set aside such matters as legality to pursue such necromancy, I believe Averran would not be happy with me were I to petition him to do so."

"You want to perform a necromantic ritual?" Sienne said, lowering her voice. She was conscious that the crowd of people, lacking a better form of entertainment, had dispersed to tables around the room, and that at least some of them were sitting nearby, trying to eavesdrop. "Perrin, we can't do that!"

"We can. It is simply distasteful," Perrin said. "Master Samretto was correct in characterizing his wife's summoning of spirits as harmless, in the sense that no living humans were hurt or killed in so doing."

"I know. I've studied necromantic theory. But still...what would be the point?"

"If we could speak with the revenant's spirit, we could learn who his murderer was."

"That might not help. Suppose it wasn't Master Murtaviti?" Alaric said.

"Then we would be no worse off than we are now. But if it was, we would gain a tremendous advantage."

"This is all premature, given that we don't know any necromantic rituals and aren't in a position to learn them," Dianthe said.

Sienne cleared her throat. "Actually, I do."

They all stared at her. "Speaking with the dead was one of the rituals they used as an example at school," she said, feeling a little defensive. "It's really simple, which is why I remembered it. I'm sure they didn't intend us to use it, but the line between theory and practice is really fine, for necromancy."

"All right," Dianthe said, "so we can do it. I still don't think it's a good idea. What if it angers Averran, and he withdraws his blessings from us? Or what if we lose control of the ritual, and the spirit gets free and turns into a phantasm? There are far too many things that could go wrong, and the potential benefit doesn't outweigh that."

"I don't know," Alaric said. "I admit knowing whether Murtaviti did or didn't murder that revenant would affect how we pursue him. My instincts are telling me he's our man, but I'd like the confirmation before we go plunging blind into the forest after him."

"What is the ritual?" Kalanath asked. "You say it does not kill, but what does it do?"

"We need a piece of the body," Sienne said, "and a few drops of the summoner's blood mixed with red wine. Then there's a ritual chant. Like I said, simple."

Dianthe shuddered. "I can't believe we're considering this. Perrin, don't you have a problem with it?"

"In the abstract, yes. But I happen to agree with Alaric that learning the identity of the revenant's murderer will aid us in our search. I also believe that so long as I do not use divine power to raise the dead, Averran will not be offended if I do so through necromantic ritual. The search for wisdom is very important to him, and I believe this qualifies."

"So...are we going to do this?" Sienne asked. The idea made her nervous and excited all at once.

Alaric nodded. "I think we are."

THE MOON ROSE, FULL AND BRIGHT, OVER THE FOREST, PAINTING THE trees silver and sending pale shadows shivering across the highway to compete with the bolder ones cast by the setting sun. Sienne settled her pack more securely across her shoulders and heard it slosh. The old man, who'd turned out to be the outpost keeper, had wanted to give her a bottle of their finest vintage, probably out of some misplaced sense of guilt. It wasn't that fine a vintage, but Sienne had still argued him down to the cheapest red and insisted on paying for it. She felt letting him give it to her somehow made him complicit in the ritual they intended to perform, and that felt unfair, making him a part of it against his knowledge.

Ahead of her, Alaric and Dianthe entered the woods, pushing aside low-hanging branches and kicking old, fallen pinecones out of the way. This was a forest no one had ever taken lumber from, and it showed in how close-growing the trees were, their branches intertwined like lovers and bent into strange angles. Alaric was hunched over, and there were pine needles in his fair hair. The branches had tugged at Dianthe's darker blonde hair too, disordering it from its neat braid. Sienne ducked and smoothed her own hair automatically. It was probably futile, but she had to try.

Within only a few steps, the forest swallowed her up as thoroughly as a monster with a gaping maw might. The heavy growth meant very little light penetrated, neither the last rays of the setting sun nor the silver glow of the full moon. Sienne took a few more steps, ensuring she was completely shielded from view of the road, and made a dozen magic lights. It was no doubt more than they needed, but she was on edge with anticipation and the darkness felt claustrophobic, more like a tomb than a forest.

She heard nothing but the background noise of millions of crickets all chirping at each other, signaling nightfall. The birds that had accompanied them all day were silent, gone to sleep, probably, and the night birds hadn't risen yet. It still felt ominous, as if the birds knew what they intended and had gotten as far away as possible.

The magic lights burned more coldly white than the moon, twelve glowing spheres like apples floating around her head. She whisked half of them away to hover beside Dianthe and Alaric, widening the little illuminated spot she and her friends inhabited. In their light, Dianthe looked as pale as Alaric, who in turn looked nearly pure white. Dianthe glanced over her shoulder at Sienne. "There may not be anything big enough," she said.

"I just need space to sit with the bowl in front of me," Sienne said. "It doesn't have to be big."

"I still say you should teach me the chant, and let me do it," Alaric said.

"I need you free to interrupt the ritual if it goes wrong," Sienne reminded him. "Don't worry. Everything will be fine."

"If there's a possibility things could go wrong, that's hardly fine," Alaric said.

"It is unlikely we will have a problem," Perrin said. "From what I understand, it is more likely the ritual will simply fail."

Alaric muttered something under his breath Sienne chose not to ask him to repeat. She'd already assured him the danger to herself was minimal, but he was, on a fundamental level, incapable of allowing someone else to face danger when he was perfectly able to. Convincing him that she was the best choice to perform the ritual had been difficult. Finally, exasperated with his stubbornness, she'd grabbed his face in both hands, kissed him soundly, and said, "Don't make me *force*-blast you, love." That had made him laugh, and withdraw his objections. Even so, she didn't expect him to be happy about it.

"Here," Alaric said, stopping abruptly enough that Sienne, rapt in her memories, almost ran into him. She looked past him and saw a small clearing. It could only be called a clearing because the tree growth was so thick elsewhere that any difference was striking. It was only about seven feet wide and a little more than that long. Old, dead needles carpeted the ground, and a broken, rotting stump off to the left suggested why there was so much space here now.

"It will work," Sienne said. She walked forward into the clearing's center and set down her pack, crouching to rummage through it. She brought out the bottle of red wine and brushed away needles to give it a flat surface to stand on. Next she removed a wide-mouthed wooden bowl, sanded pale and highly varnished so it looked almost as glossy as a pottery bowl treated with invulnerability. She set that next to the wine and pulled out a tablecloth she'd borrowed from the outpost. She hadn't wanted to draw attention to herself by making such an odd request, since the outpost didn't go in for tablecloths except for at the keeper's table, so in the end she'd had Dianthe sneak this one out of the linen cupboard. She hoped it would be in a condition to return when this was over.

She shook out the tablecloth and spread it over the ground. It was square and white, with no designs embroidered on it, which made Sienne feel better about using it for this purpose. She picked up wine and bowl and settled herself cross-legged on the cloth. "Is it full sunset yet?" she asked.

"Hard to say," Alaric said. He checked his pocket watch. "Another five minutes by the clock. But it's too crowded in here to see for sure."

Sienne set the bowl in front of her and poured a measure of wine into it. She drew her belt knife and tested the edge. "Perrin?"

Perrin removed a cloth-wrapped bundle from his pack. Sienne swallowed and reached for it. The revenant's head was surprisingly light. She didn't unwrap it. That could wait.

"Kalanath and I will stand guard," Dianthe said. "Be careful." She took a few paces away and the forest swallowed her up. Sienne glanced over her shoulder in time to see Kalanath disappear in the other direction.

"I almost wish we had that mental communication blessing," Sienne said. Perrin smiled, but said nothing. Sienne swallowed again, then unwrapped the head. It was more disgusting than she remembered, though this time the smell was too faint to make her gorge rise. The blackened skin crumbled under her fingers, and a hank of burned hair slipped off the skull and landed in Sienne's lap. Gingerly, using only two fingers, she lifted it and tossed it to one side, off the tablecloth. With her small spark magic, she set it afire, feeling obscurely that she shouldn't leave any portion of the revenant untamed. It gave off an unexpectedly bitter smell as it burned, bitter but not otherwise unpleasant. She watched it burn to ash, then turned to Alaric. He nodded and put his pocket watch away.

Sienne put the head carefully in the bowl, turning it until she was sure it wouldn't roll away. With her belt knife, she cut her left index finger, not too deeply, but enough that it bled freely. She held her finger over the head and with her other hand poured wine over the cut so the blood mingled with the wine. It burned painfully, but she gritted her teeth and endured it. Blood and wine streamed over the head and collected in the bowl.

"*From dust I call thee,*" she chanted. "*From barrow, from tomb, from desolation I call thee. I give thee breath. I give thee voice. Return, and speak with me. By blood and bone and wine I command thee. Return!*"

She tipped the wine bottle up to stop the flow and set it quickly aside, sucking on her finger. The earthy taste of the wine mingled with the sharp copper of blood. She wrapped her cut finger in a clean cloth, and waited.

The evening was still and soundless, with only Sienne's heavy, nervous breathing breaking the silence. No one moved. Sienne tried to calm her breathing, but worry had set in. Suppose she hadn't remembered it correctly? Suppose the wine was wrong, or there hadn't been enough blood?

She became aware of another sound, rising in volume and pitch. It was low enough that she was sure she'd heard it before she was conscious of it, but even as she thought this, it had gone from a low bass to a baritone and was climbing toward tenor. It was a single, moaning note sung by someone with tremendous lung capacity—or, Sienne realized, someone with no lungs at all.

Silver mist gathered in the bowl, rising off the liquid collected there like morning mist off a lake. It thickened and boiled over the edges, pooling around the bowl and over Sienne's feet and legs. "Sienne," Alaric said, his voice a warning.

"It's all right. It doesn't hurt. Doesn't feel like anything." That wasn't strictly true; the mist felt cool where it brushed her hands as they rested in her lap, but the sensation was so faint she didn't perceive it immediately. It didn't smell like anything, and when she twitched her fingers, which by now were submerged in it, it didn't move the way real mist would have. It came up against the boundaries of the tablecloth and piled up against them as if they were a hard barrier.

The mist completely covered the head now and reached Sienne's waist as she sat there, uncertain of what to do. She cleared her throat. "Spirit," she said, "tell me your name."

No response. The mist continued to boil around her. "Tell me your name," she repeated, putting more force into the command.

The mist retracted instantly, flowing backwards into the head until the thing was covered in a thick layer of mist. Gradually, the mist shaped itself to the burned head, replacing lost flesh and shoring up sagging, burned lips. Sienne watched in fascination. It was as if an invisible sculptor laid clay over an armature, building up a human head with deft, minute movements.

After several minutes, pale gray eyes opened and blinked at Sienne. Lips moved as if the motion was unfamiliar. "Pedreo Giannus," the spirit said. "That is my name." His voice echoed strangely, sounding more like violin strings than a human voice.

"Pedreo Giannus?" Sienne exclaimed. That was a name she knew. The mist shifted like flesh melting off a skull, and she drew in a breath and calmed herself until it steadied. "You lived in Tagliaveno, didn't you?"

"Tagliaveno, yes," Giannus said. "Until my death. Let me go."

Sienne examined his face. The mist had shaped strong cheekbones and a jaw you might have cracked walnuts on. His eyes were deeply set under a powerful brow. Even if it hadn't been made of mist, it was a face that would stand out. "You were murdered," she said. "Who killed you?" She was certain who'd killed him, but making assumptions seemed like a bad idea.

The lips worked again, like someone chewing a piece of gristle. "Old friend," the spirit said. "Offered me wine. Bled me dry."

Sienne shuddered. Instantly the mist collapsed, the facial features running together like a child's sandcastle when the tide comes in. "Pedreo Giannus!" she shouted. "I do not give you permission to leave!"

She felt pressure now, something building behind her eyes that felt as if it were trying to take up permanent residence. Convincing a spirit to speak was difficult, and they weren't bound to tell the truth. She drew in a deep breath and let it out slowly, calming herself. Slowly, the face reformed, though not as sharply as before. The mouth moved. "Death," Giannus said. "Vengeance."

"Tell me the name of your murderer," Sienne said.

"Killed me," Giannus said. "Repay."

"Was your murderer of average height, balding, with short dark hair and brown eyes?" Sienne recited the description Perrin had given her, not wanting to use Murtaviti's name in case that gave the spirit ideas about lying to get her to leave it alone. "A broad nose, and a C-shaped scar on his chin?" Her head throbbed, and she had to blink back tears of pain.

"I will have vengeance," Giannus said. "Let me go."

The pressure was almost intolerable. "Where did he kill you?" Sienne demanded.

"Basement," Giannus said. "Let me go."

Sienne cried out as the throbbing pain turned sharp, and she smelled blood. The mist flowed away from the head, collecting into a tight cottony ball that fell into the bloody wine and disintegrated. Alaric moved swiftly and caught Sienne before she fell face first into the wine and the head. "Are you all right?" he said. "Your ears and nose are bleeding. Sienne—"

"I'm fine." Sienne dabbed at her nose. "Well, I'm not fine, obviously, but it's only a minor pain."

Crashing footsteps through the undergrowth heralded Dianthe and Kalanath's return. "You screamed," Kalanath said. "Is it done? Did it attack you?"

"No, but I don't understand how necromancers can bear it," Sienne said. She accepted a handkerchief from Perrin and wiped her ears and nose. "Or how they manage to get any sense out of the spirits they summon."

"It was always an unlikely chance that we would learn anything," Perrin said. "I am sorry I suggested it, since Sienne suffered for no reason."

"It wasn't for no reason. We did learn something. Pauro Murtaviti definitely killed that man," Sienne said.

"But it told us nothing."

"It didn't have to. Don't you remember? Pedreo Giannus is a member of the blight. He said an old friend killed him—suppose he's why Master Murtaviti went to Tagliaveno? Also, I recognized him." Sienne looked at all of them. "From Master Murtaviti's sitting room? The portraits? He was one of them." She leaned into Alaric and closed her eyes. "What do you want to bet some of those portraits represent Master Murtaviti's victims?"

Nobody spoke for a long time. Finally, Alaric said, "We may have more of a problem than we thought."

"Meaning that our quarry is a mass murderer intent on doing

Averran knows what with the foul knowledge he gains?" Perrin said. "I think I agree with you."

"So what do we do now?" Dianthe said.

"What we set out to do," Alaric said. "We find Master Murtaviti. We stop whatever his plan is. And we do it before he kills anyone else."

9

Just as the ghoul was reaching for her throat, Sienne dragged herself out of nightmares. She lay on the hard bed in the women's dormitory and stared up at the low ceiling. In the next bed, Dianthe snored gently, a *brrrring* sound like an active beehive. By the squares of gray light hovering in the near distance, it was the quiet time just before dawn. Sienne practiced breathing regularly until her heart slowed and her hands stopped shaking. In the dream, ghouls had killed her friends, one by one, and she had run through the streets of Fioretti just steps ahead of their pursuit. It was not her favorite way to wake up.

She rolled out of bed and dressed quietly, hoping not to wake anyone else, then left the dormitory and headed for the main room. She didn't smell food, but it was probably too early to expect breakfast. Maybe she should visit Spark instead. The horse had a calming effect on her she could really use right then.

Unlike the outpost, the stables were already alive with activity as a party of scrappers prepared for an early departure. Sienne nodded a greeting at one of them, a short Ansorjan with long, flowing hair he was inordinately proud of, and slipped into Spark's stall. The horse was drowsing, but came awake when Sienne caressed her neck. She butted her head against Sienne's arm and whickered. "You're not coming with us today," Sienne whispered. "We're headed into the wilderness and it's not safe. But they'll take good care of you here."

"This is early, even for you," Alaric said, startling Sienne. His arms rested on the stall door and he regarded her closely.

"Bad dreams," she said, turning away from the horse and joining him at the door. "You?"

"Just restless. I'm eager to get this over with."

"Why is that? Is this so different from our other jobs?"

Alaric shook his head. "It's different because we don't know what we're walking into. There's a slim possibility we're wrong, and Master Murtaviti isn't the necromancer we believe him to be. But if he is, there are still unanswered questions. Like, first and foremost, why is he traveling east into the forest, away from civilization and towards Sisyletus knows what? Why did he kill that man, Giannus, in such a way that brought Giannus back from the dead? And why now? He's been a necromancer for, what, maybe forty years—what's different now that made him leave his home and strike out for the wilderness?"

"And you don't like mysteries."

"Mysteries get people killed. Not having enough information is the same." He opened the stall door and came to stand next to her. "I'm this close to calling it off and returning Mistress Murtaviti's money."

"But if we don't stop him, he might kill again. Possibly a lot of times. We can't walk away."

Alaric sighed and put his arms around Sienne's waist, pulling her close to him. "Which is why I won't call it off. We'll just have to be careful."

Sienne embraced him, laying her cheek against his chest. "I wish we were home already. There's so much I want to do."

"Mmm. Any of it including me?"

"All of it." She reached up and pulled his head down to kiss him. Kissing was so much more comfortable when they were sitting together or, even better, lying next to each other, but even this awkward embrace made her heart beat faster. "I was thinking," she went on after a long, pleasurable moment, "I could make your bed bigger. It would be more comfortable for you, not having your feet dangling off the end."

"Big enough for two?"

"If you like." She felt unexpectedly shy mentioning it, but she'd slept with exactly one other person, only a couple of times, and it hadn't been wonderful, so coming right out and saying she wanted sex wasn't something that was in her repertoire.

Alaric kissed her again. "I would like nothing better. If it's what you want."

It was, her insecurities notwithstanding. She nodded, finding herself tongue-tied and hoping he could see in her face the things she didn't know how to speak.

He hugged her, enveloping her in his arms in a way that made her feel so loved and secure she could almost cry. "Let's get some breakfast, and wait for Perrin to say his prayers. With luck, Master Murtaviti won't have moved far from his last location, and we'll catch up to him before nightfall."

She smiled. "Now who's being optimistic?"

Perrin and Dianthe were seated at one of the big round tables when they returned to the outpost. A coffee pot big enough to be called a vat sat between them. As Sienne and Alaric approached, Dianthe poured herself another steaming cup and added cream. Perrin's eyes were nearly shut and he leaned on both his elbows, his face nearly in his cup. "It looks like you weren't the only one who had a bad night," Alaric murmured. He took a seat next to Dianthe and gripped her shoulder. "Drink up. We've got a long day ahead of us."

"Kitane save me from morning people," Dianthe growled.

"I cannot pray to Averran until the sun is fully up," Perrin said. He took a long drink and refilled his cup. "It would be pointless, as I doubt he would respond."

"You'll need to control your impatience," Sienne told Alaric with a smile.

"I have plenty of patience. I just don't like waiting."

Kalanath entered and took his seat next to Perrin. Sweat gleamed along his hairline, and his color was up. "I have practiced, and now I want food," he said.

Alaric glanced over his shoulder. "Food's coming," he said. "We'll leave at ten."

By ten o'clock, though, Perrin's prayers had not yet been answered. "I dare not rush the avatar," he said in response to Alaric's grimace. "If we are to face a necromancer today, I wish to be fully prepared." He sat cross-legged in the field some hundred yards from the outpost, well away from prying eyes.

"Sorry," Alaric said. "You're right. Take your time."

Sienne looked out across the grassy meadows, shielding her eyes against the bright sun. It was hard to believe in necromancers, or the undead, on a day like this, when the air smelled of wildflowers and even the shadows seemed cheerful.

She turned her back on the fields and studied the dark forest. It didn't look ominous at all, despite the thickness of the tree growth and the way nothing moved beneath the pine branches. What disturbed her was the lack of roads heading into it. They hadn't searched for one the previous night, because they'd wanted solitude, and a road invited travelers. Now she wondered if they'd have to forge a path eastward until they caught up with Murtaviti. That sounded unpleasant. Probably she was worried over nothing. Murtaviti would need a road, too, and it was just a matter of finding the one he'd taken, something she was certain Perrin could do. If Averran ever answered his petition.

The smell of jasmine and mint brought her back to herself. Turning around, she saw streams of white smoke arising from the rice papers on Perrin's lap. Perrin opened his eyes and sorted through the blessings, setting aside the unmarked papers. "Healings," he said, "but no more than usual. Several protections. Two scryings, not one. And something unfamiliar to me, with markings to suggest it is related to sight in some way. I will have to study it as we go."

"I always get nervous when Averran gives you mystery blessings," Dianthe said. "It's like he's testing us on our cleverness. Suppose we don't figure out what it's for, and either misuse it or fail to use it at all?"

"Averran does not think that way, I assure you," Perrin said. "He has tremendous patience and a desire to watch humanity grow in wisdom and understanding. When he gives me an unknown blessing, I see it as an opportunity to learn something new. There is nothing to fear." He extended a hand to Dianthe. "The map, if you please."

The scrying showed Murtaviti hadn't moved far from his last location. Alaric took the map and examined it closely. "We'll take the highway south for...probably a mile and a half. There's a road there leading east that matches this path Master Murtaviti has been taking. As far as I know, it doesn't lead anywhere but to a before-times ruin, that and a settlement that was abandoned about twenty years ago when the water supply failed."

"More mysteries," Sienne said. She hefted her pack to her shoulders. "Let's get this over with."

As she followed Alaric down the highway, she reflected on the revenant and how hard it had been to kill. She regretted as she never had before that she lacked so many of the deadly spells. *Burn* was effective, but she didn't have *scorch* or *ice* or *shock*, or any of the spells that did damage to a group as opposed to the targeted ones like *force*. Not that *force* worked on the undead. She found herself imagining an army of undead, or a host of ghouls, and made herself think of something else.

The road, when they finally reached it, was surprisingly well-traveled. Sienne had pictured a game trail, with trees brushing them on both sides, but this was wide enough for two horses to pass each other going opposite ways. Even so, the trees grew tall enough to overshadow the road, and the temperature dropped several degrees when they left the sunny highway behind. Despite this, it wasn't eerie or frightening, just cold. Birds sang in the trees, though the needles were thick enough Sienne didn't see them, and the sound of her friends' footsteps on the hard-packed ground was familiar and comforting.

They rested at noon and ate fruit and dried meat and soft bread cadged from the outpost's kitchen. Sienne sat next to Alaric with her back against a tree and thought, as she often did, of how content she was in her new life. Even without her relationship with Alaric, she felt this was where she belonged—independent, growing in magical knowledge, surrounded by friends who knew her worth...so much better than the life she'd left behind.

"You said you had another scrying, right?" Alaric said. "Any chance you could spy on Master Murtaviti, and give us a sense of his surroundings?"

"I could certainly see our quarry, yes, but I am afraid I would see little more than that," Perrin said. He bit into his apple, chewed, and added, "I would need something else to focus the scrying on to perceive the area in which Master Murtaviti is. A particular stone, or a house. And without knowing where he is, I cannot choose the right stone or house."

"Too bad we don't have one of those location blessings," Dianthe said. "It would lead us right to him."

"Yes, that occurred to me, but I think the shortness of its duration means we would have to go quite a distance before using it, and at that point we would be close enough that it would be unnecessary. We know we are going in the right direction, and that is valuable enough."

"It's disturbing, though," Dianthe said, rising and pacing a few steps eastward along the road. She had her attention on the scuffed earth. "We should have seen more travelers, for a road this heavily used."

"There's nothing out this way for anyone to care about," Alaric said.

"But a lot of people have come this way recently." Dianthe dragged her toe across the road. "I can't tell which direction they went, east or west. It doesn't make sense."

"An army?" Kalanath said. "But an army would not take such a small road, they would approach from the south."

"And we're not at war with Omeira," Alaric said. He stood and dusted himself off, then offered Sienne his hand. "More mysteries. I hate mysteries."

"Let me think on the problem of gathering information," Perrin said. "There may be a use for this scrying blessing I have not yet discovered."

They walked on through the afternoon. Sienne began to feel uncomfortable, and it took her some minutes to realize the birds had stopped singing. "The birds," she began.

"I know," Dianthe said, "but I can't perceive anything out of the ordinary. It must be a fluke. Or there's a storm coming."

"There aren't any clouds," Alaric said.

"I know. I was being optimistic again. It unnerves me."

"We should be near the abandoned settlement," Alaric said. "Stay close together. It may not be as abandoned as we hoped. It would be perfect for bandits to hole up in."

"Maybe bandits are who passed this way recently?" Sienne said.

"Could be. I'd rather face bandits than the undead. I don't suppose it's true the undead only come out at night?"

"That is, unfortunately, not true," Perrin said. "The myth that they are nocturnal comes from the practice of necromancers to do their foul rituals under cover of darkness. However, undead eyes are sensitive to light, so they seek shadow when possible."

"That's good to know," Alaric said.

"A signpost!" Dianthe said. She trotted forward to peer up at it. "Fairglen. That's the abandoned settlement, right?"

"It is." Alaric joined her and looked up at the sign. "We'll need to search the place to be sure Master Murtaviti isn't holed up somewhere. We're very close to the last location the scrying revealed."

A dozen or so yards down the road they found a side road branching off to the south. Dianthe looked grim. "Whoever made those tracks on the road either came from here or went toward Fairglen. In fact..." She ran onward for several paces, then turned and came back. "There's no sign that anyone has traveled the road farther east for weeks. We might be in for a nasty surprise."

"Stay alert," Alaric said. "Sienne, switch places with me. Dianthe, be ready to move when Sienne calls a warning. Not too fast now."

Sienne opened her spellbook to *force*, changed her mind and turned to *burn*, then went back to *force*. Cradling the book in her left hand, she rested the fingers of her right hand lightly on the edges of the pages and prayed they weren't about to encounter an army of the undead.

Ahead of her and slightly to the right, Dianthe paced as silently as a cat, her attention flicking in every direction. "A lot of people have come this way in the last few days," she said. "I don't like this."

"Let's not jump to conclusions," Alaric said. "And be ready for a bandit attack."

The side road was narrower, barely wide enough for two of them to walk side by side, and the pines seemed to lean in, forming a tunnel through which only a sliver of cloudless blue sky was visible. The only sound was the wind blowing the tree tops in a great *swoosh* now and then, stirring the branches enough that loose needles sifted down to land on Sienne's head. She didn't take the time to brush them away.

The road widened, or the trees fell away from it, and the forest opened up into a long, broad plain. Houses, decrepit but not falling down yet, lay at regular intervals over the near end of the plain. The far end was nothing but fields, green with the new growth of first summer. Dark pines hemmed the plain in on all sides like watchful sentinels and spread out across the miles beyond for as far as Sienne could see. It was easy to imagine the forest going on and on until it fetched up against the Bramantus Mountains.

"I don't see any movement," Dianthe said. "And whoever took this road last spread out once they got this far."

"We check every house," Alaric said. "Kalanath and Perrin, you investigate, and the rest of us will guard your backs. Make it thorough, but don't dawdle. We want to eliminate this settlement as a possible hiding place for Master Murtaviti."

Kalanath nodded and walked swiftly to the nearest house. Perrin followed and held the door open for him while Kalanath looked inside. "A single room, and there are no people," Kalanath said. "There is nowhere for someone to hide."

"Good. Let's keep moving." Alaric turned his back on them to watch where they'd come from. Sienne raised her spellbook and scanned the path ahead. Nothing moved. The houses were built of logs with pine shingled roofs, most of which were still intact. A few had holes, and Sienne felt unnatural relief at seeing a squirrel scurry across a roof to one of these holes and dart inside. She'd begun to fear there was nothing living left in this settlement, and that the men and women who'd used to live here had met some evil fate rather than simply moving on when their water supply ran out.

They went from house to house, not speaking except for Perrin or Kalanath saying, "All clear." Sienne relaxed her grip on her book for the tenth time and wiped her sweaty right palm on her trousers. Her neck ached, and there was a headache beginning between her eyes. "Are we going to feel stupid if it turns out there's nothing here?" she said in a low voice.

"We never feel stupid about taking adequate precautions," Alaric said. She glanced back to see him still watching the rear and was comforted.

Dianthe swore. "Something moved."

Sienne whipped around. The settlement was as placid and unmoving as ever. "Are you sure?"

"Of course I'm sure. There, beyond the house with the tattered oilcloth in the window."

Sienne followed the line of her pointing arm. "I don't see anything—"

Something lurched into view from around the corner of the house. It moved haltingly, like someone finding their footing in a dark room, but with great deliberation. It was far enough away that Sienne couldn't tell if it was male or female, just that it was an adult and that it didn't seem to have noticed them.

Sienne brought her spellbook up just as Alaric put a hand on her shoulder. "Wait," he said. "He's not coming this way."

"We're not hiding. He has to see us," Dianthe said.

"I don't think it's human," Alaric said. "Perrin?"

"I cannot tell at this distance, but you may be right," Perrin said. "It is no ghoul, that is certain, nor a revenant. But it could simply be someone whose joints pain him into slow movement."

The man, or undead, or whatever it was, finished crossing the road ahead of them and vanished behind another house. Sienne relaxed fractionally and lowered her book. "What now?"

"I think...one moment, please..." Perrin took out his riffle of blessings and tore out one smudged purple. "I am almost certain this mystery blessing enhances sight. I think it will allow me to perceive the presence of creatures animated by dark energy within quite a large area."

"Is 'almost certain' good enough to justify using it?" Alaric asked.

"It cannot hurt, and if I am correct, it will help a great deal." Perrin pressed the blessing to the same spot between his eyes that pained Sienne and muttered, "O Lord, have patience in your crankiness, and grant me this blessing."

Perrin had pressed the paper sigil-side to his forehead, so the lines were invisible until purple light traced them to show through the paper. The light leaked between his fingers like glowing water and dribbled down his hand, evaporating before it reached his wrist. Perrin opened his eyes, and Sienne held back a gasp: amethyst light covered both eyes completely, hiding his irises and pupils and making it impossible to see what direction he was looking. When he blinked, his eyelids were pale purple from the light shining through them.

"Astonishing," Perrin said. "I can see whether my eyes are closed or open. There is the creature, passing to the left. My range of vision is increasing as time passes. There, I see another, ahead and to the left, and—"

He stopped speaking, closing his eyes and shuddering. "Dear Averran," he said faintly. "They're *everywhere*."

Instinctively the rest drew in close around him. "Where?" Alaric said.

"They are some distance away. I cannot see mundane objects, nor can I see any of you, but it is as if I were looking at a contour map edge on, the kind in which heights of terrain are represented, and each undead stands out as a gleaming pillar. And there are dozens, perhaps hundreds of them. It explains the condition of the road, but even so, I cannot imagine how they came to be here. Surely someone would have noticed their passing."

"We need to get out of here," Dianthe said. "We can't destroy hundreds of undead."

"It is peculiar, though," Perrin continued as if she hadn't spoken. "Their numbers grow greater as they approach a certain point, which is itself almost empty of undead. It is as if something draws them close, but repels them at the last minute."

"It's Murtaviti," Alaric said. "What else could have such an effect?"

"It hardly matters," Dianthe said. "We can't reach him."

"Are the undead moving?" Alaric asked.

"Less so the farther they are from the central space, but yes." Perrin blinked again, slowly, making the light dim. "They shift at random around that area until they are within...I cannot tell the distance, precisely, but there is a point after which they begin moving toward it. And then they stop."

"Then we can get close enough to reach him ourselves," Alaric said. "We just have to get past them."

"Is that a good idea?" Sienne said.

"If Murtaviti has an army of undead, that means nothing good. The fact that he's here in this backwater says he hasn't yet implemented whatever his plan is. We still have a chance of stopping him, or at least of finding out his plan so we can figure out how to stop it." Alaric let out a deep breath. "If Perrin can guide us, we can avoid the undead."

"It is not such a mad plan," Perrin said. "A necromancer keeps a tight rein on his creations. They have no volition to attack unless he has specifically given them that command. Master Murtaviti likely came to this location because it is secluded and free from interlopers. If he was not expecting visitors, he might not have given his undead the command to attack intruders."

"I don't like the amount of 'might' and 'if' in that statement," Dianthe said, "but you make a good point. And I don't want to let Master Murtaviti get away with whatever he's planning." She shuddered. "He made hundreds of undead. Where did he find that many victims? He couldn't have killed hundreds of people without someone noticing!"

"Necromancers can raise people who've died of natural causes to unlife," Sienne said. "It's faster and easier than killing people, though they do that too."

"Let's go," Alaric said, "and save that discussion for some other time, like never."

10

This time, Sienne walked behind Perrin, who was guided by Dianthe and Alaric. Kalanath paced behind them, watching their rear. Perrin moved as confidently as if he could still see conventionally, which led to Alaric and Dianthe having to steer him out of the path of houses and, once, a long-dry well. He kept up a murmured stream of instructions that seemed not to make a difference, though if he was taking them well out of the path of any undead, it wasn't as if they'd see their enemy to know it was working. They certainly saw nothing, not even any more squirrels running along ridgepoles. Sienne, holding her spellbook open to *burn*, wondered if she ought to be in the lead, just in case. But they had enough trouble keeping Perrin on his course without worrying about him tripping over her.

The afternoon felt timeless, as if the world were holding its breath, waiting for them to make a mistake. Sienne's shoulders ached with tension. Sweat slipped down her back, and she surreptitiously moved her arms to get air circulating to dry it. It wasn't that hot a day, but the sky remained cloudless and there was almost no shade provided by the low log buildings.

Perrin stopped. "Directly ahead," he said in a low voice. "We must wait for them to move on."

Sienne practiced slow breathing and tried not to imagine how many "them" might be. Two? Three? A dozen? Her lack of *scorch*, a mass of fire that could burn multiple creatures at once, suddenly seemed a serious oversight.

"Move on," Perrin said in a low voice, then "No, wait!"

A person came into view not ten yards away. It was clearly dead, yellowing flesh sagging from its bones, and completely naked, so it was obviously female. It walked slowly, but otherwise its tread was normal. Tangled, matted hair obscured its face. Sienne felt rooted to the spot, terror making her forget her spellbook. No one moved as the undead woman crossed their path, moving from one house to another.

She stopped. Turning her head, she pushed her hair out of her face and regarded them with a dead, white-eyed stare. Her eyes were, as Perrin had said, filmed over, but Sienne had no doubt the undead saw them. The creature tilted her head like an inquisitive bird. Her mouth worked as if she were chewing something hard and resinous. Then she turned and resumed her slow, halting walk. In less than a minute, she was out of sight.

Sienne let out a deep breath and heard the others do the same. "Your guess was right," she said.

"I have never been so grateful for that," Perrin said. "I hope she did not communicate our presence to her master."

"She probably couldn't," Sienne said. "Necromancers have to have a special connection to their creations to see or hear what they do, and it gets harder the more creatures they, well, connect to. With dozens or even hundreds of undead, the odds are in our favor that he didn't try."

"And undead lack minds with which a priest might forge a mental link, not to mention our Master Murtaviti is no priest," Perrin said. "We might actually succeed at this." He blinked. The purple light was dimmer than it had been.

"We should move quickly, regardless," Alaric said. "How much longer will that blessing last?"

"I have no idea," Perrin said, "and I confess I do not know how long it has lasted until now. But the figures are dimming, so I imagine it will not be much longer before it fades entirely."

They walked more quickly, Perrin giving directions in a clear, curt voice that suggested he felt the urgency more than any of them. Five minutes passed, ten minutes, and just as Perrin said, "I can see no more," Dianthe said, "We're almost out of the village."

They paused in the shelter of one of the log houses, larger than the rest, to regroup. "Another hundred paces, and we're in the fields," Dianthe said, "and we haven't seen anything of Master Murtaviti."

"The last thing I saw before the blessing faded was a large contingent of undead massing about a hundred yards away," Perrin said, "which would put them beyond the village, in the fields."

"That will give us no cover," Kalanath said. "We will certainly be seen."

"It doesn't look like the undead care anything about us," Alaric said.

"I mean that if Master Murtaviti is there, he will see us," Kalanath pointed out. "And we do not know what he will do."

"If we can get close enough, it won't matter," Alaric said. "Are we ready to go on?"

The others nodded. Sienne gripped her spellbook more tightly and prayed the undead wouldn't suddenly change their minds about attacking.

She was in the front again, with Alaric directly behind her. Compressed lips and a tightly clenched jaw were the only signs he gave that he was unhappy about it. Her heart beat rapidly enough it was uncomfortable, her palms were once again sweaty, and the strong odor of rot reached her nose, making her feel ill. *All this for one man*, she thought.

They passed beyond the last of the houses and into the fields. When the settlement had thrived, there would have been a cleared area between the houses and the beginnings of the plowed and planted fields. Twenty years later, weeds and tall grasses grew right up to the houses, pale yellow from where the sun had already begun to burn them. There was no sign that any of the land had ever been cultivated. The late afternoon sun slanted across the fields, deepening their color. It also fell on dozens of bodies, moving through the fields like harvesters. But these creatures carried no sickles or scythes, and they walked random paths that rarely intersected. They simply avoided one another, stepping out of each other's way long before collision was possible. The drunken dance sent a shiver down Sienne's spine. It just wasn't natural.

"Keep walking," Alaric said, nudging her. Sienne hadn't realized she'd stopped. She jolted into motion again, her first few steps as halting as the undead's. Dianthe, on her right, barely disturbed the long grasses as she went. Behind her, she heard the rustle of the men's passage, and the faint creak of Alaric's boots that he hadn't had mended before they left. At least it wasn't likely to draw more attention to them than anything else.

She sucked in a breath as they neared the first undead, a man dressed in rough workman's attire who showed no sign of how he'd died. Dianthe stopped to wait for him to pass. He, like the other one, turned his head to look at them, but made no other movement. After he continued on his inexplicable path, Dianthe nodded at Sienne to continue, and Sienne exhaled slowly and blinked until the spots in front of her eyes vanished.

They had more encounters the further they went, and Sienne could see Perrin was right: they were converging on a spot where more and more undead had gathered. From somewhere up ahead came a low humming sound, or, more accurately, the sound of someone singing O in a very low voice, without stopping for breath. It was unnerving. It made the increasing numbers of undead, who were now headed the same direction they were instead of parallel to it, seem like people gathering around a busker on a street corner.

"We're going to have to push through," Dianthe said, coming to a halt. "I really don't want to touch them."

"They cannot hurt you," Perrin said, "or, rather, have not been ordered to do so."

"Yes, but they're disgusting. Some of them leak. And they smell terrible."

"I think we shouldn't risk the possibility that Murtaviti gave them the command that they could defend themselves if aggressed on," Alaric said, "especially since, for all we know, touching them could count as aggression. It's time for a protective shield."

"Contact with the shield might arouse their anger, too," Perrin said, but he removed a red-smudged paper from the riffle and gestured to them to gather around him. He recited his invocation, and a pearly-gray hemisphere sprung into being around them, large enough to allow them to move freely within it. "So long as they do not attack it, it will last for several minutes."

"Let's move more quickly. We have to assume Murtaviti saw that, so there's no more need for stealth," Alaric said.

They strode forward, keeping in formation around Perrin, on whom the shield was centered. Sienne cringed as they made straight for a couple of undead who showed no sign of awareness of them. Each held a squared-off stone about head size in both hands, their arms fully extended as if the weight was almost too much for them. If contact with the shield would send them into a frenzy, the friends would soon find out.

Two more steps, and the front edge of the shield pressed up against the creatures. They stumbled, caught their balance, and looked back. Perrin kept walking, so Sienne did too. The shield pushed the undead harder, and they dropped their stones. One turned and pressed its hands against the shield, compressing it slightly. The other let the shield push it out of the way to the left, like one soap bubble sliding off another. Sienne watched the first warily, waiting for it to snarl and turn its hands with, she now saw, sharply pointed nails on the shield, tearing strips from it until it popped.

But it merely stepped away, pressing one palm to trail across it as if caressing it. "That's disturbing," Alaric said. "They're indifferent to us, even though we'll have to destroy them if we can."

"The undead no longer have human concerns," Perrin said. "They do not remember their former lives except as vague shadows—or, in the case of revenants, as white-hot rage against their murderers."

Sienne kept herself from cringing a second time as the shield bumped up against another creature. There were many of them now, almost a crowd, none of them interested in the humans in their midst. Many of them carried stones, some of which were crusted with dark loam. The droning sound had grown in volume, and multiple voices joined in the sound. The shield bubble shoved undead inexorably aside like a plow pushing up earth. "Why do you know so much about the undead?" she asked. "I know about necromancy because it was required in my studies, but they never taught us about the creatures it creates. I think they were afraid it would encourage us."

"My mentor, the man who converted me and taught me the priesthood of Averran, was in his youth a spirit hunter," Perrin said. "One who dedicates himself to destroying the undead and laying phantasms to rest. He liked to talk about those days, which is unusual, in my experience. I have met other spirit hunters and they were, with that one exception, all morose and reluctant to share stories. But Evander, my mentor, believed his work was a divine blessing upon those poor souls tortured by necromancers. He was a remarkably cheery fellow—but that is a story for another time."

"The crowd is getting thick," Dianthe said. The shield was now pushing aside four and five undead at a time. "We're almost—"

With those words, the shield displaced another few undead, and they were suddenly in a cleared area, empty of all but a handful of creatures. Those undead carried stones and walked slowly, single file, toward a pile of stones about waist-high. As each reached the pile, it set its stone atop the others and let its hands fall, then turned away and walked back into the crowd. They didn't seem interested in building a stable structure; the pile of stones was roughly conical, and as one undead laid its stone atop the cone, it rocked and then slid down to lie at its base.

Standing next to the cone, observing its building, was a man whose short dark hair receded abruptly from his brow. His dark eyes were fixed on the cone as if measuring its height against some unknown standard. He wore dark clothes too warm for the weather and a lined cloak that was too heavy for the light breeze to move. He glanced up at their arrival, then returned to watching the pile of stones. It was so clearly a dismissal Sienne almost turned to leave. She caught herself before it was embarrassing and looked up at Alaric.

"Pauro Murtaviti?" Alaric said in a firm, carrying voice.

"I am he," the man said, not looking up.

"Your wife hired us to find you," Alaric said. "She's very concerned."

"I sent word that I would be delayed," Murtaviti said.

"She never got the message."

"That's unfortunate. But this shouldn't take much longer." Murtaviti gestured the next undead to stop and measured the top of the cone with the flat of his palm, swinging it over to compare its height to his. Based on this crude measurement, the cone came to just above his belly button. His lips moved as if he were counting.

"You need to stop what you're doing," Alaric said. "And release these undead."

Murtaviti motioned to the undead to continue and finally looked up. His eyes were large and dark brown and completely devoid of emotion. "Do I? Why is that?"

"Practicing necromancy is illegal. Don't pretend you don't know that."

"And you're here to bring me in. You're rather informally dressed for guards."

"We're not guards. We're not interested in prosecuting your crimes. If you release these souls, we won't say anything about it to the law."

Dianthe made a small, somewhat pained sound. Alaric ignored her.

"How generous of you," Murtaviti said. "But I think not. I've worked for too many years to bring this plan to fruition. I'm not going to give up now."

"Alaric," Kalanath said, a warning note in his voice. Sienne swiveled to look at him and saw, beyond the shield, the hordes of undead pressing toward them. Where they had previously been indifferent to the shield's presence, they now seemed very intent on it, slowly but inexorably reaching for it with their clawed hands. The ones in front pressed up against the shield, tearing at it, and were in turn climbed on and over by more undead, until the entire back half of the shield was dark with bodies.

Alaric gave the situation a single look, then turned his attention back to Murtaviti. "That's a delaying tactic," he said. "All we have to do is kill you and your control over them is lost."

"Turning them into an army of masterless ghouls," Murtaviti said. "By all means, kill me." His mouth quirked up on one side as if he'd made a joke.

Alaric's lips thinned. "Take him," he said, drew his sword, and slashed at the protective shield. Dianthe hurried to join him. Sienne paced near Perrin, her spellbook open to *force* now. If they could knock him unconscious...

More undead circled the shield, putting themselves between it and their master. Alaric swore and slashed harder. "Don't take this the wrong way," he began.

"I feel absurdly as if I should apologize for the increasing potency of my blessings," Perrin said with a weak laugh.

The shield parted down one side where Alaric and Dianthe had slashed it. Dianthe slipped through, followed by Alaric, and came up against a wall of undead standing protectively around Murtaviti. Alaric swore again and began laying about with his sword. "Sienne!" he shouted.

Sienne emerged from the dome just as it popped and vanished entirely. Thumps indicated undead falling from where they'd been perched atop the shield, but she didn't have time to worry about that. She could barely see Murtaviti past his undead slaves.

She moved to the right, hoping to skirt them, and they followed, slowly and implacably drawing nearer. Except for the droning sound that now came from every direction at once, they were eerily silent, their white eyes unblinking, their arms outstretched and reaching for her. She bit back a scream and flipped the pages to *burn*, casting about for the best target. She needed to cut through the line of undead, but there were so many of them. Cursing herself for not having learned *scorch*, she read off *burn* and struck one of the undead with the blue fire. It kept coming for her, ignoring how the fire spread across its torso to its head.

Sienne backed up and cast *burn* again, and again, before concluding that setting the undead on fire only made them harder for the fighters to hit. She backed up again and screamed as someone grabbed her. "It is me," Kalanath said. "There are more of them coming this way."

She turned in his arms to see the approaching horde stumbling in their direction. "Can they see?" she shouted.

"I cannot tell," Kalanath said. "It seemed they saw us before. Why?"

It was worth a shot. "Let's see," she said, and flipped back a few pages to read out the summoning *fog*. The sharp-edged syllables cut her tongue, and she tasted blood, but thick mist rose up from the ground between them and the undead, completely obscuring them.

"We should move," Kalanath said, drawing her along with him. They ran to where Alaric and Dianthe fought madly, both with sword and with boot. Kalanath took up a position on Alaric's left, his staff flicking faster than Sienne could follow. The fire of *burn* was finally having some effect, and the first undead Sienne had cast it on sagged to its knees and then fell face-first to the ground. Sienne cast *burn* again, but the spell was just too slow. She needed another solution.

Pearly light flashed, and Perrin stood beside her, his left arm bearing a divine shield. "This is not working," he said as the first undead reached them and began clawing gray shreds off the shield. "We must reach Master Murtaviti or we will be overwhelmed."

Sienne watched the undead, five or six of them, scrabble at the shield. Beyond them was the clear space she wanted, but every one of them blocked her line of sight. "I have an idea," she said. "Keep the shield going."

She flipped directly to *jaunt*, near the back of her book, and began reading the summoning. It tore at the insides of her cheeks, filling her mouth with blood she swallowed. Transit spells were so *long*, it felt as if she'd already been reading the spell for an hour, though her memory of the spell's beginning had long since faded. As she read, she kept that sight of the clear space in a corner of her mind, encompassing it, picturing herself standing there. Tension built up in the muscles of her arms and back, like lifting a heavy weight high above her head and holding it there indefinitely.

She reached the end of the spell and spat out blood with the final syllables. With one last mental push, she saw herself in the empty spot—

—and she was there, not ten feet from Murtaviti. He was soundlessly counting again as he poured a dark liquid from a waterskin into a goblet that looked as if it were made of sooty glass. It was such a strange thing for him to do as battle raged only feet from him that Sienne just stared at him instead of hitting him with *force*.

Murtaviti flung the empty waterskin away. "Two hundred seventeen undead exactly," he said, gesturing toward the pyramid of stones. He raised the goblet to his lips. Sienne broke free of her reverie and started reading off *force*.

Before she could finish the spell, Murtaviti lowered the goblet and wiped his lips, which were stained a dark purple by whatever was in the glass. "Farewell, wizard," he said, dropping the goblet. Then he convulsed, doubling up over himself and dropping to his knees.

Sienne made a movement toward him, then hesitated. Touching him might be a bad idea, even if he was in pain.

She glanced back toward her friends, hoping for some inspiration. Her jaw dropped. All the undead, including the ones she'd set on fire, slowly sagged toward the ground, folding up on themselves like puppets with their strings cut. Her *fog* had dissipated slightly and was spreading—no, it was darker, whatever it was, and certainly not her spell. The dark mist arose from the undead bodies, flowing from their mouths and noses, and crept along the ground in tendrils like fast-growing black ivy. It piled up against her legs, then flowed around them, making for Murtaviti's shuddering body, racked with seizures. Murtaviti's mouth and eyes were open, and the mist flowed into them, making it look like it was choking him.

Sienne took a few steps back and bumped into Alaric. "What's going on?" he said.

"I don't know. He drank something, and then he fell down and went into seizures." Sienne prodded his leg with her toe. Murtaviti didn't respond.

Perrin picked up the goblet and sniffed it. "I do not recognize the concoction, but it smells strongly of black currants."

Sienne looked back across the field. Through the fading *fog*, she saw dozens, perhaps hundreds of undead collapsed and leaking black mist. "What do we do?"

Murtaviti's seizures were diminishing, but the black mist continued to pour into him. "Wait for him to wake up," Alaric said, "and find out what his necromantic ritual did."

"Should we...you know..." Sienne faltered.

"We don't kill helpless men," Alaric said, "even if they are evil necromancers. We're not executioners. He has to face trial." He crouched beside Murtaviti and shook the man's shoulder. He got no response.

"He is absorbing the dark energy of all those undead creatures," Perrin said. "That can mean nothing good. Perhaps killing him is not—"

Murtaviti blinked, startling Sienne. He weakly shifted his arms and legs. Alaric stepped back. "Master Murtaviti," he said, "it's over. Your undead army is gone. You have no more allies. You can come back to Fioretti with us under your own power, or under duress. Which will it be?"

Murtaviti struggled to his feet. The last traces of oily black mist seeped up his face and into his nose and mouth. He turned away from Alaric as if he hadn't heard him and flexed his arms, one at a time, testing their movement the way a fighter might before a battle. "Marvelous," he said. "I have never felt so free."

"You're not free, Master Murtaviti, you're going back to Fioretti to make restitution for what you've done." Alaric glanced around at the dozens of fallen bodies. "It's going to take a long time to bury all of these."

Murtaviti stood with his back to Alaric and let out a deep sigh. "That will certainly be a problem," he said, turning and taking a few steps to stand in front of Alaric. His eyes glowed, points of startling yellow light in his sallow face. He grabbed Alaric's collar and lifted him off his feet. With no apparent exertion, he hurled Alaric away to land sprawling in a pile of motionless undead.

11

Sienne hissed in surprise and took a couple of involuntary steps back. Dianthe cried out and ran to Alaric's side. Murtaviti flexed his arm again, a look of wonder on his ordinary face. "Such strength," he said. "I never expected that."

Perrin grabbed Sienne's arm. "We have to leave here. *Now*."

"But he—"

"No talking. Run!"

Sienne dropped her spellbook to hang in its harness and ran. Perrin had sounded adamant, but worse, he'd sounded scared. They ran past where Alaric had just gotten to his feet and picked up his sword. "What are you doing?" he exclaimed. "We have to fight him!"

"There is no fighting what he has become," Perrin said over his shoulder, not stopping to argue. "We have to get out of here before he comes to himself and destroys us."

"Alaric, now!" Sienne said.

Alaric cast a look over his shoulder at Murtaviti, who was rapt in contemplation of his ordinary-looking hands. He sheathed his sword and ran after them, followed by Dianthe and Kalanath.

Running was complicated by the dozens of bodies fallen around them, blocking a clear path. Sienne avoided them not just because she was squeamish of touching them, but because the one time she trod on one in her way, it shifted uncomfortably and nearly sent her to the ground. She lagged behind until Alaric swept her up unceremoniously over his shoulder and pelted away with her. From that position, Murtaviti was a rapidly receding black blotch against the sunny yellow field. With the dead bodies lying everywhere, it looked like the aftermath of a battle with only one survivor who stood proudly victorious while his enemies fled. And they were fleeing, no question about that.

Whatever Murtaviti had done had reached all the way into the village. A few undead lay in the streets, not as many as were in the fields. Sienne was sure his ritual had destroyed every undead in the vicinity. Destroyed them, and gathered their dark energy into himself. It had given him the supernatural strength to throw Alaric bodily through the air. Perrin seemed to know what was going on, but they were all running too quickly for conversation. Sienne clutched Alaric's shoulder to keep her balance and prayed Murtaviti wouldn't follow them.

They were all the way to the main road before Dianthe staggered and gasped, "I can't run any longer."

"Let us hope this is far enough," Perrin said, leaning over with his hands on his knees and sucking in air. Alaric set Sienne down and walked a few paces, breathing heavily. Kalanath leaned on his staff and closed his eyes. Sienne put a hand on Alaric's arm. He looked at her and nodded reassurance. She hadn't thought he was badly hurt, but it was a comfort nonetheless.

"Explain to me," he said, his voice low and menacing, "why we ran away from that little man I could have spitted with my sword without breaking a sweat."

"He was no man," Perrin said, "not any longer. He was undead."

"How could he be undead? He was alive when we reached him," Dianthe said.

Perrin drew in one last breath and straightened. "Let us walk," he said. "I wish to put as much distance between ourselves and that creature as possible. I have no idea where he will choose to go next, but it is likely our paths will coincide again, since his home is in Fioretti."

"We walk, and you talk," Alaric said.

"Very well," Perrin said.

The sun was close to setting, and they walked faster, not just because of the advancing darkness, but from an awareness of having left something terrible behind. "It is the goal of some necromancers," Perrin said, "to gain an ultimate mastery over life and death. Some of them fear death, some crave immortality, but in every case they wish no longer to be subject to aging and mortality. Their every experiment is aimed at giving up life in such a way that their spirits are not bound to God's eternal rest, but to a physical form. The resulting creature is called a lich."

"That doesn't explain why we had to flee," Alaric said.

"Liches are far more powerful than any other kind of undead," Perrin said. "They are phenomenally strong, as we saw. Their touch can paralyze. They can control the dead easily. And they are highly resistant to physical damage and immune to many spells. The only positive aspect I can see to this fiasco is that Master Murtaviti is not a wizard. My mentor faced a lich wizard once and barely escaped with his life. We were in no position to destroy our foe."

"So...he killed himself, but his spirit stayed here?" Sienne said.

"That is the gist of it, yes. The practice is, of course, far more complicated. My mentor told me it can take decades for a necromancer to undergo all the preparation for the ritual."

"And we were just the lucky ones who happened to be there," Alaric said.

"Do you suppose Mistress Murtaviti knew?" Dianthe said. "It might account for her wariness."

"I doubt it. Why would she have sent people after her husband who would witness the ultimate proof that he's an evil necromancer?" Alaric shook his head. "She knew something, but this wasn't it."

"I do not see why she sends us at all," Kalanath said, "if she knows her husband does something evil."

"Something we can ask her when we get back to Fioretti," Alaric said.

"Are we even going to bother?" Sienne said. "We found her husband, and he's a…a lich, and isn't going to return quietly. Frankly, we don't want him to return at all. We can't destroy him—"

"We can, in theory," Perrin said, "but we need more knowledge than we currently have. I know liches have been destroyed in the past, but I do not know how, nor do I know specifically what kind of attacks they are vulnerable to."

"Then that's what we'll find out," Alaric said, "because I don't intend to let Murtaviti roam free through the countryside. Sisyletus knows what kind of mayhem he has in mind."

"Maybe he'll be content to return home and live a peaceful life," Dianthe said. They all stared at her. "All right, it's not likely, but if all they want is immortality, that doesn't necessarily mean he's bent on world domination."

"The transformation from human to lich is a complete one," Perrin said. "No matter the motives, the act of becoming a lich—the murders and obscenities one must perform to reach that point— transforms a man or woman into an evil creature, even if he or she never completes the ritual. He may not be, as you say, intent on world domination, but there is no question he will continue to perform evil acts on a grand or small scale."

"I feel we should be running," Sienne said.

"We can't exhaust ourselves," Alaric said. "It's going to be a long night."

"Why is that?" Kalanath asked.

"Because we're going to ride through the night. We need to get back to Fioretti as soon as possible to figure out how to defeat him. So we'll warn the outpost—damn it, I hope they listen. It sounds crazy. I saw him transform and even *I* think it's crazy."

"We can only do our best," Dianthe said. "Whether they believe us or not is up to them."

Alaric swore. "I wasn't thinking. Sienne, *jaunt* back to the outpost and warn them. And get the horses ready."

"Good idea," Sienne said, pulling out her spellbook.

Minutes later she trotted up the short path to the front door of the outpost and flung it open. The front room was full of diners, about half of whom looked up when she entered. Under their scrutiny, her first impulse, to wave her arms and shout a warning, died aborning. Instead, she sought out the outpost's keeper, whom she found in the kitchen. "You need to clear the outpost. Get everyone out and on the road."

"What was that?"

Sienne bit back impatience. "There is a great danger coming this way, not something you can fight. An undead monster with the strength of ten men."

The keeper blinked at her. "*Another* undead monster? Miss, that's not something to joke about."

"Master keeper, I'm serious. My companions and I barely escaped with our lives. This is the creature who created that revenant— remember the revenant?"

He scowled. "I don't need you to remind me of it, miss."

"Well, its master is on its way down the road, and if it decides to attack this place, no one here is safe. Please. Help me warn the others."

"I can't go out there and tell those scrappers there's an undead monster coming our way that none of them can fight. They won't believe it. And even if they do believe it, every one of them thinks he's immortal and will want to fight it anyway."

"We—" He was right. She knew enough scrappers by now to be fully aware of their attitude toward danger, which was that it made life exciting. "We have to warn them, anyway. It's the right thing to do."

She left the keeper to make the announcement and ran for the stables, where she rousted the stable mistress and got the hands working on saddling and bridling their five horses. Spark picked up on her agitation; the little mare danced in her stall, shifting restlessly until Sienne got the saddle firmly cinched up. Sienne petted her mane and laid her cheek against Spark's hairy one. "I hope you're ready for a long ride," she whispered, and thanked any avatar who might be listening for the bright, full moon rising over the stables.

Alaric and the others still hadn't appeared when Sienne's preparations were complete. She tried not to imagine Murtaviti sneaking up on them, overtaking them and killing them all. Finally she put lead lines on the horses and mounted up. She could meet them halfway and it would give her something to do that wasn't biting her nails to the elbow.

Silvery-blue light painted the landscape and turned the narrow road through the forest into a ribbon of light. The pines leaned in on both sides, dark and menacing where just hours before they'd been a pleasant part of the journey. The wind had picked up and was making strange noises in the tops of the trees, gasps and whistles and howls that sounded as if a horde of ghouls were clambering through the branches. Sienne tried to stay focused on the road ahead, and on Spark's ears, flicking calmly every now and then. Spark was a smart horse; if there was danger, she wouldn't be so calm.

It was too dark to read her pocket watch, so she didn't know how long it took before movement in the distance set her heart pounding. In the next moment, she recognized Alaric's bulk and hopped down to go to meet her friends. Alaric put his arm around her and hugged her. "Very smart," he said. "I thought we might be walking forever."

"*Somebody* has to know *ferry*, somewhere in the city," she groused, and he laughed and kissed her.

"Mount up," he said, "and let's ride."

It was amazing how much less scary the road was when she had her friends surrounding her. They trotted single-file along the wooded trail, then spread out when they reached the highway, settling into a rapid gait that wasn't too fast for the horses to maintain. Sienne rode along following giant Paladin, whose tawny hindquarters were yellow in the moonlight. She tried not to think about what would happen when they had to stop. If Murtaviti could travel faster than they...

"I don't like that we don't know Master Murtaviti's plan," she said. "We can only expect the worst for so long."

"It could be anything," Dianthe replied.

"I hope it is not another try to kill the king and take over," Kalanath said. "I do not wish to meet the king again."

"Tomorrow, there is something I might try," Perrin said. "It is rather dangerous, but not nearly so much as continuing on blind."

"A blessing you might ask Averran for?" Alaric said.

"Not exactly. A communion. I will attempt to open my mind to that of divinity and see the world as Averran sees it. Which is to say, seeing past, present, and future as one."

"That does sound dangerous," Sienne said.

"The danger is in losing myself temporarily. The avatars are not capable of gentleness when their worshippers approach them directly in this manner. It is not their fault, nor do they wish us harm, it is simply that they are so powerful they might hurt without intending to. But I have faith that my petition will be answered."

"We'll stop at first light and get some sleep," Alaric said. "There should be an outpost somewhere near at that point. Then at noon we can try this communion of yours."

"An excellent plan," Perrin said.

They rode for hours as the moon sailed across the sky, full and white and casting soft shadows at their feet. Owls and other nocturnal birds sang mournful songs that followed the team down the road. Sienne found herself nodding off and pinched her leg to stay awake. She had to pinch herself several times—*that's going to leave a mark*—before the midnight blue sky lightened to gray, and the night birds stopped crying to one another and flew off toward the trees. Sienne listened to them go and felt sad to lose their companionship. Then she realized that was an addled thing to think, and pinched herself again.

The outpost came into view before full sunrise, when the tips of the trees were gilded with light. Sienne gratefully slid off her horse and handed the reins to a stable hand, for once forgoing the duty of caring for Spark herself. She needed a few hours' sleep, and then maybe a meal, though she was tired and anxious enough not to feel terribly hungry.

She heard Alaric speaking to the outpost's keeper, but in such low tones she couldn't make out the details and, she realized, she was too tired to care. So she went with Dianthe into the women's dormitory, found an empty bed, and collapsed into it. For once, she fell asleep faster than Dianthe.

She woke later as if to some internal prompting, not sure how long she'd slept—there were no windows in the dormitory. Dianthe still slept in the next bed. Sienne decided not to wake her and went looking for food. Now that she was rested, she felt ravenous, and she smelled coffee and hot bread, which made her even hungrier.

Alaric and Kalanath were seated at one of the tables, eating fried ham and some kind of puffy, twisted roll. "We'll let the others sleep a little longer," Alaric said when she kissed him in greeting. "Depending on what Perrin's communion tells us, we might only be sleeping four hours a night until we get back to Fioretti."

"I'm a little worried," Sienne said, taking a seat and tearing a piece off the long roll. "He made it sound like nothing serious, but exposing your mind to deity sounds potentially very dangerous."

"He will not care," Kalanath said. "He does not fear his avatar even though maybe he should."

"You think Averran is frightening?" Alaric said.

Kalanath shrugged. "It is not my way to worship. We approach God without...it is when one comes between two others to communicate."

"Intermediary," Sienne suggested.

"That is it. I have seen Perrin speak to Averran, and I believe there is something there. But maybe it is not that man should speak so closely to God in any form."

Footsteps sounded behind them. "You need not fear for me," Perrin said, pulling out a chair. "If God did not intend us to thus approach Her, She would not have taken the forms of Her avatars. Is there no coffee?"

"I had to steal it from the kitchen," Dianthe said, coming up behind Alaric with a steaming pot. "Should we really be so...I don't know. So casual? If disaster may be following us?"

"Five minutes to eat and drink coffee won't make a difference, and we can't go on without food and sleep forever," Alaric pointed out. "But don't dawdle."

Perrin poured himself a cup of coffee and downed it, heedless of how hot it was. "I am afraid," he said, "with the prospect of communing with Averran before me, dawdling increases in its attraction."

———

THEY RODE UNTIL NOON, FOLLOWING THE HIGHWAY. THE FOREST receded from view until it was no more than a smudge on the horizon. Vineyards flanked the road now, long rows of vines showing verdant green. Now and then side roads branched off, heading toward sprawling houses surrounded by outbuildings. They passed travelers going in both directions, none of whom acknowledged them. Sienne was used to this by now. Some scrappers were no better than bandits, and it was impossible to tell the difference until it was too late. It was safer for travelers to keep their heads down. But now, things were different.

"Shouldn't we warn them?" she asked the second time they'd passed a couple of men on foot going the opposite direction, back toward the outpost and, possibly, Murtaviti.

"Of what?" Alaric said. "We don't know what Murtaviti plans. And they likely wouldn't believe us anyway."

"But if he's following us—"

"There is still nothing we can do, save pray for the best," Perrin said. "Much as I would wish otherwise." He brought his horse to a halt. "There, that looks an adequate place. Sufficiently away from the road and safe from interruptions." He pointed off to the left, where a line of cypress trees marked an invisible river.

They picked their way across untilled ground covered with tall grasses and huge clumps of thistles they carefully avoided. Sienne hated thistles. She'd fallen into one as a child and had never forgotten the stinging pain. She thought about burning them, decided that would be too much effort, and gave them a wide berth.

The river was narrow, not much bigger than a stream, and burbled merrily as it flowed past. The ground under the cypresses was soft and mossy, clear of grass and muddy in places. Perrin regarded it thoughtfully. "It is not as dry as I would like, but it will have to do." He removed his vest and folded it into a pad, then lay down on the bank with the vest under his head. "If you will stand between me and the river...I would prefer not to roll into it in my extremity."

"Are you going to thrash around?" Dianthe asked.

"I have no idea. I have never successfully achieved communion before." Perrin smiled. "Granted, I have never attempted communion when my need was so great. I choose to believe that Averran rejected my earlier attempts because they were somewhat frivolous, in the eternal scheme of things."

"Is there anything else we should do?" Alaric said.

"Just pay heed to what I say. I have been told by those who know that the things one sees in communion with one's avatar rarely stay in memory. It is rather like magic in that respect. So I will speak aloud what I perceive, and you must remember it for later analysis."

Kalanath took up a position between Perrin and the edge of the bank. His lips were pinched tight together, a disapproving look, but he said nothing. Sienne stood next to him. Even after nearly a year of being companions, she still didn't know how he reconciled his own faith, in which God was approached directly, with hers, in which God was too powerful to be worshipped face to face, or however it was Omeirans worshipped. Averran had never withheld his healing or protection blessings from Kalanath, so the avatar didn't hold the Omeiran's beliefs against him, but it had to feel strange to Kalanath. And now Perrin proposed to link himself to Averran in some way. That seemed closer to Kalanath's beliefs, so she didn't know why he was unhappy about it.

Perrin arranged himself comfortably on the ground, interlacing his fingers and resting them just below his breastbone. "Silence, please," he said, and closed his eyes. No one spoke. No one moved. The sound of the river seemed even louder with their stillness. A bird twittered nearby, then flew off in a rustle of wings. A breeze ruffled the leaves, then died away. Sienne wanted to fidget, but was afraid of disturbing Perrin's concentration. He was breathing rhythmically the way he always did when he prayed, but slower, with longer pauses between exhalations.

"O most cantankerous Lord," he said, his words as slow as his breathing. "I wish to commune with you. Pray, let me see as you do, past, present, and future unwinding as one."

Silence fell again. "We face a great danger, o Lord," Perrin went on after a minute of nothing but slow, ponderous breaths. "We wish to see his plans, the better to thwart them. Please, grant me this boon—" His words cut off, and he sucked in a sharp breath. "A child—she is— no, that is memory. A field filled with workers, their faces empty of emotion, and a man standing on a balcony watching them. Master Murtaviti, touching someone who falls to the ground. I cannot see her face. Dianthe, and bars—"

Dianthe caught her breath, but Perrin didn't wait. "Glowing yellow eyes in a sallow face. We are surrounded. Roses, many roses, and Sienne, very young—that too must be a memory. I see each of us now...the unicorn, running with a dozen others of his kind...Sienne again, wielding a knife to strike at someone's heart...Dianthe on the streets of an unfamiliar city...Kalanath and a woman who touches his face...my—"

He swallowed, and a look of terrible sadness crossed his face before he regained control. "I must see Murtaviti. He is at the edge of so many visions, a dark blotch bleeding into other lives. He is on the road, heading north and west. I see a door. There is a woman, not his wife, dressed all in red. She faces him, and falls." Blood trickled from his nose, slid down his cheek to pool in his ear. Perrin's body was rigid, his back arched off the ground. "Yellow eyes. A knife, dripping blood. The staff—the staff—o Lord, have mercy, I cannot—"

The last words came out choked, and Perrin's body convulsed.

Quick as thought, Kalanath raised his staff and cracked Perrin across the temple. Perrin shuddered and lay limp and still.

"What did you do?" Dianthe said, dropping to her knees beside Perrin.

"Freed him from the grip of his vision," Kalanath said, gripping his staff so tightly his knuckles showed pale. "It was his request."

"You couldn't have known that," Dianthe said. "What if it hurt him to be dragged out of it so abruptly?"

Sienne knelt across from Dianthe and helped straighten Perrin's limbs. He stirred, and she pressed down gently on his chest to keep him from rising. "Lie still. Are you all right?"

"I will be. That was more dangerous than I had believed." Perrin opened his eyes and looked at each of them in turn, ending with Kalanath. "Thank you. I might have gone mad otherwise. You were right, touching the face of God is dangerous."

"I wish I was not right," Kalanath said. "I do not know what we learned, if it was worth the danger."

"We know Murtaviti is heading this way," Alaric said. "We know he's headed home. We know he's going to kill again—maybe already has—and if I'm right, he has a particular victim in mind."

"The woman in red," Dianthe said. "How are we supposed to find someone with that nebulous a description?"

"We don't," Alaric said. "I think our next step is to pay a visit to Mistress Murtaviti. We need to know what she knows about all this. Even if she didn't know her husband intended to become a lich, she knew something was going on. We need to learn what that was."

"What about the man watching the workers? He must be important, to be associated with Master Murtaviti," Sienne said. "But it's like the woman in red—we probably won't know who he is unless we stumble upon him."

Alaric extended a hand to Perrin. "Can you stand?"

"I need a drink. Of water," Perrin said, taking Alaric's hand and pulling himself to a standing position. He staggered, and Kalanath put one shoulder under Perrin's arm to steady him. "Thank you, both," Perrin said, accepting Sienne's waterskin. He poured some water on his handkerchief and mopped the blood from his face. "I believe I will be well enough to ride in a few minutes."

Sienne walked to the riverside and watched the rippling water. She wished his communion had been clearer, not just because it would help them defeat Murtaviti, but because his visions of each of them had been so cryptic. He'd seen her wielding a knife to kill someone. She'd never killed anyone with a weapon—didn't even have the training to do so. But she had no doubt whatever Perrin had seen was true.

"Do not think of it," Kalanath murmured. She startled. He'd come upon her silently, and now planted his staff in the soft ground and leaned on it. "If it is to be, it will be, and you cannot stop it. But it likely means something you do not know what."

"Do you mean I'm fated to kill someone? What if I don't want to?"

Kalanath shook his head. "That is not how prophecy works. It is a glimpse of a moment in time, with no sign of what led to that moment or what comes of it. The glimpse is true, and will happen. It is the sum of who and what you are at the moment it occurs. But the why...that is not in the moment. You will know when it comes what it means, and what you will do about it."

"How do you know?"

He grimaced. "It is not a story for this time. I will tell you all someday. And then you will choose."

"Choose what?"

Kalanath turned away. "What you will do with me," he said.

12

They rode into Fioretti a day and a half later, under sunny skies that felt completely inappropriate for Sienne's mood. They'd ridden as hard as they dared and slept as little as possible, which meant she was tired and achy and wanted this adventure to end already. Whatever Murtaviti's motivations for becoming a lich, she was sure they couldn't be important enough to justify the murders he'd committed or the evil he was no doubt wreaking on his way north. She resented him for his selfishness. If only he'd been content to stay with the theory of necromancy!

They stabled their horses—poor Spark looked pitifully happy to see her stall, and Sienne felt another flash of rage at Murtaviti for having made the punishing pace necessary—and set out on foot for Murtaviti's house. The sun was setting, turning the brown bricks common to Fiorettan architecture dull orange and throwing splashes of yellow light across the harbor. Sienne glanced at it as they passed and felt, not her usual pleasure at the sight of the waves, but a tired frustration that seeped into her bones along with the aches. If Bernea Murtaviti couldn't tell them anything, they were stuck trying to find the woman in red, and there were probably a thousand women in

Fioretti that matched that description. Assuming she was in Fioretti, which didn't have to be true.

Sienne tried to shrug off the hopeless feeling and reminded herself that they'd been through worse. Probably. Just because she couldn't remember anything worse right now didn't make it untrue.

Alaric pounded hard on Murtaviti's door. "I hope she's home."

"It's dinnertime. She's home," Dianthe said.

"If she—" Perrin began.

The door opened. This time, Bernea Murtaviti was dressed in an evening gown in the latest fashion. She'd piled her black hair high on her head and donned earrings made of dozens of tiny gold rings and a single diamond solitaire pendant. She was smiling as if she'd been expecting someone else. Her smile faded when she registered who was at her door. "You're back," she said. She looked around Alaric at the rest of them. "Where—did you not find him? Where's Pauro?"

"This is not a conversation for the doorstep," Alaric said. "May we enter?"

"I'm expecting guests."

"You might want to change your mind about that," Dianthe said.

Bernea hesitated. "Come in, then," she said.

The comfortable sitting room had been rearranged, the chairs and sofas grouped in small knots to allow for several intimate conversations at once. Bernea did not invite them to sit. "He's dead, isn't he," she said without preamble.

"Mistress Murtaviti," Alaric said, "why did you lie to us about your husband's necromantic pursuits?"

"What? I—I didn't lie about anything!" Her gaze flicked to the wall of portraits again.

"We already know he's a practicing necromancer," Alaric went on. "And that his activities went well beyond the theoretical."

"Did you think we'd claim you were complicit?" Dianthe said. "This isn't about you, Mistress Murtaviti. Your husband has murdered dozens of people, maybe more than that. He's raised the dead. You may not have had anything to do with that, but if you keep trying to conceal it from us, you *are* complicit."

Bernea turned away and took three steps in the direction of the empty hearth. "I didn't know," she said.

"You didn't *want* to know," Sienne said. "Some of those portraits are of his victims, aren't they? You knew that much."

Bernea turned around to face them. "Pauro's done something terrible, hasn't he? That's why you're back without him."

"More terrible than killing all those people?" Sienne exclaimed, gesturing at the portrait wall.

"Pauro wanted immortality, and he sacrificed hundreds of lives to get it," Alaric said. "We need to know how to stop him. There's no more time for you to stay silent, Mistress Murtaviti."

"Immortality?" Bernea's brow wrinkled in confusion. "I thought he wanted—I swear to you, I thought his experiments were aimed at just what I told you, that he wanted to know why necromancy worked when it wasn't divine blessings or wizardry. It was just a game, a challenge among himself and his cronies. His blight, isn't that what they call it?" She laughed bitterly. "What did he do, exactly?"

"He transformed himself into an undead creature called a lich," Perrin said. "He is on his way here. You may be in danger."

"Surely Pauro wouldn't hurt me!"

"The Pauro you knew is gone," Alaric said, "and the creature he's become is pure evil, with no human feeling left, or so our priest tells us. You can't count on him having once cared for you to protect you. Now, who are his cronies?"

"I don't—"

"We know you do, Mistress Murtaviti," Dianthe said. "If they were all trying to achieve the same goal, one of them might know how to stop Master Murtaviti. Just tell us."

Bernea half-turned back toward the hearth, closing her eyes as if it held some horrific vision. "Pedreo Giannus," she said. "Pauro went to visit him—it's why he was returning from Tagliaveno. Drusilla Tallavena. Ivar Scholten. There was the Samretto woman, but she died years ago. So did Selten Kondus. That's all. Now, get out."

"You have to leave, Mistress Murtaviti," Perrin said. "You are in danger here."

"I don't believe you," Bernea said. "Whatever Pauro might have done, whoever he's become, he would never hurt me. He's tried to protect me all these years. And I'm not going to flee my home like some coward. Get out of here. If anyone's in danger, it's you."

"It's your choice," Alaric said. "I'm sorry."

Once they were in the street, Sienne said, "Every one of those names was familiar except the last one."

"Penthea Lepporo wasn't on the list," Dianthe said.

"She died thirty years ago. That might predate the Murtavitis' marriage," Perrin said. "I think we have definitely found our blight."

"Which means we need to track down Mistress Tallavena, right now," Alaric said. "Dianthe, is Renaldi on duty tonight?"

"Yesterday and tonight," Dianthe said. "But there's no guarantee he'll know where Mistress Tallavena lives."

"The Havens, right?" Sienne said. "He might at least have heard of the neighborhood. It's worth trying."

"Since we have never heard of it, we know where it is not," Kalanath said. "I think the captain can help."

Denys Renaldi's guard post was halfway across Fioretti from the Murtavitis'. The companions stopped to eat roasted meat and vegetables from skewers sold by a round-cheeked woman who tried and failed to joke with them. Sienne felt slightly ashamed at how the woman's smile faltered and died when her humor didn't get a response. Under normal circumstances, she'd have been happy to laugh at even such obvious jokes as this woman told. But the knowledge that Murtaviti was on his way to Fioretti, and that they had no idea how to stop him, kept her from feeling cheerful.

She tossed her skewer into the basket kept for that purpose and wiped her mouth with her hand. "Thanks," she told the woman, and let her inappropriate guilt give the woman an extra couple of centi. "What do we do if Denys is out on patrol?"

"Wait," Dianthe said. "He doesn't like being approached for personal business while he's on the street. But he's likely to be there. Being a captain means more time in the guard post and less on patrol. I think he likes it. I would have thought the excitement of fighting crime directly would be more interesting, but he says all the interesting stuff comes to the guard post, and walking the streets is more tedious than not."

Alaric muttered something. Dianthe slugged him on the arm. "Denys is *not* a humorless stick."

"Be nice," Sienne said. "We want him to help us."

"I'll be nice," Alaric promised. "It's not like he doesn't know how I feel about him."

"I do not know why you are not friends," Kalanath said.

"They are. They're just the kind of friends who enjoy tormenting each other," Dianthe said. "Let's go. If we're fast enough, we might be able to speak to this Tallavena woman tonight."

They hurried across one of the many white bridges spanning the Vochus River, which flowed sluggishly now that the tide was in. It was the twilight hour between day and night, when few people trod the streets and the magic lights that burned night and day were beginning to be visible against the darkening sky. Sienne observed someone, probably a wizard, standing on a ladder and touching one of the glass bulbs, frosted with an invulnerability spell. What would that be like, to be employed doing nothing but maintaining the lights of Fioretti? Though maybe it wasn't his only job. That would be so tedious.

Denys Renaldi's guard post was located in one of the older areas of Fioretti, where three- and four-story buildings butted up against each other, their shared walls making them appear like canyons of brown brick. The presence of the guard post, which inhabited one of these tall buildings, kept the neighborhood from sliding into the near-anarchy of some of its poorer neighbors, but men and women still loitered on the street corners, eyeing passersby as potential customers. Sienne didn't meet their eyes. Nervy of them, to ply their trade just down the street from the guards, but she knew from things Denys had said that the guards weren't as interested in cracking down on prostitution as they were in stopping theft and murder.

Bright yellow globe lights on posts shone on either side of the guard post's double door. The building had once been some wealthy person's home, fifty years ago, but the changing fortunes of the neighborhood had subdivided the rest of the homes on this street into apartments and turned this one into a hub for law enforcement. Dianthe led the way up the stairs to the front door, which like all the others stood some four feet above ground level, and pushed it open.

Once, this door would have led to a narrow entry hall with doors on all sides, opening on other rooms. In converting the building to a guard post, they'd knocked out most of the walls, making the front area one big room with a single well-lit hallway leading deeper into the house. On the right, a battered desk the size of a battleship crowded into the available space. On the left, benches lined the walls, and a few people in manacles sat on them, their expressions vacant or despairing. Sienne tried not to stare, but it was hard not to wonder what they'd been arrested for, and why they weren't already in the cells that lay just below ground level.

"Jerome," Dianthe said to the large man seated behind the desk. "Is he in?"

"Ho, Dianthe," the man said with a smile. "Captain's upstairs. Maybe you can cheer him up—he's been morose and snappish all afternoon."

"That's unlike him. Thanks." Dianthe waved and proceeded down the hallway. Plain wooden doors, two on each side, lined the hall, which was floored with bare wood that creaked ominously when Alaric trod across the boards. The hall ended in stairs going up and down.

"No need to be so cheerful," Alaric grunted as Dianthe bounded up the steps.

"Aren't we in a hurry?" she responded.

At the second floor landing, Dianthe went to the first door on the left and knocked once before opening it without waiting for a response. "Denys? Is this a bad time?"

Sienne followed Dianthe into Denys's office, which was large enough that even with the five of them added to Denys and his desk, it was comfortably crowded rather than packed tight. Denys rose from his chair when they entered. He did look morose—no, he looked angry, which for Denys was so rare Sienne's friendly greeting died unspoken.

"Where have you been? I was looking for you," he said.

"Out of town, on a job. I sent word, didn't you get it?" Dianthe went around the desk to kiss his cheek.

Denys's frown deepened. "What job?"

Dianthe took a step back. "Just a job. Is something wrong?"

"You tell me."

"I don't understand."

"If you have a problem, Renaldi, come out and say it," Alaric said, his voice deeper than usual.

Denys ignored him. "Just one question," he said. "What's your surname? Your *real* surname?"

Dianthe paled. "Denys—how did you—"

"It's an easy question."

"I said come out with it," Alaric said, his voice sharpening.

Dianthe shook her head. "It sounds like you already have an answer in mind."

Denys took a step towards her. "Prove me wrong."

She shook her head again. "No. Denys, it's not what you think."

"Denys, let her explain," Sienne said.

"Shut up," Denys said. "Dianthe Katraki, I'm arresting you for the murder of Lord Georgius Pontolo. You'll come with me immediately." He swallowed. "For the love of Kitane, Dianthe, don't make me bind you."

"You'll take her over my dead body, Renaldi," Alaric said, pushing Dianthe aside to face Denys.

Denys looked up at him without a trace of fear. "You're no criminal, Alaric," he said. "This is a lawful arrest. Interfere, and I'll throw you in a cell next to hers."

"You can try," Alaric said, flexing his arms so the muscles bulged.

"Stop it!" Sienne said, grabbing Alaric's arm. "This won't help anyone!"

"Listen to Sienne," Denys said. "She's sensible." He looked past Alaric to Dianthe, whose face was white. "How could you do this?" he whispered. "Four years we've been together and all that time I thought you were...it was always a joke, that you could be a thief if you wanted, but *murder*..."

"It's not what you think," she repeated. "Denys—"

"I can't hear this," he said. "Downstairs. There's someone we're supposed to contact, to turn you over to the Sileas authorities. We'll hold you until he comes for you. Then I never have to see you again."

"That is so unfair!" Sienne shouted. "She killed that man in self-defense! Why won't you listen?"

"So you knew about it?" Denys said, turning on Sienne. "All of you? If it was something so innocent, why didn't you tell *me*, Dianthe? Did you think I couldn't be trusted?"

Dianthe shook her head. "It wasn't that simple," she said. "I thought...it doesn't matter now. I'm sorry."

"So am I," Denys said. He glared up at Alaric. "Get out of my way, Ansorjan, or I'll call in my men and this will get ugly."

"Uglier than it already is?" Alaric turned to look at Dianthe. She nodded. Alaric took a step back. He was breathing heavily and his fists were clenched. Sienne's hand closed more firmly on his arm. The muscles were rock-hard, his arm trembling with the effort of keeping his rage in check.

"Go ahead," Denys said, waving a hand at the door. He didn't touch Dianthe. Dianthe walked out the door just ahead of him, her arms held as tightly at her side as if she were bound. Sienne and the others followed in silence, down the stairs past the first floor landing and on to the cells below.

Sienne was surprised to find the cell level as brightly lit as the floors above. Somehow she'd thought jail cells would be dark and damp, possibly infested with rats, but these were open and clean. Bars divided the lower level into four cells, each with a bench and a sink with its own pump. One was occupied by a woman who slept snoring on her bench and didn't wake when Denys opened the door next to her, rattling the bars. "Keys," he said, snapping his fingers at the guard who hadn't come to full alertness immediately. "Give me your lock picks," he said to Dianthe.

"What are you accusing her of?" Alaric said.

"I'm not stupid." Denys accepted the suede roll Sienne was so familiar with, then took Dianthe's belt knife and her sword and handed it all to the guard. "You'll get everything back when they take you to Sileas."

"Denys, how can you do this?" Sienne exclaimed. "She doesn't deserve—"

"I said I don't want to talk about it," Denys said. He slammed the cell door shut and locked it, then tossed the keys at the guard, who fumbled them and Dianthe's things and managed not to drop anything. "All of you, out. You can come back in the morning."

"You can be damn sure we will," Alaric growled. "I thought better of you, Renaldi."

"Get out," Denys said, and went back up the stairs, treading heavily.

"We'll figure something out," Alaric said, reaching through the bars to clasp Dianthe's hand.

"No touching the prisoners," the guard said. Alaric turned on him, baring his teeth. The guard's eyes widened, and he took an involuntary step backward.

"Don't worry about me," Dianthe said. "You have to find Drusilla Tallavena. Stopping Master Murtaviti is more important—"

"More important than you going to your doom?" Kalanath said. "We cannot let them take you to Sileas."

"I've been expecting this to happen for nine years," Dianthe said. "It's almost a relief that it's finally come. I feel free, finally."

"Dianthe," Sienne said, and choked on a sob.

"Go," Dianthe said. "Find Mistress Tallavena. Stop the lich. I'll be fine."

"You have to leave now." The guard's voice trembled, but he stood firm in the face of Alaric's anger.

"We'll be back in the morning," Sienne promised, and they all trooped up the stairs. Denys wasn't there. The guard, Jerome, sat up and regarded them with a pleasant expression that turned confused.

"Where's Dianthe?" he said.

"Ask Renaldi," Alaric growled, shoving the door open so hard it banged against the wall, sending the sound echoing off the still street and startling the whores. He strode off down the street, faster than the others could easily keep up with. Sienne, trotting along after him, finally gasped, "Alaric, wait!"

Alaric stopped and turned on her. "We should have done something," he said.

"Like what? There wasn't anything we could do, short of assaulting Denys and getting thrown in a cell. That won't help Dianthe."

"We must do as she asked, and find Mistress Tallavena," Perrin said. "In the morning, perhaps things will look better."

"He said there is a man he must contact," Kalanath said. "If this is a man we can talk to, maybe we can change his mind." He didn't sound very certain.

"I already have a plan," Alaric said. "If we can't get her free some other way, we'll ambush her transportation on the way to Sileas and break her out."

"Alaric! We can't do that!" But the idea captivated Sienne's imagination. *Fog*, to distract Dianthe's captors, *force* to break her bonds, and if she only had *ferry*, she could take Dianthe far away, out of the reach of her enemies.

"It is premature to discuss the possibility," Perrin said. "I suggest we find a tavern."

"You...want a tavern?" Sienne said.

"Not for drink. For information. Tavern keepers meet people from all over the city, and one of them may know where The Havens is." Perrin set off briskly along the street. "We will not be in time to speak to Mistress Tallavena tonight, but it is the best we can do, I fear."

"And in the morning, we'll wait with Dianthe for this man from Sileas," Alaric said.

"What if he won't listen, like Denys?" Sienne said.

"I don't know yet," Alaric said. "But we won't let her go without a fight."

13

When Alaric pushed open the door to the guard post early the following morning, he took only a few steps inside before stopping. Sienne looked around his arm. The room was fuller than it had been the night before, with a couple of guards standing before Jerome's desk holding the arms of a prisoner, two more guards sitting on the prisoners' benches, and a woman with a sergeant's knot of rank leaning against the wall next to one of the hallway doors. They all froze at Alaric's entrance. The man at Jerome's desk, presumably the day shift, held a pen whose nib dripped ink onto the paper he'd been writing on. The guards looked wary. The sergeant openly sneered at Alaric.

Alaric recovered and continued toward the desk, allowing the others to enter behind him. Sienne stayed close to him, though she wasn't sure if it was for her own protection or for his. "We're here to see Dianthe," he told the man at the desk, ignoring the guards standing there with their prisoner.

The man swallowed. He glanced over his shoulder at the sergeant, who pushed off the wall and sauntered forward. "And what if I say you can't?" she said.

"Then I find your superior and lodge a complaint," Alaric said.

"Prisoners are allowed visitors. Deny us, and we'll see how big a stink I can make."

"Denys Renaldi is my superior. What do you think he'll say?"

"He says let them go down," Denys said, his boots thumping on the stairs. His eyes were bleary, his hair disheveled, and in all he looked as if he'd had a rough night. Sienne almost felt sorry for him, but she remembered Dianthe in that cramped cell, sleeping on a hard bench, and her pity evaporated. She wondered if he'd been down to talk to Dianthe at all. Would he still have looked as haggard if he had?

Alaric brushed past Denys without acknowledging him and headed for the stairs. "They're supposed to have an escort," the sergeant complained. "Captain—"

"Mathis is down there. He can supervise," Denys said. "I'm going out for a bit. Send a runner to the Lion when the man from Sileas arrives. I want this over with."

Sienne watched him open the door and slam it shut behind him. She couldn't imagine how much abuse that door took in the course of a day. She turned and hurried after her friends, who'd already headed down the stairs. From behind her, the sergeant called out, "I hope she gets what she deserves. After what she put the captain through—"

Sienne spun and strode back toward the woman, stopping only inches from her. To her surprised expression, she said, "So do I. Because she deserves justice. Or do you think it's fair for a woman to have to submit to rape and not fight back? That she's not allowed to defend herself, no matter what that means? If Denys is going to be a jackass about this, then *he* deserves what *he* gets. So shut up and keep your uninformed opinions to yourself, whoever you are."

She turned her back on the sputtering woman and hurried down the stairs, fists clenched. It was a good thing wizards needed spell-books to cast spells, because if she'd been able to cast *force* as easily as her spark, she'd have blasted that woman into unconsciousness.

The man seated outside the cells wasn't the same one who'd been there the previous night. He reclined in his chair, idly watching Alaric and the others standing outside Dianthe's cell, and showed no sign of distress at the scrappers who'd invaded the cells. The woman who'd slept in the adjacent cell was gone. Dianthe looked as worn out as Denys had. "—food isn't bad," she was saying as Sienne reached the bottom of the stairs.

"Hey, my mother makes that food," the guard said.

"I said it wasn't bad, didn't I?" Dianthe smiled at Sienne, and it made Sienne's heart ache that her friend, in such circumstances, was capable of reassuring her. "Mathis is a fun conversationalist, if you care about birdwatching and horse racing."

"Birdwatching? In the city?" Perrin said, turning to Mathis in some astonishment. "I would think watching pigeons defecate on the citizenry would grow old after less than one minute."

"There are lots of birds in Fioretti," Mathis protested. "There's red-coated warblers, and rock sparrows, and—"

"You got him started," Dianthe groaned. "Big mistake."

"How can you be so...so relaxed?" Sienne exclaimed. "When you're going to be taken away at any minute?"

The smile fell away from Dianthe's face. "I'm not," she said. "I'm really not."

"Did Denys—"

"No." A hard look crossed her face. "That's over. He's never going to forgive me for not telling him the truth."

Sienne cast a glance at Mathis, who wasn't pretending he wasn't listening, and decided not to pursue this line of questioning. Dianthe wouldn't want to discuss her personal life in front of her captors.

"Did you find Mistress Tallavena?" Dianthe asked.

"We learned the locations of a couple of places in Fioretti called The Havens," Alaric said. He seemed relieved at the change in subject. "Nothing specific about anyone named Tallavena. Once you're out of here, we'll investigate."

"I'm not going free, Alaric."

"We will tell this man the truth," Kalanath said. "That you are no murderer."

"It won't matter. Whoever it is doesn't have the power to free me. I have to go to Sileas and pray to Kitane they'll let me speak in my own defense."

"Then we'll go with you," Sienne said.

"*No.*" Dianthe grabbed the bars for emphasis. "You have to stop Master Murtaviti. It's a two-week journey to Sileas, and Kitane knows how long the trial will be, if there's even a trial. That's more than a month in which he could wreak havoc on the city, or worse. I'll be—" She laughed, a humorless bark. "I won't be fine. But it doesn't matter."

"But—" Tears filled Sienne's eyes, and she forgot what she'd been going to say. There wasn't anything she could say that would make a difference.

"We won't let that happen," Alaric said. He glanced swiftly at the listening Mathis and added, "You don't have to worry about anything."

"Don't you dare," Dianthe said.

"Dare what?"

"Whatever it is you're planning. I won't see you arrested or killed for my sake."

"You can't stop—"

Footsteps on the stairs interrupted Alaric. Sienne felt an irrational hope spring up in her chest that it was Denys, come to say it was all a mistake. But the man who appeared was a stranger. He was nearly as big as Alaric, but where Alaric was heavily muscled, this man was fat, with an enormous belly and round, rosy cheeks over a thick beard and mustache. He wore his brown hair long and pulled back in a tail, and his clothes were so ordinary Sienne didn't know how she'd describe them if she had to give someone a picture of him. In fact, despite his size, "nondescript" was the word that involuntarily popped into her head when she looked at him.

She heard a gasp. Turning, she saw Dianthe had sat down heavily on her bench. Her face was nearly as white as when Denys had confronted her. "Corbyn," she said, her voice almost inaudible. "What—why are you here?"

The man, Corbyn, took a few steps away from the stairs and

crossed his arms over his broad chest. "You," he said to Mathis, his voice a pleasant baritone. "You're relieved of duty. Wait upstairs until I send for you."

Mathis shot to his feet. "You can't do that," he said. "You're not authorized to give me orders."

Corbyn glared at him. "Um. Sir," Mathis added, then looked surprised at himself.

Corbyn removed a folded paper from within the nondescript vest that strained across his stomach and handed it to Mathis. His eyes never left Dianthe's. Mathis scanned the paper. His face, darker than Dianthe's, paled by several shades. "Sir," he said, this time with great respect. He handed the paper back to Corbyn and almost ran up the stairs.

The paper went back into the vest. "The rest of you, out," Corbyn said.

"They're my friends," Dianthe said.

Corbyn's eyebrows, as bushy as his beard, went up. "The kind of friends you trust with your secrets?"

"Yes."

"Well, I don't know them and I've got secrets of my own I don't want shared, as I'm sure you can imagine."

"Who are you?" Alaric said. "Because I'm not leaving Dianthe alone with you, whoever you are."

The big man smiled. "Loyal, are you, Ansorjan?"

"You have no idea," Alaric said.

"If you're here to take Dianthe away, you have to listen to us," Sienne said. "She killed that man in self-defense when he tried to rape her. She's no murderer. You can't take her back to Sileas."

"I know she's no murderer," Corbyn said.

That stopped Alaric, whose mouth was open to speak. Dianthe said, "Why are you here, Corbyn?"

He shook his head ruefully. "You're a hard woman to find," he said. "How long have you been in Fioretti?"

"Six years."

"Unbelievable. I've had people looking for you all that time. I trained you too well."

"Not too well by my standards." Dianthe rose and came forward to rest her hands on the bars. "Stop being cryptic and answer me. *Why are you here?*"

"I can't speak freely in front of these people. I don't know them."

"I do. We'd all give our lives for each other. I trust them completely. They know how to keep secrets, if that's what you're worried about."

Corbyn chewed his lower lip in thought. He took Mathis's chair and sat in it, making it groan alarmingly. "All right," he said. "But you have to understand, all of you, that what I'm about to tell you can't leave this room. If it does, your lives are forfeit. If that's not something you can agree to, you'd better leave now."

Sienne nodded. Alaric inclined his head once in assent. Kalanath and Perrin shared a glance, then nodded in turn.

"You," Corbyn said, pointing at Kalanath, "check the stairs."

Kalanath trotted up a couple of steps. "There is no one here."

Corbyn nodded. "How much has Dianthe told you about me?"

"That you taught her how to be a thief," Alaric said. "That you are a thief yourself."

"That's partly true," Corbyn said. "Only I'm not a thief. I'm a spy. King Derekian's spymaster, to be specific."

Dianthe gasped. "But you can't be. All those years—"

"I wasn't spymaster until about five years ago. Up until then, I was responsible for intelligence gathering in Sileas," Corbyn said. "Duke Randon of Sileas was one of the king's most troublesome vassals, and I spent a lot of time collecting information from my agents there and acting on it. Which meant a lot of time in the kitchens, listening to the belowstairs gossip."

"What do you mean, *was*?" Dianthe asked. Her eyes were wide, and her voice trembled.

Corbyn rocked back in his chair. "The duke suffered a sudden fatal illness two months ago. It was the kind of sudden fatal illness that was many years coming. The king is naturally quite distressed at the loss of someone so faithful, but was quick to replace him—couldn't leave one of the largest dukedoms untended, could he?"

"Did you do it?"

"That's not a question I'm at liberty to entertain."

Dianthe swallowed. "And this means...what? If Randon isn't duke anymore—"

"The new duchess spent some time going over old verdicts. To no one's surprise, she's found quite a few of them were...improperly handled. Specifically, Dianthe Katraki was found to have acted in self-defense when she killed Georgius Pontolo. The charge of murder has been expunged."

Dianthe closed her eyes and pressed her head against the bars. "Corbyn—then why the wanted posters?"

"As I said, you're a hard woman to find. My need to find you recently became more pressing. Since I couldn't reveal my identity and make a public announcement, I had to resort to other means. I'm sorry if they inconvenienced you."

"*Inconvenienced* her?" Sienne exclaimed. "Denys had to arrest her—she thought she was going off to her death—how dare you talk about it like it was some...some minor discomfort?"

"It's all right, Sienne," Dianthe said. She was smiling. "I might have guessed you'd do something like that. Why did you need to find me?"

Corbyn rose and walked forward to take her hand. "Because I'm dying," he said, "and I need a successor."

Dianthe's mouth dropped open. "Corbyn. No. Isn't there healing, or doctors, or..."

"It's not something doctors can fix," Corbyn said, "and as for healing, priests can cure my symptoms, but not the underlying cause. I've spent the last year hearing the same answer from priests of every avatar and a couple of Omeiran expatriates. But that's not important. I want you to take my place as spymaster, now, before I'm too ill to finish your training."

"She can't be the king's spymaster! She's a scrapper!" Sienne burst out.

Corbyn ignored her. "You were my best student," he said. "Better than I'd ever hoped. So many of them took to crime, but you...you never would do anything that smacked of illegality unless you were convinced it was the only way. The right way. When that murder charge came up, I very nearly disposed of Randon right then. Nine years, Dianthe. I'm so sorry I failed you."

"You didn't fail me. It was my own fault. I was so afraid, I couldn't think of anything to do but run."

"It saved your life. I was in no position to extricate you." Corbyn seemed to become aware of the bars between them for the first time and cursed. "Where are the keys? That boy must have taken them." He trod up the stairs out of sight.

"Dianthe," Sienne said, then once more couldn't think of anything to say.

"You can go home," Alaric said, clasping her hands. "Dianthe, you're free."

"I'm free," Dianthe said. She sounded stunned. "Alaric, what do I do?"

"Is spymaster important?" Kalanath asked.

"It's...dear Kitane have mercy, he's right. It's what he was training me for, all those years." Dianthe sank onto the bench and covered her face with both hands. "I'd be good at it, too."

"But is that what you want?" Sienne said. "You're a scrapper, and you're good at *that*."

"I know. I don't know. You don't understand how much I owe Corbyn. He was almost a father to me, and now..."

Heavy footsteps sounded on the stairs, echoing strangely, and Sienne looked up and saw Denys had accompanied Corbyn. His jaw was rigid and dark circles ringed his eyes, though he'd combed his hair and tidied his uniform. He held the folded paper Corbyn had shown Mathis in one hand and the ring of keys in the other. "You're free to go," he told Dianthe, unlocking the cell door. Dianthe emerged, carefully stepping wide of him so there was no chance of them touching, not even so much as their clothes brushing against each other.

Sienne looked at the two of them, at their miserable faces, and burst out, "Oh, don't be an idiot, Denys! Dianthe isn't a criminal—don't you have her pardon there?"

"It's an exoneration," Denys said. "She never was a criminal, according to this."

"See? You don't—"

"Don't, Sienne," Denys said. "Just don't say anything." He turned and left the cells, walking as heavily as if he were Corbyn.

"But—" Sienne turned to Dianthe.

"It's all right, Sienne," Dianthe said. "I screwed up. This is the result. Please don't say any more." She turned to Corbyn. "You've put me in a terrible position," she said. "I owe you everything I am, every skill, every moment your teaching saved my life. But...I have a new life now. I have people who depend on me. I don't know if I can give that up."

"Not even for what I'm offering?"

"You should know me well enough to know prestige and power never mattered to me."

"I was thinking more in terms of being able to make a difference." Corbyn put a hand on her shoulder. "The king's government is stronger now than it has been, but it's still not totally secure. You'd be in a position to support his actions, reveal traitors before they can act, give evidence that convicts criminals. You'd be able to protect women like you once were."

Dianthe's eyes narrowed. "That's low, Corbyn."

"It's the truth. Yes, I'm leaning on you. But you're the best choice for the job. I believe in what Derekian is doing for this country. He's the first Fiorus monarch in three generations who isn't corrupt. I want to leave him in good hands. Consider that before you tell me no."

"I...I'll consider it. But we have to go. There's something I have to take care of. Where can I reach you?"

"Send word to the Gray Duck tavern that you want to speak to Hector Allanze. They'll get word to me." He squeezed her shoulder. "Good luck to you."

When he was gone, Dianthe said, "Well."

"But you wouldn't—"

"Sienne," Perrin said, putting a restraining hand on her shoulder, "this is Dianthe's decision."

"That's right," Dianthe said. "And I'm not thinking about it until we destroy the lich. Now, where do we start looking?"

Alaric cleared his throat. "One neighborhood called The Havens is on the south side. Then someone thought they'd heard of an estate by that name—the woman had made a couple of deliveries there. I think we should try that one first, given how many of our blight seem to be well-to-do."

"Then let's get my things, and we'll be off," Dianthe said.

14

The journey to the estate called The Havens took them through a wealthy part of town, where manors lay spread out on ample grounds, tilled and planted to look elegant or exotic. Beyond these neighborhoods, however, the well-cultivated yards gave way to untrimmed hedges, overgrown gardens, and enormous trees that might be as old as Fioretti itself. If not for the paved roads and the magic lights on poles, dim in the daylight, it might have been wilderness rather than civilization. Sienne breathed in the warm, wet air that smelled of growing things and felt her tension drain away. Dianthe wouldn't choose Corbyn over them. She just wouldn't.

"This is it, I think," Kalanath said, pointing at a path that was all but invisible in the lush growth. A wooden sign with THE HAVENS burned into it hung from a branch at eye level.

"I feel like we're approaching an overgrown ruin," Alaric said, heading down the path, which was narrow enough they had to walk single file.

"Yes, and one haunted by carricks," Perrin said. "Not that I have ever seen a carrick."

"No fear of that so long as there's no lakes around," Dianthe said. "It's wisps you have to fear in a place like this."

"I think that is a thing you did not need to say," Kalanath said with a grimace. "I do not like wisps."

"Shh," Alaric said, then laughed, a little sheepishly. "I don't know why I just shushed you. It's just that—"

"—this place feels like a mausoleum," Sienne said. "Or a temple. But not to any avatar I know."

"It does feel rather sinister, does it not?" Perrin said.

At that moment, the trees, enormous willows that had been blocking the view ahead, came to an end, and Sienne gaped at the house before them. The manor sprawled like a sleeping cat stretched out before a fire, with two single-story wings flanking the two-story main house. Arched windows missing their glass, if they'd ever had any, gaped at them like sunken eyes. Half the windows, the ones on the left-hand side, were boarded up. Vines crept up the sides of the house, almost covering the walls on the right-hand side and racing to reach the roof of the main house. The path led through an overgrown lawn, patchy with weeds, straight to the front door, which hung ajar. There were no signs of life aside from the vulgar, verdant display.

"This can't be right," Alaric said.

"Are you sure? Because to my mind, this is exactly the sort of place an evil necromancer should live," Sienne said, stepping a little closer to him.

"Let's just see if anyone still lives here," Dianthe said, striding up the path toward the door. Sienne and the others followed her. Dianthe rapped sharply on the door, which shifted at her touch.

There was no response. "Should we wait, or poke around?" Dianthe said.

"It's *someone's* property," Alaric said, "so we probably shouldn't trespass. After all, we're here looking for someone, and if no one lives—"

The door creaked open, rising to a musical crescendo in a harmony Sienne wouldn't have thought a piece of wood and metal could make. "Yes?" said the elderly woman who answered the door. She had gray-streaked white hair falling loose nearly to the small of her back and a pleasantly wrinkled face.

She was also dressed, head to toe, in a sleeveless gown dyed bright red.

Sienne gasped. Alaric put out a warning hand. "Drusilla Tallavena?" he said.

"I am she," the woman said. Her voice was firm and not at all shaky. "Can I help you with something?"

"Are you acquainted with Pauro Murtaviti?"

The pleasant expression vanished. "Why do you ask?"

"We have some questions about his...activities."

"I don't know anything about what Pauro's doing now. I haven't spoken to him in three years." Drusilla Tallavena began to shut the door.

"Wait!" Dianthe exclaimed. "We think you're in danger!"

The door stopped. "Is this some kind of trick?" Drusilla said sharply.

"No trick," Alaric said. "Murtaviti has turned himself into an undead creature and is on his way to Fioretti. We believe he intends to attack you."

Drusilla opened the door widely. "Come in," she said. "If Pauro has succeeded, we are all in danger."

Despite its imposing façade, the old house was only one room deep. Halls sprouted from the entry chamber to extend into both wings. In the unlit chamber, dim from the shielding limbs of the willow trees, Sienne could barely make out paintings hung on the walls and a staircase, all the way at the back of the room.

"I shut up half the house when I began my penance," Drusilla said, waving a hand to indicate they should follow her. "I never have guests anymore. It wasn't as if I could explain why I took to wearing the red."

Sienne felt full to bursting with questions, but Alaric gave her a quelling glare, and she bit back the first, which was *What penance?*

The rooms of the wing seemed to have been built around the hall, which ran through the middle of them without doors or partitions, like the string on a rope of pearls. They passed through a sitting room, a dining room with two tables flanking the hall, and another sitting room, all of them tidy and dust-free, if dark. In the third sitting room, Drusilla lit a lamp on one of the many small tables scattered throughout the room and trimmed it so it cast a warm glow over all of them. "Please sit," she said, taking a seat next to the lamp. "Tell me what happened to Pauro. He managed the transformation?"

"It seems you already know something about it," Alaric said.

"It was our common goal." Drusilla laughed. "Say, rather, it was the goal we all raced toward, each hoping to be the first. I would not have guessed Pauro would be the first to succeed, though. Selten and Ivar were so much more driven than he. But Selten died, and Ivar...he seems content as he is. And now Pauro intends to kill me. What a waste of effort."

"We'd prefer it if you were less cryptic," Alaric said. "You're one of Murtaviti's blight. Why would he kill you?"

"*Was* one of Pauro's blight," Drusilla said. "It's been three years since I turned to the worship of Delanie and took the red robe of penance. I have many years yet to go before it is complete. I pray I will accomplish my penance before I die."

"You're a penitent?" Sienne exclaimed, ignoring Alaric's glare. "Is that even possible?"

"My dear, I am grateful that you are so untouched by the ways of the world to ask that question," Drusilla said. "I am assured it is possible, and the priests of Delanie would not give me false hope. She is far too logical an avatar. I try not to think that I might have had much more to atone for, as that leads me to the further sin of pride, but sometimes it gives me comfort to know I have achieved some small success."

"So Pauro wants you dead to keep you from being a rival," Dianthe said. "Is that it?"

"Yes. Oh, we all swore that of *course* any of us who achieved the transformation would use our knowledge to help the others, but we all knew we were lying. Blights generally fall apart after a decade or so because of internal rivalries. Ours has lasted nearly thirty-seven years—not that I consider it mine anymore, but you understand my meaning. At any rate, that is a long time to maintain a blight."

"So you intended to become a lich?" Alaric said.

"I did." A look of distaste crossed her face. "It seems so far away, so irrational. I don't know why I ever wanted immortality. Not at that price. Hah. Not at any price. Living forever while you watch everyone around you age and die...I much prefer the promise of God's eternal rest, surrounded by my loved ones."

"But you understand the process," Perrin said. "You can tell us how to defeat Master Murtaviti."

"Defeat him?" Drusilla smiled, the indulgent look of a parent to a pampered child. "That's impossible."

"It is not impossible. I know it has been done." Perrin leaned forward. "Is it a divine blessing of some sort? Or a spell?"

"A lich is immortal and invulnerable," Drusilla said. "They stand outside the natural order. I have never heard of an avatar intervening to destroy a lich. I believe they are capable of doing so, because I can't imagine liches being more powerful than God, but they choose not to for their own reasons. At any rate, they are immune to many spells, can endure more damage than an ordinary man, and have strength beyond mortal means. If you attack him directly, you will be destroyed."

"And if we attack him indirectly?" Alaric said.

Drusilla raised one eyebrow. "You're more intelligent than you look. If you want to destroy Pauro, you must destroy his reliquary. It is...not the source of his power, precisely, but it is what keeps his soul attached to his undead body. Destroy it, and you break the link."

"What is it? Where is it?" Sienne asked.

"It is...I'm sorry, I would show you mine, but I destroyed it when I burned the rest of my paraphernalia." Drusilla shrugged. "It takes years to assemble one, and every necromancer approaches it differently, but all must be made in part from the bones of—I would prefer not to go into the specifics. Let us just say it will be made of bone and either glass or wood, treated with invulnerability, containing a scrap of paper with ritual words written on it in the necromancer's own blood. He may keep it somewhere on his person, as I'm sure you can see would be a way to protect it."

"But if it's invulnerable, how can it be destroyed?" Dianthe said.

"The wood or glass might be invulnerable, but the bones are not —cannot be made so. They are the weak spot, because they break as readily as any bone." Drusilla laced her fingers together and rested them on her knee. "So you can see how it would be impossible."

"I don't see," Alaric said. "You've just told us Murtaviti has a serious weakness. It doesn't sound impossible to me."

"Pauro is in a position to defend himself with lethal force," Drusilla said. "The reliquary is fragile, yes, but getting at it will be more difficult than I believe—"

A distant knock sounded at the front door. Sienne tensed. "Are you expecting guests?" Perrin asked, his face still as if he were trying to see through the far-off door.

"No." Drusilla rose, but stopped when Alaric took hold of her wrist.

"I don't think you should answer the door," he said. "Is there another way out of here?"

"The back door," Drusilla said. "But it's in the main house."

"Windows?" Dianthe said. "They're big enough to fit through."

"I appreciate this, but there's no need," Drusilla said. "If Pauro has come for me, I'm not afraid to meet my God. I only hope She will be forgiving of this poor sinner."

"Not to be blunt, but we're not done with you," Alaric said. "If your knowledge will help us defeat this monster, I'm not willing to give you up to him. Now. Windows."

There were two large windows on opposite sides of the room, facing front and back. Both were shaded by creeping vines that almost completely obscured them and made curtains unnecessary. Neither was made to open. "Sienne?" Alaric said.

Sienne pulled out her spellbook. "It's going to be noisy," she warned him.

There was another knock, then a loud splintering, cracking sound accompanied by the shrill whine of metal stressed beyond its endurance. "That's not an issue," Alaric said.

Sienne read off the honey-sweet transform *break*, feeling it build inside her until the final syllable shot away from her to shatter the back window. Alaric kicked a few shards out of the frame and extended his hand to Drusilla. "Quickly!"

"Drusilla?" someone called out from down the hall. "I have the most wonderful surprise for you. Where are you, old friend?"

Sienne scrambled over the windowsill, followed by Kalanath and Perrin. Dianthe brought up the rear. "Run!" she whispered, and took off for the far end of the house.

As Sienne followed, she heard rapid footsteps, and violent cursing. Then, to her horror, her feet slipped, and she fell on her face. What felt like hands around her ankles dragged her backward. She screamed and struggled to grab her spellbook, turning on her back as she slid inexorably toward the window. Pauro Murtaviti stood there, his eyes glowing bright yellow like a cat's at night. One hand extended in her direction as if summoning her. *But he's no wizard*, she thought frantically, *and invisible fingers can't control anything so heavy!*

Hands grabbed her under her arms and hauled her to her feet. For a moment, she was pulled in two directions at once and screamed again at the pain. Then the pull from Murtaviti stopped, and she fell backward into Alaric, who got his arm around her and supported her. "What happened?" he said.

"I don't know. Get out of here. I'll stall him." She whipped open her book to *burn* and began reading. Murtaviti stepped over the windowsill and walked toward them as casually as if they were old friends he intended to greet.

"Don't be stupid. We're not leaving." Alaric drew his sword and took up a waiting posture beside Sienne just as the final syllables of *burn* emerged from her. Blue fire engulfed Murtaviti, making him step backward in surprise. His clothes caught fire, his head was wreathed in flames, and he slapped at himself.

"Get Mistress Tallavena out of here!" Alaric shouted, and ran at Murtaviti, sword upraised. Behind Sienne, Dianthe cursed, then ran past with her own slim blade drawn. Sienne circled, trying to get behind Murtaviti for another spell. She hoped Kalanath and Perrin were making their escape. It was probably a vain hope.

Alaric bore down on Murtaviti like an elemental force, raising his sword and swinging it in an attempt to behead the lich. Though Murtaviti couldn't possibly see through the fire engulfing his head, he ducked, leaped backward with astonishing speed, and rolled, extinguishing the worst of the flames and ignoring the rest. He stopped rolling and crouched, eyeing Alaric and Dianthe, then slowly rose to stand before them. "I remember you," he said, and snapped his fingers.

Alaric went up in flames.

15

"No!" Sienne screamed. She dropped her spellbook and pelted toward Alaric. Dianthe was already there, forcing him down and smothering the flames with her sleeves drawn up over her hands. Desperate, Sienne summoned as big a mass of water as she could and dropped it on them, soaking them both. Murtaviti walked past them, again with that slow saunter, ignoring them completely.

Sienne, her hands shaking, fell to her knees beside Alaric, whose eyes were wide and startled. Gasping for air, he felt about him for his sword. "How did he do that?"

"I don't know. He's not a wizard—it doesn't make sense—" Sienne rose and read off *burn* again, striking Murtaviti full in the back. He staggered, shrugged out of his vest, and dropped it to burn to ash beside him.

"Find something else," Alaric said. "It's working, but it's not slowing him enough." He rose, shook his head to clear it, and ran after the lich, Dianthe beside him. Beyond Murtaviti, a pearly gray dome of divine power surrounded Perrin and Drusilla, while Kalanath stood in front of it, staff at the ready. Murtaviti raised his hand to snap his fingers, and Kalanath spun, bringing the staff down hard on the lich's hand.

Murtaviti snatched his hand back. He laughed, a horrible cackling sound Sienne had never before heard outside the stage of a melodrama. It wasn't nearly so funny now. "You're all trying so *hard*," he said, and waved his hand. Something picked Kalanath up and flung him backwards into the dome, which compressed slightly, then bounced him off to fall hard to the ground. It was enough time for Alaric to reach Murtaviti and, with a powerful thrust, skewer him with his greatsword.

Murtaviti turned his head to look back at Alaric. "You should know that won't work," he said in a chiding tone.

Alaric withdrew the blade, which came free with a terrible rasping sound, as if Murtaviti's flesh were iron. "Didn't have to," he said. Murtaviti turned away just in time for Dianthe's sword to take him through the left eye.

The lich jerked, flinging up his hands to grasp the sword and pull it free. Black liquid oozed from his eye socket, dribbling down his cheek. "How *dare* you," he snarled, wiping away black goo as if it were ordinary tears. "I see I shouldn't have gone easy on you."

Alaric raised his sword for another head-cleaving stroke and went sailing away backward into a stand of willows. Dianthe flew the other direction. She struck a tree, head-first, and fell limp to the ground. Sienne, frantically skimming the pages of her spellbook for inspiration, screamed and ran to her side. Blood darkened Dianthe's blonde hair. Across what was left of the yard, Alaric struggled to his feet. Kalanath once more stood between Murtaviti and the shield dome, which was moving steadily away from the house as Perrin guided Drusilla's feet. Then Kalanath erupted in flames and flung himself to the ground, rolling away and dropping his staff. Sienne couldn't see what Murtaviti did next, but whatever it was, it popped the shield like a soap bubble. Perrin and Drusilla stood helpless before him, and even as Perrin brought up one of his personal shields, Murtaviti advanced on them. He was too close, and—

Struck by inspiration, Sienne ran for the house, away from Murtaviti. As she ran, she gabbled out the sharp-edged syllables of a summoning, tasting blood. It was unorthodox, and it wasn't exactly a weapon, but it might give them time. She stopped and faced her distant friends, Alaric racing to strike Murtaviti, Dianthe finally stirring, Kalanath reaching for his staff, and spat out the final syllables of *castle.*

Instantly she was falling. She struck the ground, grateful for the overgrown grass, then ducked further to avoid Alaric's powerful swing. *"Sienne!"* he shouted. "A little warning?"

"Sorry!" She stood, staggered, and looked over her shoulder. Murtaviti was collapsed in the space she'd formerly occupied. Trading places with someone was a useless transportation spell, right up until it wasn't. "We should run," she suggested.

They dashed across the overgrown lawn, not bothering to take the path. Ahead, Sienne saw the line of willows marking the edge of The Havens. Putting that between themselves and the lich would give them an advantage, though as she ran she couldn't help thinking there wasn't any way to stop him, that they'd have to go on running forever, and they were human and needed rest, but he didn't.

A wind came up, blowing the willows in a wild dance. It was so strong a wind it pushed Sienne back a few paces before subsiding. Then it was back, stronger than before, taking Sienne's breath away. She covered her mouth and nose, making a pocket of clear air for her to breathe, and staggered forward two steps.

Someone grabbed her wrist. A jolt ran through her, starting at her hand and shooting through the rest of her body. A strange lassitude followed it, all her muscles relaxing so she couldn't even support her weight. She sagged, tried to move, and found her arm was stiff as stone. Then it was her chest, her neck, her legs...every inch of her felt heavy and immovable. She couldn't even blink. She drew breath to scream and found even her lungs were unresponsive. She dragged in a slow breath, but it wasn't enough; spots were forming before her eyes from lack of air.

Though she couldn't move, she could still feel the strong wind on her skin, feel the softness of her shirt and the stiffness of her leather boots. And she could hear screaming, though her addled brain made no sense of it. Whoever it was—no, it had to be Murtaviti, this was the paralysis Perrin had said he could induce with a touch—Murtaviti let go of her wrist and she fell like a statue cut off at the knees. She focused on breathing, slowly, ignoring the panic that threatened to overwhelm her.

Someone picked her up and ran with her, every step jolting her concentration. "Just hold on, we'll figure this out," Alaric said. She was turned the wrong way to be able to see him, instead getting flashes of green as they ran through the terrible wind. Dianthe shouted something that was lost in the noise of the gale. At least Dianthe wasn't terribly injured. A head wound like that—

The wind stopped, and Alaric stumbled and caught himself. "Keep going," he shouted. "There's nothing we can do for her."

Don't give up on me! Sienne mentally screamed. There had to be *something* to remove the paralysis.

The green disappeared. Sienne caught glimpses of stone and glass, tall houses whose windows winked in the sunlight. Alaric's breathing was heavy and ragged, and he slowed, shifting her position so she could see nothing but his shoulder. His scent filled her, reassuring her that her nose, at least, still worked, and she'd just realized that was an addled thought when he stopped and gently set her on the ground, then continued leaning over, sucking in air in great shuddering breaths.

"This may not be far enough," she heard Perrin say.

"It is all we can do," Kalanath said. "We cannot run longer. Dianthe is bleeding."

"I can care for that," Perrin said. Sienne heard him mutter an invocation, but saw no green light. She hoped that was because she was looking the wrong way.

Alaric cursed at length. "We never had a chance, did we? And that poor woman…"

"I hope God will take into account her assistance to us when She judges Mistress Tallavena's soul," Perrin said.

"We need to keep moving," Dianthe said. "Master Murtaviti looked fairly preoccupied with…whatever he was doing to her…but that won't last."

"We need help for Sienne," Alaric said. "She's having trouble breathing."

"I can attempt to heal her," Perrin said, "but I am not sure—"

"Do it," Alaric said.

A hand rolled Sienne onto her back. She had a momentary mental image of how she must look, curled in on herself like a turtle with one leg extended and both hands closed into fists, and wished she could laugh. Her lungs tightened, her vision swam, and she forced herself to be calm. She'd never appreciated breathing before now.

"O Lord, this is not the common use for this one, but if you will, have patience in your crankiness, and grant me this blessing," Perrin said. Immediately Sienne felt the fist around her lungs relax, and tingling began in her extremities. She still couldn't move, but she didn't feel quite so heavy. She tried to move her mouth, with no result, so she gave up on that and flexed her toes. That worked. She was so happy tears leaked from her eyes.

"Dear Sisyletus, she's crying. Damn it, you just made it worse," Alaric said.

"No," Sienne managed, though the N was nearly silent. "No."

"It worked," Perrin said. "Or, rather, it has begun working. I imagine a blessing specific to her condition would cure it immediately, and a healing blessing simply accelerates the natural recovery process."

"Really?" asked Dianthe.

"I have no idea. It is a working hypothesis. Sienne, can you move your head? No? Can you say 'no' again?"

"No," Sienne repeated.

"Are you in pain?"

"No."

"Can you feel your limbs? Your fingers?"

Sienne managed to twitch her fingers. "Ess."

"Thank Averran," Alaric said. He lifted Sienne into his arms and kissed her forehead, somewhat awkwardly because her hands were drawn up between them. "We need to keep moving."

"But where to?" Dianthe said. "We can't go home. Suppose Master Murtaviti kills Master Tersus or Leofus?"

"We must find another of the blight," Kalanath said. "The one in Onofreo."

More bouncing told Sienne they were on the move again. "I don't really care about warning these people," Alaric said. "It was just chance Mistress Tallavena was reformed. If the lich wants to kill them, I'm fine with that."

"But he will grow stronger as the days pass," Perrin said. "And much as it pains me to admit it, we need these necromancers' help if we are to find Master Murtaviti's reliquary. They can fight fire with fire, as it were."

"He set us on fire," Dianthe exclaimed. "How is that possible? Without a spellbook—he's not even a wizard!"

Sienne had been wondering that too. Fire, wind, moving people without a touch... She grunted, and Alaric said, "What's wrong? Did I hurt you?"

"No," Sienne said, subsiding. She was in no condition to communicate anything so complicated as the theory she was still evolving. It had occurred to her that all those things were the kind of simple magic wizards could do without spellbooks, practically from birth. Not only that, but they were *exactly* the simple magics a wizard first manifested without having to be taught. Spark. Breeze. Invisible fingers. Granted, Murtaviti was capable of using them on a far bigger scale—she couldn't use her spark to set a man on fire—but there had to be *something* there they could use against the lich. She just couldn't figure it out. Yet.

She concentrated on flexing her fingers and toes. They tingled sharply, almost painfully, but she welcomed the sensation. Her wrists and ankles tingled too, more faintly, which she hoped meant the paralysis would eventually wear off.

"Onofreo is only a day's ride away," Alaric said. "We can push that —no, we can't. Sienne can't ride in this condition. And slinging her over my saddle until she recovers will wear Paladin out."

"We might try something else," Perrin said. "Though I cannot imagine what we will tell the divines about how our companion ended up in this condition."

"The divines?" Dianthe said. "You mean at a temple."

"At Kitane's temple, specifically," Perrin said, "as they specialize in all sorts of healing."

"Why do we not tell them it is a lich, and ask them to fight it?" Kalanath said.

"Mistress Tallavena was correct that divine power is useless against a lich, as my mentor told me," Perrin said. "Or, more specifically, an avatar will not grant a blessing that will destroy a lich. Naturally other blessings may be used against one."

"That seems unfair," Dianthe said. "Surely God is as opposed to liches as to any other form of undead."

"Evander never said why this was true. When I asked him that very question, he simply shrugged and said Averran's ways were inscrutable. I believe, if one could truly understand the transformation that turns a man into a lich, one would know why this is the case. But it is pointless for us to rail against the vagaries of the divine will. Additionally, even if we were to tell the divines the truth, they would be likely to slow us down with irrelevant questions and possibly demand that we turn the search for Master Murtaviti over to qualified spirit-hunters. We cannot risk the delay. What other substance might we say induced paralysis in Sienne?"

"Some poison," Kalanath said, then shook his head. "They will try to cure the poison and there is none."

"Basilisk," Alaric said. "There haven't been any in the area for fifteen years, I'm told, but they roam freely, so it's plausible."

"Very well. A basilisk encounter. The temple of Kitane is some distance from here. I suggest we hurry."

Sienne was able to flex her wrists and ankles by the time Alaric carried her beneath the portico of the temple of Kitane. She'd never been inside before, but there was one in her home dukedom of Beneddo, and her mother, a devout worshipper of the avatar, had taken her children there every year on Kitane's name-day. They all looked the same: a single round, domed building circled by a shady portico, faced with white marble, at the center of which was a bronze statue of Kitane as warrior, naked except for her helmet, shield, and sword. Four altars flanked the statue at the cardinal directions, used at different times of the year for different purposes. It would be the east altar now, she remembered, east for first summer, south for true summer, north for winter, and west for all the things that happened out of season.

"Excuse me," she heard Alaric say. "Excuse me. Our companion is in need of healing."

"Are you scrappers?" a woman asked.

Sienne felt Alaric tense. "We are."

"And what seems to be the trouble?"

"Basilisk. We killed it, but it bit her and she's semi-paralyzed."

"A basilisk? There haven't been any of those near Fioretti for years. You can thank Kitane she didn't catch its eye. There's not much anyone can do for a full paralysis, even an avatar."

"We'd appreciate your help. We're prepared to make offering, of course."

"Hmmm." Quick footsteps receded into the distance, then returned, bringing friends. "A basilisk paralysis. Have you seen anything like this, Octavian?"

"No, Reva, I have not. But I believe Kitane is willing to help. Young man, set her down here—no, not on the altar! Just below it."

Alaric laid Sienne on the floor. She blinked, and was so happy to be able to do so she flapped her hands like a trained seal and felt embarrassed immediately. The divines said nothing about it.

"Lady of Power, by your good right hand, lend me your strength," the man, Octavian, said. Golden light flared. The tingling that had been gradually moving up her arms and legs flooded through her, making her cry out in agony. She heard Alaric shout her name, but she couldn't see him—couldn't see anything with the rich golden light blinding her. The sharp pain faded back into tingling, and then it was gone. Sienne took a wonderfully deep breath and felt like crying again, it felt so good. She gingerly stretched her legs and arms, rotated her neck, and blinked. Everything was fuzzy, but she blinked again, and the world swam into focus.

Alaric crouched beside her to help her stand, and kept his arms protectively around her when she wobbled. "Thank you," he said. "How can we repay Kitane for her gift?"

Octavian turned out to be an old man with sharp blue eyes as pale as Alaric's, unusual in a Rafellish. Reva was much younger, almost too young to be a divine, Sienne thought, and her nose turned up at the end, giving her the look of a friendly pig. "One hundred lari," Octavian said, "and the answer to a question."

"All right," Alaric said, sounding wary. "What question?"

Octavian turned his sharp gaze on Perrin. "You are a priest of Averran, yes?"

"Is it marked somewhere on my person?" Perrin said in astonishment. "Yes. Is that the question?"

"No. I would like to know why a priest of any avatar should participate in lying to a divine."

Perrin blinked. "I—that is—"

"There was no basilisk. What unsavory deed did you want to conceal from us?"

Reva's mouth fell open. Dianthe shifted uncomfortably. "Not unsavory," Perrin said. "Simply...unbelievable."

"We're trying to destroy a lich," Alaric said flatly. "Believe that, or not. Our companion came in the way of his touch."

"A lich." Octavian's eyes narrowed.

Reva said, "What's a lich?"

"An evil story for another time, young one." Octavian pursed his lips. "I wish I were twenty years younger, to give you real aid. But I think...wait here." He nodded at Reva as if to say "stay put" and walked away to a door cleverly concealed in the round wall of the temple.

"Turn out your pockets, everyone," Alaric said. "We've got to have a hundred lari between us."

Sienne shook out the contents of her belt pouch. Twenty-two lari in assorted coin. She handed it to Alaric, who gave her back a couple of coins. He gave the handful of money to Reva, who took it in both hands, then looked around somewhat helplessly for somewhere to put it. Finally, she deposited it on the altar. Sienne figured that was the safest place she could have chosen.

Octavian returned holding something concealed in his hand from which dangled a long silver chain. "An artifact, from my youth," he said, extending it to Perrin. It turned out to be a round silver pendant set with a translucent yellow citrine of an irregular shape. To Sienne's eyes, it glowed with magical energy. "This grants the wearer vision beyond his own. Specifically, it will alert you to the presence of undead creatures. A small thing, but perhaps you will find it useful."

"This is a princely gift," Perrin said. "We should not accept."

"The alternative is that it continues collecting dust here in the temple," Octavian said, closing Perrin's fingers over it. "Better it be used to defeat evil."

"Then—our thanks," Perrin said. He looped the chain around his neck. "For everything."

"Good luck to you, scrappers," Octavian said with a wave.

When they were on the street again, Sienne said, "I've never been so grateful to be able to walk."

"Be grateful you're able to ride," Alaric said. "We need to get to Onofreo as fast as the horses will carry us."

"And pray Master Murtaviti has not had the same idea," Perrin said.

16

They rode out of Fioretti at nearly eleven o'clock, after a short delay to get the horses ready. Sienne felt the passing minutes as a nearly physical pull, drawing her westward. Spark's gait was as rapid and eager as ever, but to Sienne it felt plodding, like slogging through the snowy winter landscape of her youth. It was a strange comparison to make on such a warm day. The sun beat down on her head and shoulders and warmed Spark's dark mane so it smelled of her rich musk. Under any other circumstances, it would have been a pleasant ride. At the moment, it felt more like a race. Which, she reflected, it was.

She took in another deep breath and held it for a few moments. It hadn't yet gotten old, breathing easily. That paralysis could have suffocated her. Paralysis, and tremendous strength, and magic...how was that even possible? No one who wasn't born a wizard could do anything the least bit magical, and yet Murtaviti had definitely used magic against them.

"It's nine hours to Onofreo at this pace," Alaric said to Dianthe, riding beside him. "Including rest stops. That puts us there just before sunset."

"How are we supposed to find this Ivar Scholten?" she replied.

"Onofreo's not big, but it's big enough we can't expect to walk into the first tavern we see and encounter him."

"It's an Ansorjan name," Alaric said. "Let's hope there aren't so many Ansorjans that he doesn't stand out. Sienne, are you all right?"

"I feel perfectly normal," Sienne called out.

"Say something if you feel strange. We don't know what kind of aftereffects contact with a lich might have."

It hadn't occurred to Sienne that there might be aftereffects. Perrin's assertions aside, she immediately pictured herself turning into an undead, her eyes glowing like lamps. She tried to think about Murtaviti and his impossible magic. It kept her from dwelling on Murtaviti's touch or obsessing about how slowly they were riding. His magic had been powerful versions of simple things, and that suggested something to her, but she couldn't put her finger on it. It was almost as if Murtaviti had been transformed into a wizard by his ritual, and had developed magic just like an infant wizard did, but that didn't explain why his magic was so powerful. Not even the oldest and most experienced wizards could set a man on fire with spark.

"Perrin," she said, "are you sure not all liches are wizards?"

Perrin, riding beside her, drew closer so he didn't have to shout. "Very sure," he said. "But you know better than I—are not most necromancers ordinary men and women?"

"It's more that most necromantic rituals don't require magic," Sienne replied. "So even wizards who turn to necromancy don't have to use wizardry to do it. But Master Murtaviti definitely used magic, and we know he wasn't a wizard."

"You think something happened to him?" Alaric said over his shoulder. "Something that turned him into a wizard?"

"I don't know. That's supposed to be impossible. That's why I wondered if there really is a difference between a lich and a wizard who becomes a lich."

"Evander spoke very little of his encounter with the wizard lich, possibly because he counted it a defeat," Perrin said. "But he was very clear that the woman wielded a spellbook."

"How was she defeated in the end?" Kalanath asked.

"I do not know. Presumably, if Mistress Tallavena was correct, they destroyed her reliquary. But Evander was not a part of that action."

"So Murtaviti can do magic, but not wizardry," Alaric said. "That's the distinction, right?"

"Yes," Sienne said. "Magic is what we can do without a spellbook, and wizardry is casting spells. And he can do magic far more powerful than what I'm capable of."

"I noticed that," Alaric said. "What does it mean?"

"I have no idea. It feels like...I don't know."

"But you think it is something," Kalanath said.

"It's just that what he's doing is just like what an infant wizard does, how she develops. But I can't explain how powerful he is." Sienne leaned forward and took another deep breath of musk-scented air. Really, nobody appreciated breathing enough.

"So if that's happening—if he's progressing in magic the way a wizard would—what else might he learn to do?" Alaric said.

"I don't know. The rest of the simple magics, you have to be taught. Like simple illusions, or creating water. They're not...obvious, I suppose is the best word. So Master Murtaviti might not be able to use them, since it's unlikely he'll find anyone to teach him. But since he shouldn't have been able to develop *any* magic, I don't know if we can count on that."

"But he definitely can't do wizardry," Dianthe said.

"No. I'm certain of that. He'd need to be able to read the four spell languages, and he'd need a spellbook he wrote in his own blood. It's just impossible."

"Thank all the avatars for that," Alaric said.

They rode faster after that, not speaking because there was nothing to say that would propel them along the road faster. They stopped occasionally to rest the horses, ate in the saddle, and rode again. Sienne tried not to watch the sun dropping lower in the sky before them, but it was hard not to feel they were racing it, too. She watched the landscape pass, wide grasslands spotty with trees here and there that turned into forest after around five o'clock. The speed of their passage scared birds out of the trees, sending them winging away in great masses that sounded like wind rushing through the leaves.

They passed other travelers, most of them afoot, flashing past them with no time to register what they thought of the scrapper team speeding along westward. Once or twice they had to slow to pass a four-horse carriage, trundling along toward Fioretti like a lumbering bear. The drivers paid them no attention. What the passengers thought, Sienne didn't know, because in every case the curtains were drawn against the sunlight. That would make the carriage interior more stuffy, but their comfort wasn't her responsibility.

Near sunset, they left the forest behind and followed the winding road into low hills covered by vineyards and neatly laid out squares of tilled earth, beginning to show green with the first crops' growth. The sun was low in the west, slanting directly into Sienne's eyes, when a dark blotch on the horizon resolved into gray slate roofs and white plaster walls. She shaded her eyes with one hand and blinked into the light. Onofreo. The city proper was surrounded by a high stone wall that looked like it was about to fall down, an afterthought of a wall that would make no difference if an army decided to conquer the dukedom. At this distance, it was impossible to make out a gate, but Sienne figured the road had to lead right to it, if only because anything else was stupid.

"Faster," Alaric called over his shoulder. "They close the gates an hour after sunset."

Sienne urged Spark on. The little mare didn't seem at all tired from her day's journey, but Sienne knew from experience that Spark was capable of pushing herself beyond her limit and then simply giving up. It was Sienne's job to make sure she didn't do that.

Gradually, the wall loomed closer. It didn't look any more stable up close than it had at a distance. Stones the size of Spark's head seemed to fit only loosely together, with the once-sharp edges rounded off with time until the surface of the wall looked like a pebbly riverbed rather than a mighty bulwark. The gates, when they were close enough to see them, looked more secure than the wall did. Age-darkened slabs of six-inch-thick oak banded with iron stood open, welcoming travelers while reminding them the city was not defenseless. Sienne thought of Beneddo, with its six gates warding the dukedom from intruders, and wondered if she would ever see it again—or if she wanted to.

Even at this hour, men and women passed through the gates, mostly entering the city, though a few riders looked as if they intended to travel through the night, aided by the nearly full moon. Guards posted at the gate observed the travelers, but didn't stop any of them. Sienne was grateful not to have to tell anyone their business, though she was sure Alaric would come up with something more plausible-sounding than "looking for an evil necromancer."

Onofreo was a younger city than Fioretti, which was nearly as old as the wars that had torn civilization apart. It lay atop and between two hills, giving it a lopsided look. Its streets were wide and well-paved with cobblestones, and its construction was mostly half-timbered houses with stucco filling the gaps between beams, unlike Fioretti, where one could see the history of Rafellish architecture just by strolling down the right streets. Upper stories jutting out over the street to take advantage of the space gave the street they now rode down the feel of a tunnel, one lit by warm glowing lanterns that felt cozy and welcoming rather than claustrophobic.

"There seem to be a lot of taverns here," Sienne said.

"They cluster around the gates, hoping to attract road-weary customers," Dianthe said. "We should start asking about Master Scholten."

"Master Murtaviti will not need to ask. He will go there straight," Kalanath said.

"Nothing we can do about that," Alaric said. "We just have to hope our luck holds."

"Is our luck good, then?" Perrin drew closer to Sienne to avoid a huddle of amiable drunks moving from one tavern to another. "Mistress Tallavena is dead, we barely escaped with our lives, Sienne was almost killed...I cannot see anything but bad luck there."

"We're all alive despite Murtaviti's best efforts," Alaric said. "I choose to call that good luck." He swung down from his horse and handed its reins to Dianthe. "Perrin, come with me. The rest of you wait here. No sense us overwhelming the tavern keeper."

Sienne sat, not very patiently, and observed the passersby. Almost everyone was on foot, and most of those who walked past eyed the five horses speculatively. Scrapper teams couldn't be that unusual, surely? She smiled at a couple of young men who stared at her spellbook, then hastened away. Some people were afraid of wizards the way some people feared Alaric, because of the potential they represented for harm. It didn't matter that neither she nor Alaric would never attack anyone except in self-defense. Though it was funny to think of herself as a threat to anyone, with her average build and complete lack of obvious weapons. The spellbook was weapon enough.

Alaric and Perrin emerged from the tavern. "Never heard of him," Alaric said. "Let's move on."

"I think we should split up," Dianthe said. "We need to move faster."

"All right, so long as one of us stays with the horses," Alaric said. "There's nowhere to leave them on this street that won't get them hurt or stolen. Kalanath?"

"I do not think anyone will approach me, because I am foreign, and may be dangerous," Kalanath agreed.

Sienne hopped down and handed her reins to Kalanath. "I'll take the far side of the street."

"Me too," Dianthe said.

The tavern Sienne entered had a low ceiling and a taproom that smelled of warm ale, not very pleasantly. Men and women crowded the place, most of them standing because every table was occupied. She forced her way through to the bar and ordered half a pint. "I'm looking for an Ansorjan named Ivar Scholten," she said to the barkeep. "*Ivar Scholten*," she repeated more loudly when the man cupped a beefy hand to his ear. "Ever heard of him?"

The barkeep shook his head and turned away. "Ivar Scholten?" the man next to Sienne said. "Why are you looking for him?"

"A personal matter," Sienne said. "Do you know him?"

"Sweetheart, I'd *be* him if it made you happy," the man said with a lazy smile. "Why don't you talk to me instead?"

Sienne swallowed a sharp retort. She probably should have expected this. "I'm sorry, I don't have time," she said, drinking half her pint and setting it on the bar. The man grabbed her wrist and pulled her closer, his smile broadening. She smelled alcohol coming off his breath and managed not to wince. Instead, she stood up tall and twisted her wrist to break his grip, a move Alaric had taught her and insisted she practice until she could do it against men twice her size.

"You're not charming," she told the man. "And you're drunk enough you're going to be embarrassed about this in the morning."

"I don't think so," the man said. "Not if you're there when I wake up." He reached for her again.

Sienne grabbed the half-empty mug with her invisible fingers and dumped its contents on the man's head. He stood, sputtering, and wiped ale out of his eyes. Sienne made her retreat before he could recover. What was it about some men that they couldn't take "no" for an answer?

Back on the street, she saw Dianthe leave the next tavern down and followed her. "There's only one left on this side," Dianthe said. "Any luck?"

"Not even a little," Sienne said.

Dianthe held the door for her. "I'm afraid this might be pointless. What are the odds anyone will know this one person out of all the thousands living in Onofreo?"

"We don't know Master Scholten at all, so Perrin can't use a locator blessing to find him."

This tavern wasn't as full as the last, and musicians played in one corner, reassuring Sienne, though why music was a reassurance that no one would assault her, she didn't know. She followed Dianthe to the bar, where a woman was busily engaged in filling a fistful of mugs. "Excuse me," Dianthe said.

"You'll have to wait," the woman replied. "Busy night."

"I—all right," Dianthe said, as the woman sailed away toward a table where a group of burly men with the look of farmers erupted with laughter at a joke Sienne hadn't heard. They welcomed the barkeep with more laughter and exclamations over the ale she brought. Sienne cast her gaze across the room. It was too much to hope that there would be a single Ansorjan drinking there tonight, and that he would turn out to be Ivar. Sure enough, the customers were all Rafellish, with a couple of fairer-skinned Wrathen mixed in.

The woman returned, wiping her hands on her apron. "What'll you have?"

"We just have a question," Dianthe said. "Do you know an Ivar Scholten? He lives in Onofreo and we have some information for him."

"I ought to make you buy a drink, but I've never heard of him, so I don't want to taunt you," the woman said. "Any idea where in Onofreo he lives? I can direct you to most neighborhoods."

"He's probably well-to-do," Sienne said. "And he's...he might not get out socially."

"Hmm." The woman held up a finger and moved off down the bar to take someone's order. She returned, hooking a bottle off the shelves behind her. "Most of the wealthy live outside the city, on estates, but there's also Left Tit—" She laughed. "Excuse me. The Aperten Hill, they'd call it. Left Tit is what us poor slobs down in the Valley call the Hill. Anyway, there's lots of rich folks up that way. Head up the street and keep making left turns until you start climbing, and that's the Aperten Hill."

"Thanks." Dianthe withdrew money from her pouch, but the woman waved it away.

"Don't mention it. Oh, you might ask the roughnecks about your man. If he's an estate owner, they might have worked for him." She pointed at the group of farmers, now enthusiastically and loudly drinking.

"Thank you," Sienne said. The woman nodded and turned away, pouring a measure of liquor from the bottle into a small glass.

"You really want to talk to those men?" Dianthe murmured.

"Why not? If they're sober enough to get sense out of them." Sienne walked toward the men's table, Dianthe following closely.

"I've already been propositioned three times tonight," Dianthe replied. "I'm tired of fending off amorous drunks. Let's hope this is worth it. Gentlemen!" she said as they drew close to the table. "Perhaps you can help me. I'm looking for someone."

"Sisyletus bless it's me you're looking for," said one of the men, whose heavy brown beard almost obscured his smile.

"An Ansorjan named Ivar Scholten," Dianthe said, her smile never wavering. "Might be a land owner. Ever heard of him?"

Brown Beard's eyes widened. "Not *Crazy* Ivar, miss?" he said, the flirtatious note in his voice disappearing. "You don't want to see him."

"Stay and have a drink with us, ladies," said one of his friends, whose red beard suggested he might have an Omeiran in his family tree. "Ivar never lets anyone into his property unless they're delivering something, anyway."

"And it's late," a third man said. Unlike his friends, he had no beard, but his thick mustache almost made up for it. "The gates will be closing soon, and you'll be stuck outside all night if you head for his estate now."

"Thanks, but we have important information for him," Dianthe said. "Let us pay for the next round, in thanks."

"We couldn't let a couple of pretty ladies buy us drinks," Mustache said. "You sure you won't stay?"

"We can't," Sienne said. "Can you tell us how to find Master Scholten? Outside, you say?"

Brown Beard shrugged. "Don't say we didn't warn you." He gestured with his thick fingers. "Out the Widdern Gate, down the road half a mile, take the first turn on the right and the Scholten estate is the second on the left, almost halfway up the hill."

"Thanks. We appreciate it."

"Probably shouldn't have told you, for your own safety," Red

Beard said. "Crazy Ivar isn't just a joke nickname. He gets up to all manner of strange stuff out there."

Sienne patted her spellbook. "We'll be fine." By the way the men looked at her, they didn't believe her any more than she believed herself.

17

Out on the street, they hurried back toward where Kalanath waited with the horses. He didn't look as bored as Sienne would have felt in his position. "We found him," Dianthe said.

Sienne looked up the street. Alaric and Perrin hurried toward them. "Maybe they had some success, too," she said.

"I found him," Perrin said. "Outside of town. We must hurry before the gate closes."

"That's what we learned," Sienne said, mounting Spark. "And that he doesn't have the best reputation."

"I should hope not, if he's a necromancer," Alaric said, turning Paladin and trotting away toward the gate.

The guards stopped them this time. "Gate closes in five minutes," the woman said. "We're supposed to let travelers know when they leave this late. You won't be able to get back in until sunrise."

"Understood," Alaric said. "Thanks."

The woman eyed his bulk and the sword hilt showing over his shoulder. "You scrappers?"

"Yes."

"My brother's a scrapper out in Tagliaveno. Good luck to you."

"Good fortune to your brother," Alaric said, and urged Paladin onward.

They rode at a gallop the short distance to where the road branched off to the right, then slowed, as the new road was pitted with deep ruts. There weren't many lights, most of them attached to distant houses and obscured by the curves in the road, which followed the contours of the land. Dark rows of vines, their rich scent filling the air, covered the ground on both sides of the road, curving with the gentle slopes. Ahead, the ground sloped more steeply, and the vineyards ended some quarter-mile before they reached the hills.

"Let's hope we're not too late," Alaric said.

"If he found someone who could cast *ferry*—" Sienne began, then fell silent. The night was warm, but she felt cold, deep inside.

"He will not have ridden," Perrin said, "as horses and other animals find the undead abhorrent. And you yourself said you could not find anyone with *ferry* in Fioretti."

"I couldn't find anyone willing to sell the spell. That doesn't mean there aren't wizards who will take money to cast it for others."

"We can't do anything about that now. If Murtaviti is there, or has been and gone, we'll just have to make a new plan," Alaric said.

"That's it," Dianthe said, pointing. "Second left."

The second left was almost invisible in the darkness, clearly not well trafficked and completely unmarked. Presumably if you had legitimate business there, you'd know enough to find it. The road extended about fifty yards from the main highway until it came up against a white stone wall that gleamed in the light of the moon. A wrought iron gate barred the way. Dianthe dismounted and walked up to it, resting her hand upon the grille. "It's not locked," she said, reaching between the bars to lift the latch. "I wonder what the point is?"

"We can ask Scholten when we find him," Alaric said. "Let's keep moving."

Past the gate, the road led deeper into the hills and, apparently, to nothing at all. Sienne saw no house, not even the lights that would mean a house was nearby. It was easy to feel they were riding into a trap. Had it been too convenient, finding those farmers who just happened to know exactly where Scholten lived? She scowled. She was being stupid. There was no way Murtaviti could have arranged that encounter, even if he'd gotten to Onofreo before them.

Suddenly a distant flame winked into being, then another, and Sienne realized they'd come around a bend into a valley, at the heart of which was a black blotch of a house lit by lanterns. Magic lanterns, to judge by the white-cold color of the lights. Alaric pushed Paladin faster, and Sienne followed suit. The urgency was a knot of tension in her chest now. Soon enough, they'd know if they were successful.

Perrin took in a sharp breath. "Something is coming," he said. "There are undead near."

"The pendant?" Dianthe said. "Can you see them?"

Perrin shook his head. "It is more of a visible itch, which I realize makes no sense, but it is the best I can do at an explanation. There are three, and they are very near." He pointed off to one side. "There is one now!"

Something lurched out of the darkness beside the road. Alaric pulled up sharply, making Paladin rear up at the abruptness of the halt. The creature ambled toward them, its face drawn up in a silent snarl. It was a man dressed in tattered clothes, his skin pale in the moonlight. His outstretched hands were tipped with long, sharp nails dark with some substance that looked sticky. His mouth opened, but no sound emerged.

Alaric swore and drew his sword. "I think we're at the right place."

"There's more of them," Dianthe said, pointing. More dark shapes came toward them along the road, their gait slow but steady.

"We don't have time for this," Alaric exclaimed. "Press on, and don't engage unless you have to. Perrin—"

"One moment," Perrin said, maneuvering past Alaric and Dianthe with a scrap of blessing held high. He rattled off an invocation, and a pearly shield sprang up just in time for the undead to walk into it. The shield wasn't the full dome, but it was larger than the personal shield, a curved surface that reached to both sides of the road and well over even Alaric's head. The undead tried to keep walking toward them, but slid along the shield back the direction it had come. "Ride," Perrin said. "More are coming."

They rode, following the shield, which moved with them and brushed undead aside to lie flailing to get upright at the sides of the road. Sienne glanced to one side. "There are more of them coming up beside and behind," she said, pulling out her spellbook. "Damn, but I wish I had *scorch*." She sent a blast of fire toward an undead, then another. They just kept coming, though they flailed their arms as if they thought that would extinguish the flames. Sienne let her spellbook hang loose and concentrated on riding, though she didn't know where they thought they were going or what they'd do when they got there. They might just be riding into more danger. But the alternative was giving up, and giving up was unthinkable.

The lights were growing brighter and steadier, not flickering the way flames would. Lights burned on both sides of a second gate, this one of massive iron, set into another white stone wall some eight feet tall. Beyond the gate, on a small rise, more lights marked the dimensions of a house, one big enough to be a manor by Fiorettan standards. Expensive glass windows in stone arches blazed with light, and lanterns lined the road that went from the gate to the manor's front door, an impressive slab of iron-banded oak.

The shield trembled. "It is almost gone," Perrin shouted. "'Ware undead!"

They were twenty feet from the gate. Three undead stood between them and their goal. With a final shudder, the shield. Sienne braced herself for a collision with an undead body, but Alaric trampled the first under Paladin's hooves, and she rode right past and up to the gate. Dismounting, she tried pushing on it, with about as much success as if she'd tried pushing the stone wall instead. "Help me!" she shouted.

Perrin slid off his horse and ran to her side. The others had also dismounted and drawn weapons. As Perrin put his shoulder to the gate beside her, Alaric's enormous sword found the first of the undead pursuing them and took the woman's head right off. The gate continued unmoving. "It must be barred on the inside," Perrin gasped. "Dianthe!"

"Sienne, take my place!" Dianthe shouted. She sheathed her sword without waiting for a response and ran at Perrin, who crouched with his cupped hands in front of him. Dianthe planted one foot in his hands, leaped, and with the help of Perrin's boost vaulted over the gate and disappeared on the other side. Perrin immediately ran for the horses, who had started to shift uneasily at the presence of the undead. Sienne grabbed Spark's reins and handed them to Perrin, then hurried to Alaric's side.

She opened her spellbook to *burn* and cast the spell on two undead Kalanath then sent tumbling down the slope, setting the long grass to smoldering. A metallic groan issued from behind her, and she turned to see Dianthe hauling on half of the iron gate. Sienne ran to help her. "Not too far!" Dianthe exclaimed. "We just have to get the horses through. Help Perrin!"

Between the three of them, they steered the horses, now thoroughly frightened, through the gate. Dianthe shouted, "Alaric! Kalanath! Hurry!"

Sienne hovered just inside the gate, watching the men fight. Both were bloody from long, deep claw marks, and Alaric was spattered with black goo from where his sword had struck the undead. As she watched, he made one last swing, gutting an undead, and ran for the gate just behind Kalanath. Sienne stepped back, out of their way. Alaric swung on his heel and shoved the gate closed with one mighty heave. Perrin and Dianthe swung the bar down into its slots just as a creature hammered on the gate, slow and ponderous like a death knell.

Kalanath leaned against the gate, breathing heavily, while Alaric crouched and put his head between his knees. "Are there any more of them?" he asked.

"There are many clustered around the gate, and more approaching, but none on this side," Perrin said. He walked a few paces toward the manor, his head tilted like an inquisitive bird dog, then turned back to face them. "I can sense no undead in that direction. It is the oddest sensation, like having another set of eyes superimposed on the world."

"Tell us if that changes," Alaric said, standing. "Let's find out if we are in time. For all we know, Murtaviti brought those undead with him."

"Unlikely, given how slowly they move. But first, healing. I do not like the look of those wounds," Perrin said.

Alaric shifted impatiently as Perrin invoked a healing blessing on him and then on Kalanath. "If Master Scholten is dead, getting there faster won't help," Sienne pointed out.

"And if he isn't...fine, yes, you're right." Alaric used a clean corner of his shirt to wipe black ooze off his face. "Let's go."

They could still hear the undead scrabbling at the gate as they led the horses along the well-lit road lined with oaks to the manor. It was built in typical southern style, with an arched colonnade extending the length of the house and large rounded windows lining the second story. They would let plenty of light in during the day, but expensive glass filled the window openings, which would heat the house's interior to an uncomfortable temperature.

A low addition to the main house, probably the kitchen and offices, extended to the left. Lights burned at all the first story windows, which were large enough for someone to walk through, suggesting that the owner of the house wasn't worried about burglars. Living this far out of town, that was probably justified. Though with an army of undead at his command, it was more likely Scholten didn't think anyone bent on robbery would get this far.

It did make Sienne wonder how Scholten got away with having undead roam freely on his property. They might not wither or shrivel in daylight, but they were obviously not living, so how did Scholten avoid having the dukedom of Onofreo turn on him and tear him apart as a practicing necromancer?

Despite the bright lights illuminating the house, they saw no movement beyond the windows. Dismounting, they tethered their horses to the columns of the colonnade. Spark was calmer now the undead weren't within attacking range. Sienne smoothed the horse's mane and settled her spellbook securely at her side. Now that they were here, she felt nervous rather than anticipatory. Ivar Scholten wasn't a lich, and might be an ally against Murtaviti, but there was no guarantee he was friendly. A necromancer with an army of undead was far more likely to be their enemy, no matter what common cause they had.

Alaric pounded on the front door. They waited. Sienne looked around, watching for movement. All she saw was the horses shifting in place a few feet away. "I assure you, there are no undead near," Perrin murmured, making her redden with embarrassment.

Alaric knocked again. "Should we just go in?" Sienne said. "If Master Scholten is injured, or…but Master Murtaviti isn't there, and there doesn't seem to have been a struggle."

"Listen," Dianthe said. "Someone's speaking."

Sienne listened. The cadence was familiar, though she couldn't make out words—hard, sharp syllables that burned—

"Everybody down!" she exclaimed, grabbing Perrin's hand and forcing him down with her. As she did so, the door burst open. The hard-edged sound of an evocation filled the night, and several bolts of magical energy shot through the doorway, just inches from Alaric's head.

The instant they were past, Alaric rose from his crouch and flew through the door, bowling over the man standing in the doorway. The stranger's spellbook flew out of his hands to land with a crack on the tile floor. Sienne dove for it. It was larger and thicker than hers and felt uncomfortably alive, like it was waiting for its moment to writhe out of her hands and slither away.

"Ivar Scholten?" Alaric said, then grunted as a ceramic vase came flying at him and struck him a glancing blow on the shoulder. "Damn it, we're not the enemy, stop fighting us!"

Scholten twisted in Alaric's hands, bucking and kicking until Dianthe laid the edge of her sword against his throat. Then he went so still he might have been catatonic. "Thanks," Alaric said. "Master Scholten, we're here because your friend Pauro Murtaviti has become a lich and is on his way here to kill you."

Scholten blinked blue eyes only a few shades darker than Alaric's and moistened his lips with his tongue. "Pauro? A lich?"

"If I let you up, will you stop fighting?" Alaric said.

Scholten nodded. "She's got my spellbook, anyway." His Sorjic accent was thicker than Alaric's, but still perfectly intelligible. Alaric released him and gave him a hand up. "Who are you people?"

"It's a long story. May we come in?" Dianthe said, sheathing her blade.

"It looks like you already are," Scholten said, amusement touching his face briefly. Based on what they knew of Murtaviti's blight, he had to be in his late fifties, but looked a good ten years younger, his blond hair untouched by silver and only the faintest of crow's feet beside his eyes. He shut the door behind them and held out his hand for his spellbook. Sienne hesitated, then shook her head, and his amusement deepened. "Sensible girl. Very well. This way. We might as well be comfortable."

Scholten's home was very modern, the floors tiled in an intricate mosaic pattern in brown and warm gold, the walls painted a light cream rather than whitewashed. The room he led them to was sunken a few inches and filled with chairs padded with brightly embroidered cushions. Two lamps lit by magic hung low over the room, casting a cool glow over the furnishings. Scholten sank into a chair that, by its position, was his accustomed seat and gestured to the others. "Sit, please. You'll forgive me if I don't offer you anything, but I'm not in the habit of accommodating invaders."

"We're not—" Sienne began hotly, but Alaric put a quelling hand on her arm.

"We were hired by Bernea Murtaviti to find her husband, who had apparently gone missing on the road between Tagliaveno and Fioretti," he said. "We'd come looking for Murtaviti with questions about necromancy, and his relationship with Penthea Lepporo—I assume you know her?"

Scholten shrugged. "I wrote to her a few times. I met her through my acquaintance with Pauro and...I suppose there's no point in pretending I'm not a necromancer, and Pauro is a member of my blight? At any rate, Penthea's position in the blight predates mine. But go on."

"We chose to hunt down Murtaviti so we could ask him our questions. But when we encountered him, he was in the last stages of a ritual that transformed him into a lich."

Scholten laughed, a mirthless sound. "Damn him. I wanted to be first. So he succeeded, did he? You don't know how he did it, do you?"

"We're not necromancers," Alaric said. "We returned to Fioretti to find a way to destroy Murtaviti, and found Drusilla Tallavena. She told us about the reliquary, that destroying it would defeat the lich."

"Is Dru still alive? She hasn't written in years. I believed one of her experiments had killed her."

"No, Murtaviti did. He seems to be intent on killing all the remaining members of his blight, to prevent you from achieving the same state and becoming rivals."

Scholten's pale Ansorjan face went still. "Ah. Poor Dru. It's probably for the best; she never did have the necessary ruthlessness for a necromancer. And you hurried here out of the goodness of your hearts to warn me? I'm touched."

"Spare me," Alaric said. "We're here because you and we share a common enemy. We want your help to destroy Murtaviti. You'll save your life and we'll defeat a deadly evil. That's all."

"Why do you need my help? Liches are immune to most wizardry. I can't *force*-bolt him into submission, for example."

"Even one more wizard can make a difference. And I'm sure you have necromancy at your disposal you could turn on Murtaviti."

"We just need to get his reliquary away from him and destroy it," Dianthe said. "That means keeping him preoccupied rather than trying to kill him."

"It sounds like an excellent plan," Scholten said. "With one problem. I still intend to complete my research and become a lich myself. I'm as much your enemy as Pauro is. How do I know you won't just kill me as soon as Pauro is defeated? Assuming we can even do such a thing."

"How do we know you won't turn on us instead of fighting

Murtaviti?" Alaric said. "We both have to exercise a little trust if we're going to defeat the lich." He leaned forward for emphasis. "You don't have many choices. You can agree to help us fight Murtaviti, and save your own life. Or you can turn us down and wait for Murtaviti to arrive, bringing your death."

Scholten leaned forward to match Alaric's pose. "It's true I can't defeat a lich on my own," he said. "All right. Give me back my spell-book, and you have a deal. I won't turn on you, and you won't kill me."

"That's not good enough," Sienne said.

"Sienne," Alaric said, in a tone that meant *We don't have a choice.*

"I know, but I'm not stupid. I don't think we should provide him with temptation to betray us by leaving him spells he could turn on us."

A slow smile spread across Scholten's narrow face. With his pointed chin and fair coloring, he looked like a mink—a self-satisfied, supremely confident mink. "You're right, you're not stupid," he said. "But you need my magic if you intend to defeat Pauro. What assurances would you accept that I won't turn on you?"

"No assurances," Sienne said. "I'm just going to take some of your spells."

The smile vanished. "I won't allow that."

"Not permanently. I don't steal. But I'll hang onto them until this is over, and I'll give them back when I'm satisfied you're not a threat to us."

"You'll leave me with no way to defend myself against you. You call that fair?"

"Unlike you, we have a reputation for honesty," Alaric said. "We've sworn we won't attack you, and we'll hold to that."

Ivar swore a long string of blistering oaths. He rose from his chair. "I suppose we have a deal," he said, extending his hand to Alaric. Alaric considered it for a moment, then took it briefly. "When can we expect my old friend Pauro?"

"I have one scrying blessing left," Perrin said. "I will attempt to ascertain his location, if you have a map of the vicinity."

"I do," Scholten said. He glared at Sienne. "I have exact knowledge of every spell in that book. Do not think to cheat me."

Sienne glared back. "I wouldn't dream of it."

Scholten left the room. Dianthe let out her breath in a great huff. "I was afraid we might have to kill him right here."

"I'm hoping—and I realize I tarnish my soul in saying this—I'm hoping he has some necromantic secrets he can turn on Murtaviti," Alaric said. "Sienne—"

"I'm already looking," Sienne said, leafing through the spellbook. "He has some terrible spells. *Statue*, that turns a person to stone. *Change*, which lets you turn something into anything else. You could turn a man into a frog—it only lasts a short while, but it's a true transformation. Oh!" She slammed the book shut in surprise. "He has charms. That's forbidden!"

"I doubt a practicing necromancer cares much about the laws of wizardry," Perrin said.

"Well, I definitely can't let him keep those." Sienne worked the latch of his spellbook and began removing spells. "I wish we had time for me to copy some of these. He has *ferry*!"

"I suppose I can't stop you copying them out," Scholten said as he re-entered the room, a rolled-up paper in his hand. "Though it's dishonorable."

"I'd trade honestly with you," Sienne said, stung into a feeling of guilt that she'd considered just taking the ones she wanted. "Our books hardly overlap at all."

"You should consider the charms. Don't tell me a scrapper wouldn't have a use for *daze*, facing a horde of wisps or whatever monsters you happen to encounter often."

"It's forbidden."

Scholten smiled. "Only if they catch you. Clever girl like you—"

"The map, if you please," Perrin said, extending a hand. Scholten slapped the rolled-up map into it. Perrin unrolled it and held it up to the light. "This will do."

Sienne continued working. Scholten had so many spells she didn't know! And not all of them were nasty. *Fury*, the version of *force* that produced multiple bolts, and *shout*, the more potent version of *scream*, to pick two at random. "Will *shout* work on a lich?" she asked.

Scholten walked away from the low table where Perrin had spread the map to stand beside her. "To a degree. It does not incapacitate the way it would when cast on a living person, or an animal."

"And this one, *miasma*? I'm guessing not."

"Liches can't be poisoned, no. Though anything holy might as well be poison to them. They have to stay away from consecrated ground."

"So...how can they raise the dead if they can't enter a cemetery? That's consecrated ground."

"It's difficult, but it can be managed." Scholten drew up a chair and sat beside her. "May I see your spellbook?"

"You're joking, right?"

"I think any one of your companions could take it away from me if I chose not to return it, possibly by way of removing my hands. I'd simply like to know if you have anything worth trading for. If Pauro leaves us time."

Sienne laughed. "We stormed into your house, stole your spellbook, effectively made you a hostage, and you're willing to do something as civilized as trade spells?"

Scholten shrugged. "Why not? I am a wizard as well as a necromancer. Improving my spellbook—I don't have to tell you what it's like to crave knowledge."

Sienne glanced over at the table where the others were gathered. Perrin had his riffle of blessings, sadly depleted, in one hand and a stick of pastel color in the other. "All right." She handed over her spellbook, feeling a terrible misgiving that she was making a mistake. But he was helpless, and it wasn't as if he could cast spells from her book...

Scholten paged through it mostly in silence, occasionally saying, "Huh," and once, "That's interesting." It made Sienne feel self-conscious, as if he were judging her for the contents of her spellbook. "I misjudged you," Scholten finally said, with the spellbook open to the last page, displaying the spell *convey*. "You've amassed quite the portfolio despite your youth. Why the early emphasis on confusions? I presume you follow the common wisdom, and add spells in the order you gain them."

"I...the school I went to encouraged me to focus on them," Sienne said, wary of giving too much information about herself. "I like trans-forms better."

"I'm fond of summonings, myself. It's been my bad luck that I rarely come in the way of confusions." Scholten flipped back through the book. "I wouldn't mind trading for *mirror*, though it's a pity you don't have *vanish*. I always wanted invisibility. So many practical applications."

"I agree," Sienne said. "And I've been looking for *ferry* for weeks with no luck."

"We have him," Perrin said, making both of them look up. "He is traveling almost as fleetly as if on horseback, though of course it is impossible for him to ride. I estimate we have perhaps an hour and a half before he is upon us."

"Time enough to make some preparations," Alaric said. "We can fortify this place so we choose the ground we fight on."

"More than enough time for us to scribe new spells," Sienne said. "*Ferry* will give us an out if we have to make a quick escape."

"And I will attempt to pray for more blessings," Perrin said. "It is either very late or very early for me to do so, but I believe Averran may take pity on me, given the circumstances in which we find ourselves."

"Then let's get started," Alaric said.

18

Sienne tucked Scholten's spell pages inside her vest and snugged them close against her body. It felt like wearing armor, which in a way, it was, given that the invulnerable paper would deflect most edged weapons. She only cared that it kept the spells where Scholten couldn't get at them. All the charm spells, both *force* and *fury,* a handful of other spells that could not hurt Murtaviti but could do serious damage to her team. She worked her left arm, testing the small wound where she'd pierced the vein to produce ink to scribe *ferry*. If only they'd had time for more...she might not have wanted Scholten to have the ability to turn her companions into frogs, but if she could transform Murtaviti thus, even if just for a few minutes...!

She settled herself and her book more comfortably on the foot-stool placed before the upstairs balcony that looked out over the dark meadows behind the manor. The sitting room was decorated in a rather feminine style that made Sienne wonder if there had ever been a woman in Scholten's life. There was certainly no one else here now, not even servants, which made her wonder further whether Scholten used undead as kitchen help. Ugh.

They couldn't predict which way Murtaviti would come, whether he would approach from the front, which was the more direct path, or try to take them by surprise by circling around to the back, so she was set to watch the rear of the house, just in case. Perrin was on the other side of the house, similarly situated to watch the road leading to the gate. With the room darkened, she saw no movement as far as the wall encircling the estate and beyond, not even animals. What did the undead do to animals if they caught them? Probably nothing good. She hoped the horses would be safe in the stables behind the manor.

She glanced at Scholten, who sat nearby in a chair in the center of a circle charred into the floorboards. They'd removed the carpet and rolled it up to lean against the wall in one corner so he could perform a ritual, and she'd watched him doing it in between casting *break* on the window in this room and the bedroom across the hall. She'd felt a furtive excitement in seeing it, as if her observation made her complicit. It had been unexpectedly simple: spark to draw the circle and angular runic characters around the circle, some herbs from the kitchen before it was barricaded, burned in a brass bowl he'd dumped a dried floral arrangement out of, and muttered words Sienne hadn't been able to make out. Now Scholten had what he assured them was a protected area no undead could enter.

Scholten looked up from his spellbook and caught her watching him. He said, "It's difficult to believe an undead creature is on his way here, intent on killing us. Not with how peaceful the night is."

"He is. But I understand what you mean." She turned back to surveying the moonlit landscape and heard Scholten flip the pages of his spellbook.

"I wonder," he said after a minute of silence in which Sienne tried to come up with something she could talk about with an evil necromancer, "that you're a scrapper. Surely your skills are better suited to more regular employment?"

"It's what I love. I never wanted to teach, and working in any other field wouldn't give me the variety of experience I have as a scrapper. Besides, the reason I have the skills I do is due to scrapping, so there's that."

"I see." Silence fell again. "And your friends?"

"What about them?"

"No one's paying you to dispose of Pauro. I find that remarkable, given the mercenary lot scrappers generally are. What are you getting out of it?"

Telling him about Alaric's quest was out of the question. "We just feel responsible for preventing him killing anyone else."

"So altruistic of you."

Scholten's laugh irritated Sienne. She clenched her teeth to hold back a sharp answer. She wouldn't let him goad her. Instead, she said, "How much do you know about liches? How far has your research gone?"

When he didn't answer immediately, she looked at him and discovered he was examining her closely, his eyes narrowed and his lips pursed in thought. "Is this a ploy to determine whether I need killing?" he asked.

"I just want to understand what they're capable of. Master Murtaviti did things I thought were impossible, and if you know why, well, I want you to tell me."

"I don't see the benefit to me in that."

Sienne smiled. "Aside from showing off your brilliance?"

He returned her smile, somewhat grudgingly. "You have me there." He looked off across the fields again. "Immortality is everything. You're too young to understand what it's like to feel the years slipping away from you, to see your body age and falter despite everything you can do for it. To be able to slip the bonds of death...it's amazing more people don't pursue it."

"I think the fact that you have to murder to get it dissuades most of us."

"But suppose the only ones you kill are themselves criminals? Men and women whose lives would be forfeit if their crimes were known? I've never killed anyone who didn't deserve death. Doesn't that make me an agent of good rather than evil?"

"I don't believe people should take justice into their own hands." The words left her mouth before she could stop them, and they made her feel smug and self-righteous and uncomfortable. After all, hadn't

Dianthe gone on the run for nine years because she'd killed an evil man in self-defense? Wasn't that taking justice into her own hands?

"Somebody has to enact justice, and it might as well be me as anyone else," Scholten said. "And I don't think you're as upstanding as you claim. You're a scrapper—haven't you ever killed anyone?"

A memory of an emerald falcon, of green light blasting from its beak to turn men to ash, stopped her tongue from a ready response. Finally, she said, "I've never felt I was entitled to kill. That's the difference."

"It doesn't matter. You asked what a lich can do. Aside from the immortality and near-invulnerability, there's the physical changes. Great strength, enhanced senses, tremendous endurance. A lich no longer needs to breathe, so running for miles—which is, by the way, undoubtedly what Pauro has done to reach us—is no longer a difficulty."

"Master Murtaviti was surprised at the strength, like he hadn't known it would happen."

"I'm not surprised. Pauro never did care much for the theory behind the research. He just wanted to find the right ritual. How did he make it happen, by the way?"

Sienne laughed. "I'm not telling you that. Suppose it's the last piece of the ritual you need?"

"Ah, it was worth trying." Scholten shrugged. "It doesn't matter. We probably weren't pursuing the same line of research, anyway."

"So there's more than one way to make a lich?"

"Possibly. I suppose we'll find out—or not, if you all kill me when this is over."

"We won't do that." She wasn't sure if that was a lie or not.

Scholten shrugged again. "If you say so."

Hoping to deflect the conversation, she said, "What about magic?"

"What about it?"

Surely revealing this didn't matter, as Scholten would see it for himself when Murtaviti arrived. "Master Murtaviti was able to use magic. Spark, breeze, invisible fingers. But far more powerful than we're capable of. Is that something all liches can do?"

Scholten's eyes widened. "I've not heard of this. Pauro's no wizard. That should be impossible."

"I know. But it happened. We all saw it."

Scholten turned away, chewing on the tip of his forefinger. "I wonder..." he said.

"What?"

He twitched as if he'd forgotten she was there. "Nothing. I thought I had something, but it's gone."

He was so obviously lying Sienne wanted to task him with it right then. But she was certain he wouldn't tell her, no matter what she did short of torture, and she couldn't torture him. "That's too bad," she said instead. "If it was something we could use to destroy Master Murtaviti—"

"I'm sure it was nothing," Scholten said quickly. "Probably Pauro figured out some way to tap the dark energy that fuels an undead creature and turn it into basic magic. I've never heard of anyone doing it, but in theory, it should be possible."

"So would that mean he could learn other magic?"

"Unlikely. There aren't many magics that come naturally, and without someone to show him the rest—"

"That's what I thought. And he can't use wizardry."

"No. Not without a lot of training and a spellbook." Scholten stood and stretched, rather theatrically. "I'm going to see how your companion across the hall is doing. I don't want him rooting around in my clothespress."

"Perrin wouldn't—" Sienne began hotly, then subsided when Scholten laughed his nasty, mocking laugh and left the room. Fuming, she turned back to watching the hills. What *were* they going to do with Scholten when this was over? She was determined not to dwell on the possibility that they might not succeed. They couldn't just let him continue his research. Maybe they could destroy his books and other ritual paraphernalia? If he had a reliquary of his own, they could smash that. At the very least, they could set his work back by decades. She felt a tiny bit of guilt at plotting against Scholten, but not much. Even if she had to keep reminding herself that he was a necromancer, and guilty of who knew what kind of evil. He was actually pleasant to talk to, most of the time, and he'd been perfectly professional when they'd traded spells. But that was a façade, and she needed to remember that.

Footsteps in the doorway startled her out of her reverie. "I wanted to check on you," Alaric said. "Where's Scholten?"

"He went to talk to Perrin. I think he knows something about why Master Murtaviti can use magic, but he pretended not to."

"Is it something we need to coerce out of him?" Alaric sat in the chair Scholten had vacated, undisturbed by the necromantic sigils burned into the floor around it.

"I...don't think so. Not now, anyway. If it was something we could use to defeat the lich, I think he would have said."

"Perrin says we have another fifteen minutes, give or take." Alaric took her hand and caressed the back of it with his thumb. "Not enough time to do anything big."

Sienne scooted her footstool closer to Alaric's chair and leaned against his knee. "This is enough for me."

He stroked her hair, and she closed her eyes and leaned into his touch. "I can't wait for this to be over," he murmured. "I want to take you in my arms and kiss you, somewhere we won't be disturbed."

"I want that too." She looked up at him and smiled. "And I want to go dancing with you."

"I told you, I look like a performing bear when I dance."

"Maybe, but you're *my* performing bear, and even if all you do is stand there while I twirl around you, I'll be happy."

Alaric laughed. "All right. Just remember, it was your idea." He squeezed her hand once and rose. "We're all set downstairs and waiting for your signal, or Perrin's. You know what to do if someone else raises the alarm?"

"*Burn* the lich. Keep his attention on us."

"Right." He leaned far down to kiss her. "I love you."

"I love you, too."

Alaric left the room, and Sienne returned to watching. She did love him, and it was wonderful. She wished she dared daydream about what they might do when this was all over and they were somewhere they wouldn't be disturbed, but she needed to be alert. She closed her spellbook and practiced opening it to the spells she wanted, *break, burn, slick.* She wasn't sure about the last one, but she'd found in the nearly a year she'd been a scrapper that sometimes the solution was something unexpected.

The shadows of clouds sailed across the sloping hills, patches of darkness against the paler ground. Though the moon was past full, it was still bright enough that she hadn't needed *cat's eye* to let her see clearly. It was a clever spell, not like *sharpen,* which enhanced vision in darkness but made the eye highly sensitive to light. *Cat's eye* extended the eye's visual range, making nighttime nearly as clear as noon without sacrificing clear vision in ordinary light. She'd thought about casting it anyway, but she'd already used some of her reserves on *burning* Scholten's undead minions, and she was certain she would want every scrap of magical power at her disposal for use against Murtaviti.

Something moved in the fields beyond the wall. She leaned forward to look past the rail of the balcony. Whatever it was moved slowly, but steadily, parallel to the wall. An undead. In the daytime, Scholten could stand here and watch his undead meander through the fields like drunken ants following a sugar trail. The idea made her skin crawl.

She opened the spellbook to *burn* and sat back. How did Scholten control his undead minions, anyway? Something she could have asked him, if she'd thought of it. Another undead came into sight, heading the other way. No sign of anyone else.

"Here he comes," Perrin called out, and a thrill of fear and excitement shot through her. "One very bright spark, approaching from the east."

That meant the front of the house. "How close is he?"

"He is at the limit of my vision, but he comes quickly. I think— there, the undead are converging on him."

Sienne hurried to join Perrin at the bedroom window. Scholten stood at the other bedroom window, pressed against the side so he couldn't be seen. The rising wind blew with a high, thin whistle across the gaping hole where she'd shattered the glass. She didn't know if it was her imagination that the wind carried with it the smell of rotting, undead flesh. Surely they were too far away for that?

Scholten let out a grunt, like someone had punched him in the stomach. "What's wrong?" Sienne asked.

"Pauro is trying to break my control over my undead," Scholten whispered. His voice sounded taut, as if it were coming through clenched teeth. "I will not permit it."

"He can do that? Did you know this?"

Scholten nodded. His eyes were closed and his face drawn in the expression of someone intent on a difficult puzzle.

Sienne let out an exasperated breath. "Why didn't you mention this when we were making plans?"

"I didn't think...Pauro would know to do it. He understands so little...of what it means to be...a lich. I didn't think...it would be a problem."

"The undead are no longer moving," Perrin said. "Everything is still."

"He is...powerful," Scholten said, "but I...will...not..." His face was red with strain. Then he drew in a sharp breath, and sagged, putting one hand on the wall for support.

"They are moving again," Perrin said, "westward toward the house."

"He was too strong," Scholten said, sounding afraid for the first time. "How can he be so strong?"

"Can you try again?" Sienne suggested. "When he's not expecting it, maybe?"

Scholten nodded. "While he is preoccupied, maybe. If your companions can attack him..." He didn't need to say that with Scholten's host of undead on Murtaviti's side, the companions would have to fight through an army to reach Murtaviti. Of course, he also didn't know the real plan, which Sienne wasn't going to tell him.

She watched the road to the east, straining for a sight of movement. "There are many of the undead," Perrin said. "They are like fireflies drawn to a lantern. Master Murtaviti has slowed, presumably to allow them to gather to him."

"I'll go tell the others," Sienne said, and hurried into the hall and down the south staircase. They'd blocked the north stairs to force anyone who got that far into a bottleneck of their own choosing. It was important that she be the one to speak to the others, to keep Scholten from asking awkward questions about where Dianthe was, if he noticed. That was unlikely, but they weren't taking chances with the necromancer wizard.

Alaric and Kalanath stood in the open doorway to the sunken sitting room, at the end of the hall leading from the front doors. Kalanath leaned on his staff with his eyes closed, apparently meditating. Alaric looked up as she approached. "Something wrong?"

"Master Murtaviti took control of the undead. They're his minions now."

Alaric nodded. "It makes no difference to the plan. They can still only get inside one way, and we're ready for them. But the point isn't to defeat the undead."

"I know. Do you really think Master Murtaviti will try to enter the house?"

"He wants Scholten dead. I'm guessing he wants him dead at his own hand. We're going to let him believe we want to protect Scholten, and give Dianthe time to act. Go on back upstairs. We'll hear it when the fighting begins."

Sienne nodded and ran for the stairs. When she returned to the bedroom, Perrin and Scholten both stood to either side of one window. "They are near the gate," Perrin said. Sienne listened. Distantly, she heard a shuffling, rustling sound that carried far in the still night air. The gate was closed, not to prevent Murtaviti from entering—with his strength, it was a trivial barrier—but to deceive him into thinking Scholten was unaware of his approach and force him to expend resources. Scholten had been unspecific as to how far those resources might go, and Sienne thought they'd run up against the limits of his knowledge. It didn't matter. The important thing was to make Murtaviti believe they wanted him stopped.

An undead woman shambled into the light burning at the gate posts, then a man, and suddenly there were dozens of them, all moving forward and intent on the gate. They ran up against the gate and scrabbled at it, trying to get past. Sienne realized she was gripping her spellbook too tightly and forced her hands to relax. Beside her, Scholten had his book open. She didn't know what spell he'd chosen.

Even from the second floor, Sienne couldn't see past the gate, but something was pounding on it—no, not pounding, but slamming into it, making it bounce on its hinges and bowing the bar outward. The sound was inexorable, a constant rhythmic thudding that made Sienne want to scream with frustration and rush out to let him in, anything to get the anticipation over with.

A splintering, cracking sound heralded the bar's breaking, and the iron gate swung open, letting in the first undead. Sienne wondered if Murtaviti was one of them, or if he would hang back, wanting to let the undead do the dirty work. Either he was the kind of man who'd think it hilarious to have Scholten killed by his own undead, or Alaric was right, and he'd want to do it himself, but in any case, he needed to come closer so she could target him.

More bodies forced their way through the gap. They walked slowly, all taking different directions, but with intent, not the random, stumbling gait of the revenant. When they fetched up against each other, they stopped momentarily, each groping the other's face and shoulders like a blind man trying to recognize a friend.

"That's...a lot of undead," she said. "Did you really need that many?"

"It's not about need," Scholten said, and didn't elaborate.

Sienne didn't recognize Murtaviti at first. Then she saw the balding head of the man striding along near the rear of the...pack? Swarm? Alone among the crowd, he walked purposefully, without the hesitance the others displayed. His destroyed eye was a blotch of black against his undead-pale skin. She stepped back so she wasn't as obvious a target. Scholten raised his spellbook. "Wait," Sienne said. "Let them get closer."

"I know. I don't need your advice, girl."

Sienne fumed, but said nothing. The horde shambled forward, ten feet, twenty. They were picking up speed, turning toward the manor as if pulled there by invisible strings. Sienne heard once again the low O sound, a deep humming that made the air vibrate and the hairs on the back of her hands stand on end. This time, she could identify it: the undead were moaning, one low note as perfectly pitched as if they'd been trained to do it. It was beautiful, and haunting, the voices of the dead keening as if they'd lost something they could never find. It filled her with rage that Murtaviti and Scholten and their kind had wrenched these souls from their eternal rest and trapped them in undead bodies, unable to be free.

She was so angry she almost didn't notice when Scholten began reading the hard-edged syllables of an evocation. Quickly she began speaking her own evocation, the sounds burning her mouth like acid. The power built within her, a terrible pressure demanding to be free. As she neared the end of the spell, Scholten spat out the last syllables of his.

A *barrier* of fire ten feet high and fifty feet long sprang from the ground between Murtaviti and the manor, catching eight undead in its path. They thrashed just as if they were living, but soundlessly, falling forward out of the fire and lying still on the ground beyond it. Three more undead could not stop in time and walked into the fire. The others pulled up short. Murtaviti stopped, and Sienne let the spell *burn* explode from her and blast him full in the chest.

19

Fire engulfed the lich, and he took an involuntary step back as if she'd punched him. Sienne began casting the spell again, reading as fast as she dared. Murtaviti's head came up, and he scanned the face of the manor until his gaze lit on the broken windows of the upper story. He was close enough Sienne could see him smile.

Perrin shoved her out of the way, interrupting her spell. "What—" she blurted out, but Perrin shouted an invocation, and pearly light flared around his forearm, radiating out into a shield just in time to deflect the fire that splashed across the windows.

"My apologies," Perrin said, half-turned to ensure the shield fully covered both windows. "He is faster than you are."

Sienne stood beside him and looked out. Murtaviti was just getting up from where he'd rolled on the ground to extinguish the fire. The undead shambled along the *barrier* of fire in both directions, some of them accidentally getting too close and catching their ragged clothes on fire. They didn't stop to put the fires out, and one or two dropped, burning, to lie twitching as their fellows walked past or even over them. Murtaviti snapped his fingers, and more fire exploded around the window, but Sienne felt no heat thanks to the shield.

"Be ready to move," she told Perrin. "*Not* another *barrier* of fire," she said to Scholten, who'd begun reading off another evocation.

Scholten shook his head and continued reading. Sienne began *burn* a second time, letting it fly just moments after Scholten's casting was complete. Another *barrier* of fire rose up, this one encircling and completely concealing Murtaviti. Sienne's *burn* struck it and spread across its surface, blue fire mingling with red to make violet where the spells collided. "I said—"

"It will keep him preoccupied while the others deal with my poor servants," Scholten said, unmoved by Sienne's anger.

She couldn't tell him the true reason for her anger. He believed they intended to batter Murtaviti into submission. "This way, he can't betray us," had been Alaric's argument for not letting him in on the real plan.

"That was a waste of a spell," she said instead.

"That's not my fault," Scholten said.

Wind shook Perrin's shield, the powerful wind of an oncoming storm. The shield made a sound like a thin metal sheet being shaken hard, a *whopwhopwhop* that filled the bedroom. Sienne looked out the window. The fiery *barrier* surrounding Murtaviti raged as if caught in a storm, flames trailing away into the sky in loops and wheels where the wind caught it. The *barrier* looked more ragged and less robust with every passing moment. Sienne, holding her spellbook at the ready, watched the fire struggle as if gasping for air. Finally, the *barrier* collapsed into flickering embers in a circle on the road, and Murtaviti stepped over them and continued walking toward the manor. Sienne blasted him a third time, but either his hearing had improved, or his magic was more skilled, because he brought the wind up again and deflected the *burn* spell to strike an undead standing nearby.

"That's it for me," Scholten said, lowering his spellbook.

"But he's still coming!" Sienne exclaimed, momentarily forgetting the plan.

"I was going to cast *cyclone,* but he would only counter it." Scholten crossed the hall and sat in his chair inside the protection circle. "And he is strong enough to break through *prison* with no difficulties, so I don't see the point in wasting it. You do what you like. I will wait it out here."

"Sienne!" Perrin said urgently.

Sienne ran to his side. "Is she—"

Perrin laid a silencing finger across his lips. Sienne looked out across the manor's yard, which was lit brightly by the first *barrier* of fire, still burning. Murtaviti stood in front of it, directly opposite the manor door, examining it as if trying to decide whether to go around or walk through. Twenty or so undead had found their way around the *barrier* and were banging on the windows, trying to break them. Trying in futility, since Sienne and Scholten had made them invulnerable just over an hour before.

And Dianthe crept forward from behind one of the oaks lining the road, sneaking up on Murtaviti like a cat stalking prey.

Sienne bit her lower lip nervously. Dianthe was so exposed out there, visible to anyone who cared to look—except Perrin had assured them all it was not so. "This blessing," he'd said, "conceals a person from the perceptions of any undead creature—sight, sound, even smell."

"And I'll be able to sneak up and snatch his reliquary," Dianthe had said. "Can you be more specific about the location?"

"Unfortunately, no. I am aware that it is somewhere about his person, but that is all." Perrin had shrugged, and added, "It is not unlikely that he has hung it around his neck, as that would be the most typical location. Master Murtaviti has shown himself to be a rather direct and unsubtle thinker."

Now Sienne watched with her heart in her throat, willing Dianthe to succeed. She had only one chance, because once she attacked Murtaviti, the concealment would end. She moved as if she didn't quite believe she was effectively invisible, stepping lightly, one hand holding a long knife instead of her sword.

She was within three feet of the lich when he turned abruptly and walked toward the gate. Sienne sucked in a breath as Dianthe leaped to one side to avoid touching him as he walked past. *Careful!* Sienne thought a silent warning, but Dianthe paused, watching Murtaviti to see what he had in mind. Murtaviti, for his part, clearly didn't see her although he passed within inches of her. He stopped about ten feet back from the *barrier* and surveyed it again, hands on hips.

Dianthe struck. With a couple of quick steps, she stood in front of him, reaching for the ruined mess that had once been a nice linen shirt. She drove the knife deep into his belly, making him take an inadvertent step back from the force of it.

Sienne had a clear view of Murtaviti's shocked face, and it made her want to cheer. Dianthe hooked his ankle and gave another thrust with the knife, bearing him to the ground with herself atop. From that angle, her body blocked Sienne's view, but Dianthe appeared to be searching Murtaviti's clothes.

Perrin's shield disappeared with a quiet *pop*, startling Sienne. "She's almost got it," she said. From below came the sounds of undead hammering on the windows and door. The beating on the unbreakable glass was a *chink, chink, chink* like a smith beating hot iron; the pounding on the door sounded duller and more ponderous. "Should we—*no!*"

Murtaviti's hand grasped Dianthe's forearm. She shuddered, stiffened, and fell rigid to one side. Murtaviti shoved her away and got heavily to his feet. He plucked the knife out of his belly and tossed it, dark with some fluid, atop Dianthe's frozen body, then bent to pick something small off the ground. He held it up to the light of the *barrier* of fire to examine it. It was the size of a goose egg and roughly the same shape. The light glinted off glass in an irregular pattern before he dropped it into a pouch hanging at his waist.

"I have to get to her," Perrin said, heading for the door.

"No, there's a faster way," Sienne said, grabbing his arm and steering him toward the window. She opened her book to *drift*. "Count to three, then jump as far out as you can!"

She read the spell as fast as she dared. Perrin, without hesitation, clambered over the windowsill and jumped just as the spell took effect. The spell took his momentum and carried him far from the manor, over the *barrier* and past where Dianthe lay. As Perrin floated toward the ground, Sienne saw Murtaviti take a running start and leap over the *barrier,* landing heavily and going to one knee to keep his balance. She didn't wait to see anything else. She ran for the stairs, shouting, "He's coming now!" As she flew past the sitting room, she caught a glimpse of Scholten starting up from his chair, his eyes wide, then she was darting down the steps and skidding along the hall to where Alaric and Kalanath waited, weapons at the ready.

"He got Dianthe," she panted. "Perrin's with her—the lich is coming—"

"Get behind me," Alaric said. "Did Dianthe get the reliquary?"

"She did, but she dropped it when he paralyzed her and he picked it up again. I saw it. He put it in his belt pouch."

"Can you take it?"

"Maybe." Sienne rubbed sweaty palms on her trousers. "I—"

The dull, ponderous sound of undead beating on the door became a loud, sharp crack as the wooden frame gave way. The door sagged inward on its lower hinge. The moaning song rose in pitch as the masses of undead pressed forward, wrenching the door further. With a snap, it broke free completely and fell, bouncing once, to lie on the tiled mosaic floor. Undead forced their way through the opening, tearing at each other in their eagerness to reach their human prey. Their sallow, sagging skin bore the marks of the fire, their clothing was almost entirely gone, but they pressed forward, arms outstretched.

Then they stopped.

The drawn-out O sound that had filled the air vanished. The undead squirmed and thrashed like fish on a line, movements that made no sense to Sienne until she realized they were all trying to turn around in the narrow confines of the entry hall. Alaric lowered his sword. "What are they doing?"

"I think Master Scholten reasserted his control!" Sienne almost ran upstairs to confirm her guess, but realized that she would only distract him, and the real goal was down here. "Should I try to get around behind Master Murtaviti, the way Dianthe did?"

"Stay where you are," Alaric commanded. "If Perrin can restore Dianthe, they're already in position. I want you here, in case…"

Sienne guessed he didn't want to tempt bad luck by saying *in case they fail again.* She paced the room behind Alaric and Kalanath, the one with all the chairs where they'd first explained the situation to Scholten, and listened to the scuffling of the undead retreating and, hopefully, attacking Murtaviti. It was eerily silent, reminding her of another time, another battle in which their enemies also never spoke. The shouting and cries of the wounded would have been a relief, though since it was possible it was her friends who might be wounded, it wouldn't have been much of a relief.

More fire roared outside, making Sienne jump. Reflexively she checked to make sure the windows were still invulnerable, which was stupid, but comforted her. They were still frosted over the way invulnerable glass was. Alaric and Kalanath looked perfectly relaxed. She wished she knew how they did it.

Fire blossomed in the doorway, filling the hall and rolling inexorably toward them. "*Sienne!*" Alaric shouted, darting to the right as Kalanath dove and tumbled left. Sienne threw herself to the ground and felt the roaring fire pass over her, crisping her hair. The smell of char filled the air. Sienne rose to her hands and knees. The room had caught fire in places, but they weren't big fires and most of them died away almost immediately. Sienne stood. Alaric and Kalanath were once again between her and the front door, but now Murtaviti stood silhouetted against the *barrier* of fire, staring at them with one large, mad eye. His clothes were burned past repair, his short dark hair was disordered, and his pallid skin was marked with ash, but he was smiling.

"You again," he said. "Why must you continually interfere with my plans?"

Alaric didn't respond. Instead, he raised his sword to point directly at Murtaviti's heart. Kalanath took up a defensive position. Sienne hovered behind them, searching Murtaviti's form for the pouch. It hung on his right side, out in the open where anyone might snatch it. She used her invisible fingers to tug on it, gently enough that he wouldn't notice. Nothing happened. It was knotted tightly to Murtaviti's belt. So much for that plan.

Murtaviti took a few steps forward. "I'm really not interested in you people," he said. "I just want a few words with my old friend Ivar. Why don't you leave us to it?"

Sienne examined the pouch. It was made of black leather, stitched expertly along a single seam, and gathered at the top. She might untie the knot—no, it would take too long, and Murtaviti might notice. On the other hand, if she couldn't go in from the top, maybe she could tackle the problem from beneath...

"Really, you can't both fight me in this hall," Murtaviti was saying. "It's far too narrow. And you know I can't set you on fire here without burning myself, and for some reason I'm quite sick of being burned. Just step aside, and I'll let you go."

Kalanath moved forward, sweeping his staff in a complicated maneuver that ended with the steel-shod end pressed under Murtaviti's chin. Murtaviti didn't flinch. "If that's how you want to do it," he said, "I am happy to oblige."

Kalanath leaped backward as Murtaviti reached for him. Sienne took advantage of the commotion to light a spark on the pouch's seam, at the bottom where the weight of the reliquary pulled at it. She had to dart out of Kalanath's way, but kept her attention focused on the tiny flame that burned where Murtaviti couldn't see it. Just a little while, no more than a minute, and—

Alaric stepped forward to take Kalanath's place. The hall was too narrow for a full swing, capable of taking someone's head off, but there was plenty of room for thrusting and stabbing and short swings. Alaric forced Murtaviti back, keeping close to him, and Sienne had to follow or lose control of her spark. She saw smoke rising from the little pouch, smelled burning leather, and prayed to all the avatars that Murtaviti was too preoccupied with Alaric to notice.

Alaric thrust again, this time skewering Murtaviti as Dianthe had done. Murtaviti laughed and stepped away from the sword. A flood of black oozing liquid poured from the wound. "You really don't know anything, do you?" he said. "I can't be killed that way."

Wisps of black fog trickled in around the doorway, wreathing the lich's body and flowing into his mouth and nostrils. Past him, Sienne saw a couple of undead falling heavily, with black mist pouring out of them and creeping along the ground toward Murtaviti. To her horror, the wound closed up. Even Alaric seemed taken aback. Murtaviti laughed again. "I've changed my mind," he said. "I'm going to paralyze each of you. Then I'm going to kill you, slowly, one at a time while the others watch." His attention flicked to Sienne, and he smiled, a nasty, intimate expression. "You can be first."

With a faint tearing sound, the pouch's seam parted, and the reliquary dropped out of it to hit the tiled floor with a *tink*. Murtaviti's smile faded slightly. Sienne had time to notice that it looked like a red glass egg webbed with white before she had her spellbook open to read off the transform *break*.

The spell built within her, rising from hidden depths until it burst out like an arrow from a bow bent nearly to snapping. The spell shot away from her to strike the reliquary, knocking it away from Murtaviti's hand as he stooped to retrieve it. It rolled away toward the door. Murtaviti shrieked and turned to race after it. "Why didn't it work?" Alaric exclaimed. "Sienne—"

"I don't know! Bone's not as fragile as people think—maybe that's it!" Sienne pushed past Alaric and ran after Murtaviti. If she hit it with *break* often enough, it would have to shatter.

She began reading the spell and cut off with an *oof* as Murtaviti turned and lashed out with a foot, striking her in the chest. "You're definitely first," he snarled, and dove for the reliquary.

A foot came down on his reaching hand. "I don't think so," Dianthe said, scooping up the reliquary and tossing it at Kalanath. Kalanath caught it out of the air and threw it hard at the floor. The reliquary struck the mosaic—and shattered. Fragments of frosted ruby glass flew in all directions, followed by shards of white bone.

Murtaviti screamed. The sound went on and on until it seemed to have a life independent of the body that had produced it. The lich fell to his knees, clasping his head in his hands as if it hurt, then fell further to lie writhing on the floor. Black mist poured from his mouth and nose and ears and seeped from his eyes and the beds of his nails until he was swimming in it. Sienne stepped away from Murtaviti, not wanting any contact with the mist, and bumped up against Alaric. He put a protective hand on her shoulder.

The mist swirled upward, now hanging like a curtain over the lich. Faces formed within the mist, unrecognizable as anything beyond simply human, and then they were gone. The mist thinned, faded, and it, too, was gone.

Murtaviti lay motionless on the tiles, surrounded by shards of glass. Sienne saw a folded scrap of paper near his left hand, and without thinking she picked it up to read it. "Sienne, don't!" Alaric said.

"It's just words. They don't make any sense. I don't think they can hurt me." But she crumpled the paper into a ball and set it on fire anyway.

She became aware that the undead had started their moaning again. "Are they attacking?"

Perrin looked over his shoulder. "I cannot tell," he said. "I think not. But perhaps we should investigate."

"I'll go tell Master Scholten he can leave his refuge now," Sienne said. She ran up the stairs and heard Alaric following her, more slowly.

As she neared his sitting room, she heard Scholten say something unintelligible, something that sounded like barking. "Master Scholten," she began, and realized he was casting a spell just as she came around the doorway. She brought up her spellbook like a shield, and something hard and cold hit her hard enough to stop her speaking. She cracked her head on something that felt like stone, and then the lights went out.

20

It took her a few addled moments to realize she hadn't gone blind or unconscious; it was suddenly very dark. She heard Alaric shouting from very far away, and a similarly distant pounding. She drew in a deep, calming breath and winced at how it froze her lungs. Very dark, and very cold. Where was she?

She clutched her spellbook to her chest with one hand and felt around her with the other. Ice froze her palm, and she snatched it away before it could take skin. *Prison*. He'd cast *prison* on her, damn it. She had barely enough room to move in here, the ice was at least a foot thick—and he was an experienced wizard, so it might be thicker—and she couldn't see a thing. Well, that she could do something about. She calmed her breathing and made a magic light.

Her surroundings weren't any more congenial in the white light than they'd been in the darkness. She barely had enough room to move, particularly with her spellbook held before her. She raised it higher, resting it against the ice wall, and breathed in slowly. The air felt like knives in her chest. She shivered and made herself relax. If she could cast *castle*, it would serve him right, trade places with him —but she couldn't see him, had nothing of his blood or hair, so that was impossible. She shivered again. *Jaunt*, then, and she'd be out.

She couldn't raise her arm to turn the pages, so she used her invisible fingers to turn to the right spell and began reading. Her voice shook, and she stopped reading, then started again. She tasted blood, but didn't dare interrupt the spell to swallow. This time, she made it to the end, but nothing happened, no moment of disorientation, no appearance elsewhere. Still too shaky.

She wormed her hand up to cover her mouth and huffed into it. Warm air touched her cheeks, and she breathed in slowly, feeling moisture condense and immediately begin to freeze on her palm. Willing herself calm, she began the summoning again. Blood flecked her palm as she spat out the staccato syllables. Her vision was darkening, her chest ached from lack of air as well as cold, and she focused desperately on the short lines and dots of the summoning language. At the last minute, she pictured herself near the balcony of the sitting room.

Dizziness swept over her. Blessedly warm air filled her lungs, and she closed her eyes and coughed, letting her spellbook fall to hang in its harness. Alaric's large hands closed on her shoulders, and he drew her in to hold her tightly enough she squeaked. She opened her eyes and the world spun around her, nauseating her. She'd lost track of how many spells she'd cast, but surely she hadn't reached her limit yet? "Where's Master Scholten?" she coughed out.

"Went over the balcony and floated to the ground. I'm going after him." Alaric released her, and she staggered. She tried opening her eyes again, and this time the world held still. A running figure crossed the ground below, heading for the stables. She opened her spellbook to *force,* but the letters blurred together, and she made it to the window in time to vomit over the balcony rail.

"Sienne, *sit down* and stop trying to kill yourself," Alaric said. He guided her away from the balcony to sit on the floor. She opened her eyes and blinked up at him as he lifted one leg over the rail.

"*Drift,*" she said, turning the pages to the comforting curves of the transform. She felt a flash of nausea, but her stomach stayed still.

Alaric stopped with one leg out of the window and both hands on the sill. "Make it quick," he said.

Sienne made herself focus on the spell. One syllable at a time. Her mouth filled with a cloying sweetness she swallowed, making her stomach roil, but she persisted. The moment her spell struck Alaric, he shoved off from the wall, diving backward through the air as if into a deep pool and twisting in midair to face away from the manor. Sienne rose with some difficulty and clung to the sill, breathing heavily. Only a few more moments, and the spell would wear off, just as Alaric reached the ground.

"Sienne!" Dianthe shouted. "Alaric! The undead are attacking us! Where's Master Scholten?"

Alaric alit and took a couple of bounding steps before *drift* ended. Sienne clutched the rail and watched him. Scholten hadn't emerged from the stable. "Be careful—he still has spells!" she shouted. Alaric didn't acknowledge her, but she was sure he'd heard because his steps slowed, and he sidled along the wall of the stable, sword in one hand.

Movement caught Sienne's eye, not at the stable but closer to the manor. An undead came out from the shadow of the manor, stumbling along faster than usual and with frightening directness. It headed directly for Alaric. Another followed, and another, until there were half a dozen shambling toward the stable. "Alaric, *look out!*" Sienne screamed. Alaric turned to look at her and saw the undead.

A horse burst through the stable doors. It was Alaric's big gelding Paladin. Scholten clung to Paladin's back, leaning over to lie against the horse's neck. Alaric flattened himself against the stable to avoid being trampled, then ran after the horse, transforming mid-stride into the dark brown shape of his unicorn other self. Sienne raised her spellbook. If they wanted to stop Scholten, it was down to her. If she missed, if Alaric couldn't outrun him, it might be over.

The hard-edged syllables of *force* tasted like acid, and the letters blurred almost too much for her to read them. Scholten was a rapidly receding blotch against the estate wall, with Alaric a darker blotch behind him. Almost there...

The *force* bolt burst from her seconds before she once again retched and vomited thin bile all down the side of the manor. She closed her eyes and collapsed, unable to even look to see if she'd succeeded. If the bolt had flown wide, or worse, hit Alaric...

She concentrated on breathing, swallowed more bile, and tried opening her eyes. That only made her sicker, so she closed them and listened instead. The sounds of fighting drifted up from below, again eerily quiet without the shrieks and moans of the wounded. The low keening of the undead filled the air, making her skin vibrate. She didn't know how many were left, but certainly enough to kill them all. Even if she'd hit Scholten, even if that made him lose control of the horde, dozens of masterless ghouls would be just as intent on attacking her and her friends as undead obeying Scholten's orders.

She dragged herself to her hands and knees and crawled, she hoped, toward the door. If they were going to die, she wanted to be with her friends when it happened. She ran into something hard and cold and opened her eyes briefly, though she already knew it was the *prison* Scholten had cast. From the outside, it looked like a big icy lump, like a frozen haystack. She crawled around it, the cold radiating from it sucking the warmth from her skin. By the time she reached the door, she was freezing again.

In the hall, she managed to push herself upright and use the wall to stand. Blinking, she found she could see again, though not well; her vision was blurry, as if a gauze mask covered her eyes. She stumbled to the stairs. "Where are you?" she cried out.

"Sienne! Watch out!" Dianthe shouted. "The undead are coming up the stairs!"

She listened, and heard the scuffling, shambling tread of several halting feet. Her heart pounded, and she turned and fumbled her way back to the sitting room, where she slammed the door shut. After a few false starts, she managed to drag the chair Scholten had sat in to block the door. Breathing heavily, she stumbled to the window.

She couldn't see Paladin or Scholten. Alaric was surrounded by undead who pressed him on all sides. He lashed out with his hind hooves, knocking two undead away, then skewered a third with his horn. The one he impaled jerked and fell limp, sliding off the horn to lie unmoving on the ground. Of course. The horn was magical. If only it was enough!

Alaric let out a shrill scream as one of the undead scored a devastating hit on his flank, tearing it open. Sienne lifted her spellbook once more, then let it fall. Another spell really might kill her, and she didn't have anything that would help Alaric, anyway. She was too tired even to cry.

Something struck the door, hard, making her shriek and spin around. The door thumped again, and the chair blockade shifted a few inches. Terrified, she cast about for some weapon, anything that would let her go down fighting.

Her gaze fell on the circle burned into the floor. It was a gamble. Scholten might have lied about its power, or maybe it had lost its efficacy when he left it. There was no time for her to think about the possibilities. She scrambled across the floor and flung herself into the circle just as the door burst open, flinging the chair away. Two undead fell through the doorway, their pale faces frighteningly empty of emotion. They came toward Sienne, hands upraised, fingers tipped with glistening claws, eyes blank and white like pearls. Sienne screamed and crouched, covering her head with her arms.

But the anticipated blow never came. Sienne peeked up through her arms and saw the undead clawing at the air, unable to approach over the curves of the protective circle. It was like being surrounded by a glass cylinder. Sienne stood, slowly, resisting the urge to lie down and go unconscious. More undead had joined the first two, pressing against them, and the first one, pushed by its neighbor, took a step that put its foot on the burned lines.

The undead shrieked, the first human sound she'd ever heard one make. It fell into convulsions and staggered backward, knocking over the one who'd pushed it. Still screaming, it collapsed into a twitching pile near the balcony.

"Sienne!" Dianthe cried out. "We're coming!"

"It wasn't me," Sienne called out, but her voice had no force behind it, and she wasn't sure even the nearest undead heard her. She started shivering again and hugged herself. Scholten hadn't said how long the circle lasted. It was possible all her friends would die and she'd be trapped here until she ventured out to be killed herself, or died of starvation or dehydration.

Then she heard, distantly, Perrin's voice shouting, "O Lord of crotchets, spare our lives, and grant me this blessing!"

A shock wave like a silent blast of wind struck her, making her stagger almost out of the circle. Every undead in the room froze mid-motion. Then black mist poured from their mouths and noses just as it had when Murtaviti had healed himself. This time, instead of pooling and flowing across the floor, it rose in long, ropy tendrils and tumbled out the window, twisting in invisible currents of air. Sienne craned to look outside and saw the mist rising higher, quickly obscured against the black night sky.

A thump drew her attention back to the room. The undead were falling, rigid as if they'd been paralyzed, to lie motionless on the floor. Sienne stared at them. If that was a blessing, it was far more powerful than anything she'd seen before. And why hadn't Perrin invoked it sooner? If Alaric—

She gasped and ran to the balcony, tripping over a couple of fallen bodies, then had to cling to the rail to keep from fainting. Once her vision cleared, she looked down on the grassy area between the house and the wall. Undead lay everywhere, collapsed in heaps like puppets with their strings cut. Three still stood, facing Alaric, who was backed against the stables. As she watched, he reared up and lashed out with his front hooves, bringing his full weight to bear on the nearest undead. It crushed the creature, but left him open to its neighbor's attack. He stumbled as the undead reached for his throat and got his face instead, tearing it open.

Sienne turned and ran for the door, stumbling in her haste. "Alaric's in trouble!" she shouted. This time, it came out sounding normal, though she'd intended it to be much louder. She staggered to the stairs and tripped, falling to the landing where the stairs turned. "Help!"

Running footsteps came her way. "Are you hurt?" Kalanath said. "Can you stand?"

She shook her head. "Alaric's out there—still fighting—the stables—"

Kalanath released her, making her wobble, and sped for the front door. Sienne sank to sit on the top stair of the landing. "I'm not hurt," she told Perrin, who appeared as if by magic before her, "not in any way you can fix, I cast too many spells—why didn't you invoke that blessing before?"

"I was knocked unconscious briefly," Perrin said. "Things were quite exciting down here. Are you certain you are well?"

"Master Scholten's circle of protection worked. It saved my life. I didn't think I'd be grateful to him for anything." Sienne leaned against the wall and closed her eyes. "I think he got away."

"So long as we all live, I cannot find that a tragedy." Perrin helped her stand and walk down the rest of the stairs. "Did you say Alaric is in danger?"

"We should help him. I can't cast any more spells, though, damn it!"

"There is little you and I can do. I have no more shields, and that undead-destroying blessing was the only one of its kind. But let us hurry nonetheless, and provide healing, if—" Perrin's mouth shut abruptly, but Sienne could guess he'd been about to say *if it is not too late.* She walked faster, willing herself not to fall, and by the time they reached the front door, they were running.

They came around the end of the manor and headed for the stable. Undead bodies lay strewn across the short grass like victims of a fast-acting plague. Beyond them, Kalanath and Dianthe knelt beside another fallen form, one large and dark and sprawled unnaturally still. Sienne felt like she'd been punched in the stomach. "Go, go to him, don't worry about me!" she urged Perrin. He let her go and ran toward Alaric. Sienne followed as fast as she could. If he was dead—if they'd killed him—Scholten wouldn't be able to run far enough to hide from her. She dashed tears from her eyes and pushed herself harder.

Alaric lay unmoving near the stable wall, his eyes open. Blood covered his hairy brown chest and long face, and a ragged tear laid open his formerly smooth cheek. His horn, which normally gleamed like black oil, was matte-dull. Sienne sucked in a horrified breath and found her knees wouldn't support her. She landed hard on the ground and let out a cry of pain. Alaric twitched, but made no other response.

"No fear, Sienne, all will be well," Perrin said, tearing a blessing free from a ragged riffle of paper. "O Lord, have patience in your crankiness, and grant me this blessing," he prayed.

Green light flared, lighting up every wound Alaric had taken. Sienne found herself crying again. So much damage...it was a miracle he'd survived. It looked like he'd killed more than a dozen undead. The light bathed his sides, making his dark brown hide look sallow. The unicorn closed his eyes and winced as if the light hurt him, though Sienne knew from experience healing was actually pleasant.

Perrin grunted. "This is difficult," he said. "I hope..."

No one wanted to ask what he hoped, and possibly distract him from whatever role he played in the healing blessing. Sienne wiped tears from her cheeks and prayed as she never had before. *Averran, help him, please. He can't die. Please.*

The green light faded. The nasty wound on Alaric's face was gone, leaving a pale scar. Sienne had never seen Perrin's healing produce scars before. Alaric's muscles bunched and flexed, and then he was human again. He blinked. "Did someone get Scholten?" he said in a husky voice.

"He got away," Sienne said.

"I don't think so. You hit him in the back of the head with *force*, and he fell off Paladin." Alaric tried to sit up. "For that matter, what happened to my horse?"

His voice, despite the huskiness, sounded so normal that Sienne let out a cry and threw herself at him, knocking him over again. He laughed, and put his arms around her, and the tightness in her chest relaxed. She rested her cheek on his shoulder and breathed out a deep sigh of relief.

"Master Scholten is here," Kalanath said. "He is dead."

That sent a spike of dread through Sienne. "*Force* can't kill."

"But a fall from a horse can. His neck is broken," Kalanath said. "Paladin is near the wall. He looks well."

"Let me up, Sienne," Alaric said. Sienne drew back, and Alaric stood, wincing as if the motion hurt him. "I don't feel completely healed."

"I believe the wounds inflicted by the undead carried with them illness," Perrin said, "and you may require rest to recover from that. I will heal you again, though, just in case. It is my last blessing for the day. I have never before used all that my Lord has gifted me with."

"I'm at my limit," Sienne said. "I can barely see straight, and I feel I might throw up again at any moment."

Alaric put a steadying hand under her arm. "You should have said something."

"You were dying. I think that's more important."

"Not to me." Alaric turned to Kalanath. "You're sure Scholten is dead?"

"Very sure." Kalanath prodded the inert body with his staff. "And the undead became ghouls. I think that is a thing that happens when the necromancer dies."

"Then we need to search his house."

"It's full of undead!" Dianthe exclaimed. "Dead ones, but still. We destroyed Master Murtaviti, which is what we came for—we need to get out of here."

"No one's coming out here to investigate for a while," Alaric said. "And while our primary goal was killing Murtaviti, we still have a binding ritual to find, and Scholten was part of the blight. We need to find his library."

"You make a good point," Perrin said. "And we cannot return to Onofreo, as the gates will certainly be closed by now. We should sleep here, and return to Fioretti in the morning, and hope no one remembers our inquiries about the late Master Scholten to accuse us of his murder."

"I think I can arrange things so it looks like Master Scholten was killed by the undead," Dianthe said. "Possibly even that Master

Murtaviti looks like the villain. But I don't think I can sleep in a house full of corpses."

"Me neither," Sienne said. "But Alaric's right, we need to search this place."

"Then let's get started," Alaric said. "Sienne, you'll rest until you can see straight."

"I can help search!"

"Rest first." Alaric guided her back around to the front of the house and into one of the rooms they'd barricaded to force the undead into a route of their choosing. It was, Sienne was relieved to see, completely free of undead. "You have a distressing tendency to push yourself beyond your limits."

"So do you. So you can hardly criticize me for doing it."

Alaric found her a sofa and pressed her gently onto it. "Lie down, and see if you can sleep for half an hour."

"I'm too keyed up to sleep."

He bent and kissed her, a long, slow kiss that made her long to draw him down to lie beside her for more kissing. "Then close your eyes and relax. I'll be back shortly."

She watched him leave, then closed her eyes and let out a slow breath. They'd never been so close to dying. What a nightmare.

She crossed her arms over her stomach, and the pages of Scholten's spellbook pressed into her skin. Were they hers, now? Someone could make a case that she'd won them by right of combat. But she felt awkward about taking the spells of a man she'd indirectly killed. *Don't be stupid*, she told herself, *you could really use some of what he has*. The version of *force* that affected multiple targets, for one, and —no, she didn't dare take any of the charms, though putting enemies to sleep had its appeal.

Midway through mentally reviewing Scholten's spells and coming up with justifications for taking each one, she drifted off to sleep.

21

S he woke to a gentle hand on her shoulder. "Feeling better?" Alaric said.

She sat up, and the room spun around her. "A little," she lied. It was only partly a lie, because once the dizziness passed, she found her vision clear and her stomach settled. Probably sitting up too quickly was the problem, and lightheadedness could happen to anyone.

"We haven't found any necromancy books, and no rooms kitted out as ritual chambers." Alaric helped her rise and kept his arms around her when she was standing. "If you're up to it, we could use a fresh set of eyes."

"Maybe it's underground."

"Perrin and Dianthe are checking that possibility now." Alaric brushed hair out of her eyes and kissed her forehead. "I don't think we've ever been so close to catastrophe as we were this time. When that pile of ice appeared...I thought it was solid, and you were under it."

"It was almost that bad. If I hadn't had my spellbook, I might have died before you broke through." She shivered in memory, and he pulled her closer. His warm, strong embrace calmed her heart, even as it worried her that he trembled now and then. She hoped Perrin was wrong about him being infected by whatever diseases the undead carried.

They stood like that for what felt like not nearly long enough, until Alaric released her and said, "I don't suppose you can turn that disguise spell inside out? Reveal objects that have been camouflaged?"

"Unfortunately, no. But he didn't have *camouflage* in his spellbook, and even if he had friends willing to cast it for him, it doesn't last long. Where should I search?"

"The upstairs rooms. His bedroom, possibly. It would be a good place to hide anything he wanted to keep a close eye on."

Sienne nodded. "I suppose Perrin didn't want to pester Averran for more blessings to locate things."

"You suppose correctly. I didn't even ask. We've traded on the avatar's goodwill enough for one day."

Sienne still felt lightheaded as she trudged up the stairs and had to trail her fingers along the wall to keep her balance. At the top, she paused to catch her breath and saw Kalanath coming toward her along the hall. "You feel better, then?" he said.

"Much. Where have you searched?"

"All but this room." He indicated the sitting room. "It stinks of undead and I have put it off." Making a face, he entered the room. Sienne followed him as far as the doorway.

The *prison* still sat near the doorway, a lump of ice just taller than her head. Its surface was slick with melted ice, but the warmth of the evening wasn't making much headway against it. Kalanath propped his staff against the doorway and circled it like a cat examining a mouse it hadn't yet decided to eat. "You were inside this?"

"It was awful. I'm not scribing that spell. I couldn't bear to do that to anyone, not even something evil."

Kalanath nodded. "I agree." He touched the bumpy surface and sniffed his fingers. "Where does the water come from?"

"I don't know. Not out of the air, or this room would feel parched. Not to mention I don't think there's enough water in the atmosphere to make something this size. A nearby lake, maybe? Or possibly it's just created out of nothing."

"Magic is strange." Kalanath stepped over the undead bodies and crossed to the far wall, where a bookcase stood. It had been stripped of its books, which lay in loose piles all around its base. "I think there is nothing here," he said, "and yet..." He turned to face Sienne. His brow was furrowed in thought. Slowly, he walked at a measured pace from the wall to the doorway, then left the room. Sienne watched him pace from the door to the stairs with the same slow gait. At the top of the stairs, he hesitated, then turned and hurried back toward her.

"The hall is longer than the room," he said. "There is something hidden. Help me move the bookcase."

Sienne followed him, a little confused—of course the hall was longer than the room, it went the whole length of the house!—and watched him take hold of the empty bookcase. "Help me!" he exclaimed, and Sienne took one side of the massive thing and pulled with him. The bookcase didn't move.

"It's too heavy for me," she said.

"No," Kalanath said, shaking his head for emphasis, "no, it is stuck fast. Attached." He climbed up the face of it and peered at its top, sneezing once. "There is nothing attaching it to the wall. This is a door."

"Are you sure?"

"Very. We should search for a thing that opens it."

Sienne stepped back and surveyed the room. Some of what made it seem so feminine was the clutter of knickknacks covering every conceivable surface, something she associated with her mother's favorite sitting room. The fireplace mantel, painted white to match the walls, bore a tall urn with an arrangement of striped grass flanked by smaller vases, all empty but one, which contained a single white rose, half-open. A row of successively smaller tables, the smallest no taller than Sienne's knee, held an array of porcelain figures representing the divine avatars and characters from the stories in which they featured. An ornately gilded clock rested on another table that matched the bookcase in material and design. Sienne tapped its sides and heard its hollow insides echo. She picked it up with some effort and opened its case, finding nothing but a clock mechanism. "This could take a while."

Kalanath swept the porcelain figures off the largest table, prompting a gasp from Sienne. "If one of these things opens the door, it will not fall," he said. "We do not care about this place, do we?"

"I suppose not, but…" All Sienne's instincts protested against vandalism, even as reason told her no one could possibly care what they did.

Kalanath tipped another table so its contents slid off and crashed to the floor. "Could it be invisible? Or disguised?"

"He didn't have any spells that would do that. He only had two confusions, and—wait." She withdrew the spell pages from inside her vest and sorted through them. "No, I was wrong. He has *false door*, but that makes something look like an actual door, it doesn't disguise a door to look like something else. We have to use our heads. If that bookcase leads to a secret area, and the secret area is where Master Scholten did his necromancy, he wouldn't have made it impossible to find. The activation would be something ready to hand, because he wouldn't want to fumble around, and it would be out of the way, because he wouldn't want guests to trigger it accidentally."

"I do not think he has many guests."

"All right, but you know what I mean."

Kalanath stopped before upending the last table. "Let us be reasonable, then." He walked to the doorway and stood there surveying the room. "Master Scholten wishes to perform vile necromancy. He enters the room. He goes to his door—" Kalanath shook his head. "There is nothing one can press or turn to open anything. He goes to…the fireplace."

Sienne regarded the fireplace. The mantel was carved all over with fanciful creatures, dancing and playing the pipes in a rural way.

She began pressing the carvings, feeling her way across the mantel. "This can't be it," she said.

Her fingers found the round circle of a dryad's head that depressed when she pushed on it. With a click, the bookcase popped away from the wall.

"This is how it began, in Penthea Lepporo's house," Kalanath said with a grin. He ran into the hallway, calling for the others.

Sienne crossed the room to put her hand on the bookcase. It swung easily, letting out a breath of air fragrant with incense that briefly dispelled the stink of the undead.

Several people's footsteps sounded on the stairs and approached down the hall. "You weren't going to go in there alone, were you?" Dianthe said.

"You're never going to let me forget about it, are you?" Sienne said, exasperated.

"I'm kidding. Let me take a look." Dianthe pulled the hidden door open more widely and peeked inside. "Light, please?"

Sienne sent a white light drifting over Dianthe's head. "This is it, all right," Dianthe said. "To think it was here the whole time and Master Scholten didn't say a word."

"Why would he tell us?" Alaric said. "Are there books?"

"Some. Take a look. I don't think there are any traps. You don't generally set traps in a place you have to enter often, and Master Scholten lived all the way out here where nobody comes."

The hidden space was only about six feet deep and sixteen feet long, and so full of cabinets and shelves it was horribly crowded with more than two of them in it at a time. Sienne waited for Alaric and Dianthe to examine the room, then ducked inside for her turn. She traced the woody, rich smell of incense to a brazier hanging from thin gold chains from the ceiling at the far end of the room. She made a few more lights and spread them out through the room. The walls and ceiling were painted a dark blue that made the room feel even smaller. Fanciful constellations that didn't resemble any sky Sienne was familiar with speckled the chamber, dim except where the light struck them. It didn't look like a necromancer's chamber at all.

She turned her attention to the books lined up on two shelves of a bookcase. The rest of the shelves held pottery jars, tightly stoppered and labeled in ink written on their sides. It made the books look like an afterthought. "Looks like reference material," she said, paging through one of the books. "An herbal. Something about charting star movements." She gasped. "This one has rituals!"

"Let me see that," Alaric said. Sienne handed it to Perrin, who passed it to Alaric.

Sienne went back to the books. "I don't see anything that might be a journal."

"I'm going to check his bedroom again. He might have kept the journal there." Dianthe left the room. Sienne glanced over the jars. Ordinary herbs, for the most part, though Scholten did have varnwort and some other herbs Sienne recognized from several weeks' reading of necromantic treatises.

She started going through the drawers of the largest cabinet and immediately regretted it. "He kept body parts," she said, pinching her nose shut though the things didn't smell of anything but camphor. "I hope they aren't souvenirs."

"Possibly he needed them to keep his undead under control," Perrin said, looking over her shoulder.

The next drawer down held large sheets of parchment, pale in the white light. Sienne removed the topmost and held it high. It was an anatomical drawing, very fine, showing the circulatory system superimposed on a human figure. "Huh," she said. "I can't read this...oh. Master Scholten must have thought he was so clever. This is backwards handwriting."

"Backwards? That seems difficult," Perrin said.

"Yes, but it's not much of a secret code. You just need a mirror to read it." She sorted through the rest of the parchments. "They've all got notes. I hope he did his anatomical experiments on people who were already dead."

"There is a mirror in the bedroom," Perrin said. He stepped aside to give her room to exit with her find.

Sienne stepped around the bodies and crossed the hall to the bedroom, which was thankfully free of corpses. Cool wind blew through the broken window, stirring the draperies of the bed. Dianthe looked up from her search of the mattresses. "Find anything?"

"Maybe." The full-length mirror stood near the window, tilted back on its central axis. Sienne pulled it fully vertical and held up the first parchment. The mirror-writing, tiny and precise, was suddenly legible, though it was still moderately difficult to read because some of it followed the contours of the drawing, turned on its side until it was nearly vertical. Sienne scanned the text. "It's mostly notes about the circulatory system and how the heart works. It's too bad he was an evil necromancer, because this is all important research. I think. I don't know much about medicine."

Dianthe dropped the mattress and climbed up on the bed to feel around the canopy frame. "If I thought we could get away with it, I'd suggest taking them to the University of Fioretti. I'm sure they could use it."

"But we'd have to explain where we got them, yes." Sienne examined the next parchment, a detailed drawing of human musculature, and the next, fine traceries of nerves. "That's strange. He keeps referring to a 'conduit,' but there's nothing to indicate what it is. Just that parts of the body might be involved."

Dianthe grunted and hopped down. "Maybe this will help." She brandished a small book at Sienne. "It's full of funny writing."

Sienne took it and flipped through it. "More mirror writing," she said, "and in Sorjic. That's a good hint that this was important, and probably damning."

"I'll tell the others. You start reading. The sooner we're out of this place, the happier I'll be." Dianthe left the room. Sienne examined the first page. It was possible to read the reversed writing without the mirror, though slowly. She turned the book to face the mirror. The first entry was dated over five years before. *No new information from S.*, she read. *Uriane's ritual missing pieces, damn her for secrecy. She must have done it on purpose. She wants me to fail, but then I wish the same for her, so I don't know what I expected. More frustrating is the fact that this is clearly the binding ritual I need, if only it weren't incomplete!*

"Did you learn anything?" Alaric said, appearing in the doorway.

"I only just started reading, but Master Scholten believed he had a binding ritual that would do what he wanted. Who knows if it's the one we need?" Sienne flipped a few pages. "More references to this conduit of his. He's not specific about what it is, beyond that it's some aspect of the human body. I think. Sometimes he talks about it like it's not entirely physical. But all his necromantic work that wasn't focused on becoming a lich is centered on it."

"Not something that matters to us right now, though."

"No. Let me read."

Alaric came to stand behind her, reading over her shoulder. "We could take this with us and leave now. I'm increasingly disinclined to spend the night in a house full of corpses."

"But what if there's a clue in the diary that points to something in this house? We won't be able to come back, not without getting involved in whatever investigation the duke of Onofreo conducts once someone finds out what happened."

"Good point. Wait, turn back. What's that book? *Studies?*"

"He always refers to it just as *Studies*, but I imagine it has a longer title. Why?"

"I saw it on the shelf in his den of depravity. *Studies in the Calling and Binding of Souls.* No wonder he abbreviated it."

"He refers to it often. Do you suppose—"

"I'll take a look." He disappeared again.

Sienne kept reading. The journal alternated between fiendishly dull, in sections where he detailed his sometimes gruesome experiments, and fascinating, when he wrote of his interactions with his fellow necromancers. Drusilla Tallavena got a mention or two, speculations about whether her experiments had killed her. Scholten had been in communication with Pedreo Giannus and it had seemed a friendly relationship. Less so his connection to Murtaviti, whose abilities Scholten had been dismissive of.

But it was his relationship with Uriane Samretto that fascinated

Sienne. Scholten had hated her, but there was an underlying thread of admiration for her abilities and a thinly-disguised jealousy in his words. Sienne wished she had their correspondence. From what Scholten wrote, Uriane Samretto's necromantic pursuits went beyond what her husband had said, though it was possible Scholten exaggerated Uriane's abilities the way some people idolize the dead. It didn't really matter, because Uriane was no longer in a position to help or hinder their search, but Sienne was increasingly convinced the woman held the secret to the binding ritual they sought.

She turned another page. At this point, she was skimming, not liking to dwell on the less savory aspects of Scholten's research. So she almost missed it. She was turning the page when the words *not necromantic* registered. Quickly she went back and read more carefully.

I have finally found the book Uriane referred to all those years ago. Disappointingly, the rituals it contains are not necromantic. I suspect it is a hoax, as most of the rituals are simply necromantic ones with parts stripped away. The book is very old and falling apart. Still, it might be of use.

Sienne read those lines a second time. Of course Scholten would have considered it a hoax because nobody believed non-necromantic rituals existed. And altering existing rituals to make them look new and different was certainly possible. But what Sienne and her friends were looking for was exactly what Scholten described. Sienne turned the page. No more reference to the book. No title. She turned a few more pages, wanting to scream with frustration. Why couldn't he have mentioned what it was called?

She went back to skimming pages and found another reference to the mystery book. This time, Scholten mentioned using one of the rituals in a binding and failing, but in a way that he found promising. Still no title.

"Have you found anything interesting?" Perrin asked from the doorway.

"Maybe. There's a book…"

"Not *Studies in the Calling and Binding of Souls?* That one, I fear, is a dead end."

"Not that. I'm trying to find the title." Sienne read faster. It was probably stupid, but she felt in her heart that this book, this mysterious non-necromantic ritual book, was the key to their search.

"He still held a grudge against Uriane Samretto, years after her death," she remarked. "Curses her name and her deceitfulness."

"Perhaps we should pay another visit to Master Samretto. Now that we know all the members of the blight were engaged in this contest to achieve lichhood, his protestations that his wife's practices were benign seem suspect. It is difficult for one spouse to conceal major activities from the other."

"I think you're right. Wait. I—this could be it! He refers to a book called *Traverse* that he has to handle with care because it's so old. Did you see any really, really old books in the secret room? Falling-apart books? Likely it wouldn't have the title imprinted on the cover anywhere, that's a new practice."

"I saw nothing of that description."

Sienne scowled and read on. "The full title is *Traverse of Memory*. It definitely contains information about non-necromantic rituals, probably binding rituals. Damn it, it has to be here somewhere!"

"Where did he acquire it?"

"I don't know. He says...here he says he wrote to Master Murtaviti about it, but he wasn't impressed. But...later Master Scholten says some of Master Murtaviti's questions in his correspondence indicate that Master Murtaviti had a copy of his own." Sienne looked up from the book. "Maybe it's in Master Murtaviti's library back in Fioretti!"

"Let us search here thoroughly first," Perrin said. "I dislike the idea of bearding Mistress Murtaviti in her den, since we will bring news that her husband is dead. She will not be amenable to helping us, I believe."

"I'll finish reading this, just in case. I wish he'd explain what he means by 'conduit.' He was deeply interested in proving it exists, whatever it is."

Perrin nodded and left the room. Sienne made herself keep reading, though she was impatient to drop the diary and help the others ransack the house for *Traverse of Memory*. Scholten might have claimed altruism in only killing those whom the law would have punished, but his description of killing those people was so... detailed. Torture had been involved sometimes. Scholten wrote about it all as if describing an elegant meal, or the construction of a new building. Sienne longed for the time when necromancy was no longer part of their lives.

She came to the end of the diary abruptly; a good quarter of the pages hadn't yet been written in. Sighing in relief, she turned back to the first mention of *Traverse of Memory*, the one that didn't mention the name. If it wasn't a hoax, the rituals it contained were similar to necromantic ones, which meant...what? Possibly that necromancy was a degraded form of rituals that had existed centuries ago, maybe in the before times. They'd already suspected that, given that the ritual that bound the Sassaven had been created almost a hundred years before the wars that nearly destroyed civilization. But this could be the proof they needed.

She closed the book and went in search of her friends, finding them in the room where she'd slept. Alaric, Dianthe, and Perrin sat on the sofas; Kalanath, as usual, stood leaning on his staff. All of them looked exhausted. "Did Perrin tell you what I learned?" she asked.

"An old, worn book called *Traverse of Memory*," Dianthe said. "It's not here. I guarantee we've searched every conceivable place in this house."

"What about the kitchens?"

"It wouldn't be there. Too much potential for it to be damaged. But yes, we looked there too."

Sienne sank onto a sofa beside Alaric. "But it has to be here."

"Unless it was destroyed. If its condition was bad enough, that's possible." Alaric clasped her hand loosely. "We've run out of options."

"Then we need Master Murtaviti's library," Sienne said. "If he has a copy, like Master Scholten believed, we don't need Master Scholten's."

"It's after two o'clock, and I'm exhausted," Dianthe said. "But I really don't want to sleep here."

"We can't get into Onofreo until dawn, and we're not equipped to sleep outdoors," Alaric said. He shuddered, and closed his eyes briefly.

"Are you all right?" Sienne asked, feeling alarmed.

"I feel cold," Alaric said.

Sienne put a hand on his forehead. "You're feverish," she said, looking into his eyes, which were glassy and slightly unfocused. "You need rest."

"That's not something I can get in this house." He shuddered again. "Perrin, tell me about this illness the undead carry."

"Some are carriers of ordinary agues," Perrin said. "More serious are such things as grave rot and marrowblight. If you have contracted grave rot, the symptoms will not show for another three days. Marrowblight is a disease of the blood that requires several priestly blessings or intensive medical attention. That one, I do not believe you have, as it turns the skin yellow almost immediately."

Alaric looked flushed rather than yellow. "So this is an ordinary fever?"

"Very likely. I can pray for a blessing that will restore you, but it may require more than one, depending on the severity. You will still need rest for a few days and febrifuges and other treatments."

Alaric scowled. "Because what we needed was another delay."

"But we're not in a hurry anymore, are we?" Sienne said. "We stopped Master Scholten from becoming a lich. Master Murtaviti has been killed. Drusilla Tallavena and Pedreo Giannus are both dead. The blight is destroyed. All we need now is access to Master Murtaviti's library, and that's not going anywhere."

"Unless Mistress Murtaviti gets rid of it now that her husband is dead," Dianthe said.

"But she will not know for days," Kalanath pointed out. "If he did not go to his home, but went directly to Mistress Tallavena's house, she is still waiting for news."

"That's true," Alaric said. "Then I propose we set this up to look like undead killed Scholten and Murtaviti, then go back to Onofreo, wait for sunrise, and find a good inn." He shuddered again, and this time he went on shaking. "I'd rather recover at home, but I don't think I can ride for a full day."

"You should not," Perrin said. "Rest here, and let us see to things."

"I can—" Alaric tried to rise and his legs gave out. "All right, I can't."

Sienne squeezed his hand. "Everything's going to be all right."

22

It took more than an hour to arrange the bodies in a way Dianthe was satisfied with. Sienne cringed whenever she had to touch one of the undead. She was sure the stench of putrefaction had doubled in the short time since the battle was over. She helped drag the ones that had attacked Alaric nearer each other as Kalanath brought Scholten's body toward the stable. "This is disgusting," she told him.

"I will be glad when it is over," he replied. "Can we do anything about their wounds?" He set Scholten down and waved a hand at the undead.

"Even if I could cast spells yet, which I can't, any illusion to disguise their having been gored by a unicorn would fade in a few hours. We have to hope nobody looks too closely at the undead, and rely on people believing unicorns are mythical to keep anyone from drawing that absurd conclusion." She looked off toward the house. Dianthe was trotting toward them, moving rapidly but not urgently. "I hope this means we can leave."

"That's the last of them," Dianthe said. She crouched to examine Scholten's body and moved his arms and legs to sprawl more. "I think we should circle around behind the city and approach Onofreo from the other side, just in case. I doubt the same guards will be on the gate in the morning, but no sense taking chances."

"I want to wash my hands," Sienne said. "No, I want a bath. I don't think I've ever felt this disgusting in my life. Are we sure we can't catch a disease just from handling the bodies?"

"Perrin says no. I hope he's right. I've never seen an illness progress so rapidly as Alaric's."

"He's all right, though?" Sienne asked, alarmed.

"He'll be fine, Sienne. He's the toughest man I know. He doesn't take sick very often, and he's obnoxious when he's recovering. A little rest, and he'll be back to normal."

"Unless he has grave rot," Kalanath said. Both women glared at him, and he put up his hands to deflect their glares. "It is a possibility we do not need to ignore."

"Yes, but I'd rather not dwell on it," Sienne said.

They returned to the sitting room where Perrin and Alaric waited. Alaric did look worse. His fair skin was flushed, his eyes were red-rimmed, and he shivered frequently. He held up a hand when Sienne went to him. "Stay back. I don't want you catching this. There's no reason it can't be transmitted like a normal illness."

"You look bad," Dianthe said. "We could have a problem."

"I'll be fine, Dianthe. This is just a minor illness."

"Yes, but you're clearly in a bad way. They might not let you into the city if it looks like you're carrying contagion."

"I don't look that bad." Alaric straightened and wiped his sleeve across his eyes. "Do I?"

Sienne looked at Dianthe, who was chewing her lower lip. "We'll just have to risk it," she said. "The worst that can happen is they won't let us in, and we'll either have to find shelter at a farmhouse or risk the trip back to Fioretti."

"Could you cast a confusion to disguise his condition?" Perrin asked Sienne.

"Theoretically, yes, but not now. I haven't recovered from casting all those spells." Her vision was still doubled at times, and she ached as badly as if she were ill herself, not something she'd shared with her friends. It wasn't as if they could do anything about it, and she didn't want to be coddled.

"Let's ride," Alaric said. "I want to leave this place behind and never return."

Spark was as placid as if the events of the night had passed her by. Scholten must have ignored the other horses in his haste to make his escape on Paladin. She whickered at Sienne when Sienne saddled her and mounted. "No long journeys today," Sienne told her. "Just rest in a quiet stable." Spark nodded exactly as if she'd understood.

They left the gate open and circled wide around the hills behind Scholten's estate, heading south and west. Once they left the lights of the estate behind, only the partially-lidded eye of the moon lit their progress. Sienne kept a close eye on Alaric, who sat hunched in his saddle as if he were exhausted. She wanted to slump herself, but made herself sit erect. No sense giving her friends another person to worry about, though in truth they all looked like they'd had a rough night. Sienne blinked away Alaric's doubled image, and he swam back into focus. Just a few more hours, and they could rest.

She inhaled the sweet air of the short grasses covering the hills, grateful to have left the funk of the undead behind. It was a beautiful, clear night, with the stars a white dusting of shattered glass from hilltop to horizon and the light wind caressing her cheeks and keeping her from falling asleep and then off her horse. The only sounds came from the muffled tread of their horses' hooves on the grassy hillsides; no birds, no animals, not even the howl of a hunting wolf. It felt like victory. They'd succeeded in half their quest, and the other half was just a matter of time. If Alaric weren't sick, everything would be perfect.

Dianthe led them through the silent hills for what felt like hours, but was probably only ninety minutes. Eventually she brought them out onto the wide highway, turning east toward Onofreo. The sky was lightening in the east, a familiar sight to Sienne, whose usual watch while they were in the wilderness had her awake in the pre-dawn hours. The imminent dawn cheered her further, as much as her concern for Alaric would allow. None of them had spoken, but

Sienne couldn't help feeling it was a bad sign that he was silent. She urged Spark faster and drew up beside him. "Just a little farther," she said. "You're not going to fall off, are you?"

"I don't think so," Alaric replied. He was hunched more deeply now and had his eyes fixed on Paladin's ears. "I just feel cold."

"You don't look terrible."

"Let's hope that's enough to get me through the gate."

"There's Onofreo," Dianthe said, pointing at a cluster of lights on the eastern horizon. "We'll have a bit of a wait, by my estimate."

Another half-hour brought them to the city gate. The sky was lighter, but stars were still visible in the west. Dianthe rode up to the gate, looked up at where guards walked along the top of the wall, and shouted, "How long 'til the gates open?"

"You scrappers?" a voice replied.

"We are."

"Figured. Scrappers are always impatient. We'll open at first sight of the sun's rays and not before."

"Did you hear me ask you to?" Dianthe rode back to the others. "Forty minutes, give or take."

"What are they so worried about?" Sienne asked. "Fioretti's gates are open at all hours."

"Unless there is an invasion, or plague," Perrin said.

"All right, unless that, but Onofreo can't be worried about either of those things if they always close the gates at night. They aren't anywhere near the frontier, either."

"A lot of western cities do that," Dianthe said. "I don't know why. Alaric, how are you?"

"I feel like death," Alaric said. "My skin's not yellow, though, is it? What are the symptoms of grave rot?"

"Patches of gray beginning on your hands and feet and spreading from your extremities to your torso," Perrin said, "but it is far too early to worry about that. And although we cannot tell the hue of your skin in this poor light, I assure you marrowblight is unlikely."

"I hate being sick."

"The worst will be over in a few hours, when I procure the proper blessing." Perrin tied his long hair out of his eyes and added, "Though do not forget, it is possible it will take more than one. Healing disease is more complicated than healing injury. For serious diseases, it can require one blessing to destroy the disease-causing agent and another to repair the damage it does. I am afraid my knowledge of such things is rather academic."

"We can be grateful you do not need it before now," Kalanath said.

They fell silent. Sienne watched Alaric, whose breathing was heavier now, and wondered what they would do if he fell off his horse. If she tried to stop him, he'd just take her down with him, and she was certain all four of them together wouldn't be enough to hoist him back into the saddle. She eyed the eastern horizon and found herself willing the sun's disk to appear.

She wasn't sure how long it took, but it felt like much more than forty minutes before the gates of Onofreo swung open, heavy and with a low moan like an oncoming tide. Alaric straightened. "Quickly," he said. "I'm not sure how long I can hold this position."

The guards waved them through without looking closely at any of them, and Sienne breathed out in relief once they'd left the gate behind. Onofreo still slept, its morning streets a quiet contrast to the bustle and hum of the night before. The western side of the city looked much as its eastern counterpart did, though the street was wider and the signs hanging outside the shops and taverns bore writing rather than pictures of what could be purchased within.

"This one," Dianthe said, turning onto a side street that led to an inn yard off the main street. They filed through the gate and dismounted, all but Alaric, who clung to his saddle as if he'd been tied there. Dianthe handed her reins to Sienne and said, "I'll see about rooms. Go ahead and get the horses stabled."

A breeze brought the smell of fresh-baked bread to Sienne's nose, waking her stomach, which hadn't been hungry until now. To the stable hand who approached her, she said, "Do you have room for our horses?"

"Plenty," the woman said. "Here, your friend don't look too well."

"Summer cold," Sienne said.

"Well, let's get your horses stabled. Plenty of room now the scrappers are gone—but you'll be scrappers yourselves, yes?" The woman gestured toward the stalls. "Take your pick."

"We're scrappers, yes," Sienne said.

"Not headed for Fioretti?"

"Ultimately, but our friend needs rest for a few days. Why?"

The stable hand shrugged. "Last set of scrappers got word of something happening in the capital. Some call for scrappers. Don't know more than that."

"We haven't heard anything, but we've been...on the road," Sienne said, remembering at the last minute that they wanted to deflect attention from Scholten's estate.

The woman shrugged again. "Probably it's nothing."

Dianthe came out of the inn's back door at a run. "Let's get you inside," she said to Alaric, who nodded and slid off Paladin's broad back. He staggered when his feet touched the ground, and Sienne took a step forward before realizing there was no way she could support his weight. Kalanath and Perrin slung Alaric's arms over their shoulders, and step by halting step they made their way inside.

The back door led to a short hallway off which opened one door, the source of the delicious smells, and a narrow back staircase. Sienne hovered anxiously behind the three men as they made their way up the creaking steps. The staircase was poorly lit and barely wide enough for the three to fit. Alaric's head drooped, and his legs trembled with every step. It was hard not to imagine a terrible, incurable illness, and never mind what Perrin had said.

By the time they reached the second floor, Perrin was swearing under his breath, Kalanath was sweating, and the tremor in Alaric's legs was pronounced enough that they had to stop for him to rest. Sienne was grateful they didn't have to climb any more stairs. A single hall, much wider than the staircase, cut the second floor in half, front and back. A narrow carpet the color of the lightening sky covered the floor, and the walls were half-paneled in maple and painted a cheerful pink above. Dianthe had procured them two rooms with three beds each. "They're light on customers right now," she said as she held open the door to the first room. "Something about all their scrapper guests leaving for Fioretti in a hurry."

"That's what the stable hand said," Sienne said, following the men into the room. Alaric fell onto the nearest bed and lay there motionless, one leg dangling off the side. "Alaric, you need to undress."

"I don't think I can move."

"Sienne and I will see about getting breakfast," Dianthe said. "You two help him take off his boots, at least." She motioned Sienne into the hall and shut the door firmly behind them. "I'm sure the innkeeper won't mind us bringing food to the room. Then it's nap time for all of us."

"I don't think I can sleep without knowing he's all right."

"Perrin will take care of him. You know he'd be upset if he knew you were still ill, or whatever you call it when you cast too many spells."

"I'm fine."

"You are not. I bet you anything you like that you can't keep a straight line walking down this hall."

Sienne flushed and made herself walk more steadily. "All right, I'll rest. Did the innkeeper say why the scrappers left?"

"Just that they got word from Fioretti of something big and took off at sunrise. They must have taken the Widdern Gate, since we didn't see them leave. It makes me curious."

"Me, too."

After a few minutes' negotiating with the innkeeper, who put up a token protest against them eating in their rooms—mainly, Sienne thought, to justify overcharging them—they had a pot of coffee, a basket of fresh rolls, a covered platter of sausages, and a basket of apples, along with assorted dishes and cutlery. It was almost too much for the two of them to carry, but when Sienne tried to use her invisible fingers, she managed only to nauseate herself.

Eventually they made it up the stairs and back to the room. The men had succeeded in getting Alaric undressed and into bed, and

Sienne examined his face anxiously. He still looked feverish, but not yellow, and although his eyes were closed, he was still too tense to be asleep. He opened one eye as they came in, then closed it again.

"Ah, coffee," Perrin said with an exaggerated sigh. "I realize it militates against my falling asleep, but perhaps that is for the best, if it means I will be conscious when it is reasonably time to pray."

"Didn't you already pray, before the battle?" Sienne asked.

"I intend only to ask for a single healing blessing," Perrin said, "and I believe our need is great enough, and my actions humble enough, that Averran will grant it. Regardless, we will need an apothecary later today."

Sienne handed Kalanath and Perrin plates and let them serve themselves. "Wouldn't the healing take care of that?"

"It may only cure the disease and not the symptoms. I cannot say." Perrin bit into an apple. "Some diseases engender secondary illnesses that themselves require healing. I do not like the look of this fever."

"It doesn't feel wonderful either," Alaric murmured without opening his eyes.

"Do you want food?" Sienne asked.

"I'm not hungry. Maybe later."

"I doubt any apothecaries are open at this hour," Dianthe said. "I'm going to nap for a few hours and then go out. Sienne, you should sleep as long as you can."

"I want to come with you."

"Sienne, you nearly killed yourself with wizardry," Alaric said. "You need to recover."

Now that she'd eaten something, the idea of a comfortable bed had appeal. She wished she could snuggle up with Alaric and said, "I'll sleep if you will."

"Done," Alaric said, and turned to face the wall.

Sienne finished her roll and rose with her plate. Dianthe took it out of her hand. "Next door on the left," she said. "Sleep, or I'll drug your coffee until you do."

Sienne laughed. She went into the next room, kicked off her boots, and was asleep almost before her head touched the pillow.

She dreamed of nonsensical things, of chasing Kalanath through the halls of the ducal palace at Beneddo where she'd spent her childhood, of inventing a new spell that turned people into folded bits of paper that spoke in Meiric, of floating across the hills outside Scholten's estate. That last dream triggered memory, and she found herself back in Scholten's house, only it was empty of people and undead. She felt no fear, just curiosity at where the stairs led, because in the dream they went to floors that didn't exist in reality.

She came out of the stairs onto the roof, which towered high above the ground, and now she saw undead hordes pressing in on all sides, climbing over each other to try to reach her. Her spellbook was in her hand, and she read a spell written in a new language she had no trouble understanding, and the undead fell like lumps of shapeless clay. She turned back to the book—but that was impossible, there were only five spell languages, and one of them was forbidden. She strained to understand this new, sixth language—

and she woke, dragged out of the dream by reality intruding. Dianthe snored on the bed nearest the window. By the slanting rays of light, it was late afternoon. Ignoring her boots, Sienne rose and left the room to knock on the next door.

After a moment, Perrin opened it. "My petition was granted, I have invoked a healing blessing, and he is resting peacefully," he said. "Come in."

Kalanath was also asleep, his staff leaning against the wall by the head of his bed. Perrin looked as if he'd been sleeping too. "I'm sorry I woke you," Sienne said.

"I woke a few minutes ago," Perrin said, brushing her apology aside. "I had intended to fetch more water, but perhaps you might...?"

Sienne accepted the pewter pitcher and summoned a glob of water to fall with a splash into it. "Is he awake?"

"He is now," Alaric said. "Did you rest?"

Sienne sat on the edge of Alaric's bed and took his hand in hers. It was warm and dry, but not hot with fever. "I did. I feel much better. How about you?"

"Still weak, and I ache all over, but the fever is gone." He squeezed her hand gently. "Could you get me some water?"

Perrin helped him sit, and Sienne held a cup of water to his lips. Alaric nodded thanks. "I'm grateful to you, in case I didn't say it before," he told Perrin. "The last time I took ill, we didn't have money for a priest, and I was a week in recovering."

"It will certainly be less than that," Perrin agreed. "Now you simply need rest, though I believe another healing might be effective tomorrow. I believe we can head for home after two more days. You will not be fully recovered, but I estimate you will be in the cantankerous stages of your recovery, and might as well be cantankerous while we are on the road."

"I'm predictable, aren't I?" Alaric said with a smile.

"Just a bit," Sienne said.

"Well, I promise to keep my irritability to myself." He squeezed her hand again. "Now, what's this I hear about something taking scrappers to Fioretti?"

Sienne looked at Perrin, who shrugged. "That is as much as we know," he said. "Dianthe learned, when she spoke to the apothecary, that there were several scrapper teams who left this morning at first light, and a few others who departed some hours later. All but one had received communications from Fioretti about some opportunity to earn money in the capital. The last team followed the others on the basis that they did not want to miss out on possible riches simply because they had no priest to speak with someone in Fioretti."

"That's strange. Is it something we should look into?"

"I can pray for a communication blessing, yes, but I would not have any idea whom to speak to for information. But we will return in a few days, and learn the truth then."

"Or do some asking around here in Onofreo." Alaric shifted his weight and let out a deep, slow breath. "Anything that gets a scrapper team up before dawn is something we want to know about."

"We'll ask. You'll stay here," Sienne said.

"I wasn't planning to get up and run around, Sienne."

"No, but you've got that impatient look in your eye. Leave it to us." Sienne kissed his forehead lightly.

Alaric sighed again. "Promise me you'll tell me immediately what you learn. I have a feeling it's important."

"Don't worry," Sienne said, "whatever it is, it can't be that important or we'd have heard about it too."

"I sincerely hope that is the case," said Perrin.

23

Alaric mounted Paladin smoothly, with no evidence that it hurt him. Sienne thought he looked perfectly well, though he'd been unsteady on his feet walking down the stairs to the stables. "Paladin's restive," he said. "I wouldn't have thought two days of inactivity would do that to him."

"You're imagining things," Dianthe said. "You're eager to be off, so you think Paladin is too."

Alaric shrugged. "That's possible. And before you ask, yes, I still feel a little shaky, and I wouldn't want to do this ride at a full-out gallop, even if that were possible, but I'm up for nine hours of riding."

"I'm not sure I am," Sienne groused. "We're not going back as fast as we came, are we?"

"No need to," Alaric said. "Though aren't you anxious to access Murtaviti's library?" He prodded Paladin into a fast walk, and the big gelding led the way out of the stable yard.

"All right," Sienne said, "I admit to wanting to find that book. I hope Master Scholten was right, and Master Murtaviti had a copy."

"And that Mistress Murtaviti in her grief over her husband will not ban us from the library outright," Perrin said.

"I'm trying not to dwell on that possibility," Dianthe said. "I'd hate to break into her house on the off chance the book is there. Denys would—" She broke off mid-word, her lips thinned against anything else escaping.

No one spoke for a while. Finally, Sienne said, "Don't you think—"

"Denys doesn't want to hear from me, Sienne," Dianthe said. "There's nothing I can do about it. If he decides he wants to talk, he knows where to find me."

Sienne opened her mouth to say more, but decided against it. She tried to imagine what it would be like if Alaric found out she'd lied to him about something serious, and failed. Even if he didn't already know all her secrets, none of them were the kind of thing worth lying about, not like Dianthe protecting herself from an accusation of murder. But if she had, she wouldn't just let Alaric leave her, not without fighting for him...except, if she was the one who'd lied, would she have a right to impose on him like that? No, Dianthe was right. It was up to Denys to decide he wanted to speak to Dianthe, however stupid he was for being so upset.

They left Onofreo and headed east toward Fioretti, with Dianthe in the lead. She kept a steady but not very rapid gait, one that would still have them in Fioretti well before sunset. The sun was bright in the cloudless sky and beat down on Sienne's bare head, warming her enough that she wished for her true summer shirt and trousers, not the soft wool clothing that had been so comfortable up until now.

She kept a close eye on Alaric, but it seemed he was as well as he'd claimed: he rode confidently, his head held alert and high, and Paladin kept the pace as well as any of the other horses. His recovery had been quicker than Perrin had anticipated, and no symptoms of grave rot had surfaced, to Sienne's relief. He was quieter than usual, which Sienne put down to lingering illness, but aside from that he seemed perfectly well.

She sat beside him when they stopped for a noon meal and leaned against his broad shoulder. "What next?" she said.

"Next after what?"

"Well, let's assume for the moment we get the book from Master Murtaviti's library, and it has the ritual we need. What then?"

"We still have to find the varnwort potion. With luck, the ritual will relate to that somehow. Then we figure out how to turn it into a ritual to free my people. I'm afraid I have no idea what that will take." Alaric put his arm around her and drew her closer. "My hope is that seeing the ritual will give us some idea of what to do. If not, then I suppose it will be time for more research."

"I was thinking...maybe it's time I went to the University of Fioretti library. It's the biggest library in the country, and we could really use it as a resource."

"But your parents will find out where you are."

"I'm less worried about that than I used to be. They might try to drag me back home, but I have a new life now, with new friends, and they can't force me to do anything I don't want to. Besides, you wouldn't let them."

"They'd have to fight me to take you away. I'm sure I can defeat anyone they send after you, even in my weakened state." He flexed his arm muscles, making her giggle.

"Your weakened state is still more powerful than any five men."

"You flatter me. But—seriously, don't feel you need to expose yourself just to gain access to that library. We've done well without it."

"It's just a thought."

They sat in companionable silence for a while. Sienne rested her head on his shoulder and wondered what her parents would think if she came home with a giant Ansorjan (as far as anyone knew) scrapper lover in tow. All right, they weren't lovers yet, but that would last as long as it took to finish this job. Her mother would be horrified that she had a lover at all. It wasn't the sort of thing noble young women did. Sienne thought it was a bit hypocritical, given that plenty of older noble women had affairs, many of them with men half their age, but her mother was traditional, if by "traditional" you meant "humorless and stuffy."

"I wish we knew what was going on in Fioretti," Alaric mused. "I hate riding into the unknown."

"The man in the market was the only one who knew more details than just that there was scrapping work in Fioretti," Sienne said, "and he only knew the king is offering bounties for a certain job."

"Bounties generally mean collecting something. The last time the government paid out on bounties, it was a werewolf infestation near the Bramantus Mountains. So what could be overrunning Fioretti now?"

"I guess we'll find out when we reach the city." Sienne kissed his cheek and stood. "Let's ride on. I'm curious about it now."

It was almost six o'clock when they reached the gates of Fioretti, never closed except in times of extremity. To Sienne's surprise, the guards at the gate beckoned them to the side. "You here for the bounty?" the female guard said. She was tall and dark-skinned, with a scar down the left side of her face that dragged that corner of her mouth down.

"We heard the news in Onofreo," Alaric said without hesitation. "What can you tell us?"

"The usual rules about armed combat within the city limits are suspended so long as you're fighting the bounty," the woman said. "No souvenirs—they want the whole body brought to one of the guard posts. You familiar with the city?"

"We are."

"Then you'll know where to go. Any guard post will be able to issue you a claim chit, one per head. Take those to the treasury and exchange them for the bounty. Any questions?"

"The news didn't say what we'd be fighting."

The guard laughed. "Damn idiot scrappers, come from miles around on the off chance of reward without caring what the job is."

Alaric shifted his weight so the hilt of his sword bobbed above his left shoulder. It wasn't quite a threatening move, but it silenced the guard's laughter. "Sorry," he said, "I didn't hear that. What did you say the bounty is?"

The woman swallowed, then resumed her careless, defiant pose. "Ghouls."

Sienne gasped. Alaric and Dianthe exchanged glances. "Ghouls?" Alaric said. "There are ghouls in the city enough to justify a hunt?"

"If you're afraid—"

"Do I look afraid?"

Sienne couldn't see his face, but she could guess he looked angry, not afraid. The guard swallowed again. "They've been showing up in packs for the last three days. No one knows why. It's bad enough the king has authorized the payment of bounties. Don't know how much luck you'll have, what with how many scrappers are already in the city, but—"

"We should be moving. Our thanks." Alaric didn't sound very grateful. He nudged Paladin into a trot and headed through the gate without waiting for the rest. Sienne had to scramble to catch up.

"Ghouls," Alaric repeated. "Is it a coincidence? Perrin?"

"I think...not," Perrin said. "She said it had been three days since the ghouls appeared, yes? And three days ago is when we destroyed the lich. When a lich is destroyed, he loses control of any undead he raised. Master Murtaviti lived in Fioretti and no doubt did most of his necromancy here."

"So when we killed him," Sienne said, "it turned his undead into ghouls?"

"That seems likely."

Silence fell. Dianthe finally said, "I'm not sure the guilt I feel is justified."

"It's not," Alaric said. "We had to destroy Murtaviti. There was no way to destroy his undead minions first. Think of the alternative, if we'd left him alive until we'd returned here."

"So...should we hunt ghouls?" Kalanath said. "Or seek out Mistress Murtaviti?"

Alaric narrowed his eyes in thought. "I think we should proceed with our quest. That guard was right; there are probably a hundred scrappers prowling the city for ghouls right now. The longer we wait to confront Mistress Murtaviti, the more likely it is that she'll come up with a reason to deny us access to her husband's library. But I don't think I should make the decision for us. We may not be guilty of loosing a horde of ghouls on the city, but we certainly bear some responsibility. What do you think?"

"I think your reasoning is sound," Sienne said. "And I worry, too, that we've given Mistress Murtaviti time to do something rash, like burn the library or give it away. We can hunt ghouls later."

"I am not equipped with blessings to fight undead monsters," Perrin said, "and Averran did not grant me any unasked-for blessings of that nature, by which I surmise that he did not intend us to take that path today."

Kalanath just nodded. Dianthe said, "Let's hurry. I want this over with."

The stables were on the path between the gate and the Murtaviti home. They stopped just long enough to hand the horses over to the stable hands—Sienne kissed Spark's nose in apology for not settling her herself—and hurried across the city to Carissima Lane. The beautiful evening ought to have brought Fiorettans out in droves, enjoying an outdoor meal, listening to the street performers, or just strolling through the streets. Instead, Fioretti looked like a ruin recently abandoned, as if everyone had decided to leave for the country at the same time. The few people they encountered scurried along with their heads down, not meeting their eyes. Probably they were as afraid of scrappers as they were of ghouls. Given the kind of people some scrappers were, this wasn't so farfetched.

They saw one scrapper team in the distance, two men and two women striding along as confidently as if nothing were wrong in Fioretti. Sienne couldn't tell if they noticed her and her friends, though she couldn't imagine they didn't, but they behaved as if they were the only people in Fioretti. They disappeared along a side street before her team reached them, and Sienne felt unnatural relief at not having to encounter them. Normally they got along well with other scrappers—no, this wasn't true, scrappers saw each other as competition and didn't get friendly as a rule. But with a few notable exceptions, they didn't harbor any animosities toward other scrapper teams, and sometimes traded information with them. Now, however, Sienne superstitiously felt that coming face to face with another team would lead to blows. They'd win, probably, but it was the kind of delay they didn't need.

The narrow, winding streets of the south side seemed darker than usual, and Sienne found her gaze flicking from shadow to shadow, searching for ghouls hidden there. Alaric didn't say anything, but he moved closer to Sienne, shifting the position of the sword on his back for easier access. Without being prompted, Sienne drew out her spellbook and opened it to *burn*. The rough texture of the harness and the weight of the book calmed her spirits. Ghouls were no longer a mystery, after the fight at Scholten's estate, and were nothing to fear. Bernea Murtaviti's reaction to their appearance on her doorstep, however, was an unknown. If they were lucky, she'd let them in and give them access to Murtaviti's library with no resistance. Sienne had a feeling they'd run out of that kind of luck.

Alaric pounded on the door of number 34 with more force than Sienne thought was really needed. The street lay half in shadow, with some of the magically-lit glass bulbs dark and dormant. Probably no one wanted to venture out at night to renew the magic. Sienne made the ones nearest them glow brightly, surrounding them with a puddle of light that threw their shadows into sharp contrast. Nothing else moved in the street. Alaric pounded again. "Mistress Murtaviti!" he called out. "We have news of your husband!"

"Should we really announce that?" Dianthe murmured.

"It's true, isn't it?" Alaric pounded a third time.

"What if Master Murtaviti did something to her?" Sienne said. "We don't know if he went home before going to Mistress Tallavena's house. Suppose he..."

Alaric tried the knob. The door was locked. "Dianthe," he said, "maybe we ought to—"

The door flew open. "What are you doing here?" Mistress Murtaviti demanded. Her hair was a mess, her eyes were reddened, and her gown looked as if she'd been sleeping in it. "I have nothing more to say to you."

"We have news of your husband," Alaric repeated. "May we come in?"

"If this is about how I'm in danger from him, I already told you Pauro would never hurt me." Bernea made no move to indicate they were welcome.

"You're right, you're not in danger, but not for the reasons you believe," Alaric said, "and I really don't think we should have this conversation in the street, however empty it is. Please, Mistress Murtaviti. Just let us come in for five minutes."

Bernea's lips tightened. "Five minutes," she said. "Then I never want to see you again."

They followed her into the sitting room, which was once more arranged the way it had been on their first visit. Sienne sat with her back to the portrait wall and tried not to feel she was being watched. Whichever of those portraits represented Murtaviti's victims, she hoped they were free now.

Bernea took a seat opposite Alaric and clasped her hands tightly in her lap. "You said Pauro was returning to Fioretti, but I haven't seen him. Where is he?"

"He's dead," Alaric said. "He killed Drusilla Tallavena and attempted to kill Ivar Scholten, and we destroyed him."

Bernea's lips went white. "How can you admit to murder so calmly? What did Pauro ever do to you, that you could do such a thing?"

"We told you before that your husband turned himself into a lich. Destroying an undead isn't murder."

"And he tried to kill us, too," Dianthe added.

"You don't have proof for any of this—"

"Mistress Murtaviti," Perrin said, "we are sorry for your loss. It must be terrible to learn your husband was not the man you believed him to be. But I assure you, we did not act vindictively or out of malice. When he finished killing the members of his blight, he would almost certainly have turned on you next. You may feel obligated to defend Master Murtaviti out of loyalty, but please, do not align yourself with evil."

"Pauro was *not* evil!" Tears slid down Bernea's cheeks. "He was... he only..." She covered her face with her hands and let out a deep sob. Sienne exchanged glances with Dianthe, feeling torn between sympathy for the woman and a deep irritation that they couldn't just get Murtaviti's library and be done with it.

"We're sorry, mistress," Alaric said, his deep voice sounding unexpectedly compassionate. "There's no easy way to tell you this. Master Murtaviti was working toward lichhood for years. It wasn't something he decided to do in a single moment. He wasn't the man you thought he was."

Bernea lowered her hands and nodded. "I knew something was wrong," she said, "but I hoped...I hoped it was my imagination. Please don't ask me to thank you for what you did."

"We wouldn't," Dianthe said. "We're sorry for your suffering."

"Even though you're the cause of it?" Bernea laughed, a short, bitter sound. "I know. That's unfair."

"But understandable," Perrin said, leaning forward. "Mistress Murtaviti, we know you have no reason to love us, but we have a request. We would like to see Master Murtaviti's books."

This time, Bernea's laugh was longer and tinged with hysteria. "You have some nerve, asking favors of me!"

"It is nothing but what we originally asked. You told us then you would allow us access when we recovered your husband. He is no longer, forgive me, in a position to object. And his knowledge will benefit our endeavors greatly. Please, Bernea, this one boon could make all the difference."

Sienne was impressed at how smoothly Perrin had implied their interest in Murtaviti's library was altruistic. Bernea's reddened eyes closed briefly, then focused on Perrin. "I don't care anymore," she said, rising. "Take what you want and leave me alone."

"Thank you," Perrin said. "And we are truly sorry."

They followed her out of the sitting room and down a narrow hall, past the kitchen, where a woman in a white apron regarded them curiously, and up a flight of stairs at the rear of the house. Bernea opened a door to the left of the stairs and waved them in. "He didn't have much," she said. "I swear I never saw him do anything evil, and I wonder if he had some other place he went. This house isn't big enough for him to hide anything like that."

Sienne examined Murtaviti's library. Bernea was right; there wasn't much there. It was about the size of Scholten's hidden study, but barer, with only a single bookcase and a cabinet full of tiny drawers. More portraits, these full-length ones of Murtaviti and his wife done in oils, hung on the walls. A comfortable-looking armchair was drawn up near the room's one window, and a portable writing desk that fit over the arms of the chair stood on four stubby feet nearby.

Alaric immediately went to the bookcase and began removing books, examining each carefully and replacing them. Sienne was sure if Bernea Murtaviti weren't standing right there, he wouldn't have been so careful. She joined him and began searching a lower shelf. "Are these all the books he had?" she asked.

"We aren't great readers," Bernea said, her voice dull as if none of this interested her in the least.

Perrin opened one of the little drawers and closed it again with a snap. "More...souvenirs," he said. "Mistress Murtaviti, I suggest you destroy the contents of this room after we leave. Likely no one will care now that your husband is gone, but you should not risk being tarred with the necromancy brush."

"I don't want anything left to remind me. I'll burn it all."

Sienne reached the end of the shelf and moved to the next. "It's not as if anyone's left to object."

"As if I cared what they thought. Why aren't you harassing the rest of his blight? He certainly exchanged books with them often enough."

"The blight is dead, mistress," Dianthe said. She joined Perrin in looking through the drawers.

"It's not here," Alaric said, shoving a final book back into place. "Sienne?"

"No *Traverse of Memory*," Sienne agreed. She felt so discouraged she wanted to sit on the floor and cry.

"So what if they're dead? That should make it easier to get whatever it is you're looking for. Drusilla Tallavena, or that Samretto person." Bernea looked as if the names tasted bad.

"Uriane Samretto's library was sold off years ago," Perrin said. "If Master Murtaviti gave her the book, it could be anywhere by now."

Bernea's brow wrinkled. "Not Uriane," she said. "Myles Samretto. He borrowed books from Pauro just weeks ago."

24

"Myles Samretto? But he's no necromancer!" Sienne exclaimed. "You didn't mention him when you told us about your husband's blight."

Bernea shrugged. "He wasn't one of them. He just borrows books from Pauro now and again. I already told you we aren't great readers. The only books Pauro has are necromancy books. Maybe it's Myles's way of remembering his horrible wife. I don't know. Now, I want you out of here. And don't come back."

They were in the street before any of them could protest Bernea's hustling them out. Standing in the pool of light outside the Murtaviti home, Dianthe said, "Why would Myles Samretto want necromancy books?"

"I don't know," Alaric said. "But he definitely implied he knew nothing about necromancy." He shook his head. "I don't like it."

"Should we talk to him, then?" Sienne asked. "Or go back to Mistress Tallavena's house and search for the book there? Master Murtaviti might have loaned it to her."

Alaric shook his head again. "Mistress Tallavena said she destroyed all her necromancy equipment, and I doubt she has any books left. I think we need to pay a visit to Master Samretto. At the very least, he knows more than he let on. At worst, he's a secret member of the blight, and dangerous."

"That frail old man?" Perrin said. "I fail to see how he could be a danger to anything except, perhaps, a bowl of gruel."

"Do not think because he is old, he is finished with life," Kalanath said. "He has seen much and experienced much. If he is a necromancer, he has likely been one for many years. That does not sound safe."

"We'll be on our guard, at any rate," Alaric said. "Let's hurry. Those gates might be closed now that there's a real threat in Fioretti."

They ran through the darkening streets, across the Vochus River and up to the gated enclave where Myles Samretto lived. The gates were closed, and guards came to the alert as the five pelted up to them. "What's your business?" a heavily-built man said. He had bristly jowls that made Sienne think of a bulldog, set to watch his master's gate.

"We wish to speak with Master Samretto," Alaric said.

"Is he expecting you?"

"No. That is, not at this moment, but he invited us to return when we could, so yes, he wants to see us."

The jowly guard traded glances with his comrades. "Come back in the morning," he said. "Ghouls are abroad. We can't be responsible for your safety."

"Surely your enclosure is sufficient to defend against ghouls?" Perrin said.

"Master Samretto is old," Kalanath said, pushing his way to the front. "He has few visitors. You will not deny him this pleasure? What would you want for your own grandfathers?"

A thoughtful look crossed the guard's face. "Well..." He removed a large iron key from his belt and unlocked the gate. "You have until nine. That's when we set the dogs loose."

"We'll hurry. Thank you," Alaric said.

They ran faster now, past the sprawling houses of stone and glass whose colored slate roofs were dim in the twilight. The gardens were silent, the birds gone home to roost, and the sound of their feet on the cobbles echoed in the stillness. Few lights burned behind the expensive glass windows, as if the occupants wanted to draw as little attention to themselves as possible. Sienne had trouble imagining ghouls overrunning these estates, but she couldn't blame the residents for being afraid.

The Samretto house, unlike its neighbors, blazed with light at every window and from every lantern lining the path from the street to the door. Sienne, falling in behind Alaric, watched moths no bigger than her thumbnail flutter around the cold lights in confusion, beating against the bulbs and falling in a drunken spiral to the ground. She felt a moment's sympathy for them, drawn to something they couldn't understand. She couldn't guess why Myles Samretto had any interest in necromancy, or why he hadn't admitted it to them when he'd been so open about his wife's avocation.

Alaric knocked on the door a little more loudly than he probably needed to, but Sienne was sure he was as on edge as she was. She tried not to bounce on her toes restlessly. What time was it now? She'd lost track in all the running around town. If the guards were telling the truth about setting dogs loose after nine...well, *scream* or *shout* would work just as well to incapacitate dogs as any other creature, but she'd feel bad about attacking animals who were only doing their job.

The door opened. The same elderly woman peered out at them. "Yes? Oh, I remember you. It's rather late for a visit, don't you think?"

"We have an important question to ask Master Samretto," Alaric said. "We won't take much of his time."

"He's just finishing dinner. I'm sure he'd love to have you join him for a drink." The elderly woman stepped aside and beckoned them to enter.

The long hall of paintings was as brightly lit as the rest of the house. Sienne took a moment to admire the Muretti landscape, which depicted an eastern scene with the Bramantus Mountains in the background. The mountains glowed as if the sunlight within the painting were real light. It made the still lifes surrounding it look tawdry. Had Samretto painted them, perhaps, or his dead wife? He must have cared about the artist to give them pride of place next to a real masterpiece.

The small room was as brutally hot as before, the fire as bright. Even so, the elderly woman lit a lantern by the doorway, then another in the corner by the bookcases, and the room became nearly as bright as the hall outside. "Please, have a seat," she said. "The master will be along shortly."

The moment she shut the door behind her, Alaric took three quick strides that put him in front of the bookcases. "You don't think the book is *there*, do you?" Sienne asked.

"I'm not missing this opportunity to find out. Check the other shelves." Alaric ran his fingers along the bindings, pulling out books that didn't have titles imprinted on the spines. Sienne examined the other case. Kalanath and Dianthe sat in the ladderback chairs, while Perrin stood next to the fire and tied his hair more securely back from his face.

The sound of the door opening startled Sienne into shoving a book back into place and turning her back on the bookcase. Myles Samretto, wearing a dressing gown and soft-soled shoes, shuffled into the room, his wrinkled face beaming. "It's so good to see you again!" he exclaimed, offering Kalanath his hand. "*Welcome to home mine,*" he added in Meiric.

"Thank you," Kalanath said.

Sienne took a seat and hoped she didn't look as guilty as she felt.

Samretto adjusted the enormous smoked glasses covering his eyes and sank slowly into his armchair. "Tell me of your adventures. You're scrappers, yes? You must have such exciting lives. Have you heard about the ghouls infesting our city? Terrible, so terrible."

"Yes, we learned of it when we were in Onofreo," Perrin said. "The king has offered a bounty on them."

"They must be a real problem if the temples can't defeat them without help," Samretto said. "Ah, Mariane, thank you," he said, addressing the elderly woman, who entered bearing a tray containing several small glasses and a bottle of wine. "Will you join me in a drink? I admit to indulging on occasion."

"I...thank you, it is most kind of you," Perrin said. Mariane set the tray on a nearby table and withdrew. Samretto picked up the bottle and offered it to Alaric.

"Would you mind? My hands aren't what they used to be," he said. Alaric nodded and poured a measure of dark red wine into each of the glasses, then offered the first to Samretto. Samretto smiled and nodded. "Forgive my surprise, but young people today don't always have the best manners. Thank you." He drank off half his wine in one draught, patted his lips, and sighed with pleasure.

Sienne, following Alaric's lead, sipped her wine. It was full-bodied and not what she was used to drinking after dinner, but it was very good nonetheless. She noticed Perrin only pretended to drink, wetting his lips and swiftly setting the glass to one side. It occurred to her, too late, that it might have been drugged—but Samretto had drunk the wine himself, and what reason would he have for drugging them, since he couldn't know of their suspicions? She sipped again. Facing Samretto, seeing again his frailty and air of openness, made her doubt her assumptions.

"But Mariane tells me you have a question. How can this old man help you?" Samretto asked, putting down his glass and folding his hands together over his thin chest.

"Ah..." Perrin looked to Alaric for a hint.

"It's about necromancy," Alaric said.

"You do seem obsessed with it. You're not planning on going into business, are you? I'd have to report that!" Samretto laughed, a high, tittering sound that made Sienne uncomfortable.

"We were wondering," Alaric said, unmoved by his laughter, "why you borrowed necromancy books from Pauro Murtaviti."

The laughter trailed off. "Who told you that?"

"Mistress Murtaviti. She said you borrowed books only a few weeks ago."

Samretto drained his glass and set it on the tray with a *click*. "And you believed her? Why would I want necromancy books?"

"She had no reason to lie." Alaric took a step forward, forcing Samretto to crane his skinny neck to look up at him. "We're looking for a particular book and we hoped you might have it. Your reasons are none of our business."

Samretto shook his head. "I see," he said. "So this isn't a threat."

"It doesn't have to be."

"Then please, sit down. It's like looking at a mountaintop."

Alaric took a few steps back and leaned against the wall. "You're out of chairs."

"So I am. Well, that will have to do." Samretto sat up and leaned forward until he was nearly nose to nose with Kalanath. "I loved my wife, you know," he said as if he and Kalanath were the only ones in the room. "She never wanted to hurt anyone. She only wanted knowledge."

"And yet she wanted to become a lich," Kalanath said. He sipped his wine and set the glass down.

"That was only part of what she wanted. She longed for immortality, yes, but only because it would allow her greater communion with the spirits. And she wanted to best that little wart Pauro. He never cared about the spirits as people, just as counters in a game he and the others played. If she hadn't died...well, that's in the past."

"If she hadn't died, she would have become a creature of evil," Perrin said. "You cannot have wished that for her."

"Oh, I think evil is what you make of it, don't you?" Samretto's trembling hand extended toward Perrin. "It matters more why we take the actions we do. You didn't know Uriane, so you wouldn't realize that evil simply wasn't in her nature."

"How many murders did she commit on her path to lichhood?" Alaric asked, his voice dangerously low. "Or are you going to argue as Ivar Scholten did, that she only killed people who deserved death?"

"She certainly never tortured anyone. I'm sure they were all painless, quick deaths."

"You—" Sienne began, but Alaric cut her off.

"We're not going to argue over whether your wife was justified in what she did," he said. "She's no longer in a position to pursue her goals."

"That's true," Samretto said. "She's content with where she is now."

Dianthe drew in a breath. "You've spoken with her spirit. That's why the necromancy books."

"You're quick, young lady. I couldn't bear simply letting her go. I'd seen her summon spirits so often, it was only natural I follow in her footsteps. I never truly understood her passion until I performed my first ritual. It's the most extraordinary feeling. *You* understand, don't you?" Samretto's dark-spectacled gaze turned on Sienne, and she saw his eyes gleam behind the smoked lenses. "You've done it, too. I can tell. There's a look about those of us who've touched the spirit realm."

"I didn't—all right, I have spoken with a spirit, but it wasn't—it was necessary to stop Master Murtaviti. I certainly wouldn't do it for fun!" Sienne wished he'd look elsewhere. His eyeless regard chilled her.

Samretto laughed, that same high-pitched titter that set Sienne's nerves on edge. "I wouldn't call it fun, myself. Exhilarating, perhaps. Though I feel sorry for the spirits who are reluctant to respond. They fight the call. I don't force them to stay."

"You should not summon them in the first place, if they wish not to return," Perrin said, frowning.

"Oh, but you can't tell how they'll react unless you call them. Besides, some of them know so much. Ancient kings, long-dead priests—"

"I cannot bear this," Perrin said, rising abruptly enough that his chair scooted back a few inches. "We seek a particular book Master Murtaviti had. *Traverse of Memory*. Do you have it? Give it to us, and we will trouble you no more."

"Now, that's not very polite," Samretto said, his frown matching Perrin's. "I've been a good host and I think I'm entitled to a little consideration."

"We have traveled long today and are tired," Kalanath said. "Forgive our companion's outburst."

"Traveled? Yes, you said you were in Onofreo. I assume you spoke with Ivar Scholten. How is he?"

"Dead," Alaric said. "He turned on us, and it cost him his life."

Samretto's mouth fell open. "You *killed* Ivar?"

"No, he died fleeing after trying to kill Sienne and setting his undead minions on us."

"Even so—but then Ivar truly was an evil man, and I'm sure his death was justified. Or would you call fighting him evil, too?"

Sienne cast a glance at Alaric, whose dispassionate expression surely concealed more powerful emotions. "I don't think it's evil to fight for one's life," she said.

"Then you agree with me that evil is what you make of it."

"I...no, I don't. I think. I don't know what you mean."

"Evil is just a matter of perspective. If you take a life, isn't it justified if that life was someone who would have killed you, or an innocent? I don't think there's such a thing as evil in the abstract."

The wine had gone to Sienne's head, or maybe it was the conversation that dizzied her. "I must disagree with you," Perrin said. "We destroyed an undead creature whose many foul actions made him intrinsically evil. And, contrariwise, I think one would have to conclude that the avatars of God are inherently good."

"What undead creature?" Samretto sat up, looking like a curious spaniel.

"Pauro Murtaviti achieved lichhood," Perrin said. "We destroyed him, nearly at the cost of our own lives."

Samretto's mouth fell open again. Then his thin, pale lips compressed in anger. "So Pauro did it. You'd think I would have known. And you destroyed him? I'm glad to hear it. He didn't deserve immortality."

"No one deserves immortality at that price," Perrin said. "Regardless of what you may think about your wife, she would have become evil if she had succeeded in her quest."

"You keep saying that," Samretto said, rising to face Perrin. He wasn't trembling. "You know so little and yet you are so convinced you are right. I assure you, things are not as black and white as you insist."

Dianthe rose to stand next to Perrin. "Why would you have

known about Master Murtaviti?" she said in the quiet voice she used when she was thinking hard.

Samretto turned to look at her. "Did I say that? I should have been more careful, but you surprised me." He raised his hand to remove his dark glasses. "Though I imagine I have a few surprises for you, as well."

His eyes glowed with an unholy, yellow light.

25

Perrin staggered backward, gripping Dianthe's arm and drawing her with him. Sienne went for her spellbook, but found herself held by an unseen force that froze Perrin in the act of reaching for his riffle of blessings. She couldn't even move her head to see if Alaric and Kalanath were held as well, but heard no movement. Blinking was nearly impossible.

Samretto set the glasses down on the arm of his chair and chuckled, a more normal sound than the tittering laugh. "I intended not to reveal myself. You're nice young people, after all, and there's no reason we should come to blows. But when you said you'd killed Pauro—well, that and your complete wrongheadedness about the nature of my transformation—at any rate, it would be only a matter of time before you came after me. You'd probably think it was your duty or something tedious like that."

"The amulet—" Perrin mumbled through stiff lips.

"Amulet?" Samretto felt around Perrin's neck until he found the citrine amulet, then swore and thrust it away, waving his fingers as if they burned. "It lets you perceive the presence of the undead, is that it? I perform a ritual every morning that disguises my nature. I could hardly worship in a chapel, or pay my devotions at a temple, if that weren't the case. You see? How can you consider me inherently evil when I'm a faithful follower of Delanie?"

"If you have to disguise your nature, you must be conscious that Delanie and her servants would reject you if they knew the truth," Perrin said.

"How are you holding us?" Sienne said. "You're not a wizard, are you?"

"Not at all." Samretto slid Sienne's spellbook out of her hand and lifted the harness from around her shoulder. "It's a part of the ritual to become a lich. Ivar called it opening a conduit, but I'm afraid I never understood his research. It doesn't matter. I have no need for magic—well, except in circumstances like this." He put the spellbook on the seat of his chair. "Normally I use a drink I distill myself, one that renders my victim pliant without harming him. But I had no idea you were a threat to me. I suppose I'll have to do this the hard way."

"What 'this'?" Alaric said.

"Well, I can't let you walk out of here knowing my secret. I could make you my undead servants, but I have enough of those that it's becoming difficult to conceal them. I'll just have to kill you and bury your bodies behind the house. Nobody questions old Myles Samretto puttering about in his garden."

"You can't hold us forever," Alaric said. "We've killed one lich and we can certainly kill another."

Samretto approached Alaric, his hand raised as if to caress the big man's face. "You—"

Sienne snatched her spellbook with her invisible fingers and slung it at the back of Samretto's head.

It hit him hard enough to bounce. The old man cried out and clapped a hand to his head. The grip holding Sienne vanished, and she snatched the spellbook back, flipping it open to *change*. She had to force herself not to read too quickly, for once resenting the honey-sweet taste of the transform and how *slow* it was.

Quicker than thought, Samretto was in her face, grabbing her shoulder. A well-remembered jolt ran through her, and she cried out as the lassitude that followed it dragged her to the floor, her muscles unable to support her weight. Her spellbook fell from her nerveless hands, which turned stiff as stone. She tried to cry out again in protest, but her lungs wouldn't respond, her throat was paralyzed, and she couldn't even roll her face away from the scratchy rug that smelled of dust and old smoke. Spots formed before her eyes as her lungs struggled to draw in air.

"Sienne!" Alaric shouted. "Don't let him touch you!"

It's a little late for that, Sienne thought. Her eyes ached from dryness. She made herself breathe shallowly, but it wasn't enough, she was going to suffocate—

A hand rested on her shoulder again. "O Lord, have patience in your crankiness, and grant me this blessing," Perrin gabbled out. Instantly Sienne's muscles relaxed, and she collapsed onto the carpet, sucking in air. "Do not rise until you can breathe freely," Perrin said, and then he was gone. Sienne didn't need the advice. She breathed deeply, hating the stink of the carpet, until her vision cleared. Then she carefully sat up, gathering her spellbook to her.

Everything was confusion. Kalanath was pinned to the ceiling by Samretto's unnatural magic. Dianthe and Alaric both had drawn their swords, but the room was too small for them to wield them properly. Perrin gripped his riffle of blessings, clearly at a loss as to which one to use. Little fires burned everywhere, threatening the walls and the books, and another erupted near the door as Samretto flung fire at Alaric, who dodged. Sienne opened her book once again to *change* and read as quietly as she dared. So long as the others kept Samretto distracted, she had a chance.

She'd never cast *change* before and had no idea what to expect. It felt as if something were resisting her wizardry, pushing back against the image she held in her mind. The syllables of the spell came more slowly, almost slowly enough to ruin the casting. She made herself stay focused on the smoothly curving lines of the script, on the image in her head, and with the final syllable felt the spell burst away from her like a falcon stooping to its prey.

Samretto jerked. Kalanath, still on the ceiling, dropped and landed catlike on all fours. Samretto's body blinked, and vanished. Sienne tossed her spellbook aside and dove on what he'd become. Her fingers closed over smooth, slick skin that writhed in an attempt to get away from her. With a shriek, she dragged the frog close to her chest and, panting, held it against its struggles. "Somebody help me! He'll remember what he is in a minute!"

Alaric's huge hands closed over hers, taking the frog away. "What did you do?"

"Transformed him. It won't last—you have to kill him *now!*"

With an unexpected look of squeamishness, Alaric's hands closed on the frog. It gave out a strangled croak, and fell still. Alaric tossed the little body into the fire, but as it hit the logs, it blinked again, and Samretto lay there, half in the fire, half lying on the floor. Alaric dragged him out of the fireplace and laid him out on the hearth. "Ew," he said. "That was anticlimactic."

"It is not over," Perrin said. The fire gave off a dark, stinking smoke that stung Sienne's eyes. "We have not destroyed his reliquary."

"But his body can burn. There will be nothing left," Kalanath said, retrieving his staff.

"My mentor learned this the hard way. A lich's spirit is powerful enough to reconstitute its body from whatever is handy. We saw Master Murtaviti heal his wounds from the dark energy that fueled his undead. We do not know how many undead Master Samretto made, nor where they are. His spirit could be anywhere by now. We must find his reliquary and destroy it before he is restored."

Sienne summoned water to fall over Alaric's hands. He wiped them dry on the back of Samretto's armchair. "The *reliquary* could be anywhere. Would it have been transformed with him?"

"I don't think so," Sienne said, "not with as much necromantic power as they pour into them. He didn't have it on him."

The door opened, startling all of them. "Master, it's—" Mariane said. She had a small tray in her hands with a cup and a pitcher of water. She looked down at where Samretto lay on the hearth. "Master? *Master!*"

Alaric grabbed her, knocking the tray out of her hands and dragging her into the room. "Did you know what your master was?" he growled.

"Let me go!" the woman shrieked. "If you've hurt Master Samretto, I'll have the law on you!"

"The law will be on our side. Destroying the undead isn't a crime."

"Undead?" Mariane's eyes flicked nervously from Alaric to Perrin and back to Alaric. "I—he isn't—"

"You knew something was wrong," Perrin said. "Do you imagine anyone will believe you were not complicit?"

Mariane sagged. "Master Samretto is a good man," she said. "We all know it. He never hurt anyone..." Her voice faded.

"You're thinking. Good," Alaric said. He released her, but stood between her and the door. "Did your master have a...a special object? A trinket? It might look like a large pendant, or a jewel."

"I don't know anything about it!"

"Start searching," Alaric told the others. "You, Mariane. Did your master have any secret places? Where did he do his necromancy?"

Mariane's lips tightened. "I won't help you destroy him."

"Your master murdered his way to becoming an undead thing," Perrin said, pausing in his search of the knickknacks on the mantel. "However good he was to you, does that negate the evils he has committed?"

"They were all deserving of death. Murderers, rapists..." But she looked uncertain.

"Neither you nor Master Samretto are entitled to decide the fates of others," Perrin went on. "If you knew his victims were evil, why did you not turn them over to the guard, or the magistrates, or even the sanctuaries of Averran? You chose to allow their deaths to fuel your master's mad quest. You are as guilty as he."

"I am *not*," Mariane replied. Her eyes went wide, and her hand went to her throat. Black mist poured from her open mouth, and she convulsed, choking and thrashing as she fell to the floor. Perrin took a step toward her.

"Stop!" Alaric shouted, shoving Perrin to the side. "It's Samretto!" He brought his sword up for a heavy two-handed swing at Mariane's head.

Mariane rolled out of the way as the sword came whistling down at her, coming to her feet in a move too agile for a woman of her age. Her eyes glowed malevolent yellow. "You're much smarter than I gave you credit for, mountain," she said. "I will make you suffer for forcing me to kill Mariane. She was a good, loyal servant for many years."

"That was your choice, lich," Alaric said, advancing on him.

Samretto/Mariane backed toward the fire, away from him and out of reach of Dianthe as well, before coming up against his own dead body. "You'll never find my reliquary," he said. "It's well hidden, far away." He smiled as if at a private joke. "Far, *far* away..."

Alaric swung. Samretto caught the blade between his palms, stopping it inches from his face. "Your young Omeiran friend can do this," he said. "Well, maybe not *this*." He switched his grip and, with no apparent effort, broke Alaric's sword in half.

Alaric stepped backward, lowering the broken sword. Samretto threw the fragment of blade into the fire and advanced on him. Sienne opened her spellbook to *change* and began reading. Something picked her up and hurled her at the door, which flew open under her weight. She coughed, scrambled backward, and tried to read again. The resistance was greater than before, slowing her reading, blurring the lines of the transform together, and she knew the moment she'd failed. She tried again, focusing harder.

Samretto's magic picked her up and held her mid-air, then shook her hard until the spellbook fell from her hands and dangled in its harness. "I won't let that happen again," he said, his words the more menacing coming from Mariane's lips, and threw her down the hall to hit one of the alabaster vases. She cried out as her head and arm cracked against the wall, and she bit her tongue, tasting blood. Stunned, she lay still for a moment, then pushed herself upright and screamed at the pain in her right arm. Broken. She used her other arm to get herself to her feet and swayed with dizziness. So, not *change*, and *force* and *scream* wouldn't work, but she couldn't sit around and do nothing.

She staggered back down the hall, leaning against the wall with her left arm to keep her balance and knocking a few of the still lifes to the floor. They were ugly things, not like the Muretti—

Sienne stopped in front of it. It was a stupid idea, but it would take all of two seconds to prove. She grabbed the painting awkwardly by the top of the frame and lifted it off the wall.

Behind it was a wall safe.

Sienne stared. "*Dianthe!*" she screamed, and staggered toward Samretto's study. Kalanath was on the floor, with Perrin crouched over him; by the sprawled, graceless look of his body, Samretto had paralyzed him. Dianthe and Alaric had Samretto flanked, though he seemed unconcerned about this. Alaric had thrown away his broken sword and stood with fists raised in a defensive stance that would do him no good if the lich got his hands on him. Dianthe's sword was gory with reddish-black ooze, showing she'd gotten in at least one completely ineffectual blow. "Dianthe!" Sienne screamed again. "Over here!"

Dianthe's brow furrowed. "What—"

Sienne used her invisible fingers to open her book to *castle* and backed away until she was in the hallway next to the safe. Swiftly she read off the summoning, swallowing more blood, until she felt the welcome jerk and pull of the spell, the dizzying drop, and blinked to find herself on the floor behind Samretto. Instantly she willed her book open to *change*. She was going to keep trying until it worked, damn it. "The safe!" she shouted at Dianthe, and began reading the spell.

Samretto cursed and gestured. Alaric flew toward the ceiling, flailing for balance. Then Kalanath was there, his staff spinning. "You will not win," he said, "and I am sorry I ever felt compassion for you."

"I liked you," Samretto said. "I'm sorry to have to kill you."

Kalanath whipped his staff around to catch Samretto under the chin, knocking him backward into Sienne, who lost control of *change* and had to scramble away one-handed to avoid his grasp. Kalanath pressed the attack, slamming into Samretto's borrowed body again and again. It didn't seem to hurt him, but Alaric dropped, landing more heavily than Kalanath had. Samretto snarled and gestured again, and Kalanath went flying, but Alaric was there, laying into him with his huge fists. Sienne scooted away farther and tried *change* again. They just had to keep him occupied—and pray he didn't have so many precious possessions he had more than one secret place to hide them.

"Back away!" Perrin shouted, and Alaric flung himself backward just as a pearly gray shield sprang up around Samretto. Mariane's body looked horribly beaten, and black blood poured from a wound low on her back, but it moved as smoothly as ever. Samretto threw himself at the shield, pounding on it once, then stepped back and summoned fire—not on the shield, but on Alaric and Perrin.

Sienne screamed and summoned the largest mass of water she could, which wasn't enough. She did it again as the two men fell and rolled on the floor, trying to put out the fire. Sienne could hear Samretto laughing, not the horrible titter but something deep and sinister. She wished she could set him on fire, but the shield protected him, something she cursed Perrin for even as she knew it was the smartest thing he could have done.

Then Samretto's eye fell on her, and suddenly the air was full of fire, and she incautiously gasped in surprise and sucked in a lungful of fire. She dropped and beat at herself with her good hand, trying not to scream. The fire, and her broken arm, hurt too badly for her to summon water. Then there were other hands, and someone threw a rug—the horrible smelly rug—over her, smothering the flames. She gasped, and tears came to her eyes from the pain, but the fire was out.

"I've got it!" Dianthe shouted. Sienne sat up in time to see her rush into the room, holding a prism made of bone and black glass that gleamed in the brilliant light from the lanterns and the fire. Something swept her off her feet, flinging her at the ceiling, but she flung the thing hard at the floor. It bounced.

All four of them dove for it, with Kalanath getting there first.

"Break it, Sienne!" he shouted, tossing it toward her. It stopped midair, changing direction to fly toward the shield, and Sienne snatched up her spellbook and let the syllables of *break* roll off her tongue, sweet and oh so slow.

The shield popped. Samretto held up his hand to catch the reliquary. Alaric threw himself at the lich, bearing him down and making him miss his catch. The reliquary struck the far wall, bounced again, and rolled toward the fire. Samretto screamed and gestured just as the final syllables of *break* shot away from Sienne.

The spell struck the reliquary. The bone cracked all along one of the prism's long sides. Samretto screamed again, a high, shrill sound that went on far longer than human lungs could sustain. Black mist poured from Mariane's abused lips once more, filling the air and then dissipating into nothing. Mariane's body sagged under Alaric, and he rose, stepping away from her with alacrity. He was breathing heavily. Sienne dropped her spellbook and closed her eyes.

"Is it over?" Dianthe asked.

"It's over," Alaric said.

"No, it isn't," Sienne said. "We don't have the book." She incautiously tried to pick up her spellbook with her right hand and hissed with pain, closing her eyes.

"Hold still," Perrin said, kneeling beside her and resting one hand on her arm above the break. He muttered an invocation, and green light played along Sienne's forearm, filling the air with the scent of jasmine and mint. Sienne took a deep breath and flexed her arm. It was the only part of her that didn't hurt.

"Are you well, Sienne?" Alaric asked. When she nodded, he said, "We have to get out of here. It's not going to look good if anyone finds us here, with Samretto vanished and Mariane very dead."

"But we need the book."

"Then let's split up and search." Alaric went back to the bookcases to resume his search. "Unless it was in with the reliquary."

"There was just money in the safe," Dianthe said. "We need his secret room, assuming—"

Heavy footsteps sounded in the hall, and Sienne turned in time to see a couple of armed women in the uniform of the Fiorettan city guard push through the broken door. "On the floor, all of you!" the heavier of the two shouted.

26

"This is a misunderstanding," Perrin said, holding his hands up in a placating manner. "If you will allow us—"

"I said *down!*" the woman shouted, drawing her sword. "Invading this man's home, stealing his goods—you think I won't use this if you cross me?"

Sienne, who was still sitting, joined the others in lying face first on the floor. Now the awful rug smelled of fresh smoke and char as well as dust. One of the guards snatched her spellbook from around her shoulder, and she resisted the urge to protest, even though despair threatened to engulf her. Alaric was right that it looked bad. They needed someone who knew about the undead to prove they'd destroyed a lich, and the odds of these guards letting them contact anyone like that were low.

More footsteps sounded in the hall. "What happened here?" a man said. Not Denys Renaldi, thank all the avatars.

"They broke into this house and killed these people. Looks like they intended to rob the place, and the owners surprised them," said their captor.

"That's not true," Alaric said.

"Shut up. You'll have your chance to argue your case. Sir, did you see the safe?" The footsteps retreated.

"Sienne, quick, take the reliquary," Alaric whispered. Sienne turned her head. The room was empty of guards. The reliquary lay about a foot from her face. She whisked it toward herself with her invisible fingers and tucked it into her belt pouch just as the footsteps returned. Someone leaned over her and fastened iron manacles on her wrists, binding her hands behind her.

"You're not going to give us any trouble, are you, wizard?" the woman said.

Sienne shook her head. "We're innocent," she began, and the woman slapped her. Alaric growled a warning.

"So he's sweet on you," the woman said with a laugh. "Don't worry, big fellow, we won't hurt her. We're not criminals like you lot."

The woman hauled Sienne to her feet. Around her, more guards were doing the same for her friends. "Where are you taking us?" she asked.

"A nice little cell," the woman said. "For now."

Sienne let them march her out of Samretto's house, which was surrounded by guards. She wondered if the enclave guards would still let the dogs loose if the city guard was roaming free. Probably not.

The guard station they were taken to was only half a mile from the enclave, but in a much more rundown area than Denys's post. The guard post itself had a much seedier look to it, its gray brickwork crumbling and its front door sagging on leather hinges. Inside, the plaster walls were cracked, the paint peeling, and the front desk tilted as if two of its four legs were the wrong length. The woman at the desk regarded their little group with a complete lack of interest. "There's only two cells free," she said.

"They can share. They're all such good friends," the guard said with a sneer. "Downstairs, the lot of you."

These cells looked much more like what Sienne had expected—cold, dank, dark, and rustling with some kind of verminous life. She made herself submit to being searched and her belt knife, boot knife, and pouch removed. She almost made a grab for the pouch, with its precious contents that were all the proof they had that their story was true, but remembered in time she didn't want to draw attention to it. Then she shuffled into the cell with Dianthe and sat on the moldy bench as the guard locked the door on them.

Across the narrow corridor between the cells, Alaric gripped the bars as if he wished he could throttle them. "Is everyone all right?"

"I'm just fine, precious, thanks for caring," a high pitched male voice said from the depths of the next cell over.

Alaric ignored him. "We're probably here until morning, so let's see if we can get some rest," he said. "Tomorrow we'll send to the temple of Kitane and see if we can't get that divine, Octavian, to speak for us. He can testify that we were hunting a lich, and that we destroyed the reliquary."

"Will that be enough?" Dianthe said.

"That, and the increased—"

"The ghoul presence in Fioretti will redouble," Perrin said, over-riding Alaric. "This will either be evidence in our behalf, or the guard will be too busy dealing with the renewed bounties to be overly concerned with our fate."

"Shut up, people are trying to sleep," a woman in the cell next to Sienne's said.

"What if they won't let us send a message?" Sienne asked.

"Then I will pray for a communication blessing that will allow me to speak with Octavian," Perrin said. "Do not fear, Sienne, this is merely a temporary setback."

"I said *shut up!*" the woman shouted.

Someone thundered down the stairs. "All of you, shut it or I'll make you wish you'd never been born," said the woman from the desk.

"Let me out and we will see who suffers," Kalanath said, gripping the bars tight.

The woman looked him over. "You're too skinny to be worth my time," she said, and turned and went back up the stairs.

Kalanath blinked. "I have not been dismissed like that before," he said. "It is strange."

"Try to sleep," Alaric said, clapping Kalanath on the shoulder. "I admit it seems unlikely."

"I think there are roaches in here," Sienne said, shuddering. "I'm afraid to touch anything. And this bench smells like old cheese."

"It's jail, Sienne," Dianthe said. "It's not supposed to be pleasant." She sat on the floor with her back to the wall and tilted her head back, closing her eyes.

Sienne wormed her way around on the bench until she found a marginally less uncomfortable position. She curled up on her side and tucked her hands under her head for a pillow. Silence fell, broken only by the breathing of seven or eight people and the skittering of insect feet. It was not how she'd pictured her first night back in Fioretti. She'd hoped to spend it with Alaric. Now who knew how long it would be before they were free, before the ghoul problem was resolved—they would have to join in the hunt, not because of the bounty but because it was in one sense their fault—and before they found the book? If they even could. It was unlikely they'd be allowed to search Samretto's things, even if they were exonerated of guilt in his death.

Dianthe let out a gentle snore. "Oh, for the love of Kitane, somebody muzzle her!" the irate woman exclaimed. Sienne grinned, and let the arrhythmic music of Dianthe's snoring lull her exhausted body into sleep.

She came out of a dream of Alaric tickling her face with a feather to find the tickling was real. "*Oh!*" she exclaimed, sitting up fast and batting the roach away. "Oh, oh, that's so disgusting!"

"They're cleaner than we are," said Sienne's neighbor. Sunlight leaking through the narrow, barred window at the end of the row of cells revealed her to be a hard-lived middle age, her hair as messy as Sienne's no doubt was and her face round and plump. She stood leaning against the bars as casually as if they were in the woman's own home. "Cleaner, and more sociable."

"I don't think that's true," Sienne said.

Dianthe came awake with a gasp, then shut her eyes as if even the wan light pained her. "Have they fed us yet? I don't suppose there's coffee."

The woman laughed. "No coffee. You'll have to do without."

Dianthe groaned, prompting a stirring from the men's side. "You have said the terrible word 'no' in conjunction with the blessed syllables of 'coffee,'" Perrin groaned. "We cannot get out of here quickly enough."

"Don't get your hopes up, darling, the guards don't care about the likes of us," the thin man in the next cell said, rising and stretching like a cat. He had a silent cellmate, someone hulking and broad as Alaric, but a foot and a half shorter, making him look like an animate wall.

"I intended to wait to petition Averran until the day was rather more ripe than it currently is, but under the circumstances I hope he will understand my importunacy," Perrin said. A confused frown crossed the face of the silent wall, as if he only understood half Perrin's words.

Perrin sat cross-legged on the hard-packed earth of the floor and patted his vest. A look of chagrin touched his eyes. "They have taken my blessing papers."

"Do they have to be rice paper? I have my notebook still," Sienne said. "Though they took my pencil. I don't know if they thought I might try to stab someone with it."

"Averran once made footwear out of three lengths of canvas and a pair of forks," Perrin said. "He understands improvisation."

Sienne used her invisible fingers to send her palm-sized notebook across to Perrin, who tore a few pages out and ripped them into smaller squares. He settled them on his lap and closed his eyes, resting his hands loosely on his knees. "O great and crotchety Lord," he said, "forgive the earliness of my appeal, for we are in need."

"Is he a *priest?*" the woman exclaimed. Sienne shushed her, though she knew from experience Perrin could pray amid terrible distractions.

"We have performed a great service," Perrin went on, "and have received what are traditionally the wages of a good deed, namely that it does not go unpunished. I must communicate—"

He broke off mid-sentence, and his tanned skin visibly flushed. "My Lord, are you *laughing?* I do not think—well, yes, I suppose it is somewhat humorous—actually, I have spent a most uncomfortable night without the promise of blissful coffee—" He went silent again, his lips pressed hard together. "Your mirth is less than salutary in these circumstances, o good and cantankerous Lord. Now, if you are quite finished—"

A sizzle of white smoke, a whiff of jasmine and mint, and Perrin opened his eyes. "He thought the entire adventure hilarious," he muttered. "Sometimes I do not understand the divine mind." He sorted through the papers on his lap. "Here, this one will allow me to communicate with one person. I hope the divine is willing to help us."

Footsteps sounded on the stairs. "Breakfast," said an older man in a guard's uniform who bore a tray laden with bowls. He was followed by a younger man twirling a ring of keys on his finger. "Back away from the doors."

Sienne obediently backed up to the wall, but stopped short of leaning against it. Some of the stains looked fresh and oily. She waited for the guard to set two bowls of porridge inside the door and lock it again before moving forward. The porridge tasted as oily as the walls looked, but she ate it without complaint; her stomach felt ready to mutiny from hunger. She couldn't remember when they'd last eaten—they hadn't had an evening meal before confronting Mistress Murtaviti.

Alaric downed his food in silence, his grim expression the only sign that he hated it. Kalanath ate swiftly, then took hold of the upper bars of the cell and started a series of chin-ups. Perrin eyed him skeptically. "Your commitment to your exercise regimen is laudable, but I do not think I could maintain it under these circumstances."

"I am bored," Kalanath said. "When I am bored, I fidget or I exercise."

"Very well. I will attempt to make contact with Octavian." Perrin once again settled himself on the floor, closed his eyes, and clasped his hands loosely in his lap. Sienne watched him. Nothing happened. Kalanath went to the bench and began doing push-ups.

The older guard came thundering down the stairs again. He opened the cell opposite Sienne's and gestured to the thin man. "Pay your fine, and you're free to go, Larussi," he said. "As usual."

"Are you arrested often?" Sienne asked, unable to stop herself.

"I'm a familiar face around here, precious," Larussi said with a wink. His stolid cellmate didn't react to his leaving, just sat and stared at Sienne. "Goodbye, all, and here's hoping your fines aren't too stiff."

Perrin opened his eyes and let out a deep breath. "I have done all I can," he said, "and now we must wait to see what will happen."

"Did he say he would come?" Dianthe asked.

"I have no idea. I did not, as it were, pay for a response. The blessing was to send a message only. But I hope I piqued his interest."

Kalanath stood and stretched. "If that means you make him want to know our story, then I hope so too."

Alaric, who'd been uncharacteristically silent, turned and paced the confines of the cell. It didn't allow him much room for pacing. "Samretto said he normally drugged his victims," he said. "I wonder..."

"Wonder what?" Dianthe said. "You don't think—isn't it a bit of a coincidence if he'd stumbled on the potion we're looking for?"

"No more than if he had the right book. We were looking for a potion that went with a binding ritual, right? Someone has to have the book, and there's no reason it couldn't be him."

"You're necromancers," the woman said, backing away from Sienne into a corner of her cell. "Guards! *Guards!* Somebody help me!"

"Oh, for Kitane's sake, we're not necromancers," Dianthe said.

The woman kept shouting. This time, a female guard they hadn't seen before came down the stairs, a guardsman's truncheon in her hand. "Shut up, you," she said, smacking the bars and making them ring dully.

"They're necromancers! You can't leave me in here with them! I'm as good as dead!"

The guard looked at Alaric, whom she clearly saw as the biggest potential threat. "What's she talking about?"

"I have no idea," Alaric said blandly. "She's probably still drunk. Been babbling all night about monsters."

"Liar!" The woman shot forward and gripped the bars. "He's lying —they were just talking about potions and rituals—they're going to use me for their evil magic—"

"You're all in separate cages. Give it a rest." The guard smacked the bars one last time and went back upstairs.

"If you're afraid we're necromancers, you really ought to be more polite," Alaric said.

"We shouldn't discuss this in public," Sienne said. "We have to wait, and hope Octavian comes soon."

Alaric shrugged. "You're right. It's not as if we can work our evil magic in here."

The woman cringed. Alaric smiled a pleasant, non-threatening smile. "Stop taunting her," Sienne said, but she couldn't help laughing as she did.

They waited. The sunlight slanted across the cells and turned into a diffuse afternoon light. No one came to feed them at noon. "Two meals a day," Dianthe said, making Sienne wonder what experiences she'd had to be so certain. She sat on the stinking bench and practiced her small magics, spark and invisible fingers and ghost sound, the last of which sent their neighbor into a frightened huddle. Sienne tried to feel bad about it, but it wasn't as if ghost sound could hurt anyone, and the woman was unnaturally skittish.

Finally, as she was about to tear the hem of her shirt so she could practice magically mending it, footsteps sounded on the stairs, and three people came into the jail. One was the female guard with the truncheon. The second was a strange man dressed in magistrate's robes. The third was the divine Octavian. Sienne shot to her feet and gripped the bars.

"These are the five I spoke to four days ago," Octavian said. "They informed me they were pursuing a lich—a powerful undead creature."

"I've never heard of a lich," the magistrate said. "I don't see what it has to do with the very serious matter they're charged with."

"We have not heard the charges against us," Perrin said.

The guard said, "Entering someone's home illegally. Attempted robbery. The murder of Master Myles Samretto and his house-keeper. We're still working on learning what more they might have done."

"We did not kill Master Samretto," Perrin said. "He was a lich. When his body was killed, he took the body of his housekeeper, the woman you found dead."

"I can't believe you're confessing to these crimes. Don't you have any sense of self-preservation?" the magistrate exclaimed.

"It is no crime to destroy an undead," Perrin said. "Our defense hinges on proving that we speak the truth. Pretending we did not do what we did would work against us in the long run."

"This was the lich you were pursuing?" Octavian said.

Perrin hesitated. "No. We found and destroyed that creature else-where. We did not know Master Samretto was a lich until he attacked us."

"*Two* of these creatures?" The magistrate laughed. "This sounds ridiculous. I'm inclined to leave you here pending trial."

"When did you destroy the lich? The second one?" Octavian asked Perrin, ignoring the magistrate.

"Last night, sometime before eight o'clock," Perrin said.

Octavian closed his eyes and cursed fluidly, making the magis-trate's eyebrows go up and the female guard emit an uncharacteristic giggle. "The ghoul presence in our city increased markedly yesterday evening," he said. "As would be expected if a lich died and lost control of his undead. My lord magistrate, this man is telling the truth."

"You can't expect me to believe this nonsense? And even if I do, it sounds like they're responsible for setting the ghouls loose on this city."

"That wasn't our fault!" Sienne exclaimed, then subsided when Perrin glared at her with an unspoken *Let me do the talking.*

"It was an unfortunate side effect," he said, "and I assure you if there had been an alternative, we would not have allowed it to happen. But the lich attacked us, and we were forced to defend ourselves. As proof, I offer Master Samretto's reliquary, which is intact save for the crack that prevented the lich's spirit from remaining connected to the material world."

"You kept a dangerous necromantic device?" The magistrate took a step back. Sienne wanted to slap him. If he was representative of what passed for justice in Fioretti, she almost wanted to take her chances with the lich again.

"It is not dangerous, my lord magistrate, certainly not if it is damaged," Octavian said. "Where is it?"

"With our belongings, in a belt pouch."

Octavian turned to the guard. "May we see their possessions? If he is telling the truth, I will recognize the lich's reliquary and can attest to its witness on their behalf."

The guard nodded and went back upstairs. "You've had a busy week," Octavian said. "Two liches. I don't suppose you want to go into the spirit hunting business? Kitane would be happy to sponsor you."

"We've had enough necromancy to last three lifetimes," Alaric said. "Though we have a great appreciation for those who make spirit hunting their life's work."

"Well, I'm sure we can arrange for some kind of compensation." Octavian turned as the guard came back down the stairs. She had all their belt pouches dangling from one hand, which she held well away from herself as if she feared contagion. "Which one?"

Sienne pointed to hers. As Octavian opened it, she experienced a moment's terror that someone had stolen the reliquary, that their story had no proof and she was going to live in this awful cell forever. Then he withdrew the black glass prism, and she sighed. Octavian held it up to the light. In the light of day, Sienne could see the cloudy glass pieces were held together by a network of fine bones, not those of a child, but surely a woman's bones, and she was gripped by a certainty that she was looking at the remains of Uriane Samretto. She swallowed bile and tried not to think about it.

"This is indeed a lich's reliquary," Octavian said. "My lord magistrate, these people have done the city a tremendous service. They should be freed immediately."

"They have to face official charges," the magistrate said, somewhat pompously, Sienne thought.

"With the city in the turmoil it's in?" Octavian frowned. "They ought to be out destroying ghouls, not rotting in a cell. Come, young man, show sense."

The magistrate eyed Alaric. "Two hundred lari fine, for disrupting the peace, and they're free to go," he said.

"What!" Sienne exclaimed.

"That's acceptable," Alaric said, shooting a warning glance at her.

The magistrate nodded to the guard, who unlocked the cells. Sienne tried not to leave the cell at a run, but it was hard not to imagine the door closing on her again.

"Thank you," Perrin said to Octavian. "We are once again in your debt."

"It's a small way for me to be involved in fighting evil," Octavian said. "Now, be on your way. I'll keep this, if you don't mind?" He held up the reliquary and turned it so the remaining glass caught the light.

"Please do," Perrin said.

They collected the rest of their gear and spent some time scrounging money for their fine. Finally Perrin removed the amulet from around his neck and laid it on the pile of coin, saying, "I pledge this against our returning with the rest of the money. I assure you it is more valuable than the fine, and it had better be here when I return."

The guard at the desk held it up by its chain and let the citrine catch the light. "It's magical," Sienne added, and the guard hastily put it down.

"The rest of the fine to be paid in the next twenty-four hours, or it's forfeit," she said. Perrin nodded agreement, and they were out the door and blinking in the soft afternoon light.

"Sienne?" Alaric said.

"Let's start walking," Sienne said.

"What are we doing? Should we fight the ghouls?" Kalanath said.

"We've got one last shot at finding whatever Samretto had," Alaric said. "His house is probably being watched, so—"

"Five full-body *imitates*, coming up," Sienne said, opening her spellbook.

27

S ienne made herself walk the way the female guard at the jail had, hips loose, legs swinging in long strides, arms hanging relaxed at her side. But it turned out not to matter. No one was guarding Samretto's house. It hadn't been wasted wizardry, as the confusions had gotten them past the gate with no trouble, but it did feel anticlimactic.

"Spread out, and let's be quick," Alaric said.

Sienne chose the short hall leading to the kitchen, though she wasn't sure she'd find anything useful there. It wasn't likely Samretto had mixed his potions there—or maybe she was too fastidious, and nobody else found the idea of brewing necromantic potions in the same place they made food disgusting. She searched the cupboards, anyway, and checked both ovens, which were cold. The cupboards held only ordinary foodstuffs, no strange herbs and certainly no varnwort.

Another door led outside, into a kitchen garden that at this season was still new and undergrown. At the far end of the kitchen garden, a shed squatted just inside the gate that led to the main gardens. Sienne crossed the path of hard-packed earth and opened its door, summoning a handful of magic lights to illuminate its interior. It contained nothing but garden implements, all hung neatly on the walls within the chalk outlines of their shapes. Sienne sent her lights into all the corners and saw nothing more than a spider web and a blobby, multi-legged body scurrying off into what shadow was left. She shuddered and called the lights back to her, shutting the door.

She returned to Samretto's study, where Alaric was making neat piles of the books on the floor. "Anything?" he asked.

Sienne shook her head. "I'm hoping Dianthe finds a secret room."

"None of these books are about necromancy," Alaric said. "At least, none of the ones I can read. That small stack is books in Meiric, if you want to take a look."

Sienne knelt and sorted through the pile. "Poetry. A history of the lost city Ma'tzehar. I'd love to see that someday. Or is it mythical?"

"Maybe a job will take us to Omeira. Though I'm not sure Kalanath wants to return home." Alaric handed her another book. "I know he misses it, but whatever he left behind, it's worse even than Dianthe being wanted for murder."

"That's pretty bad." Sienne sat back on her haunches and looked up at him. "What will we do if the book isn't here?"

"Keep looking. I'm not giving up."

"I didn't mean give up, I meant…I don't know. We're running out of places to look. Depending on chance seems like it could take forever."

Dianthe and Perrin came into the room together. "There aren't any secret rooms in this house," Dianthe said, dropping heavily into one of the ladderback chairs. "If I didn't know better, I'd swear Master Samretto was no necromancer."

"I cannot imagine how he did it," Perrin said. "He implied his interest in necromancy postdated his wife's death. Becoming a lich in less than five years…much less, if I am correct…it is unprecedented."

"There's nothing here worth taking," Alaric said, dropping the last book to fall on the floor with a thump. "Where's Kalanath?"

"He was out back exploring the garden," Dianthe said. "Looking for an underground lair, or something. I'm afraid all he'll find are hidden graves."

Sienne shuddered. "I still don't understand how Master Samretto could justify murdering people."

"Let's go," Alaric said. "Whatever Samretto's secrets, he kept them well. We should see about hunting down those ghouls."

They trooped through the house and out the kitchen door, through the garden to the gate. For all Samretto's main gardens were raw and unfinished-looking, they were beautiful, with beds of flowers in all stages of bloom and trees casting shade that in true summer would be wonderfully comfortable. Kalanath strode toward them, a look of disgust on his handsome face.

"I do not think we should dig here," he said, "but maybe we should tell someone about the bodies. There is one fresh grave by the toolshed and another under a tree. I think there are more that a priest can find. They should have real burial."

"We can tell Octavian. I'd rather not try to explain Samretto to a different divine," Alaric said.

"You didn't dig them up, did you?" Sienne exclaimed. Then she said, "Wait—what toolshed?"

Kalanath gestured over his shoulder. "There is a toolshed at the edge of the garden, near the back wall."

Sienne turned to look at the shed just inside the kitchen garden. "This estate's too small to need two toolsheds," she said. "Especially if Master Samretto was the only one tending it."

Alaric followed her gaze. "What are you saying?"

Sienne turned and ran for the kitchen garden. "I don't know which one he'd use. Would he want it close to the house, or far from prying eyes?"

She threw open the shed door and stepped inside, once more summoning lights. It looked and smelled like a toolshed, dank and musty and smelling of compost. Sienne reached for the nearest rake. Her hand passed through the handle.

"This is it," she said to her friends, who crowded in round the door. "It's *seeming*. Master Samretto got someone to cast a permanent confusion on this shed."

"And then killed the wizard, no doubt," Alaric said darkly. "Why didn't it disappear when you touched it?"

"*Seeming* is one of the most powerful spells you can cast," Sienne said, waving her hand through a few more tools. "Even if you know it's a confusion, your eyes can't not believe it unless it was cast to exclude you. It takes divine magic to counter it."

All eyes turned on Perrin. "I think…" he said, looking through his handful of blessings. "Healing…shield…I believe Averran does intend us to hunt ghouls today, here are more of the undead-destroying blessings…ah." He held up a ragged-edged piece of Sienne's notebook paper. "This is intended to break an ongoing magical effect. It disrupts rather than dispels, so it will not be permanent, but it should last long enough for us to perform a search. O Lord, I thank you for your foresightedness, and I ask you to have patience in your crankiness, and grant me this blessing."

Orange light flared, spreading outward from Perrin's hand like fire. It crackled across the floor, walls, and ceiling of the little shed, revealing black paint stippled with tiny pale blue writing where ordinary planks and paneling had been. The tools vanished. Cabinets and bookshelves painted the same matte black as the walls and floor appeared in their place. A long table against the far wall was stained dark with old blood, and manacles hung from its corners. Sienne swallowed bitter bile and tried not to look at it.

"Unbelievable," Alaric said. "Let's be quick."

They spread out, each taking a cabinet or shelf. Sienne ended up going through a shallow cabinet whose shelves contained nothing overtly necromantic, but some of whose objects shone with magical light. "He must have been collecting these artifacts for *years*," she breathed, picking up a knobby chunk of metal whose use she couldn't begin to fathom. "Most of them are broken, but…" She set the metal down and touched a silver ring engraved with a winged serpent. "I don't know what they do."

"Take them all," Alaric said.

"I'm not sure that's a good idea. Someone will eventually see all this, and if it's obvious things have been stolen, all it takes is one blessing to trace the stolen things to us."

"Perrin said the confusion will be restored after a while. How will anyone ever see it?"

"I...that's a good point. I still think we should be careful." She nodded at a peg on one wall. "That cloak is magical, too. I've never seen an artifact made of cloth before."

"We could probably take that," Dianthe said, rummaging through a box on the floor. "Is any of this magical, Sienne?"

Sienne shook her head and turned her attention back to the cabinet. Rings, necklaces, more chunks of metal encrusted with cabochon gems, and a box the size of her palm and fingers, about four inches deep, that alone among the items did not radiate magic. It was lacquered red, with strange angular letters engraved on the top and stained black. Sienne didn't recognize the alphabet. She slid the lid off and almost dropped the box as magical energy blinded her inner eye.

Carefully, she tipped the box over, and a deck of cards fell into her hand. They were old, the corners worn down, but the purple and gold pattern on the backs gleamed as if freshly painted. Sienne turned over the top card. The duke of crowns looked back at her, his perky blond image scuffed from years of play. A hazard deck. She looked at a few more cards. An antique hazard deck, based on the style of the paintings. The images weren't as bright as the backs, but for something that had to be hundreds of years old, they were remarkably well-preserved. She counted quickly; all seventy-eight cards were present. What magic could a hazard deck possibly contain? Luck, for winning at hazard? Or...people used hazard decks for fortune telling—what if the fortunes actually came true?

She tipped the cards back into the box, took several other items, and rearranged what was left on the shelf so it didn't look like anything was missing. This was too big a mystery to let slide. Whatever the deck really was, she intended to find out.

Dianthe was examining the cloak, which was of heavy twilled

cotton imperfectly dyed a streaky dark green. Its hem was worn and fraying, and it had once had a hood, but someone had cut it off and not repaired the rent properly. "You're sure it's magical? I can't imagine cloth lasting half a millennium, unless it's that ugly rug in our sitting room."

"It radiates magic," Sienne said, turning the fabric to look at the lining, which was dark green satin much nicer than the outer layer, except for the patches. Someone had mended holes in the satin with random pieces of fabric that stood out against the dark green. "These look like bits of old tapestry. I wonder why they didn't try to make the patches blend in."

She picked at the corner of one patch, which was coming loose from the cloak. "Probably we could—oh!"

"Sienne?" Alaric said.

"I'm fine, it's just—" In her hand she now held a silver fountain pen where the blue and gray patch had been. There was no hole in the satin, nothing to show a patch had been there.

Sienne and Dianthe stared at each other. Dianthe took the pen from Sienne. "What kind of magic is that?"

"A transform, and a powerful one," Sienne said. "What happens if you put it back? *Can* you put it back?"

Dianthe shrugged and pressed the pen to the lining of the cloak. Instantly it vanished, and once more a blue and gray patch of heavy woven fabric clung to the inside of the cloak. "We have to take this," Dianthe said. "Suppose it works for anything?"

"I found it!" Perrin exclaimed. He held up a book bound in tattered pale brown leather. "The title is on the inside."

"May I?" Alaric said, extending a hand. Perrin gave the book to him. Alaric opened it, taking great care with the binding that flaked away as it flexed. He turned a few pages. "It's not what we thought," he said, his voice flat with disappointment. "It lists rituals, yes, but it's more a compendium of references to where the full rituals can be found."

"That is still more than we had before," Perrin said. "It may yet be useful."

Alaric closed it with a snap. "We'll have to study it later. Now we need to get out of here before *imitate* wears off and someone wants to know our business."

Sienne followed him through the house, her new finds nestled deep in her pack. Dianthe had the cloak bundled up under one arm. Sienne tried to summon up feelings of guilt at having stolen from a dead man, but failed to evoke anything more than mild distaste. The artifacts might be able to help her friends, and it was the least Samretto could do, given that he'd nearly killed them. Not to mention creating an army of undead who were now plaguing the city. Time for them to go hunting.

————

COLD MAGIC LIGHT PLAYED OVER THE GHOUL'S FACE, TWISTED IN A FINAL rictus of death. Death, or whatever one called it when the undead were finally laid to rest. Sienne breathed shallowly through her mouth, trying not to smell the stink of rot coming off the body. With her spellbook held at chest height, she cast *float* once more and watched the thing drift off the ground to hover a few inches above it. Kalanath prodded it with his staff, and it drifted away toward the others.

"That's seven," Alaric said. "I think we can call it a night. Sienne? Perrin?"

"I'm coming up on my limit," Sienne said. In fact, the lights had blue and green halos around them that made trails of color whenever she moved her head too quickly, but she didn't want to mention that. It was only a warning sign, and she felt no other discomfort or pain.

"That was the last of the undead-destroying blessings. I choose to take it as a sign," Perrin said. He tore off a green-smudged blessing and approached Dianthe. "Let us heal that wound before we proceed."

Sienne put away her spellbook and stretched. It was after one o'clock in the morning, and they had the street to themselves. The last set of ghouls, a trio considerably more decayed than the others they'd dispatched, had gone down quickly in the face of Perrin's blessing. Sienne felt they were becoming expert at dealing with the undead. She wondered how much the bounty was. That two hundred lari fine had made a serious dent in their purses.

A hand closed around her upper arm. "You're weaving," Alaric murmured. "How honest were you about your condition?"

"I'm not at the exhaustion point, if that's what you're asking."

"Sienne, I know you don't like being fussed over, but you shouldn't conceal your exhaustion. You're the only one who knows when you're close to collapse. Perrin doesn't hide it when he's low on blessings."

Sienne scowled. "You're right. I...might be a little closer to the edge than I implied."

"Come here." Alaric put his arms around her and rested his forehead on the top of her head. "I told you I have trouble not trying to protect you. I know that makes you reluctant to admit you're not well. I'll make more of an effort."

She put her arms around his waist. "Thank you. For caring, and... for everything."

He kissed her hair. "Let's get these turned in."

Kalanath said, "We are close to Denys's guard post."

Everyone looked at Dianthe. "We can go elsewhere," Alaric began.

"No," Dianthe said. "It's late, we're all tired, and I'm not interested in walking across town with a floating load of corpses. Besides, we might not even see him."

"It's up to you," Alaric said. "Let's start towing."

Kalanath had tied ropes around each ghoul's torso, and now they all took up a rope and walked toward the guard post. With *float*, the bodies swung back and forth, bouncing off each other and forcing the companions to tug harder to straighten out their trajectories. Sienne felt weary almost immediately. The floating cargo meant they had to walk side by side, so it was fortunate they weren't doing this midday, fighting the crowds that thronged Fioretti's daytime streets.

"Tomorrow, we will have the amulet again, and tracking down our prey will be easier," Perrin said. "I intend to retrieve it at first light. I have no desire to give those guards any opportunity to sell it."

"Is that what we're doing tomorrow?" Sienne asked. "Fighting ghouls, I mean, not getting the amulet back."

"That depends on how much the bounty is," Alaric said. "We're no longer pressed for time as far as finding the book goes. I admit to being discouraged. I hoped—"

"But you said it tells where to find rituals," Kalanath said. "That is something."

"Who knows how old the book is?" Alaric tugged on the ropes in his hand, making the grisly burdens sway. "Some of what they reference might not exist anymore."

"Let's not worry about that until we've identified the ritual we need," Sienne said. "And I've decided to tackle the University of Fioretti library. I don't care if my parents find out where I am. I'm not going back. This is my home now." She didn't feel as defiant as she sounded. Her parents had always been good at making her feel like a dependent child rather than a self-reliant adult. She wasn't sure how well she could stand up to them on her own. Fortunately, she had four other people to stand with her.

"I think that's a good idea," Dianthe said. "Let's plan on spending tomorrow evening studying that book."

They turned a corner, and the guard post came into view. The streets were empty of whores, for once, but several people went in and out of the guard post, some of them carrying bodies over their shoulders. Sienne was suddenly struck by the absurdity of it all, how quickly handling the dead had become normal for scrappers. They were towing *corpses* behind them, floating corpses, by all the avatars! She had to swallow a giggle she didn't feel like explaining to her friends.

Getting the bounties through the door proved to be a problem, but one easily solved. One of the sergeants on duty came outside and down the stairs to examine the corpses. "How long until that wizardry wears off?" she asked.

"Another two hours before the first one does," Sienne said.

The sergeant shrugged. "Clever solution. I'll have someone take them away. That spell makes it easy on us. Come inside and collect the bounty."

Jerome wasn't at the desk, but the man sitting there recognized Dianthe. Sienne guessed he knew at least a little of her story by the way his lips compressed in a tight frown when he looked at her. "Seven bounties at twenty-five lari a head," he said, addressing Alaric and ignoring Dianthe.

"That seems fair," Alaric said.

"I don't know. I just handle the money." The guard reached below the desk and came up with a sizable metal box. He counted out seven large brass tokens into Alaric's hand. "And you might think about taking any others you kill to a different post."

Alaric made a fist around the tokens and slammed his other hand down on the desk. "You have a problem?" he said, his voice dangerously low.

The guard leaned away from him. "I can have you arrested for threatening a guard," he said, his voice trembling slightly.

"Alaric, don't," Dianthe said. "It's not worth it."

Alaric turned toward her. "I don't—" He stopped, looking past her shoulder to where Denys had just emerged from the corridor. He was talking to his companion, but went silent when he saw Dianthe. Sienne saw him close one hand into a fist.

Dianthe's face was pale, her jaw rigid. "Let's go," she said, but her eyes were on Denys. Sienne hesitated, then followed her friends out into the street.

Alaric handed Perrin the brass chits. "You'll need to redeem them, but it's more than enough to pay off the rest of the fine and get back the amulet. We—"

"Dianthe!"

Sienne was close enough to see the look of pain flash across Dianthe's face at the sound of Denys's voice. Then it was gone, and Dianthe turned around to face him. "What?" she asked, her voice empty and colorless.

Denys came down the stairs and took a few steps toward her.

"Dianthe," he repeated, then seemed to be searching for words. Dianthe regarded him in silence. Sienne was afraid to move, even to back away and give the two room. Finally, Denys said, "Why didn't you tell me?"

Dianthe shook her head. "It doesn't matter now."

"It matters. I need to know why."

"Because I didn't want to put you in a position to have to choose between love and upholding the law," Dianthe said. "I don't know if I was more afraid you'd turn me in, or that you wouldn't. I hoped...it was stupid, but I hoped it would never come out and we could just go on living our lives. I'm sorry."

"You could have trusted me."

"Trusted you to do what, Denys?" Tears trickled down her cheeks. "To do the right thing, and turn me over to the authorities? Or to become a stranger to yourself, someone who breaks the law when he has a really, *really* good reason? I couldn't do that to you. I just couldn't bear it."

Denys took a few more steps toward her. "Am I so rigid, then, that I only care about the law? You were defending yourself when you killed that man. I would have done anything to see you received justice—actual justice, not whatever that bastard of a duke wanted. Or did you think it meant nothing when I said I loved you?"

Dianthe shook her head. "I thought I was protecting you. Maybe I was only protecting myself. Maybe I thought what we had was too good to be real, and your love only went so far."

"I wouldn't have asked you to marry me if that were the case."

Sienne drew in a sharp, startled breath, but neither Denys nor Dianthe paid her any attention. Dianthe said, "I don't know how to tell you I'm sorry in a way that will mean anything to you. I didn't tell you about my past because I love you and I didn't want you to be hurt. I wish by all that's holy I'd told you the truth and let things fall where they would, but I didn't, and I can't change that." She swiped water out of her eyes and added, in a voice made husky by tears, "We won't come back here again. It's the last thing I can do for you."

She turned away, and Denys said, "Wait."

302 | MELISSA MCSHANE

Dianthe stopped, but didn't turn back to face him. Denys walked the rest of the way toward her, stopping when he was close enough to touch her. He let out a deep breath that seemed to come from his innermost soul. "I'm sorry," he said. "I'm sorry I let you think I couldn't be trusted to choose you over every damn law on the books."

Dianthe turned, startled, then flung herself at him, drawing in a great harsh breath that was just shy of being a sob. Denys drew her into his arms and held her tightly enough Sienne could see the tendons standing out on his arms. She backed away from the two of them, slowly, and bumped into Alaric, who put his arm around her shoulders and pulled her close. The warmth of his embrace filled her. She found she was crying and didn't know why.

Dianthe and Denys were talking again, too low to make out, though Sienne didn't want to intrude on their privacy any more than they all already had. Dianthe nodded, and Sienne heard her laugh. Then she and Denys kissed, a long, lingering kiss that made Sienne turn away out of embarrassment at having witnessed it. In turning, she met Alaric's eye, and he was smiling in a way that again made her warm all over.

"Not tonight," he said in a voice pitched for her ears alone, "but soon."

She didn't have to ask him what he meant.

28

S ienne slept through the morning and into the afternoon, waking only when her bladder pressed its demands on her. When she returned from the privy, she found the kitchen empty of everyone but Leofus, busily preparing dinner. "Sitting room," he said without looking up.

Alaric sat on the sofa with the brown book open in front of him and a scattering of papers across the too-low table. Perrin, in the armchair, held a sheet of paper spread over his knee and was reading it with his brow furrowed. Kalanath lounged against the wall near the bookcase, reading something titled in Meiric. "Where's Dianthe?" Sienne asked.

"She went out," Alaric said. "I can't believe I'm saying this, but I hope she went to Renaldi."

"You like him, admit it." Sienne sat next to Alaric on the sofa. "You don't think...will she marry him? I can't believe she didn't tell us he asked her!"

"I don't know. It's up to her."

Sienne, who'd been about to put her hand on his knee, withdrew. "You're in a temper."

"He has had his head down over that book for several hours," Perrin said. "It is a wonder he has not erupted."

Alaric sighed and put his arm around Sienne. "Sorry," he said. "This is really slow going, and I admit I'm thrown by learning Renaldi wants to marry Dianthe. I shouldn't let it bother me, but—"

"You feel it would break up the team," Sienne said. "Lots of married scrappers go out on jobs. There's no reason Dianthe couldn't still work with us."

"She is his sister," Kalanath said without looking up from his book. "Reason does not matter."

"I'm not unreasonable. I'm not going to stop her, am I?"

Sienne leaned into him. "We don't know what she'll decide, so there's no point worrying. Tell me what you've learned from the book, instead."

Alaric nodded. "It's better than I thought. Well-organized, for one. Whoever wrote it made detailed notes on where he found the information. He just didn't reproduce the actual rituals. I gather that would have made the book three times its size."

"That is not the best part," Perrin said. "Our unknown writer *did* include recipes for potions. It seems some of the rituals refer to potions by the name of their creator, without specifics as to how they should be brewed. The writer collected recipes that might be the ones referred to, attached to their references. And we have narrowed down those recipes to three that might be the one we seek."

"Which means we also know what rituals they're associated with," Alaric said. "Five rituals, to be specific. Non-necromantic and very old."

"So where do we find those rituals?" Sienne asked.

"This is my third time through the book. I'm making note of every book this man refers to that's related to our five rituals. Book, or letter, or pamphlet—he was thorough. Then we hope at least some of these are still extant."

"Do you want me to take over? Give you a rest?"

"I'm already familiar with the man's handwriting, which I can tell you is hard to make out. You can look at the list of sources and see if there's anything you recognize."

He pushed a sheet of paper toward her. Sienne picked it up and scanned the contents. She refrained from commenting on Alaric's handwriting, which was also spiky and hard to read. Fellic wasn't his first language, after all. "None of these are known to me," she said, "but one or two of the authors sound familiar. I'm amazed there are so many of them. I would have sworn the only rituals anyone wrote about were necromantic."

"It is unfortunate in one respect that our quest is well focused, as we might otherwise add to the body of Rafellish knowledge on the subject," Perrin said. He rose from his seat. "I will ask Leofus if he has some of these ingredients. I presume we intend to concoct these potions, and learn which is correct?"

"You presume correctly," Alaric said. "Though I don't know where we'll do it. I doubt Leofus will be willing to let us use his kitchen."

"We will find a way," Perrin said, and left the room.

Alaric went back to making notes. Sienne leaned back and watched him. She loved looking at his hands, how agile they were despite their size. "I'm hungry," she announced. "I hope dinner is early."

"You slept a long time," Kalanath said. "I was glad to sleep in my own bed finally. And tonight we will hunt ghouls again?"

"Tomorrow," Alaric said, handing Sienne another sheet of paper. "We deserve a night off."

Dianthe appeared in the doorway, prompting Sienne to exclaim, "You're back!"

"Did you think I wouldn't be?" She sat in the chair Perrin had vacated.

"No, I just...did you see Denys?"

Dianthe shook her head. "I went to talk to Corbyn."

A chill went through Sienne, settling in her stomach. Alaric said, "Oh?"

"This is why I love playing hazard with you, Alaric. You are terrible at hiding your emotions." Dianthe leaned back in the chair. "I turned him down."

"Turned who down?" Perrin said, entering the room. He held a small sack in one hand and his paper in the other.

"Corbyn," Dianthe said. "It was the hardest thing I've ever done in my life. His job is...well, it's difficult, complex work, and I'd be good at it. It would be a challenge, true, but I've never backed down from a challenge, and the truth is, I think I'd like it. But it would take me away from all of you, and I'd hate that." She paused for a moment and carefully studied her fingernails. "And it would take me away from Denys."

No one spoke for a moment. Finally, Sienne said, "Have you... made up your mind? About marrying him?"

"Thank you for not challenging me on not mentioning it to you," Dianthe said dryly. "He only asked me two weeks ago, before we went to the Lepporo estate, and then everything was so busy...well, you know what happened. But now...I think we should wait a while longer. This business with the murder charge has showed us both we need to be more careful of our relationship. We need time to get past the misconceptions we both had. However, you should all know I do intend to marry him. I'm just not sure when."

Sienne rose and flung her arms around Dianthe. "I'm so happy for you!"

Alaric laid the book down. "So am I," he said.

Dianthe laughed. "You are not."

"I'm happy for your happiness. I'm sorry I'm selfish enough to want to know what that means for us."

"Well, I won't live here anymore, that's for sure," Dianthe said, "but I don't see why anything else has to change. Denys and I certainly can't afford for me to sit around taking care of his house while he goes to work every night. And I love what I do. So I'll still be part of the team."

"That is good to know," Kalanath said. "We would miss you."

"Corbyn took it better than I thought," Dianthe said. "He's disappointed, but he had to admit nine years is a long time in a person's life, and I'm not the same young woman who had to disappear from Sileas back then. If it hadn't happened...my whole life would be different now. That's such a strange feeling, to know I might have been another person."

"Everyone can say that," Alaric said. "It's not everyone who has such a clear view of who that other person might have been."

"I feel so good. Like I could float away, except I'd want to come down eventually." Dianthe squeezed Sienne's hand and released her. "So what have you all found?"

"Recipes, and rituals, and direction." Alaric closed the book.

Sienne stood. "There's plenty of time before dinner for me to make a first visit to the university library. You've given me pages worth of references. I'd like to see what I can find."

"There's no rush, Sienne."

"I know, but—" Sienne let out an awkward laugh— "if I don't do this quickly, I might lose my nerve."

"Then we should go with you."

"They won't let you in unless you're a student or a graduate of an affiliated school. You'd just wait around outside. Don't worry, no one's going to accost me and lock me up until my parents can arrive."

"All right," Alaric said, "but if you're not back by dinnertime—"

"Storm the library for me."

The afternoon was pleasantly warm, and Sienne had time during the short walk to the University of Fioretti grounds to dwell on all the unpleasant possibilities. For all her bold words, she really wasn't sure what her reception would be. She'd visited the university twice on school trips, and been awed and inspired by the beautiful library. She'd never gone in her own name before. What if they didn't believe she was who she said she was? She was certain Stravanus didn't send lists of its graduates to all the other institutes of higher learning in Rafellin. Well, if they turned her away, her team would at least know where they stood.

The university was a collection of red-roofed buildings east of the palace, which crouched on its island like a lion guarding Fioretti. Unique in Fioretti, which had a long history of repurposing buildings far beyond their initial design, the university had been designed by a single hand and constructed about one hundred and fifty years before. It bore the marks of that period: lots of arches, lots of marble, and bas-reliefs rather than statuary. Even if her family had been able to afford to send her there after her schooling in Stravanus was complete, Sienne didn't think she'd have wanted to go. The place was cold and forbidding, suggesting that those who studied there were aloof from the concerns of the warm, human world.

The edifice housing the library was a three-story terror with three peaked roofs above round windows, which in turn lay above a row of arches defining a colonnade circling the second floor. There were three doors, two of which, Sienne knew, were for the use of faculty and graduate students. The third was the main entrance. Sienne swallowed a nervous lump in her throat and opened the door.

There was no entrance chamber; the door opened directly on the library. Sienne stopped inside the front door and gaped, not caring if it made her look like a back country yokel. She'd remembered correctly the smell of a hundred thousand books, rich and welcoming like a High Winter garland or her father's rose garden. She'd remembered how brightly lit the place was, with magic lights outshining the sunlight that would damage the older, frailer books. What she'd forgotten was how *big* the place was: three stories of galleries filled to bursting with books, two doors leading to the annex that had been added forty years earlier, pillars holding up the galleries and long tables filling the center of the hall where people sat and read or took notes.

She breathed in the scent again and felt a sense of peace envelop her. She'd never been an outstanding student except where magic and languages were involved, but this made her wish she was a true scholar.

She walked forward to a lectern where stood a red-gowned academic flipping the pages of a book. "May I help you?" the woman said, adjusting her spectacles on her narrow nose.

"I'd like to use the library," Sienne said. "My name is Sienne Verannus. I'm a graduate of Stravanus."

The librarian raised one thin eyebrow. "Verannus? Are you related to Duke Pontus Verannus?"

"He's my father."

"I see. And you went to school in Stravanus."

"I graduated almost two years ago. I don't...I didn't bring any proof of that."

The woman waved a hand dismissively. "Very few people claim credentials they don't have. We're more concerned that you treat the books well. Don't worry, we won't make you wait while we send off to Stravanus for your records." She smiled, a thin-lipped but pleasant smile. "Have you used our library before?"

"Only visited. But they explained your system."

"Do you need more help than that? We're short on staff today, but I'm sure someone can show you around."

"No, I think I can manage." She felt wary of revealing what she was looking for. The whole situation made her nervous that they'd change their minds and throw her out, the nice librarian notwithstanding.

"Very well. The catalogues are along the back wall, along with paper and pencils. No ink pens allowed, and of course taking notes in the margins is forbidden. If you have need of a book for longer than a day, speak to me and we'll arrange for it to be held for you. No reserving books for longer than six weeks. Do you have any questions?"

"Not yet."

"Then—good luck, my lady."

Sienne didn't correct her form of address. Probably she was still entitled to the honorific, even if she felt she'd left it behind. She crossed the room, furtively peeking at what the other patrons were reading—she loved the feeling of kinship when she found someone reading a book she knew—and ended up facing the row of lecterns where the catalogues were kept.

The huge volumes, each three to four inches thick, gave her a fleeting feeling of despair that she would ever be able to find anything useful. They were labeled by subject—mathematics, linguistics, philosophy, and so forth—and their edges were ragged with pages that had been inserted after they were bound, to allow for writing in new acquisitions. Sienne realized in dismay that she didn't know what subject a book about ancient, non-necromantic rituals would be catalogued under. She read the pages Alaric had given her. Mostly titles, a few authors, but no hint as to subjects. She'd just have to guess. *Or read the entirety of every catalogue volume,* she thought, and tried to suppress that little voice of pessimism.

She decided to start with the history catalogue, on the grounds that all of the books on her list were probably ancient. Some of the pages were printed, but after each printed page were three or four pages of handwritten entries. The university acquired books often, Sienne saw, and it was hard not to feel more despair when she saw just how many there were. She squashed that feeling into a corner of her mind and kept looking.

The sound of the university bell startled her out of the reading fugue she'd fallen into and made her drop her pencil. She bent to pick it up and found the librarian standing beside her. "We close in half an hour," she said. "Did you not find what you were looking for?"

"Oh! No—I mean, yes, I did, but I wanted to be thorough—I think I should come back tomorrow." She'd found, to her surprise, two of the titles Alaric had listed and exhausted the possibilities of the history catalogue. She also realized she was hungry. She returned the pencil to its bin, smiled at the librarian, and made her escape.

Two titles. Out of...she'd forgotten how many were on the list. And she'd only looked through one catalogue. It was more success than she'd dreamed possible. She had to fight the urge to skip all the way home.

Sunlight slanted low and in her eyes as she turned the corner onto Master Tersus's street. The smell of roast pork wafted down the hall when she opened the back door. "Sienne?" Dianthe called out. "We were almost going to come looking for you."

Her fingers were gray with pencil lead. "Just a minute," she said, stepping into the bath house to wash up. She splashed water on her face as well, relieving her tired eyes.

The others were seated around the table when she entered the kitchen, and Leofus had just set down the pork roast in front of Alaric. Sienne took her seat next to him. "What did you find?" Alaric said. He took up knife and fork and began carving. "You have a look that says you found something."

Sienne accepted a plate and passed it to Kalanath on her other side. "We'll know tomorrow. But it's a promising start."

"I have to say I never thought scrapping would ever end up being research," Dianthe said, taking her own plate, "but this isn't the first time we've had to look up information on ruins. Not that these books are ruins. But the principle is the same."

"Did anyone give you trouble over your name?" Perrin asked.

"No. But it's only a matter of time before it gets out. I've decided not to worry about it." Sienne took a bite of roast. It was juicy, and delicious as all Leofus's meals were, and she savored it.

"Let's hope it's a long time coming," Alaric said.

After dinner, Perrin said, "I believe I will go for a walk before bed. I—what is it?"

Kalanath blushed. "It is nothing."

Sienne had caught the edge of the skeptical look Kalanath gave Perrin and agreed silently that it didn't look like nothing.

"You wish to know what illicit things I do on my evening walks," Perrin said. "It is nothing sinister, though were I to be discovered, I would be chastised. I go to see my children."

"I thought you were disowned. Does your family let you do that?" Dianthe asked.

"Not at all. In the eyes of the law, I have no children. I observe them in secret." Perrin laughed. "I probably look like a criminal, examining a rich house for points of entry, but I merely wish to know they are well."

"How can anyone take your children from you?" Sienne exclaimed. "You're their *father*. A law can't change that."

"Certainly not in my heart." Perrin shrugged. "I likely should have told you sooner, on the chance that I am arrested one of these nights for loitering and you are summoned to pay my fine. But it is...humiliating."

"It is not," Sienne declared. "Any of us would do the same."

"Just be careful," Alaric said. "Lysander Delucco is a vindictive man. He might yet do worse than disinheriting you."

"I am ever careful," Perrin said, saluting him with a self-mocking smile. "I will return shortly."

When he was gone, Kalanath said, "I did not think it would be that, but it is not a surprise. I will practice before bed. We have studied all day and I am restless."

"And I'm off to see Denys. I'll spend the night there, so don't wait up," Dianthe said.

"That leaves us," Alaric said when the two left the kitchen. He put his arms around Sienne and pulled her close for a kiss. "Alone, and with nothing and no one demanding our time."

Sienne was stricken with an unexpected shyness. She kissed him again to cover it and said, "So what shall we do?"

"I don't know. Maybe you should look in your room," Alaric said.

"My room? Is something there?"

"Go find out."

Alaric's mysterious smile sent Sienne up the stairs to her room. She pushed the door open and stopped, breathless. A beautiful dress, red like the heart of a rose, lay spread across her bed, its full skirts winking with sparkling crystals that would shine like diamonds under the lights of a dance hall. Its bodice scooped low enough that it would slide over her head easily. She walked forward and fingered the smooth satin. "Beautiful," she said. "How did you know?"

"I see your face every time Dianthe goes out dancing with Renaldi," Alaric said. She turned to look at him, standing in the doorway, and he smiled. "It's true I'm not much for dancing, but anything you want that much, I'm happy to do for you."

Sienne crossed the room and took his hand, pulling him fully into the bedroom and using her invisible fingers to shut the door. "I love it," she said. "I love *you*. Thank you."

"It's my pleasure. Go ahead and change, and I'll wait for you downstairs."

Looking up at him, at his eyes shining with love for her, her shyness evaporated. "Tomorrow night," she said. "Tonight I have something else in mind."

His eyebrows went up. "Then you'd better move that dress."

Sienne's invisible fingers whisked the beautiful dress off the bed and hung it neatly on a peg on the wall. "Is that what you had in mind?"

Alaric put his hands around her waist and lifted her, making her laugh before he stopped her laugh with a long, breathless kiss. "My love," he said, "it's just the beginning."

SIENNE'S SPELLBOOK

Summonings:

Summonings affect the physical world and elements. They include all transportation spells.

Castle—trade places with someone else

Convey—teleport an object

Fog—obscuring mist

Jaunt—personal teleportation

Slick—conjure grease

Evocations:

Evocations deal with intangible elements like fire, air, and lightning.

Burn—ray of fire

Force—bolt of magical energy, hits with perfect accuracy

Scream—sonic attack, causes injury

Confusions:

Confusions affect what the senses perceive.

Camouflage—disguise an object's shape, color, or texture

Cast—ventriloquism

Echo—auditory hallucinations

Imitate—change someone's entire appearance

Mirage—visual hallucinations

Mirror—creates three identical duplicates of the caster

Shift—small alterations in appearance, such as eye or hair color

Transforms:

Transforms change an object or creature's state, in small or large ways.

Break—shatters fragile things

Cat's eye—true darkvision

Drift—feather fall

Fit (object)—shrink or enlarge an object; permanent

Fit (person)—shrink or enlarge a person; temporary

Gills—water breathing

Mud—transform stone to mud

Purge—transmute liquid

Sculpt—shape stone

Sharpen—improve sight or hearing

Voice—sound like someone else

The Small Magics

These can be done by any wizard without a spellbook, with virtually no limits.

Light

Spark

Mend

Create water

Breeze

Chill/warm liquid

Telekinesis (up to 6-7 pound weights)

Ghost sound

Ghostly form

Find true north

Open (used to manipulate a spellbook)

Invulnerability

ABOUT THE AUTHOR

In addition to the Company of Strangers series, Melissa McShane is the author of more than twenty fantasy novels, including the novels of Tremontane, the first of which is *Servant of the Crown;* The Extraordinaries series, beginning with *Burning Bright;* and *The Book of Secrets,* first book in The Last Oracle series. She lives in the shelter of the mountains out West with her husband, four children and a niece, and four very needy cats. She wrote reviews and critical essays for many years before turning to fiction, which is much more fun than anyone ought to be allowed to have.

You can visit her at **www.melissamcshanewrites.com** for more information on other books.

For news on upcoming releases, bonus material, and other fun stuff, sign up for Melissa's newsletter at http://eepurl.com/brannP

SNEAK PEEK: SHIFTING LOYALTIES (COMPANY OF STRANGERS, BOOK FOUR)

Cold magical light reflected dully off the black stones of the corridor, as if they were made of something that sucked the light in and held tightly to it. Moisture slicked the walls, but despite the warmth and wetness, nothing grew on them. Sienne heard water dripping, somewhere in the distance. The noise came at irregular intervals, probably from more than one source. Knowing that didn't make the sound grate any less on her nerves. A regular *plink*, she could have ignored, but the erratic *tap-tap, tap, taptaptap* kept her on edge, listening for the next one. The smell of old stone, sour and damp, filled the air. It was like being inside the digestive tract of some oddly angular beast.

The stone swallowed up the sound of her footsteps and that of her companions just as it did the light. It was a strange corridor, as wide as it was high and seeming without end. Sienne pinched her nose against a sneeze and summoned another couple of magic lights. Their light banished the darkness a few paces, but didn't illuminate the corridor more than about ten feet away. She sent the new ones flying ahead and heard Dianthe curse. "Too bright," her friend exclaimed.

"Sorry. This place has me on edge. No lanterns, no torches, not even brackets to hold lanterns or torches." She shifted her spellbook to a more comfortable position.

"Nobody's been down here but us for decades, maybe centuries," Alaric said without turning around. "There's nothing to be worried about."

Sienne eyed the giant Sassaven's broad back. "Then why are you tense?"

"Because I could be wrong, and someone's already retrieved the salvage from this place."

"Am I the only one who believes this corridor has gone on forever?" Perrin said. "With no discernable landmarks, I cannot imagine how we could tell if that were true."

"I have marked the walls," Kalanath said, demonstrating by drawing the steel tip of his staff with a *skree* across a stone at head height. "But there is no turn, or door, so it does not matter."

"It relieves my mind," Perrin said. "Pray, do not stop."

"The corridor turns here," Dianthe said, "and there's a door up ahead." She vanished into the darkness. Sienne came around the corner to see her examine the thumb latch, then try it. "Not locked."

"That could be bad," Alaric said. "Let's see what we have."

Dianthe pushed the door open and waited for Sienne to send her lights through before entering. Sienne followed Alaric and moved to the side to allow Perrin and Kalanath to enter. The sour smell was stronger in this room, which was vast enough Sienne's lights, clustered around the door, didn't illuminate the far end. Chairs with disintegrating cushions stood in groups here and there throughout the cavernous room. Damp, rotting tapestries whose subjects were lost to time hung from the walls, which for once bore patches of moss. They seemed the only healthy, thriving thing in what Sienne was increasingly inclined to call a lair. The ceiling was unexpectedly low, though no lower than it had been in the hall. In this vast room it felt as if it were poised to fall and crush them. Sienne shivered and stepped closer to Alaric.

"It's empty," she said. "Should it be this empty?"

"Reva Nocenti was killed before she could retreat with her possessions," Perrin said. "But there are records enough of her underground palace that other scrappers may have looted it in the hundred-odd years since her defeat."

"This was an entrance," Kalanath said, prodding one of the cushions with the tip of his staff. "A place for people who wish a thing to come."

"An antechamber," Sienne said. "That makes sense. Though not much else about this does. Why would a wizard care about ruling a dukedom? Particularly a wizard who was as interested in research as Nocenti was?"

"Power does strange things to people," Alaric said. "Why would someone spend three fortunes building an underground palace when an aboveground palace is half as expensive, and has windows?"

"There are two doors," Dianthe said. She'd crossed the room, trailing a light, and the far wall was now visible. "Anyone have a preference?"

"You sound like you're in a hurry," Alaric said.

"Aren't you? This place gives me hives. See, I'm scratching." Dianthe rubbed her forearm. "Let's find this salvage and get out."

"I apologize for not being able to direct us more, ah, directly," Perrin said.

"You got us this far. And figured out there was something here at all. I call that more than enough help," Alaric said.

Sienne brought a light closer to the door nearest her, the one on the left. It was nearly as tall as the ten foot high ceiling and half that wide, carved all over with scenes of a beautiful noblewoman dressed in the style of a century past, passing judgment on groups of people —merchants, peasants, even other nobles. "I think we should take this one."

"Why is that?" Perrin said.

"Because it probably leads somewhere interesting. That other one is plain and I bet it leads to the storage room."

"She has a point," Dianthe said.

Alaric nodded. "Then left it is."

The room beyond the carved door was as cavernous and claustrophobic as the first. More rotting tapestries hung on the walls, more mossy growth gleamed verdantly in the white light. Directly ahead, on a dais reached by three shallow steps, stood a throne carved of black marble, unrelieved by cushions. The wall behind the throne was carved in a bas-relief whose details Sienne couldn't make out at that distance. She crossed the room to look up at it. It showed the same woman with her hands held out in a pose like the Mercy card in a hazard deck, water overflowing her cupped hands.

"I sense a theme," Perrin said.

"We already knew Nocenti was arrogant," Alaric said. "Though this certainly proves the point. Dianthe?"

"I see no signs of any concealed doors or rooms," Dianthe said. "But I'm not sure she'd want her treasury where so many outsiders go, even if it's well-hidden. The only exit is that archway over there." She pointed.

"I think perhaps we should be certain we are not leaving anything behind," Perrin said, removing his riffle of blessings from inside his vest. "Not to disparage your abilities, Dianthe, but Averran sees better than we do, and if the wizard Nocenti knew the *seeming* spell, it might be beyond all of us to find what she hid. I have several of these today, and I daresay that is a hint I should use them." He tore a purple-smudged square of rice paper from the little bundle and held it high, bowing his head and murmuring an invocation. Purple fire consumed the paper, and a bright violet light outlined all the stones of the walls, turning the moss a dusty gray color. When it faded, Perrin said, "Nothing."

Alaric was already headed for the archway, in which drifted shreds of a filmy curtain that might once have been red. "Between the two of you, I think we have an excellent chance of finding the lost treasury."

Sienne took up her place in the middle, cradling her spellbook in the crook of her left arm. "I hope nobody else found it first. It's so disappointing when we make a find and it's been cleaned out already."

Once again, the walls of this corridor were clean of moss. She wondered what made the difference. Nothing obvious, at any rate.

"My augury blessing suggests strongly that whatever is here is worth our time," Perrin said. "I, for my part, hope it is a non-magical treasury. Selling off gold and silver is much easier than haggling over artifacts, however more potentially valuable the artifacts are."

"There's a door ahead, and the corridor branches right before it," Dianthe said. "The door's not locked. More specifically, it can't be locked."

"We might as well check it first," Alaric said.

The room beyond was clearly a barracks, with three rows of bunks devoid of mattresses or bedding filling the space. "Nothing worth looking at here," Dianthe said. She crossed the room to the door on the other side and reached for the latch, only to snatch her hand back as if she'd been burned. "Somebody trapped this door. Recently."

"How recently?" Alaric said, joining her at the door.

"Not recently by our standards. A year or so."

"That's recent." Alaric glared at the door as if that would disarm the trap by itself. "Can you disable it?"

"I could, but it will take time. We're probably better off seeing if there's a way around it. Though the fact that there's a trap there tells me somebody found something worth hiding."

"Or they intend to deceive other scrappers," Perrin said.

"Or that. In either case—"

"We move on," Alaric said.

They backtracked and took the second corridor, which ended in a T-junction where they went right. The next room they found was an armory, stripped bare of all but a few rusted swords and armor stands. Sienne examined the walls of the corridor outside the armory. "Strange," she said. "There's moss growing here where there isn't any just ten feet on in the cross-corridor." She leaned close and sniffed the moss. It smelled reassuringly green.

"This place has mold growing all over it," Alaric said. "There's probably some quality of the walls that encourages it, or inhibits it."

"Probably," Sienne said.

Far in the distance, something went *thunk*. Sienne froze. "What was that?"

Alaric raised his head like a pointer scenting game. "I don't know. It didn't sound like something falling. Did you knock something over?" he called to the three still in the armory.

"No," Dianthe said, and a moment later she joined them at the door. "It sounded like a door slamming, or a portcullis dropping."

"Huh," Alaric said. "Did you find anything hidden?"

"No, and Perrin's blessing didn't either. Let's move on."

"Aren't we worried about that noise?" Sienne asked.

"There's nothing we can do about whatever it is," Alaric said. "We'll just have to hope it's not some gate trapping us in here."

Sienne shivered. "You could have kept that thought to yourself."

Turning left at the T-junction led them down a winding corridor to a dead end. "I guess we'll have to tackle that trap, after all," Dianthe said as they turned and headed back.

"We're not in a hurry," Alaric said, "and I don't—what's that *smell?*"

Sienne sniffed. A breeze brought the scent of something rotting to her nose. Something rotting, tinged with the burning, acrid odor of a strong acid. Her heart pounded faster. "Could there be ghouls down here?"

"Nothing for them to eat," Alaric said. "I don't think anything could live down here except bugs and rats."

Dianthe stopped at the corner leading to the T-junction. "You know," she said in a too-casual voice, "we haven't seen any rats down here at all. Or beetles, or spiders."

Sienne drew closer to Alaric. "What does that mean?"

"It means we might be in for a fight," Alaric said. "Let's not be carried away by our imaginations, all right? Lack of vermin doesn't have to mean anything."

Sienne realized she was shaking and clutched her spellbook tighter. She was being ridiculous. She and her companions could defeat anything this lair could throw at them. She couldn't stop shaking. Her arms and legs vibrated with it. Just as she realized the vibration was coming from outside her, Alaric said, "Something's coming. Something big."

They had nearly reached the T-junction. Sienne's lights illuminated the short corridor clearly. No one was there. The vibration had grown to the point that it was audible as a low hum that sang through Sienne's bones and teeth, rattling her skull. She stepped in front of Alaric and opened her spellbook to *fury*. It sounded big, and anything this big needed more than one *force* bolt. She wasn't taking chances.

Behind her, she heard the rasp of Alaric's sword sliding free from its sheath. The sound comforted her. She held up a hand, reminding them to stay silent. It was possible whoever this was didn't know they were there.

The lights danced in the air, caught in the vibration. The smell of rot and acid was so strong Sienne could taste it. She swallowed hard and clenched her teeth together, blinked away tears from the stinging, acidic air, and focused hard on the T-junction corner.

The air rippled, and two of Sienne's lights went out.

She blinked. The rippling in the air didn't stop. Something was there, something almost invisible in the now-dim light. She made more lights and flung them down the corridor. As they sailed into the junction, they vanished.

"Kitane's eyes, look at that," Dianthe breathed. A rat danced— danced!—into view, reared up on its hind legs. Its fur was almost gone, and bone shone through in places. Sienne covered her mouth to hold back a shriek. She still had nightmares about undead monsters, and maybe this rat wasn't big enough to hurt anyone, but it still horrified her.

She brought up her spellbook and flipped back to *burn*. *Force* had no effect on the undead. But as she began to read, Perrin said, "Dear Averran, it is floating. There is something there, carrying it."

Sienne took another look. The air before them shimmered, and as another light went out, Sienne realized the rat wasn't moving its limbs. Perrin was right—something was carrying it, something nearly invisible that moved slowly into the T-junction. "What is that thing?" she exclaimed. Now that she was looking more closely, she could see other things embedded in the field, or mass, or whatever it was: tiny stones, wisps of what might once have been moss, more small furry bodies nearly eaten away, the twisted remnants of a lantern bracket.

Kalanath stepped forward, his staff extended. Its steel tip prodded the thing. "It feels like a jelly," he said. The thing reached the wall and stopped. Kalanath pressed harder, then yanked his staff back as the wood below the steel cap began to smoke. "That is fire-hardened oak," he said. "It is a powerful acid, whatever it is."

Sienne summoned more lights. "But what is it for?"

Alaric chuckled. "I think we just met the cleaning staff. Look—Sienne, shine a light up high there. It's exactly the same shape as the corridor."

Sienne did as he directed. With a dozen lights shining on it, it was visible as a cube of some thick, clear liquid, its skin shimmering with oily rainbows. It was almost pretty.

The vibration began again. Kalanath took another step back. "Ah," he said, "it is moving again. Toward us."

"It's not that fast. We can stay out of its way," Alaric said. Then a peculiar look crossed his face. "But this is a blind corridor."

They all looked at each other. "I think we should back up," Dianthe said.

They retreated around the corner, all the way back to the blind end. "Sienne, can you get us out of here?" Alaric said.

"I can get *some* of us out of here," Sienne said. Her palms were sweaty, and she surreptitiously wiped them on her trousers. "Moving all of us with *ferry* takes all my reserves, and I've already cast spells today, to get us in here. But I can try *force*-blasting it."

"We can fit two of us across the corridor," Alaric said. "Maybe if we hit it hard enough, we can get it to reverse its course."

They ran back down the twisting corridor. The cube hadn't advanced very far, though it had consumed more of Sienne's lights. Sienne opened her spellbook and read off the evocation *force*. The syllables of the spell were hard and etched with acid, burning her mouth the way the acid in the air burned her eyes. She kept from blinking until the spell shot away from her in a tremendous burst of force.

It splashed against the cube and vanished.

"Burn it," Alaric said. Sienne flipped pages and read again, tears trickling down her cheeks from the burning sensation. *Scorch* would be more powerful, but it would also burn everyone in the area, so she stuck with its lesser cousin *burn*. Dark blue fire shot away from her to strike the cube, flickering across its surface.

This time, she got the thing's attention. A high, wavering scream joined the low hum, creating a discordant melody that felt like needles being stabbed into her ears. Alaric grabbed her and pulled her back as the cube accelerated toward them. It still wasn't moving faster than a brisk walk, but the way it just kept coming, inexorable and ponderous, made Sienne want to flee.

Alaric squared up to the thing and swung his massive sword in a great two-handed blow. It struck the cube, which made no effort to get out of the way. The sword sliced through the membrane of its skin, and a thick, clear liquid spurted out, striking Alaric in the chest. He shouted and sprang backward, swiping at himself. The stench of acid redoubled. Sienne stepped in front of him and read off *burn* again. The blue fire struck the cube, turning it a translucent sapphire color briefly. It sped up again. Sienne saw no other indication that her spell had affected it.

Sienne turned to Alaric and nearly screamed at the sight of his chest, the jerkin and shirt burned away, raw red burns covering his chest and stomach. Alaric was paler than usual and grimacing with pain. "You need to get out of here," he panted. "Take Dianthe."

"I'm not leaving you. Don't be stupid."

"Sienne—"

They'd backed almost all the way to the dead end. Hands grabbed Sienne and pulled her away from the oncoming juggernaut. Then Perrin said, "O Lord, have patience in your crankiness, and grant me this blessing." A pearly gray wall went up between them and the cube, which was now only ten feet away and closing fast.

"Smart," Alaric said. "But will it last long enough?"

"I have no idea. We did not see this thing earlier, so perhaps once it reaches the end of its route, it will return to wherever it lurks when it is not on duty." Perrin stepped forward to the edge of the gray barrier. "Unless it does not consider itself finished until it touches the wall behind us."

Dianthe swore. "This is ridiculous. We haven't seen a single blind corridor in this whole damned labyrinth until now. I refuse to believe there's no way out of here." She pressed her hands to the wall and closed her eyes, feeling her way along it.

Sienne stood watching the cube advance. She felt Alaric put his arm around her shoulders and squeeze gently. "Get out of here," he said.

"Make me."

"I would if I could. Sienne—"

The cube pressed against the gray barrier, which started to sizzle. The scent of jasmine and mint mingled sickeningly with the stench of acid. Sienne and Alaric backed away. "I have one more shield blessing," Perrin said. "I will not go without a fight."

The shield popped like a soap bubble. The cube lurched forward. Perrin invoked another blessing, stopping the cube three feet from them. Sienne stared through the barrier at it. "At least we know which corridors are safe," she said. "The ones with moss still growing on the walls. I wonder why those don't get cleaned."

"If I remembered which ones they were, I could make a guess," Perrin said.

The barrier shivered. "Dianthe, if you're going to make a discovery," Alaric began.

"Shut up, mountain," Dianthe said through gritted teeth.

With a pop, the shield vanished. The cube once again advanced. "Well," Alaric said, "it's been—"

A whoosh of dank, sweet air free of acid taint blew past them. "Save it for later," Dianthe said, grabbing Kalanath and hauling him through the gap she'd just opened. "Move!"

Made in the USA
Lexington, KY
27 November 2019